Black Oxen

ALSO BY ELIZABETH KNOX

The Vintner's Luck

Black Oxen

A Novel

ELIZABETH
KNOX

Picador USA
Farrar, Straus and Giroux
New York

www.picadorusa.com

Picador® is a U.S. registered trademark and is used by Farrar, Straus and Giroux under license from Pan Books Limited.

For information on Picador USA Reading Group Guides, as well as ordering, please contact the Trade Marketing department at St. Martin's Press.
Phone: 1-800-221-7945 extension 763
Fax: 212-677-7456
E-mail: trademarketing@stmartins.com

Library of Congress Cataloging-in-Publication Data
Knox, Elizabeth.
     Black oxen: A novel / Elizabeth Knox—1st Picador USA ed.
         p. cm.
     ISBN 0-312-42049-8
     1. Fathers and daughters—Fiction. 2. Twenty-first century—Fiction. 3. Latin America—Fiction. 4. California, Northern—Fiction. I. Title.

PR9639.3.K57 B58 2002
823'.914—dc21   2002066241

Visit the author's Web site: www.artistnz.telecom.co.nz/knox

First published in the United States by Farrar, Straus and Giroux

First Picador USA Edition: July 2002

10 9 8 7 6 5 4 3 2 1

For my friend Madeline

Whether we fall by ambition, blood, or lust,
Like diamonds we are cut with our own dust.

—John Webster, *The Duchess of Malfi*

Contents

Characters
xi

PART ONE: *Autism*
(A story by Carme Risk for her narrative therapist) 1

FIRST INTERMISSION: *Transference*
43

PART TWO: *Pérdida Total de la Memoria*
(An amnesiac's journal) 47

SECOND INTERMISSION: *Transference*
167

PART THREE: *Anesthesia Dolorosa*
(Carme Risk's journal and memoir) 171

THIRD INTERMISSION: *Transference*
347

PART FOUR: *The Autokinetic Effect*
(Carme Risk's journal) 351

FINAL INTERMISSION: *Countertransference*
431

Characters

EDEN

ABRA CADAVER, a foundling.

CARLIN CADAVER, Abra's guardian, a former RAF pilot.

CASSANDRA, Carlin's wife, a librarian.

ULAW, an immigrant upstart and a patron of Abra.

GENEVIEVE, Ulaw's wife.

ASTRELLA, one of Ulaw and Genevieve's daughters.

TWARKY, a boy with shopping bags.

DEVLIN HUGHES, an escaped convict.

LEQUAMA

AMBRE GUEVARA, a healer and former prostitute.

MADLENA GUEVARA, Ambre's elder daughter, a Lequaman revolutionary heroine and breeder of polo ponies.

EMILIO RIVERA, Madlena's father, a member of the Pola Pastrez, the Security Forces of the former regime.

TOMÁS JUILIANO, Madlena's husband.

ROSA, Madlena's daughter.

FERNANDO SOLA, chief of the Taoscal, a revolutionary hero.

CARLOS and AURELIANO JUILIANO-GUEVARA, Madlena and Tomás's twin sons.

IDO IDEA, aka WALTER RISK, an apparition.

RICARDO PASTREZ, former head of the Pola Pastrez, a smooth and polished murderer.

DON MARCOS PASTREZ, Ricardo's son, Minister of Education in the revolutionary government.

JUANITA PASTREZ, Ricardo's daughter, a lonely and neglected girl.

ENRICO GARCÍA, furniture maker and former head of security at the Presidential Palace after the revolution.

COLONEL MARIA MARIA CONCHITA CONCHITA GODSHALK, the commander of Battalion Amazonia and a revolutionary heroine.

ARAMANTHA VISISTATION, a psychotherapist.

MARGUERITE MILLAY, Aramantha's lover, a ballet teacher.

ANTON XAVIER, a surgeon and general practitioner.

FRANCIS TAYLOR, an Australian photographer: landscapes, wildlife, ethnographic interests, weddings and funerals.

MORGAN GRAY, an American journalist.

MAJOR WARREN S. MUNRO, of U.S. Military Intelligence, held captive in Lequama.

JON SCOTT, a British anthropologist.

GILLIAN McINDOE, a Canadian entomologist.

LEE McINDOE, Gillian's son, a dull, rude, unfinished boy.

JIRON PÉREZ-FARANTE, a Peruvian entomologist.

JULES FREI, a venerable and beloved Lequaman poet.

LENA GUEVARA, Ambre's mother, Frei's lover.

OLIVER, a New Zealander.

HANS, a German.

SAN FRANCISCO, BAY AREA, AND LOS ANGELES

CARME RISK, a specialist in multi-drug-resistant TB, in therapy in her forties.

SEAN HART, Carme's narrative therapist.

BELLA FREI, a grand-niece of the famous poet, a professor of cultural studies at Berkeley.

FIDELA GUEVARA, Ambre's younger daughter, a child star.

BOB RENZI, an entertainment lawyer, Fidela's husband.

EDWIN MONEY, a frail and elderly billionaire.

NATHAN WRYTOWER, his secretary.

PART ONE

Autism

A story by Carme Risk for her narrative therapist

Some years ago a young man and a boy of fifteen were walking along the banks of a river, looking for a good place to fish. Or rather, the boy had some memory of a better place he'd once tried, only a little farther on. They weren't particularly good at fishing, or interested in it, but they liked each other's company—in a contentious and unsettled way. Fishing, they could be together, but about some business, with no commitment to conversation.

The man was the boy's guardian, and had been for eighteen months. Other adults were involved—a welfare agency, a doctor, a developmental psychologist—but the man was the only one who had really taken the boy on, who was affectionate, bossed a little, and asked to have his own feelings considered.

For this man everything had happened at once, in a momentous two-month period a year and a half before. First, he found he was the sole beneficiary of the will of a well-regarded and wealthy grandfather he'd scarcely known, and was suddenly in possession of a lovely house, a bit of land, and a portfolio of investments that his grandfather's executor said was in fine fettle. Next, he had to deal with what he'd dreaded and tried to postpone, the results of some tests he'd been obliged to take because he'd had a few too many short blackouts at the controls of his jet. Blackouts induced by the g forces—he flew fighter jets for the RAF. The tests detected some "cumulative damage." He would always have to look at the world through a swarm of gray amoebic shapes that were, in fact, blood cells loose between the retinas and lenses of his eyes. Eyes and brain had been too hard-pressed, and had thereafter to be left in peace. He had to give up the jets. So he took a disability discharge and gave up the air force altogether. He didn't want to assess the performance of cadets in simulators or teach theories of flight.

He drove up the country to take inventory of his grandfather's house—and kicked a loose tile back and forth along the terrace while it rained. For a time he stared at the green smoke of spring willows down the valley, then asked his grandfather's gardener, "Are there fish in that river?"

There were fish, yes, brown trout and perch. There was a living once in fishing here, and some ancient fishing rights were accorded the people of the village. "But it's gone now—that village. See?" said the gardener. "Over there is the remains of a mill. The place was inhabited up until quite recently. Most of the people moved out only a little way, to Gatelawbridge—or thereabouts. Oh, no, Mr. Cadaver—it was nothing like the clearances."

At a specialist shop just south of the border, the man bought a rod and chest-high rubber waders. Then he used the waders as a jelly mold for a party in his flat near the base. He formed the mold with three dozen packets of jelly crystals and two gallons of vodka—which made a stiff blue-and-red jelly. He cut the waders open with a scalpel to have the jelly out intact.

Two days after the party, still dehydrated, he was woken at 5 a.m. by a scraping boom as part of the squadron went out on a scheduled exercise. A moment later, when he was sitting on the edge of his bed, mustering energy for a walk to the bathroom, he heard a noise, a loud pop, which he knew was the sound the stainless steel kitchen countertop made when it was depressed and then released. (He'd made that sound himself climbing through the kitchen window once when he'd forgotten his keys.) He found the nearest weapon and went out to investigate. He crept to the kitchen, turned on the light, and hefted his *shoe* to threaten a skinny boy with matted

4

hair, who was about to go out the window with an armload of party leftovers, including a chicken carcass that had sat about sweaty and neglected all evening at the party and was probably a health hazard. Concerned about this, the man leaped across the room and grabbed the boy's ankle.

"Hey! You!" he said. The boy gave a start, but didn't otherwise make any move to go. He let his ankle be held. He looked up, apparently amused by the shoe, and then into the man's face, with a slow, awed widening in his expression—like, the man later told people, Balboa in the jungles of the isthmus, sighting the Pacific and saying: "*Dios mio!* This isn't the ocean I've crossed."

The man noticed several things at once—which is how things happened to him, how his mind worked, and also what he came to expect from the world (he'd never asked anyone to justify an act with one good reason, he always wanted ten). He noticed that the boy was sticky to the touch and had a powerful musky aura, where bodily health had somehow converted dirt to the ozone of rain on dirt. The boy was thin and had snaky red scabies scars at his hairline, and his dark eyes darkened more, giving way onto a capacious gulf of expectant attention.

"Hey," the boy echoed. "You."

It was the first thing he'd said for ten years.

The man's name was Carlin Cadaver. There was a Genovese ancestor. When Carlin Cadaver and the very proper but overextended authorities had scratched together the boy's intermittent records, they discovered the child had been named three times in different incarnations at institutions the length of the country, always by diminutives of very commonplace names. That was the effect he had on people—a combination of tender protectiveness and an associated desire to make him somehow *more ordinary*. The boy was "Jimmy" before he went missing at five (his foster family hadn't ever really got over it). He was "Billy" when he appeared, perhaps eight years of age but wordless, at a hospital emergency room in Leeds. He had pus-streaked patches of scabies on his neck, in his groin and armpits, and between his fingers. The authorities had possession of him for a year after that—little Billy—and two different child psychologists examined him and put up quite convincing arguments for both elective mutism and autism. Billy ran away again—and didn't reappear officially till the police had him two years later. He was "Fredo" then, because of the huge hoard of chocolate Fredo frogs among other shoplifted goods filling his packing-case nest—a thin, utterly silent, mostly passive child who wouldn't meet anyone's eyes but who had a surprisingly sound set of straight scummy teeth, and good bones. Fredo escaped from a locked van transporting him to a "home." There was a female constable in the back of the van with him. She said that when the van stopped at a red light with a long cycle, Fredo tried the handle. She had just warned him—"Here! You sit down, that's locked!"—when the door opened and he got out, gave her one quick little look (the only eye contact he made), and shut the door. The constable found herself locked in and watching Fredo walk away along a traffic island.

"Jimmy, Billy, Fredo," the caseworker said to Carlin Cadaver. "He never answered to any of them. So it's your choice—"

"Call me Ishmael," said the boy, his nose in a book.

"He's not pretending, you know," Carlin said, almost squawking with indignation. "He says he taught himself to read."

"There's writing everywhere," the boy said, and looked up at them, making eye contact. He had gone to the opposite pole and did this more readily than most people. He was trying to find out from their faces why it was surprising that anyone should teach themselves to read, being surrounded by road signs and billboards. He put his face back behind the book, saying, with a faint air of accusation, "I told you I wanted to read *true* stories or stories about animals. This isn't really either."

Weeks passed. Carlin tried "Jimmy" and "Billy" and the boy just echoed—which he always did when he was upset.

There was a lot of fuss about moving caseworkers, but Carlin Cadaver did have a home to offer—a *stately* home—or big, anyway, as lovely as a Victorian glasshouse-cum-wedding cake, by the same architect who built Dickens's house at Gad Hill. There was a very good developmental psychologist in the neighborhood. And a good school, an experimental school, but with traditional houses, boarders, boys and girls; with languages, French, German, Spanish, and

Cantonese; and it offered twenty sports including *fencing*. (Carlin was trying to sell all this to the caseworker.)

"I want to learn how to kill with my bare hands," said the boy, who was reading a brittle paperback copy of *To Russia with Love*.

"Billy——" Carlin admonished.

"Billy," the boy echoed, in a hollow whisper. Then, "Who could conquer the world with a name like Billy?"

Carlin said that the boy was a smart little sod, and he supposed the boy wanted to be called Bond, James Bond. Well, he was going to sodding adopt him and call him "Abra" and that would show him.

The boy laughed, getting it, and said that was fine by him. Though later, when he was working his way backward through Nobel Prize winners, he once raised an irritated face out of *East of Eden* and complained that Abra was a *girl's* name.

Carlin and Abra, their fishing rods waving like the antennae of field radios, had reached a place where the river seemed to put out into its stream a pinching thumb and finger of shingle spits. Each spit originated on a different bank where the river turned around two rock outcrops, but both spits lay straight in the current, sculpted by water. It was a quiet place, sheltered by low hills and by the willows and chestnuts beyond the track to the river. The nearest road was a quarter mile off, and never busy.

"I thought it was here." Abra had been looking for the place he'd found the previous Saturday, a place where the river split around what might have been an island, with its own stony beach and trees, hawthorn, hazel, and rowan, roots exposed where the water had eroded the bank. On one side of the island the channel had been narrow, deep, and green, and Abra had seen a big, dappled shape drift momentarily up into the light.

The boy stopped and looked about him. "It can't be the next bend because there's the bridge." He seemed very puzzled. A truck crossed the bridge; they could hear its mudguards slap the asphalt where the bridge had been resealed, a tad too high for the road beyond it.

"You know how good my memory is," Abra said. He had been uncertain, embarrassed, disappointed just for a moment—now he felt suspicious.

"This is a fine place though," Carlin said. He squatted and opened his tackle box, began to fasten hooks along his line.

Half an hour later they had coffee and a cold meat and mint sandwich. They watched the tiny pulls their lines made on the surface of the water. There was more traffic, the post van, early, and Abra watched Carlin watch it pass, watched him wonder about postcards from someplace NATO exercises had taken his mates—last month it had been Malta. Abra was always noticing things, then not knowing what to do about them. He noticed that when the sun came up, it lit a streak of slick reddish mud on the gray stones of the upstream shingle spit. Because he couldn't think of anything to say—about the post—he got up, balanced his coffee cup on a flat stone, thrust the handle of his rod into the beach, and walked away. He crossed from the spit on his shore to the spit on the far shore by wading through the river. It came up to his thighs and was so cold his legs burned once he was out of it.

"Now you're wet you'll want to go back, I suppose," his guardian said, mild.

Abra studied the wedge of red silt, studied it up to what should have been its point of origin, where it stopped, thick still but sharp-edged, as though something had sat there keeping the shingle clean. Abra said to his guardian, "Things aren't like this."

"Things aren't like what?" Carlin had faith in the boy. He never mocked, never hurried—after all, little Jimmy had, by report, been manipulating buttons through buttonholes at twenty months and how many children could do that?

Then Abra's line twitched. Carlin grabbed the rod and said, "Quick!" The boy loped back through the river to reel in his fish.

Three fish later, and on the way back, Abra left the track through the weeds, following a very fine trail of broken stems. He ducked into a place where some dry thorns were tangled with hanging willow fronds. Carlin came when called. There was a lean-to about the size of two closets and made of hardboard and some flat timber shingles. It had shelves inside it, along the back wall, which held blankets wrapped in oilcloth—real oilcloth, canvas sealed with paraffin—and a musty old army surplus anorak. There was also a bicycle, its chain loosened and well greased.

Abra looked at his guardian, his eyes wide. He was waiting for a reaction.

"Do you expect me to mind?" Carlin asked Abra. The lean-to was on his land.

"Someone comes here," Abra said.

"Well, yes, obviously."

Carlin received one of those black, unfathomable, I-don't-understand-why-you-don't-understand looks. He felt unhappy, and there was a kind of panic in his unhappiness. Abra was being "obscure." The psychologist said Abra's autism had, to a degree, mysteriously resolved itself—as sometimes happened—but that there would probably be "whole registers of human interaction that would always be beyond him."

Abra sighed and shifted his feet and put one finger on Carlin's wrist. He'd looked blank, but suddenly had an expression of such beauty that it should have been love or joy or gaiety but was only eagerness and impatience. "Look," he said, "there is camphor in the paraffin of the oilcloth. But the wool isn't itself treated." He wriggled a pale fingertip through a hole in one blanket. "See? Here's a moth hole. The oilcloth is homemade."

"Yes? And the bike is a Raleigh, as in Walter, so I suppose we should keep our eyes out for the fabled city of gold?" said Carlin.

"Okay," Abra said. He slid, shrinkingly, past his guardian and picked up his rod from the path and went on home. Carlin followed, and continued patiently to ask what it was he'd failed to notice, and what Abra *meant*.

When he wasn't at school, Abra kept an eye on that bend in the river. It was summer. He'd take a book and lie in the shade along the long trunk of a fallen willow, near enough to the place to see in, but not too near. One day he arrived to find that the bike wasn't in the lean-to. He hovered for a bit, then climbed into his tree to wait. He finished his book. Then he practiced patience. Carlin called him in to lunch—his voice floating down the valley. Abra blocked his ears and waited. Later he sucked on a stone—having read somewhere that this helped with thirst and hunger. He got down from his tree and, though he knew he shouldn't, he drank a little river water—then played a game making patterns with slime on his feet and letting the sun dry them.

He managed to keep his back turned to the ticking of the bike's wheels and to the squawk as its brakes were involuntarily depressed when he was seen. There was a stealthy silence, then a slight stealthy noise as the bike was run on, and the thorn screen before the lean-to was moved, then resettled. When Abra turned around he saw a red-haired boy about his own age, sitting in the grass surrounded by plastic shopping bags.

"Hi," said Abra.

"Hi," said the boy.

Abra got up and minced over, trying to keep his feet immobile in order not to break the now stiff spirals and stars of blackened river slime. He introduced himself and asked for a name.

The boy thought for a bit. As he thought he scratched his neck—his shirt was wool and it was hot. "Twarky."

"What kind of a name is Twarky?"

"A family name," said the boy, with dignity.

Abra forgot his spirals and stars and began to sway from foot to foot. He told Twarky he should reciprocate.

"I don't know what that word is—so I can't," Twarky said, stolid.

"You should say, 'What kind of name is Abra?' "

"I was brought up to have better manners," said Twarky. Then, "Why don't you go? Can't you hear you're being called at for your meal?"

Abra stopped swaying. He considered this odd "at"—then went back to the river to wash his feet and retrieve his boots. He came over to sit by Twarky while he put them on. He asked who the boy was waiting for.

"My big brothers, to help me carry all this."

"*I* could help."

"You're being called." Twarky was staring at Abra's footwear—camel-colored desert boots, of which Abra was very proud.

"You don't have an accent," Abra observed.

"No?" Twarky pretended interest, not understanding what Abra had said.

"Well, I'll be off," said Abra, and got up.

"Yes. Good-bye," said Twarky and offered his hand.

"Abra Cadaver," Abra said, taking it and shaking.

"Yes, I'm sure," said Twarky, improvising again.

Abra walked away, then, out of sight, doubled back around the nearest hill and came up over its crest, crawling low through the long grass. He could see the red head and the white bags. He lay on his stomach and kept watch.

At dusk Carlin called again. Then Abra heard Carlin's cousin, and the cousin's wife, who also lived in the house, add their voices. He heard the three calling adults spread out, giving the occasional holler. After a time the cousin and his wife must have gone back in—but Abra saw his guardian on the bridge, his big silhouette, looking upriver, then down into the water under the arch. Carlin switched a torch on and pointed it down there.

Below, the boy with the bags hunkered down in the grass, drawing the bags to him.

Carlin pointed his torch upriver, made shadows behind each stone. Agitated, animated shadows rushed back and forth in the path of the torch. Carlin held it still. Twarky cowered in the grass. Carlin switched off the torch and left the bridge. Twarky sat up slowly, and drew a jittery breath.

The insects came with the dark and began to make a meal of both boys. Abra felt quite giddy with the itching. The headlights of the odd car on the road behind the hill showed the insects about him, a billowing net with black knots. He was in great discomfort, but he stayed still. He stayed still, but the insects gave him away to the boy with the bags.

Abra heard the grass move, heard, "So, it's you!" Then Twarky hit him over the head with the hard leather sole of a shoe. (Abra reflected afterward that this was bound to happen to him sooner or later, it was in his stars, the shoe that threatened.)

When he came to, struggling up out of sharp pain, nausea, vertigo, he heard voices, plastic rustling, and people walking through the river. He heard words he couldn't understand. He got to his feet, found all the hills and trees nearer and blacker than ever and outlined in pink. Below him he saw the water flash, he saw white bags, he saw—he *saw* a thick fur of shadow in the middle of the river where before there was only unquiet water in braids of light. He thought he saw the trees of his island.

He had to go down there. But one of his feet wouldn't take his weight—there was a stabbing pain in its sole, so severe that he lost his footing and tumbled—rolled over in the grass and sat up. He discovered that his boots had been taken and the sole of his right foot was slick with blood. He felt the stud of a thorn, tried to pull it out, but couldn't get purchase on the greasy blood. It hurt, and he'd been *comfortable* for so long—had even learned how to sleep in a bed—that he'd forgotten how to ignore pain. Instead of giving chase, Abra stayed still. He sat on the hill and listened. He heard the voices of the two men and the boy recede—he couldn't understand what they were saying. He heard a marsh bird boom. Behind that was something he had never heard, and *couldn't hear*, that he worked out only a moment later—when he did hear a truck on the bridge—was the sound of many square miles of antique silence, the silence of a place without engines.

Abra got up to limp home. The sky was blue again—and by its light Abra could see that his island was still there, with its stand of trees, some of their roots showing in the red clay bank where the water had carved at it, making a slick of silt on the stones. Just over the treetops Abra could see the island's end, more river, and the bridge as usual.

It took him an hour to get home—and he made a good entry, limping across the lawn to the house just as the police arrived to look for him.

Abra didn't tell his guardian what had happened. He said he was mugged, but was unhelpful in describing his assailants—unhelpful even as to their number or the time and place of the assault. He said that he couldn't remember.

When he recovered he continued his stakeout of that dexterous bend.

It was at this time that he and Carlin got a favorable answer to his request about taking a few classes in anatomy and physiology at the nearby university. His psychologist threw his weight behind this decision. Abra was possibly as mature mentally as he'd ever be, given his developmental disorder. Abra was also "in the genius bracket" and should be extended in whatever direction he desired. (Abra read the psychologist's letter, laughed, and said, "Freudian slip," to which Carlin said, "What? What?")

Abra started his classes at medical school, and was only saved from his rather reckless dabbling in all the available prescription and nonprescription drugs *not* by his desire to work—the drug-taking scarcely affected his concentration, stamina, and memory—but by the little dance of dependence he got into with his psychologist. The man made errors, he looked along his nose and made rarified remarks about Abra's clinical "coldness" and his "residual bodilessness." Provoking. The man said later that the boy had mistaken attention for intimacy, *he* thought he had fostered a healthy therapeutic bond, but perhaps should have expected something like this—*Oh God*—*at least from the boy, if not himself*. It was messy, and formative for Abra—but it's not what this story is about.

It was winter before Abra had a few days entirely at home. The motorbike he rode back and forth to his classes was at the local garage having something done. Carlin, Carlin's cousin, the cousin's wife, and some other adults were running a holiday math camp for some disadvantaged kids, and none of them had time for him.

Abra had climbed into bed with his guardian that morning to be told that, One, he was too big to do this and, Two, he always had been too big.

"The floor's cold and I want to talk to you," Abra said, snuggling. "I liked it better when it was just us."

"You're not, you know, a lifelong project," said Carlin—and squeezed back. He was a very affectionate man with, so far, no one to lavish it on but Abra.

"I am. I'm enough," said Abra.

"What an ego," said Carlin. "The alpha and the sodding omega."

"You're a very good parent," said Abra. "That's what I tell people. I tell them how you try very hard never to swear in front of me and corrupt my language, so instead you do this quaint 'sodding this' and 'sodding that.' "

Carlin pushed Abra out of his bed. "You know," he said, staring at the ceiling, "you used to notice everything *except* what people did. Now you notice that too. Not always nicely."

"Is that bad?" Abra said.

Carlin looked at him. "No. It's just—I think your psychologist must be mistaken, about the autism."

"He can't be. There is nothing else in the book that describes how I was and the way things seemed to me. Besides, if he's mistaken I've acted on his mistakes—or at least with him I have."

"So—have you read 'the book'?"

"You know I read."

Carlin waved a hand. "Okay. Good. Go read. Or call back one of those people who keep calling you, and failing to identify themselves," he said, disapproving. Then, as the door was closing, "But don't disappear."

Abra put on several layers of clothes, took a few supplies, and went out, on the off chance—but armed—to conceal himself in Twarky's lean-to. He waited without, he thought, much patience. He remembered having once been capable of great patience, like a hungry dog who can wait for the crumbs to fall.

Late in the afternoon, when he'd decided to go, a damp breeze came in the door, plucking the flap of curtain aside. The breeze was warm, and through the thorns Abra could see the tops of those anomalous trees. They weren't evergreens, but were in full leaf in winter. He heard a woman calling out, words he mostly missed the meaning of, but for "matches" and "Band-Aids." He heard Twarky reply—in another language. Then he heard the woman again, more distant, call out her good-bye.

Abra realized he was lying in wait at the wrong end of Twarky's shopping expedition, but by that time it was too late, and Twarky had pushed the curtain aside and had stopped still, staring at him, paralyzed by surprise. He was wearing Abra's boots.

Abra hit Twarky in the throat. The boy rolled about on the ground gagging. Abra sat on him and began to unbuckle his own belt. Twarky looked at this with popping eyes. Abra made a loop in the belt and slipped it over Twarky's head; he rolled the other boy onto his stomach and pulled the noose tight. He took out his pocketknife, opened it, and held its tip under Twarky's ear. "Stay still," he said. "You struggle, you choke." He studied Twarky's clothes, saw a thong fastening one shirt cuff and pulled it free to use on the boy's wrists. As Abra did so he was obliged to shift a bracelet, a cord on which were strung three gold rings—Twarky's currency. Because he'd paused too long to look, there was some struggle and a small but very bloody nick appeared below Twarky's ear. The boy burst into tears and put his face down in the stiff white grass. He begged Abra not to kill him.

Abra said, "Are you hungry?" in a tone that was almost mad with nervy insinuation. Twarky just moaned. Abra moved the knife to fish a mashed chocolate bar from his jacket pocket. "Mars Bar?" Abra suggested. He bit off a big chunk, which he kept between his teeth. His free hand worked the cap off the bottle still in his pocket. He dropped a pill into his palm, then pushed the Mogadon into the pinkish caramel of the Mars Bar, smoothed the place with his thumb, took the bar out from between his teeth, and said, "Here." He fed Twarky several pieces, including the piece containing the pill. That ought to make him more manageable.

Abra got Twarky up and walked him back toward the river. He could see the wet red clay bank and the trees exhaling steam in the winter air. "How long is it here for?" Abra asked.

"It's on a waning cycle, so seven hours, about."

"Your English has improved."

"No, all our talk about the Shuttling Wood is in English." Twarky told Abra that someone called Ulaw had studied, described, and charted it. In English, said Twarky. Then he said that his mother was from Dougalbrae but had kin in the village that once was here. "That was both here and there," said Twarky.

"Step down into the water," Abra said. He was concerned about the depth of the cut near Twarky's ear, so held the noose close and leaned behind the other boy to lick, once, twice, three times, till the sluggish red lacquer was cleared.

Twarky was shaking—but Abra reasoned that he had his feet in the river and it was very cold. Abra propelled his captive across the stream, shoved Twarky before him up the slippery bank, used him as a man uses a horse fording a swift river. They lay together on the bank, panting and coughing in the condensation and mixed air. The ground was warm, and Abra could feel the sun at two angles. He was scared and moved, so leaned close to his prisoner for reassurance—which was far from reassuring to his prisoner. Abra then explained to Twarky that his psychologist had told him that he suffered from feelings of exclusion because he didn't understand normal social interactions—but lately he'd been suffering from feelings of exclusion because this warm little island had kept its back to him.

Twarky moaned again. Abra got him up roughly and marched him forward. They were on a path that wriggled its way through the wood on the island. The steam followed them along the path a short way, then turned into still humidity. *There* began the long reach of silence Abra remembered, and had feared he'd never hear again. "I thought my life was over," he confided softly to Twarky, who strained his head and rolled an eye back. "I thought I'd never *know*."

The trees thinned. The sun was low on the other side of the sky, which was the color of melted butter. A marshland lay before them, haze making its horizon streaky. The captive saw this, and for some reason gave a faint self-satisfied "Huh!"

Abra used the belt to slow Twarky and bring him nearer. He said, "Show me the way."

The way was, at first, uncomplicated. A track descended into the marsh, then went along between low fresh rushes and, immediately beyond them, hummocks of mixed dead vegetation with living rushes atop. After a time Abra noticed he couldn't see the horizon—though he could still see the trees of the "island." The track narrowed and there appeared bundles of brush on its wet patches—some form of reinforcement. Stepped on, the bundles contracted and black water oozed through their branches. It was stinking hot.

Twarky asked to stop—croaked when he spoke—then squatted to plaster some black mud on his red hair. Abra watched him and wondered. He wondered how far Twarky and his brothers were normally prepared to lug plastic shopping bags in this heat.

They walked on. For one moment Twarky seemed uncertain of the path. Abra pulled hard on the belt so that Twarky staggered backward and dropped onto his knees. "This isn't the way," Abra said.

"It is," Twarky whispered. He was trying to insert his fingers between the belt and his throat. At his end, Abra wrapped the belt around his hand. "It changes," Twarky said. "How can you believe in the island, but not trust me that it changes?"

Abra saw that the other boy was weeping again; there were white trails uncovering the freckled skin on his muddy face. Abra said, "I'm sorry." He loosened the noose and his grip a little. Twarky raised both tied hands to wipe his eyes on the back of his wrists—then suddenly lunged forward. The belt slipped out of Abra's hands and Abra fell face forward in the mud between one hummock and another. The reeds stabbed at his face and he shielded his eyes. The instant he was down he got up again, without pause, erupted out of the mud and followed the splashing sounds and the sight of a hummock coming up again. He saw no red hair, only footprints filling with welling black water. He lost the tracks, circled looking for them. Before and behind him two islands of reeds were rising slowly, their cherry-red roots coming up again, glistening. *Which way?* He could hear only birds, half a dozen swifts in a dogfight against the shiny sky. Abra jumped onto a higher hummock, which teetered and gave him a view, as he turned, only of the marsh. The trees of the island had passed out of sight.

Abra found footprints again and followed them to the place where one set became two, and he and his captive had parted ways. After that he climbed the nearest tall mound of scratchy brown vegetation and scanned the marsh.

From the horizon a light flashed green as the rim of the sun disappeared. The heat lessened. Abra could see that the sun had gone down in a slight gap between the serrated horizon and a fine even cloud cover. He listened to the *scree scree* of the swifts, who were stirring up the still air, circling obliquely on an updraft from the hot marsh. A booming bird began to boom, then a heron cried, harsh.

When he climbed down from his vantage point Abra saw that the ground below him had become quite obscure. He waited for his eyes to adjust and, keeping them off the still-bright, buttery sky, he began to look for a quick way out of the swamp. It was hot. But at least, with his hands free, Abra was able to remove his jacket and jersey, to tie their sleeves together and sling them over his shoulder.

The air around his head began to whine. The insects aimed first for the rims of his eyes and his nostrils, where they could smell blood closest to the surface. Abra brushed at his face and thought about a book by André Gide that described that flash of green light. It only happened over the sea. So, as he went, he paused now and then to taste the marsh water. As he went, he remembered the librarian at the university who, whenever Abra was checking out a huge stack of books, would say, "Here comes the safety-conscious prodigy, who knows that a *little* knowledge is a dangerous thing." Abra thought, muzzily, about other books he'd read, and passages in those books where one person had walked about alone. Like Yossarian in liberated Rome, or Lucy Snow on a fête day in *Villette*. "I am by myself," Abra thought. Two years before he had always been solitary, but hadn't been conscious of it. Every time he blinked the world came back dimmer, but still perceptibly swarming. This was what Carlin saw—blood cells loose and magnified against the very apparatus of sight. Abra thought how strange it was that after all, everything had turned out to be wet and organic, despite an island that came and went, and a silence like a future he didn't have to plan for—what courses to take next year, whether to cut his hair, what profession to enter.

It was then that Abra fell into a sink of mud. He went straight down into it up to his ribs, his arms out, so that they slapped its gelid surface. The whole thing happened with a strange dry sound like that of a cork being put back into a bottle. A full bottle—there wasn't any air anywhere underneath him. He kept still, but sank a little. He put his head back and felt the mud suck at his long hair. For a moment he was so afraid that he closed his eyes and encased himself in himself—in his own thick, unfeeling body. Then, breathing slowed, he came back out to slide his hands across the mud, searching in a circle about him. A slimy solid something met his touch, he felt that it was a stick, perhaps the diameter of his wrist. He closed his hand around it and pulled—it gave, it came toward him. Abra paused, breathed, and the insects settled on every part of his face and throat and threaded their needles down through his skin. After a moment he had the stick in both hands like a quarterstaff. He extended his arms and rowed with it, across the mud, sank some, moved forward some. On his fourth reach, when the mud was already sucking at his armpits, one side of the stick struck something solid. On the next rowing motion the other side struck. Abra thrust the stick as hard as he was able up and forward, till both ends caught and he could pull himself a good way toward the solidity. Slowly—sobbing with effort and pulling every muscle in his upper body—he dragged himself out of the tepid constriction of the swamp.

He lay among the reeds. Maybe he slept—and saw a waterspout that came walking through his dream, white, swaying its hips and throwing salt over its shoulders. When he woke he thought for a time about a discussion he'd overheard between his guardian and one of those first doctors, about how widely spaced his eyes were, and fetal alcohol syndrome, and poor impulse control, and whether he was able to recognize danger as danger. But what "sense" or simple set of instructions would have kept him out of the swamp? he wondered. It was as if these health professionals and his guardian inhabited a different world from the one he was in—a world like a fenced-off section of his own.

He sat up and, when he was up, he saw the lights. Two of them, not far, not near, yellow and moving very slowly. He heard voices carrying through the still air, and the hollow slap of water against wood.

He swallowed, lubricated his throat with phlegmy spit, and called out. "Help me!" It was the first time he'd ever said it. The blood rushed to his head and he covered his ears—the sound of his own cry for help frightened him more than all the things he was asking to be helped from.

The lights moved together and came closer, till he could see figures and faces, and that the lights were held high at the bow and stern of a long flatboat. He saw too, by the light, that the dry place where he perched was formed around a broken tree, a piece of flotsam, and that whereas one side of it was the mud hole in which he'd nearly died, the other was a sizable channel that probably came from the sea at the ragged edge of the marsh.

A man with hair and beard the same dull bronze red as Twarky's poled the boat in toward the tree. Abra clambered down. The people in the boat put out their hands meaning "careful," but he swarmed over the water and into the boat. He fell into an inch of bilge and lay panting. A lamp was put down beside him on the seat. Two of them helped him up, wrapped him in a blanket, and sat him in the bow. A girl sat beside him. The other three were all men—two young, the helmsman middle-aged. The men were all from the same family, almost certainly Twarky's.

"I'm Astrella, Ulaw's daughter. My father sent us out to find you," the girl said. She looked at him, hard, her eyes like two cold lamps. "I'm here to make sure they don't hit you over the head and sink you somewhere."

Abra saw his best option and took it. He curled up on the narrow seat in the bow, closed his eyes, and went to sleep.

Manhandled, he stayed down, sulking under the surface of consciousness. Like that original and disastrously tempting dappled fish, Abra found himself patrolling a small but deep pond—his own young, uninformed brain. He felt himself undressed and let it be done, his pliability practiced. ("He doesn't speak, but he does everything practical he should, on cue—has even been toilet-trained. He only puts up *meaningful* resistance, as if . . ." *As if he wasn't deaf enough.* He closed his ears. It was a caregiver and caseworker who spoke, about Jimmy, who had closed his ears—but remembered now what they said.)

Warm water and scented soap; he could feel grit under his elbows and buttocks, the silt from the swamp. He opened his eyes and got up and took a towel from the woman in the green dress—not young, not so old she shouldn't mind that *he* minded her seeing him naked. Her dress was good, brocaded silk, but all one color, a glistening olive green. She had green eyes too, but she was obviously the mother of the blue-eyed girl in the boat. The other woman wore a big white apron and had the same voice that had asked for "Band-Aids" and "matches" all those hours ago.

The towel hurt. The skin on his face, throat, and forearms was tight and lumpy. The women took the towel away from him, told him to keep still, then lathered the bites with cold, chalky calamine. He got an erection and they laughed. The one in the green dress stood him on a mat and combed out his hair while the calamine dried. She didn't offer him a towel to wrap around himself, and she wouldn't speak English. She giggled, spoke too loud, and gestured in an airy, girlish away. The other woman kept testing the poultice on his face. When it was so dry and hard it had pulled his nostrils wide, she gestured he should come with them. They gave him a waffle-textured cotton robe and led him out of the bathroom with its marble bath but—Abra noticed—no taps, and to a big bed under a gold-fringed canopy and curtains of gauzy, embroidered silk.

Later, he rolled over to find a man—not young, but too old, Abra thought, to be lounging around in the state of undress—on the edge of the bed, studying him. The man looked over his shoulder and said, in English, "He's awake, Genevieve, come and look at his eyes."

The airy woman asked if he was hungry.

The man leaned closer. He was very good looking—or he had been, and had carefully preserved the superficial luster of his youth. His skin was clean, pale, and nurtured, his hair glossy, even its gray. "Listen," he said, in a friendly word-to-the-wise way, "Twarky turned up last night, raised the whole village, to tell us about his abduction. *All* about it. I just had to see for myself. Your brutal, devious, unsavory behavior has saved you, because it caught my interest."

"I'll try my best to keep it up," Abra said. Then, "I only wanted Twarky to *share*."

"You know you look like a monster," the man said. "Knobby and misshapen."

"That's right, keep his spirits up," said the woman, who was dressing. "Does he have to stay in our bed, dear?"

"You even have blisters on your eyelids," the man continued.

Abra just regarded him, dumbly, wondering why, since he was so completely in this person's power, he was being controlled by insults or—if that wasn't it—he was being told something as *irrelevant* as how he looked?

"Do you think *I* should share?" the man asked him.

Abra considered this, then suggested, "I could bring you books."

"I have a library full of them. And I could send Twarky for more. I could get them for myself—except I'm not going back there."

"Would Twarky know what to get?" Abra studied the man a moment, then added, "I read a good one recently, Patrick White, *The Twyborn Affair*. It's about three people: a young woman, a man, and an older woman—but really they're the same person."

The man addressed his wife over his shoulder again. "Do you hear that, Genevieve? Patrick White has a new novel." He looked back at Abra and said, "You're a shrewd creature."

"Patrick who?" Genevieve said. She was dressed now, and was plaiting gold braid into her thick black hair.

"Ignorant woman," her husband said fondly.

"*I'm* not ignorant," Abra promised.

The man asked his name.

"Abra Cadaver."

"Related to old John Cadaver?"

"He was my guardian's granddad. He's dead."

"He used to come here. In the 1930s first, then the island disappeared for ten years, or so he said. Cadaver thought the island had two different regular cycles, one like a lunar cycle, the other like a comet's long orbit. I first came here when my mother met and married someone. When our family reached our quota of advantageous marriages on this side, we settled." He gestured about the big, luxurious room. "This house is Ulaw—and I am its lord. Therefore call me Ulaw."

"We have a party, dear!" his wife called out.

Abra put a hot, lumpy hand on the man's leg. "There's a marsh and inlet. I've seen only those so far . . ."

Ulaw smiled. "There's farmland and forest just out these windows. There's a lake, and around the lake a town with castle and Queen. It's the capital of a whole country with two rivers, at the mouth of one a marsh and an inaccessible beach heaped with whale bones and rainbows, at the mouth of the other a great port. There's a vast, rambling 'monastery' that sends doctors and teachers and vets and engineers all over the country. There are two coastal borders, two mountainous; and, beyond that, a whole world about which I know a great deal, enough to have married one of my daughters to a prince."

Abra lay looking at the man with what—if he wasn't too swollen—would be recognized as a sad and speechless look.

"A boating party, with *music*," the woman said, tapping her foot now, right behind her still undressed husband.

"What have *you* got?" the man asked Abra.

Abra thought, then volunteered, "Your attention?"

He ran a fever for four days and Genevieve had him moved—he was making their mattress damp. He was installed in the smallest guest room and waited on by servants—including the cook, Twarky's mother, who made him feel her disapproval and her power by telling him how easy it would be for her to feed him something that would really set him back. "But you're just a boy," she finished, and tucked him in so firmly it was an oppression.

He improved. Genevieve came in one afternoon and apologized. She'd been terribly rude and cruel—to turn an invalid out of the best bed. She got him up and took his arm to lead him out along the loggia that ran around the central courtyard of the house on its first floor. They went in through the door of the master chambers.

"You must think me heartless," she said as she turned down the bed. "You look much, much better—only a little like a peach the hail has caught." She fluffed his pillow and smoothed his hair. Then she perched by him, faintly flustered, breathless, blushing. She waited to catch his eye, then began to coax, one by one, out of their loops, the small mother-of-pearl buttons on the bodice of her dress. Abra was mesmerized. She took his hand and put it in between what was warm and yielding. He felt her heartbeat and, under his light touch, tiny hairs in her cleavage lift, pulling her skin up into goosebumps. He sat up, following his hand, the blood singing in his ears.

"Rip the dress," she said, and threw back her head and freed one bony, shapely shoulder.

"Why?" Abra asked.

She told him not to be so cautious and cold-blooded, then swooped at him and pushed him down so that her nipples brushed his chest. She took a deep breath, bared her teeth, and gnawed along his jaw, all the while moving her own skirts. Then she found him, without looking, and she took hold of him and got him in the right place. "Good," she said.

In a rush he upended her. She laughed, "Even better!" Then she pinched his chin and made him look into her eyes again—which was difficult, because he was angry with her. Angry and confused. She whispered to him. Commanded him to hold still. She said things, a kind of commentary on what she felt, on its growth, while making her muscles talk too, or *chew* on him. He did as he was told, but watched her sullenly as she caught with her tongue the string of spit from his slack mouth. Then she said, like those coaxing caregivers to the suddenly silent little Jimmy, holding out a biscuit: "What do you say? Hmm? What do you say?"

Abra said please, and she let him move.

Afterward, she said *sixteen* was even younger than she had thought. Then she laughed for a while, a musical chuckle, and tangled her feet in his. "The youngest yet!" She fanned herself, then she grew still when he leaned his head sleepily on her arm. "*Now* you trust me," she said, surprised.

Abra said he didn't trust her, he liked her, and that *that* was the first time he'd done that without a condom. It felt so good—even better than a mouth.

"Sixteen," she said again, cradling his head. "What a responsibility. But I'm not going to take you on."

Abra yawned. He said he was going back to Carlin Cadaver, the only person in the world he loved—then amended: in *any* world.

Ulaw was piqued. His wife sat up in the bed and mussed her own hair and said, "First in, first served." And then they began to argue about his intentions, and her perception of his intentions, and some lover of his who had "stepped over the line," and another lover of hers who had refused to recognize Ulaw's rights as the *supporting* parent of a certain child, and then they argued more earnestly about someone it seemed they once shared—and somewhere during all this Genevieve got up, examined herself closely in a full-length mirror between the room's two big windows, and, slapping herself firmly on her silver-stretch-mark-webbed but neat potbelly, exclaimed, "Ha!" as if highly satisfied by something she could see. Then she raised her arms and did a little whirling dance across the room. Her husband fell silent.

Abra got out of bed, tried to make a toga of a sheet, and got hopelessly tangled. "This is all getting a bit too much like Edwardian pornography," he said, trying for dignity. "Although I've not read any," he admitted. "But since I suspect that if I hang around with you two I'll end up heavily kohled and in a sailor collar, I'll leave." He began to look for his clothes.

Ulaw had erupted into laughter.

Genevieve told her husband, gloatingly, that Abra had the loveliest smell of anyone ever—except her babies of course, delightful objects, in the short term anyway.

Abra found his clothes and put them on. He told Ulaw that he didn't need an invitation. "I don't mean to your wife. I mean here. This world. I'll just go around you."

"I'm the bosom of Abraham," Ulaw said—serious again.

Abra shrugged, collected himself, and went out.

He found the cook and had a talk with her. She drew him a map. She said, "We people who live along one side or the other of the Shuttle, we have to behave responsibly. This place doesn't want bandits with ballistic weapons, or mining companies."

"No," he said, "that's not what I'm interested in. I like the difference. It's so quiet here—a whole land like a person who won't speak. Besides, I'd never settle. Never. I'm doing medicine. I'm going to make *discoveries*."

"You wait till I tell Ulaw that, he'd welcome a trained and equipped doctor. He's a bit of a hypochondriac. It's half his reason for settling here—he'd swallowed all that stuff about, what was it, allergies and food additives?" She was cutting Abra some sandwiches for his walk. "You might have to wait in the marsh till the trees come," she reminded him. Then she mused on the word "allergies," pleased to have summoned it. "My children have such patchy English. But their father is from here, so we speak both languages in our house. Ulaw's children are word-perfect in both." She pointed at the elderly woman at a thatched washhouse—she was walking him out then. "Now, if you spoke to her you'd hear a broad Australian accent. She had no traditional connections, but just tagged along with those of us who came in on the final exodus. A bridge that connected the village to the road washed away in 1968. The county council wouldn't rebuild it. So we all left."

Abra asked how many chose the other way, and was told of families in Gatelawbridge, her own brother on the oil rigs somewhere, another cousin of a sort who was a beekeeper back in Closeburn, who had claimed that he couldn't shift his hives. "That was his excuse for staying. My eldest had her eye on him—but he wasn't as keen on her." She stopped where the fields began to drop and get a little dank, and waved Abra on.

Carlin was so distraught and incensed by Abra's long absence that Abra had to tell him everything, and take him there right away. But the wooded island had disobligingly disappeared.

Carlin strode up and down the icy riverbank. "You come back—battered—and tell me the plot of sodding, fucking *Brigadoon*." He stopped, struggled, wiped his eyes. "I thought you were more normal than that." He held up a finger. "Give me one, just *one* good reason not to ground you."

"You wanted ten before," Abra said, placid. "Ten good reasons, you said." Then he gave them again. "I was led into another world.

But the one who led me lost me. I nearly drowned. Insects ate me alive. A couple had me rescued, and nursed me in their house. I was knocked about, and feverish for four days. I wanted to know enough to know how to come back. I wanted to know whether it was worth it. I needed to know if it was safe. I had to wait for the island to cycle back to that side, and then to this."

Carlin was red-eyed but spiteful. "They'll never let you practice medicine, you know, because you're not mentally stable."

"Why would you think that, and not that I was insulting you with a silly lie?"

Carlin stormed, he kicked the stones.

"Look at me," Abra said, and waited till Carlin did. Abra's face coming and going in the veil of his breath. "I'm the evidence of your senses," Abra said. "Where did I find the biting insects?" He gestured around at the bare trees and the river edged with rime.

"Why are you like this?" Carlin said, miserable and exasperated. Then he turned his back and walked away.

Carlin met Abra's psychologist to discuss strategies to manage this latest problem. It was suggested he monitor what Abra was watching on television. "Perhaps that's where this stuff is coming from," the psychologist said. Carlin had hoped he'd be told that Abra's "other world" story was just a lame excuse for his having wandered off, for drug-taking and sleeping rough—ordinary adventures.

Carlin came home from the meeting to find Abra parked in front of *Sapphire and Steel*. He sat down and *monitored*.

In the program there was a boy whose parents had been consumed by a vortex in the wall of his sister's bedroom. Carlin observed that this story wasn't very *grounding*.

Abra's eyes stayed on the screen. "Says the grounded pilot. Is grounding good, then? A good grounding—good training for a daily grind."

Abra's word games always made Carlin uncomfortable. Carlin said that he'd meant that it wasn't real. "No real problems. No real solutions."

"It's more real than . . ." Abra trailed off. Sapphire had somehow walked into a painting, she was trapped in it and under attack.

Carlin watched Abra's face, his open mouth, his beautiful, self-forgetting idiocy.

The moment passed. Sapphire was saved.

Abra said he'd had his first human dissection that morning in anatomy. Before beginning his whole class was talked to—counseled. Carlin *had* signed Abra's permission form—he'd needed one because of his age. Of course they'd all found the dissection horrible and hard, and all tried to be as steely as they could. "I was very steely," said Abra. "More than most."

There was an ad break. Abra looked away from the screen and at his guardian and was immediately at flashpoint. His eyes ignited and voice colored up. He hadn't been boasting of a strong stomach. "I wasn't moved in that way. Listen—what's so real or *right* about the fragile interdependence of human organs?" he asked. Then he observed that a dead body was different from a living one.

Abra had a way of stating the obvious. It was as if he wasn't registering the difference between a dead and living body as a *fact*, but as something about which he had a feeling. A powerful, instructive feeling.

"I could feel the difference," Abra said.

"I'm sure you *all* could. Obviously. Temperature, texture, smell—everything."

"No." Abra's eyes wandered, but not to the television, just away from Carlin. "I don't mean the obvious difference between my body and the body's body—I can't say cadaver to you without feeling too weird. I could feel the difference between her body as it was, on the table, ten weeks in formaldehyde, gray, pickled, and how it had once been. It wasn't my imagination. Anyway, we all went back to the classroom and looked at our textbooks and our 3-D model. And everyone was thinking about how a map is not a landscape—except me. I know I'm not supposed to say that I know what other people are thinking. I've been told I don't. *Far from it*, I've been told. And I've been told not to imagine I'm thinking anything very different from the next person. These are mutually exclusive recommendations, I might say. To imagine correctly that I'm thinking more or less what everyone else is, I'd have to be able to imagine *what* they're thinking. Or am I just supposed to have faith?"

Carlin was bewildered. He wished Abra had never read *Alice in Wonderland*. To get Abra out of his mirror maze of logic, Carlin asked, "What were you thinking?"

"That it was unbelievable. That what really happens to people is unbelievable. Like—a mistake, with a remedy."

The program resumed. Abra was swallowed by the small colored vortex in the wall.

Abra arrived home one evening, four months after his "lost week," with a small, blond, bright-eyed, black-browed woman. Abra introduced her: "Cassandra, a cataloguer. She'd like to look at your library."

"By all means—this way." Carlin was flustered for some reason puzzling to himself. He led Cassandra to his library, opened the curtains wider to let in the last of the light, switched on some lamps, and apologized for the wrinkle in a rug and the poor placement of one massive, immovable couch. Then he stood, fiddling and staring at her. She touched spines and asked questions. Who dusted, for instance. She knew that Abra *read* the books. "I'm cataloguing the library at Ulaw."

"Excuse me?" said Carlin.

"Oh." She looked at him, taken aback. "Abra said he told you. I'm cataloguing Ulaw's library."

"The—the—" Carlin couldn't get it out. He pulled faces. He put a finger in the collar of his polo neck and stretched it so hard a stitch popped.

"I'm a little tired of it—or perhaps I'm addicted to exhaust fumes." Cassandra was tentative. "But my son is at school over there and he won't speak anything but Esindu."

"Oh, fine, mock me!" Carlin said. He stamped a foot. "Ha! *Brigadoon*! Gene Kelly in a Tyrolean hat, Cyd Charisse in plaid. A hundred years among the heather!" He was red in the face, and would have asked her to leave if her clear, sympathetic gaze hadn't stopped him.

"Why does it have to be Brigadoon?" she said. "Why not the mystic isle of Avalon?" Then, "I knew your grandfather. *He* had some imagination."

Carlin regarded her skittishly, as though she might explode.

"I shouldn't stay too long, because of my son. Though the cycles have been reliable for over thirty years." She put out her hand. "Come on," she said. "Come and help me woo my son away from the eels in the marsh. We can try promises of toys, or a trip to an amusement park." She came up to him and took his hand in hers. Her palm was rough, its biggest callus, however, still a writing callus. "Abra is hurt that you're so determined to think him mad. You're pretty much his home base when it comes to the whole human race, you know."

"How long have you known him?" Carlin was a prickle wrapped in ice.

"A few months. Time moves the same here as there, it's quite convenient," Cassandra said. "It's not like Narnia." She tugged at him. "Come and see."

Carlin yielded, with the oddest sensation, as if his scalp thought it was the only part of him still sane and under its own volition and it had decided to creep away somewhere without him. He clapped his free hand on his hair and went with Cassandra.

It was flattering how quickly her son took to him. The boy had been born in his gatehouse when Cassandra was staying with her mother, John Cadaver's housekeeper. The boy was called John after Carlin's grandfather, though there wasn't any connection other than sentiment. John's father was dead, pushed out of a moving train in Turkey while tussling for a money belt. He and Cassandra had been on a journey of self-discovery—cheap ganja, nice beaches, bed lice, exotic landscapes and people. She came home.

Carlin and Cassandra were sitting on the step of her little drywall stone house. Carlin was trying, valiantly, to mend a toy sailboat, somewhat distracted by a cavalcade passing through the village. There were men and women on horses with bows and arrows and hooded hawks and horns and flags—the Prince Consort and some other courtiers, Cassandra said, and that Captain of the Palace Guards who was such a charmer. The boy took the boat back saying he'd try himself, saying it in English, to his mother's satisfaction.

Abra came along the road after the hunting party, on foot with a group of younger members of Ulaw's family. They ambled along in a loose knot, Abra at its center. He halted before Cassandra's house and half the group stopped too.

Cassandra told Abra his pharmacology text was on her kitchen table, then asked how wet the road was. She had thought to go around the shore that afternoon. She had noticed that the girls' dresses had muddy hems.

Ulaw's blue-eyed daughter, Astrella, was telling Carlin about Abra's "political questions." She said Abra did a "foreigner in need of guidance" act, then asked uncomfortable questions about the laws of the land. "There was quite a crowd on the lakeshore, half of them keen to answer Abra's questions and several getting very testy. Then the Captain of the Guards stopped off on his way with the hunt and made some cautionary remarks about noisy assembly."

Cassandra's son had put the mended boat in the lake's shallows, where it stood straight. Carlin applauded. Cassandra said next time he came they should go to the nearest port and see all the sailing ships. Carlin nodded, then looked sharply at Abra, whom he had found the other day, at home, with a library book, poring over a diagram of rigging on one of the great tea clippers. Carlin had the feeling he was being conspired against—manipulated somehow. He got up and reminded Abra, "We have to get back for your exams. If you don't get an A this time you lose your scholarship. And I'm not taking you to Italy with me if you don't get an A."

They went up to Ulaw's house to take their leave of—Abra said—the two bosoms of Abraham. They found Genevieve manicuring her husband's hand. They were by the fountain in the central courtyard. The long stretch of engineless silence was sampled there without cattle or voices or birdsong—unless the birds passed right overhead.

Ulaw had already got a report on Abra's "questions" from one of the group who hadn't paused at Cassandra's door. He said Abra was going to get himself killed.

"Asking questions?" Abra was incredulous.

Ulaw raised his brows at Carlin. "He's gathering crowds and preaching on lakeshores. And you named him after a magic charm."

"It's only a pun. And it diverts people from all the bloody dead body jokes *I* had to suffer."

"I want to change it to something with a similar rhythm," Abra said. "I had thought 'Agrippa.' "

They laughed. Then Carlin, more gentle: "But your psychologist says I should do everything I can to help you to a stable sense of your own identity. Since you have problems with self-definition."

"My psychologist has problems getting his tongue far enough into my asshole," said Abra, annoyed.

Genevieve whooped, unladylike. Ulaw scowled at her and said really it was too much, she couldn't sleep with Abra and laugh so hard at his jokes.

Abra, who cared about the questions he'd been asking, began talking to Ulaw about refugees, and asking how come the king in the country to the north whom everyone spoke so badly of had still managed to convene a council of commoners. Carlin reminded Abra that his psychologist had explained that, given his childhood autism, he could be expected to be attracted to ideas about social organizations, but to be blind to social behavior. "You'll get it wrong, don't you see?" Carlin said.

"But I am learning how to read people."

"*Read*," said Carlin, significantly. "Apparently, you can learn anything." He pointed at the pharmacology text under Abra's arm, wrapped in oilcloth.

"But I like this world, and it's so far only mildly infested by books," Abra said, not quite taking Carlin's meaning.

Ulaw was smiling at him, rather proud and possessive.

"And"—an anxious line formed between Abra's straight black brows—"and I'm *unlearning* some things. There are things I can't do anymore. I'm forgetting how it felt to do them. You think I'm the skinny little alien I was, but I've changed so much it feels—evolutionary."

"I worry about you," Carlin said.

"Don't worry too much, Cadaver," Ulaw promised. "I'll protect him. Assiduously. If he stops sleeping with my wife."

"*Sleeping*. The sweet, defenseless, post-orgasmic snoozer," said Genevieve, looking at Abra. Then to her husband, "Dear—it's not like you to be so euphemistic." She said that, anyway, she might not *have* to sleep with Abra anymore. As she said this the cook came in to tell them that Twarky said they were in luck, the trees had appeared a little earlier than expected. Carlin hustled Abra out. Ulaw retrieved his hand from his wife and said, "Meaning what?"

In high summer, Abra was on his way back home from his classes one night at ten in a blue dusk. The Cadaver estate was on more than one border, was in the north where the summer nights were long. Abra was riding his Honda, and had slowed for the bridge, because of the country's unintentional speed bump of bad seal, and because he always took a look from the apex of its arch to see if the island was there yet. He had a copy of a chart Ulaw had made, mapping the cycles of the Shuttling Wood, as they called it. (Years later, when Abra was in one of those enclosed, reversible bridges that shuttle across the runways at Dulles Airport, Washington, D.C., from terminal to terminal, he turned to the elderly poet whose escort he was and said, "This reminds me . . ." Jules Frei welcomed any sentence which began that way, never having been tortured by a toastmaster: *That reminds me of a joke. A poet and a doctor are in an airport shuttle at Dulles and the doctor says to the poet, 'This reminds me . . .'* ")

I'm sorry, I was doing so well, but I'm afraid of this. I'm afraid that when I come to the end of the story you've set me to write, you'll know what I mean by making a joke of these repetitions.

Abra slowed his bike, pushed up his visor to see better, and saw the wood. He coasted down over the bit of bad seal at the bridge's end. He opened his throttle.

A big figure rose up from behind the wall at the bridge's end and wrapped its arms around him. The bike shot out from under Abra and skidded on its side, sparking, along the road. He was flung down the bank. He kept his arms close to his body and rolled fast and neat to the foot of the bank, bruised by the odd prominent stone and jarred by the larger one with which his helmet connected.

He got up fast and went back up the bank, where he could see a headlight casting its eye here and there as his assailant struggled to lift the bike. The sight of the struggle misled Abra. He mistook it for muscular weakness, but it was spilled gasoline and the problem of getting a grip on something splashed and slippery.

Abra launched himself at the man, hesitating halfway as he got a sense of the man's size. He hit hard. The man dropped the bike to catch him—caught him, and put a foot back to keep his balance. Abra found himself up off the ground like a dog that has leaped into its master's arms.

The man simply tossed him away again. Abra relaxed—as he'd been taught in his karate classes, and as it came to him naturally—and watched the edge of the road pass underneath him as he sailed, feeling fatalistic and silly, over the edge of the bank once more. This time he came down on his hands and knees. The pain and the gas fumes made him gag.

Abra didn't often lose his temper. He got up feeling grim and vicious, and climbed to the edge of the road, where he found that the man had the bike up on its wheels. Abra unfastened his bike jacket, got out his Zippo, flipped it open, and tossed it into the glossy patch of spilled gasoline.

Gasoline, bike, man, all went up in gentle, hazy, blue-based flames. The man gave a grunt, then closed his mouth against the fire, flung past Abra and down the bank, where he fell in the deep place and disappeared, all but his gasps, in wildly disturbed gleaming water and a confined pall of smoke.

Abra watched the river seethe, heard boulders grinding together as they were trod by someone floundering and furious. He waited for the man to emerge from the river—waited to see what would happen next. The river looked oily in the firelight. Abra saw a slick black head appear in its slickness, a broad orange-clad back, and one huge, white-knuckled hand grasp a patch of wheezing waterlogged turf on the bank. A big square knee in scorched orange cloth appeared, and a blackened boot splashed on the bank.

The man was wearing an orange coverall, he was lanky, long-boned, monstrously tall. He raised his face and looked at Abra.

Abra pulled off his helmet and put it down at his feet.

The man came slowly up the bank and stepped onto the road. He stood, his shoulders drooping, and watched the bike burn. His hair gradually separated into dripping rattails. He brushed it out of his eyes. Then he addressed Abra. "It's hard to form an impression of someone when you first meet them," he said. The man's voice was deep in timbre but shallow somehow, reticent. They both watched the bike burn.

"I can help you," Abra said.

"I'm not really desperate," the man said. "They're probably not swarming about the countryside heavily armed and looking for me."

"Uh-huh," said Abra —who, being capable of violence himself, recognized a dangerous person when he met one.

"I'd have liked to get home to see my parents. At their own hearth, with the cats," the man mused. "You see—they can't bring the cats when they visit. I only get letters about the cats."

"Uh-huh."

"Really all rather whimsical on my part," the man said. "A whimsical prison break."

Abra watched him. Then he asked the man if he was a murderer.

"Yes," the man said.

"And was that whimsical too?" Abra asked.

"A moralist," the man said, "who thinks a person's acts must be consistent with his character."

Abra studied him for a little longer. The light was fading. The man's face was so exhausted it was incapable of expression. Abra asked the man to follow him—but the man just drooped and dripped. Abra was forced to touch him—to take his wrist. He felt flattened links and an oval disk curved to the shape of the wrist. He asked what the medic alert bracelet was for.

"Epilepsy," said the man.

"Any medication?"

"Yes. My muffler, I call it. It retards the fits, and makes me feel hungover and watery."

The man let himself be led along the road, out of the light of the burning bike, and to a notch in the road's shoulder, where a track went down to the narrow beach under the willows.

Abra wanted to know whether the man would die without the drugs. He wasn't pleased with the answer. Possibly. It was rather a strong dose. The man said he hadn't been looking after himself, before or after—delicately declining to say before or after *what*. Too many late nights in clubs with loud music and lights, the man explained. And there was the ephedrine and amyl nitrate, and the little speedballs. "None of it mixed well with my medication—so I just took more of the anticonvulsive."

It was very dark on the riverbank, the stones giving only a hint of pallor in the lower hemisphere of their vision each time they blinked and their eyes registered anything at all.

Abra asked the man his name.

"Devlin Hughes. And why should I follow you?"

"I can keep you out of prison."

"That's quite a promise." Devlin Hughes sounded amused.

Abra asked how he'd do without the drugs if he took proper care of himself: exercise, diet, early nights, not too much stress.

"I'd have the odd fit. Maybe small. Maybe not. If I was alone I could die. Why?"

They reached the ford. Abra pulled Hughes down into the river. The man staggered, found his footing in the thigh-deep water, and then took hard hold of Abra by his jacket, lifting him up till their faces were together. "Where *are* you taking me?"

Abra grabbed at the man's shoulders to get the pressure of his collar off his jaw. His palms settled against the thick bands of muscle on the man's bunched neck. The river water was cold, but the skin warm. Abra was bewitched by his close proximity to pulse, tremors of tiredness and effort. The man's small jaw muscles jumped and jumped. Abra had never felt more absorbed.

He told Hughes that if he'd stayed by the burning bike the police would soon have had him. No matter what happened now, if Hughes just stepped up this bank and sat down for a short while under these trees, the worst of it would be a few hours of darkness and discomfort and uncertainty—but at least at liberty.

Devlin Hughes put Abra down, stepped up the bank, and leaned against a tree. "You're doing the voice of reason, but I'm afraid of you. You don't make any sense." He said that the person he'd killed had been not much older than Abra, and that it was more ineptitude than malice on his part—violence that went too far past the consensual. "And there's society's typical intolerance of certain practices," he added, almost pious.

"Uh-huh," said Abra.

The shadow that was the man against the shadow that was the tree said, "I'm trying to tell you that it's dangerous for you to touch my face and say—possessively—that you can save me." Hughes stopped, sighed, and began again. "My parents are very decent people. In every way, political and personal. They make goat-milk cheeses. They run a boutique cheese shop in Bristol for the lactose intolerant. It's called Intolerance, in D. W. Griffith lettering. Of course, after the notoriety of my crime the shop's name did rather look like a challenge to the community. But people *have* been good to them." He was silent for a while, then said, very quietly, "Boy— it's best for you to try to sound as if you're *good*. A decent person."

Abra didn't say anything. He peered at the shadow—this unsavory, dangerous man. He imagined he felt a weird dark warmth coming off the shadow.

"They're very sweet," Hughes went on, about his parents. "My father writes poetry."

"I like poets," Abra said.

"Oh? Do you know any poets?"

"No. But I know I'd like them—poets, and caviar, and haggis, neeps, and tatties—I'm very flexible."

"I hope to find out," Hughes said, flirting and threatening.

This made Abra hot all over, and restless. He jumped up. "Come on, we'll go to the other end, where the marsh might be. I think I can smell the sea."

He put out a hand, and the man took it.

A few weeks later a boy of maybe seventeen came and draped his arms over the high glass counter of a boutique cheese shop in Bristol. He said to the man behind the counter—white hair, white apron, exceptionally tall—"Excuse me. Are you Mr. Hughes, the father of Dev Hughes?"

The man in the white apron looked pained, then he steeled himself. This wasn't a detective—or even another reporter, unless he was from some college paper. He said yes, he was the father of Devlin Hughes.

"I know where he is. He'd like me to bring you and his mother to him."

It was impossible for Dev's father to be guarded, even after everything. Tears filled his eyes. "Where is he?" he said.

"He's safe with me," said the boy.

One other thing has to be told—as a story—not reported.

Abra wasn't "maybe seventeen"—he *was* seventeen. Two years later, at nineteen, he was in the warm, weathertight salon of a ship he'd built, trying to settle his two-year-old daughter down. The ship was out in the current at the river mouth, anchored stem and stern. The *Thresher* wasn't swinging with the tide, but Abra could see that the water had climbed the piles of the wharf and he knew the ship was about to weigh anchor. He wanted to go on deck, to take what he was thinking of as "a last look."

Dev came into the salon with his trunk and they discussed the disposition of their belongings and how, once Carlin had his master's ticket, they could dispense with this extra captain and could all shuffle cabins.

"We are stopping somewhere, though?" Dev said, worried. The *Thresher* was to sail south.

"It makes no sense to trade out of this port," Abra said. "It's too small." Then he said, "I can't get Carme settled. Whenever I get her front end down, her back end comes up."

"I think that putting a child to bed is not something you can do expediently, love. You know, Carme is actually more complicated than your money-making schemes. And she's just lost her mother."

I'd just lost my mother. Ulaw died in an accident, and after the funeral Genevieve took my sister Astrella aside and had her promise she'd do her best for her younger siblings. "Especially little Carme." She was stroking my back. I was in her lap, and listening. However this was the limit of her sobriety, because then she giggled and said, "If any of them *let* you."

She killed herself. No one guessed she'd been planning to. She'd been mute and miserable, and had suddenly improved. Genevieve was happy once she'd decided not to try to live without her husband. She didn't believe in the afterlife, but she went off like a bride going to her bridegroom.

In the salon of the *Thresher*, Dev delivered a lecture. Abra must try to be a parent. He, Dev, was worried about me. As he talked, he manipulated his trunk into the trunk-sized space under the washstand. He had his back to us. My father was facing me. I was on the bed—my front end up. My father signed to me, in the British sign language that someone had taught him in his own childhood as an alternative to speech and that he'd never deigned to use. He signed a joke, a pun, which I could read, but couldn't understand. "He wants me to be apparent," he signed. Then, as he often did, "Don't speak, baby. Don't speak."

Carlin came in to stow his sextant in its case; it was noon and he'd taken the reading. He complained about the complexities of sailing. Far worse than a jet's controls. A jet's instruments were all self-explanatory, with digital readouts and so forth. A ship was mute and mysterious by comparison. Then Carlin asked Abra why they were going south.

"Bigger ports, better weather," said Abra. Then he launched into an apparently irrelevant exposition of the wrongs of the world. Dev turned around and straightened, till his hair brushed the beams on the ceiling. He and Carlin grew still and watchful.

Abra spoke about some religious refugees he'd met, on their way to a settlement they had in the big southern port. "They have a *religion*, unlike the priests here, who are a sort of secular sect, a priesthood of the rational who regard things like ghost stories as rather heretical." Abra asked if Carlin and Dev knew that only those born to the sect, of that race, could study law or medicine, or that the priests and priestesses had to go where they were sent and couldn't own anything. They weren't allowed to enter business—so that, for instance, most property and business law was practiced by lawyers from the country to the north. Did they know that the present Queen, though high priestess of the sect, was racially so dilute that it made nonsense of the sect's essentialism, their ideas about peoples of different temperament having different tasks in life? Then he said that he wouldn't take any of it up in this country, whose Queen was a friend of his friend, Ulaw—but that the southern country had the same distorted system.

Dev remarked, quietly, that they were going farther from his parents. He didn't push this point, because his parents had left him, had settled where they could raise goats and make cheeses, near enough for visits, but where they wouldn't have to watch their son—wouldn't feel that, despite his apparent happiness, they had to keep an eye on him. Dev always had his hands on Abra. It was affection as much as possession, but seemed to cause Dev's parents some anxiety.

"This journey is just another remove from home," said Carlin. "But maybe you never felt at home, Abra."

Abra pointed out that, for him, there had been many more removes. "I'm starting to forget how I felt and who I was in the years I wandered. It's like trying to retrace my steps through a swamp."

Carlin wasn't listening. He wanted to know what Abra was removing himself from. "Who is on your tail?" he said.

Astrella put her head around the door to say they had the tide, and that Carme should be in bed.

When they were all gone, Carlin to the helm, Dev to the capstan to do something useful with his weight and height, my father picked me up and began to pace the salon, up and down. I watched the sunlight come in as the ship came about. I watched light ripple on the ceiling like a school of ghostly fish. I admired the odd-shaped marine cabinets, the hanging stove, the cot with its—to me—vast, white, inviting mattress. My father was warm, and he was talking to me, softly, as if afraid of being overheard. He said, "I'm sorry about your mother. I didn't make any difference to her. She loved him better than anyone else. But I love *you*. I love *you*."

He paced.

Then it was dark, and I woke up when someone touched me, tucked me in. I heard Dev say, "This child's hair is damp." Then, "Ah. You"—possessive, and pleased to find what he perhaps saw as a sign of my father's feelings, his humanity.

And what is so right—so real to me, telling this story—is how Dev didn't use my father's name. "You," he'd say, more often than not, or "love." Or "little one," interchangeably to my father and me as we grew, in our different ways got bigger. Dev wouldn't use my father's name. Perhaps he saw, before anyone else was able to, that "Abra" was only a name my father was using.

And that's my story. It sets us on our way.

I've invented some of the details here—though I had much of it by report, piecemeal, over the years. I had it from Astrella, the girl with the very blue eyes—who is one of my two half-sisters. I had it from Dev Hughes and Carlin Cadaver and Carlin's wife Cassandra. And I had it from my father, who, like Patrick White's Eudoxia and Eddie and Edie, has gone by a number of names. Has come and gone by a number of names.

In addition to writing a story you asked me to draw two pictures, "In some way meaningful to me"—that was your prescription. One I drew, and it is of a tall ship, burning, at a list and turning in the convection current of fire. The other is a color photocopy of a plate from a book, a reproduction of a page from one of the "bark books" of the Taoscal people of South America, held in the British Museum. It shows black oxen being led into the temple, Turoc Iddu. Or, perhaps, the picture shows the progress of one animal, dark-eyed and decked with flowers, then white-eyed and with a great wound in the hump of muscle at its neck, then on its knees and wreathed with blood.

Transference

(A therapist's rooms, Northern California, 2022)

My first question, the first *rational* question I had for Carme Risk, was, why me? Why did she choose me to be her therapist?

Dr. Risk seemed comfortable. She had removed her shoes and put her feet up on the couch. Between us was a low table, on it her story and pictures, and two steaming cups. She explained that her nephew was in a class with a boy I saw. A special needs class. Her nephew was born with congenital anesthesia, which meant that he couldn't feel pain. He'd learned strategies to avoid injury. "His relation to sensation is rather like yours or mine to electricity," she said. "For example—the other day my freezer began spontaneously to unthaw. I didn't put my hand into it to unload frozen food because, as well as unthawing, it was spitting and popping. I turned off the power. My nephew checks the thermometer before he gets in his bath. He has faith in the existence of the intangible as we have in the invisible—electricity, for instance."

Carme Risk told me the name of the boy I saw, my young client, who spends our sessions rolling back and forth across my floor and sometimes talking to me. Once, when I left the room for a few minutes, he took apart the oxygen pump in my fish tank. There wasn't even one drip on the floor. Luckily, I missed its bubbling before my fish stifled.

I was being told—in a disarmingly detailed way—what amounted to "I got your name through a friend of a friend." I said that we should acknowledge that there were two remarkable circumstances in her having chosen me. I waited; she only smiled.

Carme Risk was a beautiful woman in her mid-forties. (How careful and cowardly of me to qualify that "beautiful" by stating her age.) She gave the impression of being glad somehow to be "losing her looks"; she was careless and easy and even better-looking for it.

"There's the difference in our ages," I said. "It's *conventionally* the wrong way around."

Her friend Bella had remarked on it, Carme said. When she reported to Bella what her therapist was like—in the ordinary order of importance: gender, age, name, favored school of treatment—Bella asked why Carme was taking her troubles to someone so much less *lived*.

"Why are you?" I asked, thinking that she would acknowledge the other remarkable circumstance. I waited. I worried. How could I be professional?

"First," she said, "it's your candor, your readiness to admit your lack of the usual human credentials—a family."

I watched her curl her toes, as if to dispel a cramp. Her expression, her thin compressed lips, could indicate pain. But I suspected it was pleasure and suppressed laughter.

She said, "To use your words, you told me that you were an 'adult foundling.' And you looked embarrassed. My father once said to me that embarrassment is what's available when shame is busy with heroes." She waited again, watching me.

"I won't be ashamed of what I can't help," I said. "But being unembarrassed is beyond me."

Carme Risk told me that she thought I could bring my unique experience to her story. "Abra Cadaver was a foundling."

"But not an amnesiac."

As though offering a bribe, she said, "There's an amnesiac in the next part."

"More background to *your* story?"

"My story is that my father kept disappearing on me. The first time for eleven months when I was ten."

"Did he ever disappear for good?"

"I'm sure *he* thought it was for the best." She watched me out of her too-widely-spaced eyes. Dreamy, cold eyes. If her nose hadn't been small and shapely it might have looked like a muzzle between those eyes. "My friend Bella drove me here today," Carme said. "We sat in the car till you came and unlocked your door. Did you see us?"

"Yes."

"Now that she's seen you Bella is satisfied."

"About the age difference?"

She nodded.

"Because she noticed the other remarkable thing about your having chosen me?"

"Yes. You look like me. I'm a childless woman, but you could be my son."

"Transference," I said. Then I gave its definition—the generalization toward the analyst of feelings the patient has toward other people in the patient's life. "But, for a start, you're not my patient, because *you* are the expert on your own experiences. And I'm not an analyst, I'm a narrative therapist."

Carme said she wasn't trying to *fix* herself, only to understand. She wanted me to help her find a more hopeful interpretation of her story.

But I had a problem with her story. It wasn't that I knew she was testing me, professionally, by writing about Abra's psychologist's rigid negative characterization of Abra as "autistic." She was warning me there, and I respected that. My problem was my choice. History or fiction? Should I respect her use of metaphor, her "other world"? She'd asked me to enter into a contract with her, to talk about her story as though it was the literal truth. But where would that take us?

I looked at her. Her face was the only one I'd ever seen that looked like *family*.

I picked up one of her pictures. For a moment I took refuge in the burning ship. Above the ship a tall flame, like a flathead screwdriver, wound the vessel down into the sea. I found myself speaking: "Your story says the world is big, open, as endless as two worlds putting their heads together."

"Therapist and client," she said. "You and me."

I told her that her story was about possibility, about open doors. But I had to point out that she had entered a therapeutic *conversation* with a story that characterized silence as positive, an unpolluted silence, like paradise. I said that the only dark note in her story was that Abra, her father, imported evil into his Eden in the form of the murderer, Devlin Hughes. Abra had confounded darkness with mystery, but wanted mystery. "Your story proposes your father's homosexuality, or his promiscuity, as a problem. What do you think?"

"I think you want to call the other world Eden," she said. "Shall we? And maybe Abra's *autism* was the problem."

I said that, by and large, her story seemed to side with her father against that diagnosis.

We'd begun. I saw her relax further. I said, "But whereas your story mostly concerns possibility and paradise, your pictures show a sacrifice and a catastrophe." I put the burning ship back down on the hacked, collapsing black oxen.

"Which is the sacrifice?" she asked. She said she had three journals for me to read. The first was her father's 1987 journal. The others were hers, 2003 and 2010. "I've transcribed them. I'd like to know what form you want them in, digital or paper?"

"Transcribed *and* edited?" I asked.

She didn't answer, except to say she was serious.

I told her I'd like the texts in a form I could read in the bath, if I wanted. Paper and bound.

"So we're back to electricity," she said, "and our faith in the invisible."

PART TWO

Pérdida Total de la Memoria

(Spanish medical term for total amnesia)

An amnesiac's journal, Lequama, 1987

Journal: La Host, Lequama, August 1987

This morning the women were whispering outside my door. Ambre and her daughter Madlena. Ambre told Madlena to lower her voice, because I was still asleep. I'd been up all night playing dice in the Plaza Bar, and Madlena said, loudly, that under those circumstances she didn't see any need for consideration.

Ambre, still whispering: "Under what circumstances *would* you see the need?" Then she told her daughter that I was gambling for my airfare to London, and Madlena asked, distressed, "Is he leaving us again?"

In February of this year I found myself standing in the dusty sunlight that stretched from the doorway of La Host Cathedral. I was inside already, past the font, my fingers dry. In that first moment I felt *endowed*. I felt that an unknown friend was standing behind me, and that the sun was like a warm hand between my shoulder blades. But I took a step forward and the feeling of that friendly hand fell away from me.

Out of the sun my eyes adjusted. I saw a woman beside the stepped candles at the feet of the Virgin. She looked like she'd come to have a stern word, she was scowling at the statue, her brows knitted and her chin lowered. She glanced at me, and I saw that she recognized me. I saw alarm and, behind that, a kind of wild gratitude.

I asked her, "Do I know you?"

She said, "You're Ido. From the Black Room."

She told me later that I laughed and said, "Well, at least I have an address." Then I gave her the passport I held. A passport with my photo in it, with all the right stamps, and a name—Walter Risk, British citizen.

She put my passport with the four oranges and two spiny chokos in the string bag looped over her arm. She took my hand and led me out of the cathedral and into the street. We paused on the steps, and I realized she was waiting for a reaction. For recognition.

The Plaza was wide and unsealed.

We walked into the sun, were painted with warmth. The ground was dusty, and the white-and-yellow flag on a pole at the far end of the Plaza was coated with dust.

I read aloud the year "1935" in raised letters above a wide awning, the underside of which was studded not with bulbs but empty sockets. An old cinema.

"It's 1987," she said.

I was amused. She seemed taken aback by my amusement. "What a strange laugh you have. I didn't think it would sound like that."

A bus howled past, its engine in low to cope with its load of passengers inside and on its roof, packed as thickly as flower wreaths on the top of a celebrity's coffin.

"Hambre!" We were hailed by a tiny woman with a dowager's hump. She wore a floral shawl over a silk slip, a pillbox hat with sequined veil, and her feet were puffy in tight, red pumps. Her heels danced among the dry indents in the ground as she advanced on us by small increments of movement. I had time to say to the woman at my side, whose name I had heard for the first time, "Your name is 'Hunger.' " And she had time to explain, "My mother had twins. Twins run in my family—my daughter has twin boys. My sister and I were 'Hunger' and 'Hungrier'—though we *were* christened. I don't know by what names. My sister drowned when we were under

50

three, and Mama never moved beyond my nickname. These days almost everyone calls me Ambre—amber—which is nicer. You must too."

"My *curandera*." The old woman panted. "Can I come tomorrow about my aridity?" Ambre told her, certainly, come in the morning. The woman left us.

"She is the secretary of the Prostitutes Collective," Ambre said. "We hope to build them a resource center on my property."

"Aridity?"

"Don't be so nosy."

"*Curandera?*"

Ambre sighed. She led me up and over the arched back of a stone bridge—below us was a brown river with one torquing vein of black silt at its far bank.

"La Mula," Ambre said. "Mixed, like a mule. A very lovely river where it is young. Yes, I am a *curandera*, a healer."

We walked into the lesser streets. In time we reached her house, which was near to the front of a deep lot covered in parched trees and fat succulents. Along the road was a hedge of aloes and mother-in-law's-tongue, and a broken gate. The house had two floors, one wedge of attic making a third, the roof otherwise flat and with wide red-painted eaves. There was a veranda, skewed at one corner by a heavy mass of red bougainvillea. The vines grew over something else at the side of the house, something low and square, a wood shed, or an outhouse, or a derelict car.

Something shuffled out from under the steps. It looked like a small bear. It stretched, fore and aft, shook itself, and barked. A Newfoundland.

"Barabbas," Ambre said to the dog. "Don't make a fuss."

She ushered me through the gate. The dog came and sniffed me, whuffled, and dropped big spots of drool on my boots.

Ambre turned, her face aglow. "This is where I live now, Ido. Flores Negras—a house of my own. Why do you think I wouldn't remember who you were?"

It was difficult to answer her. I was so taken by her large, heavy-lidded eyes, their brown irises blurred and somehow poorly contained so that their sclera looked stained. The scent of her body, flesh or clothes, was extraordinary, smoke and perfume, like burning sandalwood. I stood near her, immersed.

Barabbas sneezed.

"Uh." I sounded a little stupid. "Excuse me. *I'm* the one who doesn't remember." I found myself reassuring her, wanting to sink the look of alarm surfacing on her face. I wanted to take hold of her so badly that I felt I was losing cohesion, my cells swarming away like iron filings following a magnet. "Don't worry," I said. "It's all right."

I could see that she was forming a resolution of some sort, her glow had faded, and that, when she put out her hand again, saying, "Come inside," she had accepted me as a responsibility.

The following morning Ambre's daughter arrived and found my boots on the veranda.

I woke in the room Ambre had given me—a room right under the rooftiles—to the sound of a peevish voice. I got up. The horse-hair mattress made a silky rustle as it adjusted itself to my absence. I put my head out the window but couldn't see past the veranda's old tar-paper roof.

I could hear, though. Hear someone berating my host about *men.* "Juanita told me what you did, Mama. How you stole that actor right out from under her nose at Plaza Bar Two. Have you any idea what it's like for her, being upstaged by a leathery forty-five-year-old woman?"

Ambre was mischievous. Goodness, Madlena, she said, Juanita really *must* want Enrico back. But was it a good idea to work her way around to him again through his brothers?

"I suppose it's all right for you to date old Papa García." Ambre's daughter was prim. Then, in response to some expression or gesture invisible to me, she exploded. She said that she knew her mother was trying to get pregnant. And that every time it didn't take—and Ambre did give each candidate a few cycles—she'd move on to someone new. "You were screwing Papa García last week, someone else before that. And you know—" she made a big gesture, because I heard silver bangles slide down her arm and chime like the

52

bell on one of those fairground piledriver test-your-strength machines "——there were others. You even 'flipped the pancake' with that Peruvian entomologist, that *eugenicist*, Pérez-Farante. How could you? An Airan?"

"Must we all adopt your husband's mispronunciations?" said Ambre.

I heard them move indoors and went to listen at the head of the stairs.

The young woman was in an ascending spiral of anger. She demanded to know whose boots were at the door, whose *British* boots.

"*Madlena.*" Ambre was reproachful.

They crossed the small patch of tiled living room floor visible to me. Ambre was drawing on a pair of patchwork gardening gloves. Her daughter dogged her steps, a thin, speedy young woman in a crackling cloud of crisp black hair.

Madlena accused her mother of not telling her about a phone call. "Juanita said you came off the phone with your hackles up. That it was Emilio Rivera—*my father.*"

"Your father is dead, dear," Ambre said. "It was only an old crony of his from the Security Forces. Not a pleasant person." Ambre went outdoors and Madlena pursued her. I crept down the stairs and watched them from the shade of the doorway. Ambre was hoeing between her rows of corn. Her daughter hovered, in some awkward place between irritation and anxiety.

"The phone call was yesterday morning," Ambre said. "And in the afternoon I went out to the cathedral."

Madlena said, uncertain, "Did you go to confession? Or are you enlisting the *Church* against Security Forces sorcerers?"

I noticed the two children in the yard. Twin boys, perhaps three-year-olds. They looked very like their mother, had her pouting frown. Despite the hard sunlight they had seen me in the doorway. They got up and came to me, stared—two solemn faces bearded by dog hair, as if they had just eaten Barabbas.

"I went to the cathedral," Ambre repeated, then stood straight and looked at me.

Her daughter spun around. She started toward me and barked, "You! British boots!" Then she staggered as though tripped.

Ambre watched, smiling.

Madlena slowly climbed the steps and stopped before me. She put out a hand to touch me, seemed to test my solidity. "Oh," she said.

And I said, "Your mother put me in the room under the roof." Polite, propitious, pacifying. Because I didn't *know* anything—including whom I might vitally need.

Madlena had her friends at Foreign Affairs make the usual inquiries, and a few unusual. Madlena was the Minister of Foreign Affairs here for a year following the revolution, till resigning after a bust-up with her *compañero*, Fernando Sola.

"More a dust-up," Fernando explained.

"A bitter quarrel," said Ambre, then turned to mouth at me, "All *his* fault."

I'd known Fernando for perhaps an hour. He seemed to know me: I'd had some sort of correspondence with him, apparently, because he said, "You wrote . . ." then quoted me. Ambre introduced him as "my daughter's friend," and something about Ambre's tone had me suspect I was being told he was trouble. He looked it, with his broken nose and gaze like the clear fuel thrown ahead of a flamethrower's burst of fire.

Madlena's colleagues made this report.

The Walter Risk of my passport was a vulcanologist. He'd not made an impression on his teachers at Cambridge—but of course so-and-so, the professor who had apparently supervised Risk's master's thesis, *died* a few years back on a guided climb of Everest, shortly after writing a letter of reference for Risk, who had been looking into a job with a geothermal company in Iceland. But the company received no application, and, although Cambridge forwarded Madlena's friends a copy of the reference, Risk's enrollment forms were missing from his file. His age was impossible to pinpoint, the name yielding only a birth certificate for 1933, but *that* Walter Risk was killed in the blitz.

The magistrate in Bristol who signed the proof of identity on

Risk's passport photo had petered out in a series of strokes over the last several months. His wife was drunk when Madlena rang her, on her fourth sherry and in stitches about "petered," since the magistrate's name was Peter and he "never was very handy with his you-know-what."

Madlena put the phone down and glared at me. She said to know for sure I'd have to hand in my passport to the British Embassy.

"No," Fernando said. "Better a passable fake than no passport at all."

And so I became Walter Risk, officially—my address care of Ambre Guevara at Flores Negras.

Madlena's husband, Tomás, explained to me later that Madlena disliked the way her mother collected strays. When I arrived Morgan Gray was in residence, a burnt-out American journalist who camped in the iron lean-to attached like a stoma to the side of the house, and only tolerable because it was insulated by vines. Madlena was in and out of her mother's house, often sleeping over, though she, Tomás, and the twins lived on a ranch fifteen kilometers out of town.

(That was a clue—I never felt the need to translate metrics, so wasn't American. And I hadn't dipped my fingers in the cathedral's holy water, and made my genuflection, so wasn't a Catholic. I collected clues, and my collecting was methodical, like Madlena's phone inquiries. But when I caught each clue my heart would hammer.)

In my first weeks in Lequama Madlena monitored her mother's compassion in regard to me, and Tomás ran around after both women, anxious to please his wife and baffled by his mother-in-law. While Fernando Sola kept his eye on all of us.

They explained themselves to me—took it in turns. And, as I listened, it became clear to me that some of them coveted sole ownership of their shared history.

Fernando Sola was Tomás's friend, but had once been his commander. Despite Lequama's supposedly socialist egalitarian principles, there were people who thought that, in marrying Tomás, Madlena had *married down*. When Madlena had a ministry in the revolutionary government, Tomás was only a bodyguard—Fernando's bodyguard.

Fernando and Madlena were the most famous of the four youngest ministers in the 1983 revolutionary government. The other two were Don Marcos Pastrez, who was still the Education minister, and Colonel Maria Godshalk, who gave up her Armed Forces portfolio to return to soldiering. Maria never came down from the mountains, I was told. All four were demagogues.

I found the ranks a bit of a puzzle—*Colonels* Guevara and Godshalk? *Commander* Sola?—till someone explained. Apparently the colonels were planners, strategists. Madlena and Maria Godshalk went back and forth between the several scattered guerrilla forces, coordinating their efforts. For instance, Battalion Nuevo, made up of Taoscal Indians, was not wholeheartedly with the Frente Democrático Revolutionario (FDR) till the eve of the revolution. As Madlena explained it: "The struggle wasn't ideological to them—only territorial."

Fernando added, "Mutual trust evolved out of mutual interest. And Maria Godshalk was clearly a very talented soldier. We—the Taoscal—admired her. Madlena—for her part—was someone the different forces had to work through for support, money, arms."

"I had connections," Madlena said. "I was young and invisible. I'd been to Cuba and Nicaragua, and had trained with guerrillas in Costa Rica. I used to set things up—meetings—but there were people I never met."

"Me," said Fernando.

"It wasn't a *chain* of command. I mean—the FDR was founded on revolutionary 'cells,' and many of our leaders were in prison in the final years. It was a *net* of command, difficult to unravel, hard to ruin. Imagine. Fernando and I—most FDR soldiers—didn't even know that Don Marcos was the notorious saboteur 'Pico Hermano.' *Maria* was his liaison. What a shock when we found out! It was three in the morning on the first day of freedom, and I'd arrived at the TV station in La Host. Don Marcos had come from the main La Host power station, which he and a few other civilian rebels had secured, and I was introduced to him. 'Pico Hermano' was Marcos Pastrez, the sports-car-driving playboy son of Ricardo Pastrez, the devil, the head of the Security Forces!"

Don Marcos Pastrez, Madlena Guevara, Fernando Sola, Maria Godshalk. In August of 1983 they were heroes.

Now thirty-one, Fernando was the eldest of the four. He was proprietorial toward his friends and the families of his friends. He was intensely possessive, an orphan, and addicted to involvement. He had—how to explain it without recourse to parody—enormous life force. He was *too* much, but seemed to make a joke of it half the time. I noticed that Madlena watched him *all* the time, often with a bleak, bewitched, unhappy expression. Fernando didn't notice—only Ambre seemed to guess that her daughter was in love with the wrong man.

They took me to La Casa de la Mujer—the House of Mothers—the general hospital in La Host. I was escorted by the principal interests—Ambre, Madlena, and Fernando. I was presented to a doctor, Anton Xavier.

Dr. Xavier, the best physician in the country, was once a resident in an emergency room in the United States, but came home two years after the revolution. Everyone in La Host was doing their best to welcome, appreciate, if possible *remunerate* Dr. Xavier. He was short, solid, and ring-eyed like a panda—a pregnancy mask in a woman, in a man possibly a sign of kidney problems.

Dr. Xavier examined me. He took blood, had me look here and there, manipulated my head. He noted that I had scabies scars at my hairline on the back of my neck. Though my passport suggested I was of the educated middle classes, this, he said, was a clear sign of childhood poverty and/or neglect.

While he examined me he talked to Madlena and Fernando about the war that was simmering along the northwestern border. Fernando and Madlena had inside information. At her HQ in the field Colonel Maria Godshalk was questioning two captives, consultants from the highly euphemistic U.S. International Military Education Training Program.

Madlena looked at her watch. "At 4:00 p.m. Armed Forces are due to inform the U.S. Embassy that we have them."

"Should be interesting," the doctor said. "Are they well?"

"They're fine. They're being moved away from the border. Farther in." Fernando gave Dr. Xavier a smug little smile. I gathered that "in" meant the mountains, the jungle, and under *his* influence.

Dr. Xavier turned to me. He asked me if I knew what he was doing. Checking, I guessed, for confusion or disorientation. I told him what I *knew*, used certain technical words, which came up like a green crop through damp soil. He listened till I finished.

Dr. Xavier said he felt he really should do a head-to-toe. He herded my minders out of the room and had me remove my clothes. He had a good look—as army doctors do—at my skeleton and musculature and, I gather, my personal hygiene.

He was saving on gloves, I felt him touch my buttock with the tip of his pen. He said, "I believe—" hesitated "—I'll need to get a better look at that lesion." Very formal. Would I please bend over.

When I refused to move he took a mirror down from the wall and asked would I prefer to squat, and look too. At that I did bend— knowing he'd report to Ambre, or Madlena, or Fernando, that there was something I didn't want to see, or to be seen. The "lesion" was a scar. A burn mark on my anus. I had scabies scars in my groin also— red tendrils like custom paint flames on the wheel rim of a hot rod. Ha ha.

The doctor showed me scars of surgery that overlaid a knife wound—and what he'd already noted, the narrow slash on my left collarbone and a purple notch near my carotid artery. "Your scars are these: those caused by a disease of neglect; three wounds, a slash, stab, and a shallow incision, probably all knife wounds. The stab wound has been subsequently operated on, well after it had first healed. Probably to clear out adhesive scar tissue. You have one sign of torture. None of these injuries is recent."

I listened as I put my clothes back on. He fell silent, perhaps waiting for me to speculate or ask a question.

My minders were shown back into the room. Dr. Xavier didn't repeat to them what he had just told me. Businesslike and hasty, he seemed to forget that I wasn't a child; he began to button my shirt, stopped as I took up the task myself. He asked me to come with him, telling Ambre, Madlena, and Fernando to please remain behind in his office. They looked like penned sheep, Fernando a sheepdog piqued to find himself on the wrong side of the closed gate.

Anton Xavier introduced me to a woman who sat propped up in bed in a big ward—an aging woman with empty holes in her earlobes. She pressed her silver-and-amethyst earrings into the doctor's hand as he stood by her bed. He left them on the coverlet.

We read her history. Dr. Xavier watched me read her history. I had some trouble with its unfamiliar expressions. Handing me his stethoscope and a blood pressure kit, he asked me to examine her. I lingered over her feet, her bluish nails. I asked for a flow meter and used it. For a long time I listened to her heart. Then we both thanked her, and she asked me to help thread the earrings back through the near-navel-sized holes in her lobes. I did this and then the doctor and I went out into the corridor. He asked me what I thought.

Angina. There were two ways I knew to treat her, I said, one involving fresh grape juice, nightshade, and a preparation derived from the sap in seedcases of baasera—salicin, digitalis, and baasera, all in the long run only palliative. The other option that occurred to me, I said, was ultrasound and a balloon angioplasty.

Anton took my arm and led me back to his office. He told Ambre he thought I was either a medical student or possibly a doctor and that I spoke and read fairly serviceable Spanish.

Ambre looked smug.

"We don't have ultrasound," Dr. Xavier said. "But we do have some cutting-edge cardiac drugs a French company would like us to trial."

"No!" Madlena said, appalled.

He looked at her hard and asked, "What would *you* do if you couldn't do anything?"

To me he said that he didn't know this drug derived from— "What was it?"

"Baasera."

"Is this naturopathy?"

My mind reached, as minds do, for what it knew, had seen, a

beautiful vine with fleshy flowers—the image in an iris, which irised out to black, showing me no soil, patio planter, vase, or hand holding the flower; no environs, no clue permitted me.

"What is it?" Fernando asked.

"I don't remember where I saw it. Baasera. A flower on a vine."

And how, the doctor asked, did that make me feel?

I felt as though I had slipped underwater, my hand parting from the hand of another. I was under the river now, chilled and deafened.

Anton Xavier sat down at his desk. He began to write.

"Ido was always very poetic," Madlena said. My character divested of all biographical apparel.

"Other than a considerable but healing bruise on his head," Dr. Xavier said, "he has no recent visible injury. But I'll venture to say that someone has tried to harm him, and that his memory loss is possibly post-traumatic."

I reminded him that *total* memory loss is very rare.

He said, more to Ambre than to me, that he'd recommend I see Aramantha Visistation, a psychotherapist—very good and, like him, only in Lequama for reasons of family. No one was to imagine Ms. Visistation was another mad quack like Lydia Yahanova, capitalizing on a chance to experiment on the people of a country where no one sued.

Like the French drug company, Madlena said. And was ignored.

"If, so far, he's managed to find a flower and a river, he'll find the whole landscape, his friends and family, and his own cozy bed, eventually." The doctor handed Ambre the address.

At the door, faced with the corridor and a weary line of men, women, and children, I said to the doctor, "If I wasn't mad I'd be useful."

"What makes you say you're mad?"

"Or bad. Maybe I'm bad."

He touched my arm. "Tell Aramantha that. She can help you."

And—last thing—Fernando turned back to remind Anton Xavier to report on the blood sample. "Its status."

Ambre wasn't happy to follow the doctor's advice. Someone had given her the appropriate New Age labels so she muttered to everyone about "Western medicine." Then she went out into her garden and, in a patch of shade free from the gray, spiny succulents that overran the place, she started to dig. By twilight she'd dug a shallow grave, two feet deep and otherwise in my size. She explained that this was an earth coffin and that she expected me to lie in it. No, she wouldn't fill it in over me. My problem, she said, was that I was out of touch with the terrestrial element, I must steep myself in its energies. The virtue of its patience.

The coffin was cool, its earth dry and friable. I lay under an oblong lid of sky where the light dissolved slowly, first losing color, then volume, till it was only its empty skin. I could smell cooking—eggplant and bell pepper, chilies and tomato and red beans. Ambre came out, knelt by the lip of the grave, had me sit up and spooned food into my mouth. My hands must remain in contact with the soil, rooted, she said. She blew on the spoon herself; her breath, controlled, depressed the surface of the stew without causing it to overflow. Fed, I was made to lie back down. I slept for a short while, then woke with my relation to everything changed, no longer horizontal, but like a saint in his niche who gazes not on worshipers or a church interior, but on God. I was extinguished by a slow torrent of stars, or shot full of holes.

Fernando came to speak to me. He seemed to expect me to speak first, to ask him what he wanted. The others would have. They played prey to his predator.

"You're very obedient," he said.

I didn't answer.

"I know you're awake, I can see your eyes. Their liquescence."

After a moment he reached down to touch my face. I turned a little so that exhaled air warmed the few millimeters between my lips and his fingers. He removed his hand. He said that he knew I wasn't Ido from the Black Room—perhaps I was his body, Ido's body, Ido's soul had come by itself last time. Fernando left. Later Madlena came and sat by me. She asked me how I was. Didn't I realize her mother was a silly, superstitious old woman? I told her that Fernando had spoken to me, that he didn't seem to like me.

Madlena was gleeful. "Of course he doesn't." Then she told me that an encounter between Fernando and Ido during the Black Room episode had resulted in Fernando's bout of hysterical mutism. "He wouldn't say what happened to him, so he couldn't talk at all."

She told me that the exorcist priests, who were camping in the palace in January of 1984, said that the Black Room demon tried to drag Fernando by his feet into the stairwell in the East Wing, where someone had died bloodily just weeks before. The exorcists thought the Black Room demon was trying to kill Fernando. "But from their description, I think it was trying to haul him through into what *I* call 'bus-shadow land.' You know—when you're traveling on a bus with the sun low in the sky and the bus's shadow, with your own shadow inside it, is one moment right up close on a stand of trees, then the next far away on a hill, then close again on a house wall? That's how spirits usually appear and disappear. They don't just go *pop!* and materialize." Madlena was pleased with her explanation.

So, I said, I was "Ido from the Black Room," but not the Black Room demon.

"The demon was Ricardo Pastrez's magical ally," said Madlena, happily informative, and quite deaf to my skepticism. "The exorcists couldn't tell between you till *you* saved Fernando."

Ambre delivered me to Aramantha Visistation's office. We admired the room—beeswax on the billowing floor, boards over subsided piles. There was a table by the old leather sofa, on it a potpourri of dried rose petals and seed heads, and a vase of red aspidistra, like birds with braced necks. The room's air was scented with the same herb oil that Ambre always dabbed in the hollow where her collarbones meet.

Ambre, in parting, made a few dire hints about what she'd do to Ms. Visisitation if she recommended ECT—as Lydia Yahanova had for Fernando in 1984 or, for that matter, hospitalization with the nuns at La Host's only psychiatric hospital, who used those lidded baths to "treat" the few poor lunatics still in their care.

Ambre finally left and Aramantha said, "Well, I won't be putting myself forward for the role of mother." She made a pot of tea. We reviewed what Anton had told her—concentrated on the fact that my "caregivers" knew me as "Ido," while my passport belonged to Walter Risk, neither of whom I knew. She asked me if I had a name for myself.

"I'm answering to Walt and Ido."

"But you are . . . ?"

I shook my head.

Aramantha set the boundaries. The duration of the therapy—an hour, twice a week, any "marathons" to be agreed upon by both parties and appointed in advance. She told me how she would deal with any inappropriate or dangerous behavior. She outlined the possible course of the therapy: exploration; hypnotic regression, Amytal-assisted perhaps, if she could obtain any; the management of any abreactive episodes toward therapeutic release; then griefwork.

She asked me to tell her what I knew about Ido, and I did, all of it from report. "They tell me, very confidently and persuasively, that Ido was a spirit or a demon, who came through 'the Black Room'—which they haven't sufficiently explained—in December of 1983. Tomás tells me Ido stole his uniform and shut him in a cupboard. But since they assure me that Ido was an apparition I can't think what he'd want with Tomás's uniform. Someone who thought 'Ido' was an alias, invention, or delusion, took to calling him 'Idea,' which, instead of usurping 'Ido,' was respectfully adopted as a surname—'Señor Idea.' People conversed with Ido in graffiti on something called 'the Wall.' Fernando found him objectionable. He called Ido a know-it-all—on 'the Wall.' Ambre argued with him on 'the Wall.' A Mexican photojournalist called Jesús Mendoza managed to capture Ido in one of a series of photographs taken in and around the Presidential Palace during a New Year's Eve party—photos that show drunkenness, nudity, group groping, horses ridden up staircases, and one apparently levitating body. Mendoza photographed Ido coming out of midnight mass at the cathedral. Madlena showed me the photo. It *is* me, wearing the uniform of a soldier of the FDR, and what looks like an aura or halo. They say that Ido made the Black Room go away, defeated Ricardo Pastrez's demonic ally, took his leave on 'the Wall,' then left."

"And what do you think about Ido?" Aramantha asked.

"The story makes me nervous. But it's typical of their magical thinking. I'm not saying I don't believe in magic—what do I know? But if I filter their world view out of the story I'm left with some dallying impostor, a bulletin board flirt, a know-it-all."

"So you don't think very highly of Ido?"

"No."

"And how do you *feel* about Ido?"

I stared at her. "What I think is how I feel."

She explained. She had to regard my amnesia as somehow related to the signs Dr. Xavier reported of early abuse and neglect. She had patients who were doing griefwork because of the trauma of torture. For example, she was treating a *compañera* who had been released from Los Muertos, the Security Forces prison, without the socially therapeutic public *telling* of her story that—say—a celebrity like the poet Jules Frei experienced. "She was expected to deal with the loss of self she experienced as a prisoner by getting on with her interrupted life. Whereas Frei—who was found in a coma in the prison infirmary when Los Muertos was liberated—once he'd come out of his coma, got to tell his story endlessly, in national and international forums. If my patient reads an article that says, 'Frei is telling the story of all Lequaman detainees,' she feels canceled out. She thinks her own experience is shadowy and inessential. Any Lequaman presenting to me with a degree of amnesia and physical signs of torture, I would treat as suffering from post-traumatic stress disorder. That is Anton's suggestion in his referral. But you have this Walter-slash-Ido business as well. Plus *old* signs of abuse and torture. Therefore I am planning to explore your amnesia as a possible product of a disassociative identity disorder."

"Is that 'multiple personality'?"

"Disassociation doesn't necessarily involve actual alternative personalities."

"I hope not. It seems so morbid and deceitful."

She got up, went to her bookshelves, stood on tiptoe—and I watched the muscles bunch in her calves and buttocks—to take down a post-revolution collection of the poems of Jules Frei. She gave it to me and sent me away with my homework. I was to write a journal during my therapy. She even supplied me with a notebook, with deckle-edged pages, marbled endpapers, a padded cloth cover, and a silk ribbon. And she told me the title of her favorite Frei poem: "Saint Peter in Prison."

SAINT PETER IN PRISON

At first he sees the blue spark
As his jailer's steel club on the bars
He comes reluctantly back to himself
At four points on a mattress of metal mesh

The blue light plays over him
He moves his mouth
Yes
I *do* know him
I was with him
We were breathing together

(Truth got off, not at its usual stop
And is reported exercising its old right
Wholeness
No free assembly required)

There is a stranger in the room
Hand alight, electric blue
Against the bolted grid of bars
Pain falls back from holy terror
His wounds pucker up for the kiss of life
The door swings wide

He will save himself, and other orphans
He will follow this hope's
Late unlawful entry.

                                    Jules Frei
            (translated from the Spanish by Walter Risk)

65

By "status" Fernando had meant my HIV status. He wanted a report on the blood sample. This gave me another clue. If I was only Ido's *body*, and Fernando was looking to Ido's blood for knowledge of his history, his missing soul, then I was forced to conclude Ido's soul was a pretty low character. In Fernando's estimation.

Madlena paid for my therapy. It wasn't much. There were perhaps forty families in the whole country who could afford Aramantha Visistation at the fees she was used to. And Madlena was a propertied person. Her father had been a member of the Pola Pastrez, Lequama's so-called Army of National Salvation, the Security Forces of the previous regime. Emilio Rivera had been declared dead only a year ago. In his will he left his estate—a house, Flores Negras, and a polo pony stud farm thirty kilometers out of La Host—to his daughter's *husband*. In a trust till she married, then to her husband. Madlena told me that Emilio Rivera didn't trust Ambre. They were always ill-suited—when they first met he was a junior officer and she was a whore called Hunger.

"A novelty whore!" Madlena whispered. "Three hundred pounds. The other women would roll her out in a wheelbarrow." Presumably, either to astonish or to tempt selected customers. "Like the dessert trolley! So—Emilio had a thing for fat women."

Madlena was hanging head-down in my earth coffin, her hair warming my throat. "So," she said, using the word as punctuation, avoiding anything rigorous, like logic, order, or the popping sinews of good speech. We were speaking English so I made excuses for her, then discovered that English is her *first* language, and that Ambre's mother is an English-speaking El Buon Indian from the Caribbean coast of Lequama. "So," Madlena said, "Papa was one of Ricardo Pastrez's sorcerers. And when he met Mama again, she was into that too. Sorcery. They got together—they got married. Mama was corrupt in her own way, but when she found out about some of the vile things Emilio was doing with the Security Forces she left him. Actually she left Lequama, leaving me with a friend of hers."

I asked Madlena how old she was then.

"Seven. But the damage was already done. Mama's experimentation. I mean Ambre. Everyone says I grew up wild. I was never in bed at night. Mama *likes* people to be overexcited. She used to tease me till I had tantrums, then she'd stand back and laugh at me." Madlena was indignant. "That is why she has you in this coffin. You're just such a *mess*, and she loves that."

Madlena wanted Aramantha to restore me to myself. I was an image they had—the spirit from the Black Room—but an image out of alignment.

As part of my therapy they planned to bargain for microfilm of "the Wall," or "Democracy Wall." They told me that the U.S. Embassy began to photograph Democracy Wall every evening, beginning the evening of November 1, 1983. Whereas the Lequaman government only started in April 1984. They knew the Americans began earlier because something written on the Wall in January '84 was used as evidence at an inquest into the death of an American student, Brad Powers—the levitating man from the Mendoza photos.

December '83 and January '84 the Wall was full of the Black Room.

Madlena and Fernando were talking more to each other than to me, persuading themselves to go to the trouble of bargaining with the embassy, when I interrupted to say that I felt the way I had on buying a copy of *David Copperfield* at an English-language bookshop in Rome, only to find on opening it that it commenced at page 11: *"Mercy on the man, what's he doing!" cried my aunt, impatiently. "Can't he speak?"* Very frustrating. I'd got out my American Express guide and looked up words and phrases. Between "Shopping" and "Motoring" I cobbled together a complaint. I went back to the bookshop and said to the girl at the front counter: *"La mia libra no s'accende"*—"My book won't start."

They all stared at me. Ambre, Madlena, Tomás and Fernando, Don Marcos Pastrez, and his little sister Juanita, who said, "You're beginning to remember!" and clasped her hands together against the bodice of her blue broderie-anglaise blouse.

Don Marcos raised an eyebrow. "Do you recall how the book goes on?"

I quoted the beginning, from *"Whether I shall turn out to be the hero of my own life . . ."* to *"I was privileged to see ghosts and spirits"*—where, naturally, my sense of timing dictated that I stop.

We looked at each other.

I said, "The cover of the Amex guide said 'Rome.' Why I was there, who with, and *at what age* I can't tell you."

Fernando's face hardened.

"I mean—I can't remember."

"However, you do have remarkable recall," Don Marcos said.

"We know Ido liked to quote," his sister reminded him.

I said, "I have no idea what you *mean* by 'the Wall.' Back up a little."

Democracy Wall ran along the stone quay by the river, one of the high barriers surrounding the Presidential Palace. The quay was part of the Old City—a collection of nineteenth-century buildings. Around the Plaza these were three or four stories high, with the same heavy columns and squared capitals found in railway stations, banks, and libraries the world over. Signs of the world's empires— in Lequama in the form of the United Fruit Company, Dewhurst Mining, and Florida Sugar. All the buildings had been originally owned by American companies, or were the places of business of importers who served only the "three percent," the members of fifteen families who, until the revolution, owned seventy percent of Lequama's arable land. Fronting the Plaza were the García Bank and the opera house where Don Marcos and Juanita's mother first caught the eye of Don Ricardo Pastrez when she sang the page Cherubino in a touring production of *The Marriage of Figaro*. At the southern end of the Plaza was a hotel, named for its address, and a big cinema, its front portal embossed "1935." The northern end was stopped up by the stone nave of a cathedral, a building otherwise made of corrugated iron, not exactly a whited sepulchre, but false-faced. On the broad avenue that led away from the Plaza to the river were the National Library and Archives; the police barracks, once the headquarters of the Pola Pastrez; a terrible prison, Los Muertos, now empty; one stone bridge that arched over La Mula; and the stone quay, from which everything and everyone once came and went. The quay had the usual history—roads improved, the airport opened, the river port once strictly for bulk, later tourists, and, after the revolution, people loitering by Democracy Wall.

The wall was sixty meters in length and four meters high. It had tungsten lamps arching over it from the grounds of the palace, some still intact even after the firefights of August '83. The lights were hard and bright but made hazy by the bodies of insects, opulent moths in velvet and jewels, beetles in shot silk. (A jungle out there.) The wall was of brick coated in smooth cement plaster, its surface pale in shade, but only ever cleared of slogans nine days before the final offensive.

I was told there was a reason for that, a reason connected to disconnections, to piles of melted flex—power leads and phone cords—found smoldering in a palace lightwell. The palace had been silenced, wiped clean, emptied out.

"All the jacks were torn out of the central switchboard, and burned with every other power lead," Fernando said.

"They destroyed their documents, of course. But the outside wall was already covered in *our* slogans, not *their* secrets," said Madlena. "The Pola Pastrez didn't need to whitewash the Wall, but they did. It was like—well—whenever you come into Mama's house and find her scrubbing the walls. Scrubbing and muttering. She's not being a cleaning freak, she's planning to do sorcery."

Dictator General Nestor Galen's government stood emptying their files and gorging their shredders in the time-honored fashion. The same thing was happening at the U.S. Embassy. Followed by more customary stuff—big army choppers on the roof of the embassy and lawn of the palace. While this was going on the core officers of the Pola Pastrez went about the palace unplugging computers and phones, smashing telex machines.

The old regime was ousted.

People came and wrote on the Wall.

The leaders of the FDR installed themselves in the palace, in the creaky seat of government. Security was lax at first and the main gate was always open—the people came and went; mothers of the disappeared, or of dead soldiers, lined the hallways outside Armed Forces. Elders of the three tribes—Taoscal, El Buon, and Mneone —camped outside Indian Affairs and scorched the carpets with their cooking fires. A young private, Pablito Masolan, came and set up a stall by the bullet-pocked concrete gateposts and peddled three-tiered coffins made out of altered wardrobes. "For families who've sacrificed several members to the great revolution," Pablito said. (They talked for a long time about this person, still resentful about his insolence, violence, poor taste. But when I asked what became of him they exchanged glances, then shrugged.)

People who didn't want to camp, but wanted to be heard—having, suddenly, the luxury of free speech—came and wrote on the Wall. Slogans at first: "*Venceremos Lequama!*" "Maria Maria Conchita Conchita Godshalk for president!" (Fernando explained. The people, who loved her, always used her full name. Maria had had an older sister, Maria Conchita, who'd died before she was born. Her parents had reused the name by repeating it in Maria's; they crossed their eyes when they looked at her, then signed the register seeing double. Maria was commemorative from the day she was christened, which perhaps explained why she was so reflective a person.)

People began to "share information," Madlena said. "That was how they put it then. *Share.*" The gossip began, the rumor-mongering, snitching, slagging off. Madlena wrote a poem about the boots of soldiers tramping through "her nights," which the popular imagination chose to interpret as "her bed." Compelled to be piously polite face-to-face, in front of the great moral heavyweights of the revolution, the younger government members took their jokes, banter, and intoxicating talk out of the palace and onto the Wall. They were seen—Don Marcos, Fernando, Maria, Madlena—late at night, cigarette in one hand and felt-tipped pen in the other, checking left and right, then writing. It was as though the palace had turned itself inside out, and its thoughts appeared, as a mute demonic's cries for help might appear etched in blisters on her skin.

Democracy Wall. Who called it that? How did La Host come to an ironic consensus on its name? The slander, storytelling, and rumors *were* democratic, even the official disinformation was democratic, for, it seemed then, free speech was a genus while truth was merely a species, a dependent branch on the evolutionary tree. "But Democracy Wall was filled with the threats of the powerful," Juanita said, her tone rising plaintive although no one interrupted her.

"Not threats, just banter," said Don Marcos. "At least according to Fernando when he and Madlena were being taken to task by the Disciplinary Committee."

Fernando and Madlena laughed.

But—Juanita told me—Madlena, or someone imitating her hand, wrote in late '83: "Pablito you're a dead man" to Masolan, the pop-eyed, hopheaded, compulsively obscene private of her battalion who, two months later, was found faceup ten feet from the roadside on one of the jungle-lined roads west of La Host, with tear-along-the-dotted-line perforations across his chest, bullets from an AK-47.

Fernando said, "Juanita, every soldier carried one."

"Maria Godshalk threatened Pablito Masolan on the Wall," Juanita told me. "She kept writing that she hadn't *forgotten* him."

"The threats were epidemic," Fernando said.

Juanita looked at me. She told me to imagine the *gaiety* of their threats. And of threats following slogans like an afterbirth, as though it was malice that sustained their political will.

Aramantha was pleased that we had established a friendly relationship, a relationship of mutual trust. Madlena had told her that I was compliant, active, and adaptable. "If it wasn't for your amnesia, Walt," she said, "we would be tempted to imagine you are in very good mental health."

Forgetful, but sane. Forgetful *and* sane. Forgetful *therefore* sane.

Aramantha crossed her legs. She wore jeans with a hole in the knee, denim so soft that something soft had ruptured it—the knee, smooth, tanned, and oiled. Aramantha remarked that all I did in our sessions was to ask questions about the people I was living with. "Do you think you are perhaps committing yourself to the present because you mean to remain amnesiac?"

"Maybe asking questions is what I normally do," I said. "And it is their pasts I am asking about—appropriating."

Aramantha was very careful, but ventured an opinion. They—the Pastrez siblings, Don Marcos and Juanita, and Madlena and Fernando—those four at least, were arguably themselves still post-traumatic. "Madlena was tortured by the Pola Pastrez at fifteen, that's in her official biography. Fernando is the sole survivor of a massacre that took place when he was under five, which Taoscal tradition takes only as a sign of great luck, although it must have had an enormous negative impact on him. His surname, Sola, is the name of his razed village. And I believe the Pastrez children lived in an appalling domestic situation. Unfortunately Madlena, Fernando, and Don Marcos were very badly served by a colleague of mine—Lydia Yahanova—who persuaded the Disciplinary Committee to impose a questionnaire on government members and palace security in late '83. After 'incidents.' I believe she meant to test for personality disorders. The government was very susceptible to the 'personal is political' idea then popular, a kind of consciousness-raising-group version of being 'struggled' by the Chinese Cultural Revolution."

I asked Aramantha to elaborate and she frowned. "See?" she said. "I'm pandering to your appetites. Who *are* you?" she asked. "Where do you come from? What happened to bring you here, making a curdled mess of my throw rug and pouting at me because I won't fill your head with stories?"

I asked her, how did she think I should behave? Depressed? Shifty? Self-centered?

One evening in early March Anton Xavier turned up at Flores Negras.

I was busy in the swept-earth front yard, in a mess of sweat and dog hair, clipping the coat of Barabbas, the heat-tormented Newfoundland. Barabbas had been cohabiting with snakes and scorpions under Ambre's front steps, the place where moisture from the cracked cistern finally collected. No one had thought to clip him. I took it on, stopped twice to sharpen the shears and then had to lure him out again into the light. A breeze had come up and bits of black fleece were flying all over the yard.

Fernando arrived and parked his jeep blocking the gate—to show he didn't mean to linger, I guess. He came into the yard.

Ambre had brought me a drink—thick and mauve, fruit and oil and bitterness. I told Fernando she was experimenting on me.

"I'm sure she's *treating* you, just as La Visistation is."

Ambre agreed with him and growled that she knew what she was doing. She offered Fernando a drink—coffee, a coke, lime and water?

Just water. He was fasting. He was off to the pyramids for a week. Purification ceremonies. And he had to see to his prisoners, the men from the U.S. International Military Education Training Program. He'd wanted to tell me that he hadn't yet managed to swap the captured consultants for microfilm of Democracy Wall. Part of the problem was *language*. The government couldn't call the men "hostages," because the U.S. had a policy about hostage taking that rendered hostage takers helpless. The Lequaman government was trying to decide what charges to bring against the men, to decide its respectable legal position and what to put in press releases. The IMETP was funded by the U.S. government. But did the U.S. government actually *send* the consultants? How to prove it? Armed Forces wanted to get the international press bitching about the U.S. backing of the Contras. It had been out of the headlines for too long.

Fernando said, "Of course Armed Forces only *has* the two Americans inasmuch as Battalion Nuevo now has them. Taoscal soldiers. I'm the chief of the Taoscal. And I'm not interested in publicity." He shrugged. "I know I have to release the men, but I want something to show for it. Something maybe meaningful to *you*."

I said, "That's remarkably altruistic, Fernando."

"Drink your medicine," Ambre said to me, imperious. I drank it off, then began on Barabbas's forelegs, placing one soft hoof of a paw in my lap and trimming his hair into long ridges.

Dr. Xavier arrived, pulled in behind the jeep, and wound his window down to open the door using the outside handle, his car old even for Lequama. He came in through the gate, removed his hat, and smoothed his hair. Barabbas, who is morbidly afraid of hats, lumbered off and wriggled under the steps. A snake emerged and

Fernando placed his boot on it, tilted his foot and pressed—the hard edge of his sole crushed the base of its skull; it ceased to writhe and began to shiver.

Dr. Xavier wanted another blood sample. The one he had was contaminated.

"What does he have?" Fernando asked.

I laughed.

Anton Xavier mopped his brow. "I said the *sample* was contaminated, not the blood."

We all went in, me to wash my hands and arms so Dr. Xavier could draw some more blood.

Fernando followed Ambre into the kitchen and I could hear him asking her about some Taoscal sorcerer who had been tortured by the Pola Pastrez. What did she know about it? Wasn't her husband, Emilio, involved? But, having realized that Fernando had come looking for information, Ambre became mockingly demure. She did her dubious old lady voice, responding, "I don't really know, dear," to every question he asked.

Ambre turned people out of her house, wanting a little peace and quiet, a break from "other people's problems." Fernando left for the pyramids at Taosclan, the capital of the tribe's old empire. Madlena was busy training her polo ponies. Her husband, Tomás, had just started as deejay on the last shift before shutdown on La Voz, La Host's only radio station. Juanita Pastrez was completing her music degree at the Universidad; she had a final coming up. Don Marcos was about the business of government. The American journalist, Morgan Gray, was still in residence at Flores Negras, but ate out, came and went by the back door.

Ambre burned scented oil and entertained a García brother— the only one who no longer lived in Lequama, the one who played Latino villains on American TV shows. The García wanted me out of the way altogether. I overheard them in the hallway on their way to her room—her throaty laughter as she soothed him: "Oh, Ido's harmless—only a boy."

"*Sí*, harmlessly and boyishly appealing," the García muttered.

Aramantha kept trying to surmise an *event*. She asked very general questions, until I felt that I was completing a survey. She kept going back to parenthood—she was encouraging, said that I was entitled to opinions, though I may not be a parent, everyone *had* parents, even abandoned children had absences in the shape of mother and father.

In trying to surmise an event—bad parenting in some baroque form—Aramantha wasn't in her own culture, but in the culture of psychotherapy. All around her she had people suffering, to one degree or another, the trauma of loss, their fear, silence, paralysis due to the Security Forces' culture of terror. But in me she was looking to treat something she was equipped to meet. She could see herself taking me by the hand—like a good mother—and helping me to confront the monsters in my dark closet. My black room.

I say "good mother," but once, when she was called away for a moment to sign for a package, I sneaked a look at the top page of her open notepad. I read: "Don't *suggest* anything—this one will feign integration. His 'split' is a triumph of the imagination, but he's deflating somehow—his speech slow and blurry. His mindlessness, his sexualization, his stupor."

After one session, on my way back from Aramantha's office to Flores Negras (to the exhausted scent of hot lemon balm and silence as opaque as flesh at rest), I went past the fruit stalls in the Plaza.

Something happened to me there.

I recall being jostled by a group of girls, all in shabby leotards and leg warmers—like a juvenile detention center on its way to ballet class. I remember the two army trucks that entered the Plaza, snarling, overladen, and in low gear. I recall watching a mother turn and put a hand back to her tall eight- or nine-year-old to hurry the girl out of the path of the trucks. I saw that, as they moved, mother and daughter had a small struggle to see whose hand went on top—it had been a while since they'd held hands and their relative heights had changed. Watching this I seemed to feel a little ghost clasp my hand, a touch without temperature—the neuropathy of my amnesia. For an instant I was nearly blown over by a feeling of compounded tenderness and panic.

Then I came to on the stone quay, smothered, it seemed, and trying to suck in air that was a hand's breadth from me beyond an invisible gag. When I could breathe again, I stooped and cupped my hands over my nose and mouth, slowly stopped hyperventilating, and restored my oxygen-saturated cells to their usual equilibrium. To judge by the sun I'd lost only an hour, but hadn't lost my straw bag of mangoes. Where I'd been, and what I'd seen, I had no idea. What I *did* know was this: when I came to I felt not panic or disorientation, but despair. Despair at three atmospheres, as thick as the air of a larger planet.

In the last week of March I took to wandering the city, trying to keep ahead of the frightful fiend of my lost time. I had fugues. Once I "woke up" and found myself eye to eye with the swiftly moving surface of La Mula, opaque with mud and full of submerged snags.

I walked and tried to stay conscious. Or I followed Ambre into the kitchen to help her cut vegetables, as if we were feeding a houseful instead of just herself, me, and, alternately, García or the young drama student she was now bringing home. When the men weren't at Flores Negras she and I sometimes sat together in front of the TV and watched Venezuelan soap operas. When she had company I slept or went out.

On one walk I met Francis Taylor, whom I had heard mentioned as one of the "gringo foreigners" with whom Madlena Guevara had been infatuated. (I think I was being warned. The Guevara women, mother and daughter, were often represented as predatory.) Francis was photographing a flowering squash, which grew on a wall beside the faded pink lintel of a doorless house, in one of those unsealed streets where the houses are painted with colored whitewash. There was a trickle of water in the center of the street, from a blocked or broken drain, and black chickens pecking near bare-legged children or thin dogs.

I stood behind Francis and asked him had he thought of photographing *that* dog. Would he consider it.

He didn't remove the camera from his face. "The goal of art is beauty," he said in an Australian accent.

For the dog the proximity of two men proved too much, it looked at us across its ulcerated shoulder, mauled ears back, anticipating trouble. It got up and walked a little way off, stood with drooping head and shivered.

"And why not?" the photographer said, still fiddling with the focus, "when the goal of life—or at least my life—seems to be exception and nonsense."

I said, "You're very frank."

He took the shot, turned around, blinked, then stuck out a hand. "Frank Taylor."

We shook. He was slender, blond, tanned, blue-eyed, looked good-natured, if a little febrile.

I managed an introduction. Opted, as I do, for Walt.

"*Ah—Dios—sí!*" Francis shouted. "Ido the Idea! Christ, you're beautiful. I'm allowed to say that. I'm a connoisseur. Can I take your picture?"

I stood very still and frowned at him.

He gestured at the dog. "With the dog, by all means." And he flapped his free hand at me, herding me toward the animal. It hadn't the energy to retreat farther, showed its teeth, its black lips tacky and clinging to its inflamed gums. I found a spot on its brow free of ulcers and still covered in its own short chestnut coat. I petted it, and it closed its mouth and whined. The whine came from way back in its throat but involved its whole body.

Francis advanced with his camera obscuring his face. "The ugly, unredeemed patient face of matter," he said, quoting me. "You've been writing poetry on the Wall."

"A little. I've stopped. Well—I think I've stopped."

The dog shivered under my hands, its shivers a wordless litany, as if its bones were asking their way out of its skin. I made an inventory of its ailments. So many, so far advanced—so far gone. I had the oddest feeling, in either my hands or my head, or somewhere between the two, like the *click-click* of a failing telephone connection. I decided what to do. I shut the dog's muzzle with one hand, put the other down to hold its shoulder, and pushed its head around in the opposite direction, fast. I felt resistance, vertebrae grate, then burst. It gave one final shudder and went limp. I laid its head down on the road, pushed its ears forward for the first time and closed its eyes.

When I got up and turned around Frank was staring at me. Then I saw his hand, the hand with the camera, move a fraction upward, and I put my hands over my face. Frank came and pulled them away, told me off, about sores and diseases, staphylococcus that could get into my eyes and blind me. He led me back into the broader streets and found a square with a tap and tank. He borrowed a cake of soap from a woman washing her clothes there, lathered and rinsed my face and hands.

When he had finished with me, Frank said, "Sun over the yardarm." And asked me to go have a drink with him.

We went to the Plaza Bar and met the American journalist Morgan Gray, who was shacked up in Frank's room at the hotel. She decamped from Ambre's, she told me, because she "hated to see a woman do that to herself."

We were in Bar Two, the upstairs bar. Bar One was, Frank said, the roughest public place in Lequama, "Bar *one* that is, the Pig Club in Leonarda."

Morgan leaned forward to shout over the din. The Pig Club was rough because it was about fifteen to twenty kilometers from the movable front line and full of soldiers from Amazonia, Maria Godshalk's battalion—fifty percent women—and could those chicks party. The Indian battalion, Nuevo, was sent back to the camp near the capital after the big offensive in '85, when they suffered a twenty-percent casualty rate. "The Pig Club was even wilder back then—Friday nights measured eight on the Richter scale."

Frank said, "Plaza Bar Two is gringo backpackers, locals with some cash, army officers, and government and embassy types." He gestured around us. "Bar Three is hotel guests and their guests only. Bar One is all students from the Universidad, working-stiff locals, and grunts from Nuevo. *Heavy* scene. Go in there and it's best to keep your back to a wall and your wits about you—which rather defeats the purpose."

We could hear Bar One, the thud of amplified music throbbing through the floorboards. Bar Two was scuffed and shabby, but had big mirrors with beveled edges, red leather booths, and a long shallow balcony with opulent iron fretwork clogged by coat after coat of brown paint—it looked as if it had been chocolate-dipped.

Frank and Morgan were drinking the strong local beer, but urged me to at least *try* mountain wine.

Frank: "It's a spirit. Distilled, not just fermented. Don't let them kid you. It has coca in it, and yagga."

Morgan: "Yagga's what local magic practitioners use to take trances. Yagga root mixed with some kind of flower. The flower is one of those drugs that slows your bowel. Like codeine. Yagga is an emetic—one counteracts the other. Tricky dosages though. Frank tried a yagga preparation, and very nearly ended up color-blind."

Frank: "Everything went this pretty monochromatic blue and stayed that way for four days. I was pissing myself. But, hey, at least I wasn't shitting myself." He grinned.

A flushed kid, who couldn't have been more than sixteen, loomed over our table. "When is Señor Idea doing his CMT?" he asked.

"Compulsory military training," Morgan translated, then asked, "Have you applied for citizenship, Ido?"

The kid went on. "I believe they teach poetry composition as part of the literacy module of the training. Señor Idea badly needs lessons. He also needs the discipline. Badly. In fact his head badly needs to be blown off."

"Fuck off, kid," Frank said, cheerfully.

The kid fucked off.

"His brother is screwing the old bat," Frank said. "A drama student. The kid thinks you are too. Not a drama student—screwing the old bat— Ambre. Are you? Morgan's slept with her, I only ever got a grope."

"Frank!" Morgan went red.

Frank sucked on his bottle, smacked his lips, then said with admiration, "The *leathery* old bat."

I said that Ambre was only interested in my well-being.

Frank cocked an eyebrow. "I see." He looked at Morgan. "Sensitive subject. You do know she's trying to get pregnant? That's what Madlena thinks. *I* suspect she had a bad experience with a creep, a Peruvian entomologist—so-called—who only wanted to inspect her moral health. He hurt her confidence. She's just climbing back on her bike."

"Poor Ambre. She's forty-five and menopausal. She should face it." Morgan shook her head.

I leaped to Ambre's defense—an attractive woman still full of life and sexual appetite. "If she's still blowing spunk out of her sinuses at seventy, then so what?"

Morgan gaped. Frank looked impressed. "Spunk in the sinuses. There speaks the voice of experience."

I got up. My chair fell over. I went up to the bar to buy myself some mountain wine.

After that I remember watching, at close quarters, Madlena and Tomás talking and laughing—Madlena's eyes tiny inverted *c*'s. I was at their table, making Madlena laugh, being told, "Ido! You're dronk!" Dronk and fonny—in their Cordillera Pacifica accents. They'd sent Juanita to the bar to buy them another round. It was a kind of endurance test. If Juanita wanted to drink with them she had to push her way through a press of officers, three deep.

"She'll do it!" Madlena shouted at me.

Then Tomás, his broadcast-quality baritone carrying better: "Juanita is very lonely."

When General Nestor Galen's government fell in August of 1983, Juanita was fifteen and at a finishing school in Switzerland. She watched it all on television—Tomás said—and saw her father, Don Ricardo, standing behind a fat, deflated Galen at a press conference in Miami, his eyes like hot oil, like oil at its flashpoint. Don Ricardo called Juanita, he wanted his daughter to join him in exile, he sent her air tickets—destination Miami, with a two-hour stopover at JFK. Juanita went around her schoolmates, raised some money, sold her amber beads, her pearls, her watch. She got on the plane.

At JFK she went to a currency exchange, swapped her francs for greenbacks, and bought a ticket for Panama City. No airlines were flying into Lequama at that time.

In Panama Juanita bought a bus ticket to El Real, in the south. From there she hitched to the border. She walked across the border wheeling her Louis Vuitton suitcase. A patrol from Amazonia found her resting at the side of the road. Wasn't she headed the wrong way, they said, in her nice shoes, with her nice luggage? Juanita asked to be taken to her brother Don Marcos Pastrez, and three days later she was delivered to him at the Presidential Palace.

Don Marcos had no time for her. Madlena showed some friendly interest but was distracted, had her own troubles. The head of palace security, Enrico García, took Juanita to task now and then for behavior he saw as delinquent. Juanita had no job and didn't attend school. But in December of '83 she did find a piano, tuned it herself, and wheeled it into the only unoccupied room near to where she slept—a room with patchy black paint on walls, ceiling, and floor . . .

"The Black Room," Madlena said, in case I'd missed the point.

Juanita reappeared with an uncapped bottle and three glasses clutched in her near-two-octave hand span. She asked whether all those full bottles were mine.

"He's getting drunk," Madlena told her.

Juanita was worried. I should keep a clear head. She seemed to think I was in peril. She began to tell us about something that happened a few nights before, when she was with one of her dancer friends at Marguerite's. Marguerite Millay was a dance teacher and Aramantha Visistation's lover.

Juanita put her hand over mine and said, "Please pay attention."

They were all drunk, Juanita said. Her friend was cuddling her—just cuddling. "But Marguerite was trying to get us *going*. She took off Aramantha's top and rubbed massage oil on her breasts." Juanita brushed the back of my hand, her fingertips at play over my most prominent knuckle, perhaps a stand-in for my therapist's nipples. "The whole time," Juanita said, "all Aramantha seemed able to do was talk about *you*. Or insult Ambre. She's amazed that Ambre put you in therapy. She said, 'Ambre Guevara thinks mental torment is ridiculous.' And Marguerite laughed and said, 'No, she thinks mental *activity* is.' " Juanita withdrew her hand, waved it, and told us that Aramantha then said something about how spirit possession was the local metaphor for multiple personality disorder. "She said that we think Ido is a *spirit* possessing Walter Risk."

"She's a heady cooze," Madlena said, almost admiring.

Juanita told Madlena that she was only trying to get me to absorb certain facts. "We all just *threw* Ido at a therapist, then made ourselves scarce. We treated him like a Christmas kitten."

I drained a bottle and said, "So, I'm not cute anymore?"

Juanita had activated their interest, and Madlena leaned, *loomed* across the table. I was questioned at length about Aramantha. My answers made Madlena giggle—then, at something I said, I'm not sure what, "Hey!" she protested, her face stiffening.

Apparently psychologists were bogeys to these people. The only other psychologist they'd encountered was the Russian Freudian, Lydia Yahanova, who was brought in by the FDR's Disciplinary Committee near the end of '83. All because—Madlena claimed— Don Marcos had a breakdown. She spoke about his breakdown as something between womanish hysteria and being a tetchy little spoilsport. "The people" of La Host had dug up his mother's body and paraded it around the streets—a blond mummy in a white satin evening gown, dead for five years. "And he got all hysterical!" Madlena's eyes were wide, a pantomime of disbelief.

"She was my mother too," Juanita said, so quietly that I apprehended her only by reading her lips.

Tomás reminded Madlena there had been a few other incidents. Other people behaved in an unstable way.

"*Sí, sí.*" She waved her hand at him.

Lydia Yahanova was brought in not as a counselor, but with a series of questionnaires. When they filled in her questionnaires Yahanova decided all the younger government members had personality disorders, or worse.

"Tomás and I have just been going over all this," Madlena told me. "The actual papers." She was intoxicated and enunciating very carefully. "According to Yahanova I was an hysteric and a sado-masochist."

"And a repressed homosexual," Tomás added, very thorough. "Don Marcos was a deluded deviant alcoholic with a death wish."

"True! True!" Madlena shrieked.

"And he's the only one of you who still has a ministerial post," I said.

"*Sí!*" Madlena was gleeful, as if I'd proven some point she had. "And Fernando was a masochist, drug addict, and megalomaniac. 'A dangerous combination, particularly in an Indian,' Yahanova wrote."

"And she got fired," Tomás said. "Because *no one* could bad-mouth the chief of the Taoscal. Well—he was only heir then, but it was the same thing. Yahanova never *did* finish her report on Maria Godshalk's questionnaire. A classic. I just stole it from the files at Health." Tomás unbuttoned a pocket along the outside of his thigh, pulled out a wad of papers, and waved them around. He and a friend were going to make a rap track using the questionnaires. He was thinking of going up to the border to get Maria herself to do some of the vocals.

Madlena put an arm across my shoulder and poured me some more mountain wine. "So," sweetly, "do you like living with Mama?"

It was all I knew, I said. And I hoped I was useful to her. I told them how upset she was the day she'd slid a soup bowl across the kitchen table to me and it "tripped" on a knife gouge, splashing my shirt. I'd borrowed a plane from the furniture-making García brothers, planed and sanded the table down. I demonstrated the new, smooth, exfoliated surface by doing as I had with Ambre, placing my hand over Madlena's and drawing it across the table. Ambre's hand had caressed the silky wood; Madlena's stopped short of a patch of spilled liquor. She removed her hand and frowned at me. Then I said what I thought. About Ambre.

She looked as if she'd last forever. She looked cured—her smooth, loose, dark skin—smoke-cured. Her half-mast eyelids gave her the look of someone only partly present in any moment, half an eye always in another internal world, perhaps her past, perhaps only her body.

Did I say any of this? I can remember Juanita rolling her eyes and Madlena telling me that I talked a load of nonsense.

Too much drink taken. I left before midnight and found the long narrow stairway between Bar Two and the street lined with the overflow from One and Two, with bodies, as though the two bars had fallen into the same orbit and docked. I was stopped by two Americans trying to talk to me, to bum a smoke. Then near the bottom I was jostled by some soldiers from Nuevo who called me "Anglo."

"Hey, he's a friend of Commander Sola, I think," someone warned, and they drew back, but not before I'd caught a forearm in the moving machinery of my body and felt, for the second time that day, a moment of resistance, then breakage. He didn't even cry out, just fainted, and his friends, drunk and unsure, held him up and hustled him down behind me, to give him air. They didn't even realize he was injured.

I ran away—stopped in a quiet street to repeat what my body did to his with no body present. As if in a chess game the move I made to break his arm suggested several following moves. I imagined another body—specific dimensions, contingencies—and danced, solo, among the puddles, this move and that, my skin insensitive and body off balance because of the mountain wine, but still full of a graceful, gruesome competence I never knew I had.

At Flores Negras Ambre was alone, but smelled of cologne. She put me to bed, scolding and tut-tutting. I made it hard for her, held my boots on my feet by arching the foot inside each boot. I watched her hair flop, her breasts flow down against her cotton robe, the droplets of sweat beading the sides of her long nose. My T-shirt was hauled over my head, the smell of my sweat hit me, sweet and meaty, not acrid. She pushed me down onto my back and touched my buckle.

I said, with drunken dignity, "You'd better leave the pants."

"Oh nonsense. Don't fancy yourself."

I put my hands over hers and gave her a very serious look. "You mustn't unbuckle my belt if you don't really mean it." I didn't say this—except with my eyes, soberly, I think.

She said, "Bah!" in disgust, and got off the bed.

In the morning, I was sitting on the steps, feeling just a little fragile and hungover, when Dr. Xavier arrived. He lowered himself onto the step beside me. After a moment he picked up my hand and extended my arm, turned it over to inspect the braided veins on the inside of wrist and elbow. He was so quiet and attentive that I found myself contemplating this arm, skin, its subcutaneous coloring, as if I too had a diagnosis to deliver.

"The sample wasn't contaminated," he said. "You have phosphorus in your blood—at levels incompatible with mammalian life. I imagine I can see it now, it must be in all your cells." He didn't release my arm, held it not to comfort me, or keep me still, but as though he needed proof of my corporeal existence. "Don't ever give blood," he advised.

I could both see and feel his pity change pitch as he opened his mouth to say, "You realize that you're not—"

I put my fingers in my ears, but I saw his lips move. I got up and walked out the gate.

(Excerpt from Madlena Guevara's responses to Lydia Yahanova's questionnaire. October 1983. Translated from the Spanish by Walter Risk.)

Q: What is your worst memory?

A: Finding my uncle's body in our yard when I was six. He had been in detention. They "returned" him—threw him out of a car.

Q: What memory most influences your actions?

A: That one. It awakened me to the evils of the oppressive regime.

Q: Do you ever have bad dreams? Describe.

A: I dream a government bill is passed forbidding me to be non-monopolies [*sic*]. I am dragged to the cathedral and married to a teddy bear. Then I'm made to blow up all the mountain wine stills.

Q: Do you enjoy your work?

A: Yes. I am powerful and I am never bored and I am helping the country and I am loved by people who don't know any better for the work I do.

Q: Do you have any sexual problems? Describe.

A: I cannot get enough and my partners say I make too much noise, shouting and kicking the wall, etc.

Q: Does your partner have any sexual problems? Describe.

A: When I talk about my stomach he gets omnipotent [*sic*]. Also he gets angry and omnipotent when I tell him what to do, or talk about other partners.

Q: Do you ever feel persecuted?

A: Yes. Everyone keeps calling me by my name—"Madlena, Madlena"—as if I don't know it!

It was in early April that Aramantha tried to hypnotize me and failed. The hypnotism wouldn't *take* without Amytal. She promised to get me some. She wasn't disappointed. I lay on her couch, facing away from her, and she sat down in the crook of my knees. She meant to console me. She said, "I can't sense any resistance."

Her attention was a caressing pressure all over me. I turned my head to look at her, and she kissed me, plunged through those boundaries she had so carefully set up and had me consent to. She sighed, sucked the breath out of my mouth, and drew back, my drawn breath a shaft between our open mouths. I rolled over and she pushed up my shirt and stabbed her palms with my stiff nipples. Then unbuckled, unzipped, released, sighed again, was admiring, praised me—"thick, sturdy." The little blowhole in its end exhaled its salty oil. She tasted. Exquisite. Her skirt climbed her thighs, and I threaded my arms through her legs to lift her, supporting the small of her back, to my face.

It was quite unfamiliar—that firm, hot lip between my lips and my chin wet.

She moved away, poised a moment, then descended, enclosed me. Her bra was fastened at the front, I managed the catch, caught the weight of her breasts. She was panting above me, her nipples in my palms as hard as scabs. I felt my penis push against the tough bud of her cervix.

"You will let me," she panted—her decency stripped down to desire—"yes, let me." She bent to my mouth, her hair came loose of its French roll in a sudden slippery rush against my face. "Let me use the drug," she spoke into my mouth. "The needle."

She came, I came, and we were both still a moment—or she was swaying toward collapse—then she found more hunger in untouchable tenderness, me still in her, not yet soft, and she started again, crying as if in pain, and we continued, blind and deaf and as lubricious as greased pigs.

A week after that Francis Taylor and Morgan Gray went up to the pyramids at Taosclan and took me with them. Morgan said they'd better get me out of that house. Frank leered, said I was looking more succulent by the minute.

Forty miles by jeep on tree-encroached, slick, silty yellow roads. We drove into the rain shadow, then the mountains. We got out and walked into a big flat wedge of valley, pasture, and jungle. Morgan was met by a Taoscal elder and taken off to observe a female rite of passage—she'd asked a year ago and they'd only just made up their minds. I went on with Frank, who was to photograph the pyramids in an annular eclipse—due tomorrow, he said. He was shooting for *Geo*, had a commission. He had sold his last Lequaman shoot mainly to *Geo*—except his photos of wim-wims nest-building, the first time ever the birds were photographed in color. Those pictures were sold to the highest bidder. Frank's fee was enough to raise a mortgage on a house in Surrey Hills, Sydney, for the time being leased, but if Frank kept his head down for a few years and got lucky, all his someday.

"It's a very pedestrian dream," Frank said, and photographed me again. Then he said it was about time someone filled me in a little on the Black Room, and on Jiron Pérez-Farante, the Peruvian "eugenicist" with whom Ambre had "flipped the pancake."

Frank said that he'd arrived in Lequama in January of 1984, at the very end of the Black Room episode. He found himself in the middle of what seemed to him to be a citywide experiment in altered states of consciousness. Everybody was seeing ghosts. Time-

honored tribal practices were being taken up by foreigners and fad-
dish La Host kids. People were doing yagga and cocaine, and even
spider venom. Jesuit exorcists had taken over one wing of the Presidential Palace, and no one seemed ever to sleep. But then I saved
Fernando and fixed the Black Room as if it were some kind of snag
in a sweater—and I'd turned the sweater inside out and pulled the
snagged thread back through the weave. (The exorcist priests who
were camping in the East Wing all reported seeing me pull "shadows" back into another world. Their descriptions varied. Some saw
me walking away along a winding path above the turquoise rapids of
a glacial river; some saw me in a carpeted hallway with tall windows. It was night—one said—and out the windows he could see a
harbor, and a burning ship adrift on black water.)

With the Black Room fixed things began to seem more ordinary.
Frank began experimenting with yagga and lost sight for a while of
his Lequaman friends. Ambre was depressed, and Madlena and Fernando were working up to their big public quarrel. Frank had his
bad experience, and thought he'd go color-blind. He holed up in his
room at the Plaza Hotel. He had to be ferreted out by some of
Madlena's colleagues from Foreign Affairs, showered and shaved,
and displayed to a man from the Red Cross. Frank's friends in Sydney were scared that he'd been *disappeared*. At that time the British
and American embassies were still investigating the disappearance of
an English poet, Norton Lawrence, and the death of an American
student, Brad Powers. Disappearances and unsolved murders were
in the news.

"Lawrence, Powers, Pablito Masolan," Francis said, and looked at
me. Hard. He stopped in his tracks on the trail. Our young Taoscal
guide stopped too, although he kept his back to us. He had Frank's
Walkman on, leaking a tinny tune, a tape of Frank's; the band was
Hunters and Collectors, the song "It's Like Talking to a Stranger."

"I guess no one has told you about them. Lawrence, Powers, Masolan," Francis said. "And since I'm not sure of my facts, I'm not the
one to do it, okay?"

Francis said that even after the Red Cross and Australia's Minister of Foreign Affairs got themselves involved in his fate, he'd kept
up his chemical experimentation. Eventually, he was hospitalized at

La Casa de la Mujer. And for days he raved. Then suddenly his mother was hovering over him in her safari suit calling, "Frank, Frank." She'd always insisted on "Francis" before, but her latest lover was a Francine and she clearly wanted to avoid any incestuous associations. Frank's mother was worried that he was going to get away before they'd *resolved their issues* and *achieved communicative integration*. "*You* try having a mother who is only seventeen years your senior and convinced you 'stole her youth.' "

Francis paused. He stopped talking and hurried up to tap our guide on the shoulder. The guide turned, pulled the headphones from his ears—releasing music. Francis pushed the red button on the Walkman. The guide listened, then his face relaxed and he pointed off the trail. Francis signaled "Wait here" to him, motioning the same to me.

But I followed him. We climbed through vines like trip wires, and broadleafs like lily pads suspended on the softest water imaginable, a layer of steam on the forest floor. I let the incomplete silence, the little unsourced sounds of the jungle, soak into me. Frank paused to take the cover from his camera and held it up by his shoulder as he went on—toward the undistinguished busy wheedling of a pair of birds. Again he stopped, five meters ahead of me, sank into a crouch, and raised the camera.

The wim-wims were tiny, vivid yellow, and were perched on a branch, twigs in their beaks, hitting each other. Frank explained later that the Indians say the birds duel. In fact a bonded pair coat twigs for their nest with scent from the glands in their necks—the nests reek in a way that discourages the smaller snakes who live on the eggs of little birds. Wim-wims were thought extinct, harvested from the jungle in great numbers from the late nineteenth to the early twentieth centuries, prized from Adelaide to Archangel as ornaments on women's hats—listed in hat catalogues as "dwarf South American canary."

When he'd shot off a roll, Frank walked away backward, then turned into me, eyes wide with surprise.

He took my arm and pulled me after him, back onto the trail. Then when it was safe to speak he said, "Do you know what you're like? You're like nothing on earth."

He told me that the first time he photographed wim-wims, on his initial trip into the jungle, he'd photographed other things as well. A helicopter gunship, American-made but unmarked, brought down by a rocket launcher on that ridge. Over there. (He pointed at a far, precipitous hill, dark green and scarred by red mudslides.) He took pictures of a mass grave unearthed in the Cordillera Pacifica. Photographed it before a team of forensic archaeologists went over it. Anton Xavier had arrived in the country with them. The team's money came from some human rights group in the Federal Republic of Germany. *National Geographic* bought the mating wim-wims; *Geo* the slow-exposure shots of early-morning ground mist around the base of a Taoscal pyramid. He was hard put to make a sale on that tattered litter of bodies, but *Mother Jones* took it when they profiled one of the forensic archaeologists.

Francis reminded me: "The goal of art is *beauty*."

He had a friend in Sydney, he said, who was thinking of making an artwork of film footage of a First World War shell-shock patient paralyzed by what paralyzes people of whom too much has been asked—who, if well, are to kill; who, if well, are to be killed. Frank shrugged. "Serious stuff. But me, I can't do those difficult things, can't make the ordinary extraordinary. I have to traipse around in a jungle only twenty miles from a civil war, photographing rarities of nature so rare they are almost *super*natural. Or," he smiled winningly, "I can just point my camera at you."

And then Francis told me about Pérez-Farante and the "Airans."

Jiron Pérez-Farante visited Lequama in late '85. His arrival coincided with that of a "colleague," Gillian McIndoe, and her son, Lee. The McIndoes claimed to come from Winnipeg in Manitoba. Pérez-Farante was authentic, had a lectureship at the university in Lima, and a list of publications in scholarly journals. Gillian McIndoe had no verifiable qualifications.

At first glance—at *second*—they were all very ordinary. Lee maybe a little slow and rude, an article of furniture made of undressed timber. Lee's hair was like a brush, straight bristles, his skin coarse-grained, eyes a dull moss-green. A slow big boy still tagging around after his mom. He called her Mom. "Mom, Señor Pastrez took our picture, he followed us along the street." This right in front of Don Marcos, only days after the Minister of Education had taken it on himself to follow and observe the McIndoes—who, when they arrived, had started to ask questions. For example: "The Western press has written that people around here regularly see ghosts. Have *you* ever seen a ghost?"

It was true that reporters had tried to write features on the Black Room episode, illustrated by pictures of the priests camped in the East Wing, or the famous photo by Mexican photojournalist Jesús Mendoza of the murdered American Brad Powers floating a foot from the ceiling in a palace basement corridor. A feature writer from the *Guardian* tied himself in knots about hysterical millenarianism—more than fifteen years before the millennium—about the reassertion of the irrational in times of massive social change, his theorizing supported by stories printed in local papers like "Woman Gives Birth to Two-Headed Chicken." Stories that the Lequaman government blamed on the Contras, who they said were peddling omens and portents to suggest that if the social order was overthrown, then God was dethroned and nature corrupted. The foreign media dealt with the Black Room that way; it was their version of anthropologist Jon Scott's little talks on "phenomenology" and "belief systems." (I was bound to meet Jon Scott, Frank said. Jon came and went; a British anthropologist who did his Ph.D. on the Mneone. A man full of comfortable theories.)

The McIndoes asked about the Black Room *not* as if they were looking for local color, or an example of a narrative from a different "belief system"—as Jon Scott would say—they asked about it as if they were making up an accident report, or were paralegals researching a case. And they began to narrow the focus of their questions so that, in the end, they were only asking about "Ido."

Madlena had her friends at Foreign Affairs ask the Plaza Hotel for all their guests' passports. She and Juanita even bribed hotel housekeeping to let them look around Pérez-Farante's room—and found only what one would expect: camera bag, insect traps, specimen bottles, a killing jar.

The questions continued, not the usual questions embassy officials had put to Enrico García's security personnel and government members resident in the palace: "Who was on the palace roof that night with Norton Lawrence?" or "Do you think Brad Powers had enemies here?" These questions had a different slant. And Ambre, Fernando, Madlena, and Don Marcos followed after the questioners, asking, "What did they want to know?" Warning, ineffectually, "Don't talk to them anymore."

Finally Ambre arranged a meeting. It was held in Plaza Bar Three on the hotel's second floor. Francis was there.

The McIndoes and Pérez-Farante were very attentive, but not very forthcoming. Frank did manage to discover that Ambre had tried to track "Ido" by somehow using his infatuation with her to boost her own power. Frank blurted out at the meeting his version of what he'd experienced. He told the McIndoes and Pérez-Farante that the old bat had buttered him up. He'd thought she just wanted the use of his car, himself as chauffeur. They'd gone driving in the salt flat southeast of La Host, between La Mula and the cane fields, where Ambre jumped out of the car. Francis got out too and pursued Ambre on foot. He found himself in mist, and met a man herding sheep who was a gringo, like him, fair-skinned and blue-eyed, but who didn't speak English—or Spanish, for that matter.

Gillian McIndoe listened with interest. She and Pérez-Farante showed no bafflement or incredulity. The whole story was oddly navigable to these "Canadian and Peruvian entomologists," it seemed. Then Gillian asked Ambre, politely, if she had managed to *locate* this Ido.

No, said Ambre, she hadn't.

And Madlena had put her lips to Frank's ear and asked him to notice that Lee, who had scarcely spoken, was imitating their body language. Lee studied each of them in turn, and mimicked. They watched as Lee's face changed from an ugly approximation of Ambre's expression—the haughty tilt of her head, her hooded gaze; to Fernando—his relaxed open posture, throat exposed, a well-fed jaguar at rest out of reach twenty feet above the forest floor.

Then Gillian asked Lee if he was *wondering* how much of this was true—sacrificing all the attentive neutrality she'd projected so far.

And Lee said that several Lequamans thought that Ricardo Pastrez knew more, and was responsible. They believed that Ido was something Ricardo had summoned, but that it had all backfired. After "something" Lee added in parentheses a number of words in Indian, Meskito, Spanish, Taoscal, and Latin—varying in meaning from "demon" to "fetch," "ally," and "familiar"—each word perfectly pronounced. Lee said that Francis Taylor regarded himself as a skeptic and believed that Ido was one of many drug-induced hallucinations. "And," Lee said, "Commander Sola thinks that Ido was what I am. And——" Lee went on, despite the fact that his mother had raised her hand to halt him, "Señora Guevara is wondering whether Jiron would like to sleep with her." Lee's mother made dampening motions with her hand, and Lee stopped speaking. His eyes glazed over and he began clicking his tongue against his palate.

Then, Francis told me, Fernando jumped up and yelled that Lee was reading his mind. Madlena lost her temper with him, and accused him of acting as if it only concerned him, and *his* was the only mind in the room worth reading. Then Ambre stood up and said that the meeting was over. She looked at Jiron Pérez-Farante and said that she believed that they wanted the same thing—to find Ido—and should be able to cooperate.

Later Madlena decided that the McIndoes and Pérez-Farante were sorcerers themselves, with very definite ideas of dos and don'ts in magic. They'd had the air of health inspectors listening to testimony from food handlers accused of unsafe practices. "They thought we'd *mishandled* the Black Room," Madlena said. "We didn't remember to wash our hands after taking a crap. They were *squeamish*."

Tomás agreed with his wife. He said that Gillian McIndoe struck him as some kind of racist. "Like Nazis talking about being fine Airans," he said. "They want to clean things up—*cleanse* things."

"Tomás meant 'Aryan,' " Frank said, and laughed. "But we adopted his blooper."

Weeks later, Frank said, Madlena was still fuming with indignation about the "Airans." He'd gone home to Sydney for a short visit and the same night he got off the plane from Bogotá, the plane from Los Angeles, the plane from Sydney, Madlena turned up in his hotel room and bent his ear. "My feet were swollen and the lights were strobing and there she was."

Francis said that the McIndoes were very creepy, and *unheimlich*—uncanny. But indignation didn't seem quite the right response to their creepiness. "On the other hand Señor Pérez-Farante was personable, urbane, *very clean*." Francis did a Filipina bar-girl voice. "So Ambre tried to approach him for more information. Madlena is disparaging about this. She thinks her mother was only after a sexual adventure. Whatever, four months after the McIndoes and Pérez-Farante left, Ambre went to visit the Peruvian in Lima. She came back very, very depressed. And as far as I know, no one got much sense or substance out of her. She did say he treated her like some kind of criminal, without coming up with a crime. He seemed to feel that all the people she loved most should be separated for their own good. He talked as if he were a junior officer under orders. Spoke vaguely about perils, like a nun substituting 'sin' for sex education. Ambre came home, burned a lot of herbs, washed her walls, wore her clothes inside out, and plaited locks of Madlena's, Tomás's, Juanita's, Don Marcos's, Fernando's, and even *my* hair into her own. She muttered away to herself about psychotics, and how her heart was breaking, and how she'd not be allowed to grow old with 'a little dignity.' Pérez-Farante had terrified her—horrible, lukewarm man.

"That was eight months ago," said Francis, turning right around to me on the jungle trail, finishing his account just before the arrival of a large and engulfing crowd of skinny Taoscal kids. "And now you appear, Ido, in the flesh—except you don't know who you are."

The children swept us up. The path broadened, opened into a delta of paths, lined by bright green fields of coca, softer green of corn, coils of flowering bean vines, then, in the clearing, tin, canvas, and timber huts surrounding three great pyramids of gray sandstone, four-sided with tapering shallow steps in which there were large portals and ramps of muddy flagstone going down into darkness. At the apex of the nearest pyramid was a square-pillared donjon, pillars decorated with fading yellow-and-white FDR banners. Between the pillars lounged men with semiautomatics. Fernando appeared beside one of these and waved to us. Francis lifted his camera to his eye and said to himself, "A man among men."

A meal was cooked in a pit full of hot stones wetted to make steam, onto which more leaves were layered, then parceled food. The whole was then buried. The mounded oven steamed like freshly solidified magma.

We ate late, the pit uncovered by firelight. I had sweet potato seasoned with slices of yagga. Cooked, its hallucinogenic enzyme was neutralized. Ingested, it gave me the same mellow buzz to be had from one toke.

There was pale meat that fell apart in the steaming leaf. Goat meat, Francis said. He ate, then set up his tripod to do some slow exposures by firelight. He was particularly interested in the long strip of matting near the fire where the tribe's small children had been sent to lie shortly after the meal. They were allowed to listen to the stories and talk, but not to leave the meal. They made a beautiful picture, all thin and smooth-skinned, seminaked and in assorted sizes. Some had closed their eyes, meaning business, or had turned to lie with their thick-skinned soles toward the flames; others were reclining but awake. Among the children first—because I was thinking of progeny, I guess—but then among the adults, I noticed a few individuals with the same uncanny yellow-irised eyes Fernando has. Something unique to the gene pool. I watched the children and picked little bits of Spanish out of the Taoscal talk.

Fernando, who hadn't been at the feast, sat on the other side of the fire from us. He was fasting, but watched others eat. His chest was bare and printed with a blackish handprint over his heart—dried pigment, I thought, chalky in the firelight. But it was blood, not pigment, for I noticed his injured hand upturned against his knee, his palm stiff with blood dried in a network of cuts.

When Francis left his tripod and went around the fire to Fernando I followed him. I was in time to hear Fernando's answer to Frank's inquires after his health.

Fernando said that being chief was a demanding privilege. He had to match certain influential elders excess for excess, deprivation for deprivation, hour for hour. It was hard work.

"You're keeping up your fluids, I hope?" I said.

He looked at me. "How pedestrian you turned out to be," he said. Then to Frank: "I'm correct in my observation of ceremonies. I cultivate trust. Or I humor them, perhaps. I wait for someone to make a slip."

"What kind of slip?" Frank asked.

I told Fernando that dehydration would often result in depression and a sense of impending doom.

Fernando seemed somehow condensed into a fractionally smaller space, his muscles and flesh taut, closer to his bones. His face was set hard, and his eyes were several shades lighter than usual. He peered at us, eyes struggling to focus, then answered Frank's question. "They have a secret from me. A secret *about* me. I can't seem to crack it—and I've been trying for years."

"Perhaps they are its best custodians," I suggested.

Fernando said, "Aren't you glib."

The next morning, the day of the annular eclipse, it was overcast. Francis was in a very bad mood. He had set up his camera at an angle to the biggest and best-preserved pyramid, having calculated that if the sky cleared, the black-silhouetted moon would appear, ringed by the sun, to one side and above its apex. Francis explained to me that he wasn't aiming for symmetry. He stood, cleaning a filter with a puffer brush, grumpy, his shoulder hunched against me. Then he told me to piss off.

"Is there a secret?" I wanted to know. "About Fernando? I do know he wants to find out about the sorcerer the Pola Pastrez tortured to death in their black-painted room. He was asking Ambre about it."

Francis swung around and aimed a kick in my direction. So I left him alone. I climbed the pyramid. Forty steps up, I felt myself climbing out of the worst of the warm steam that seemed to have collected in the muddy clearing. The pyramid's steps were narrow and there was really no place to pause, so I continued on to the top, where there was a kind of pavilion, an open rectangle edged by sandstone pillars carved with rows of portly, flattened warrior figures. The pavilion was paved by a broken mosaic. Between the tiles were channels from which beaten silver had been stripped—there were still a few tarnished fragments remaining—and pockmarks where precious stones had once studded the floor. The mosaic formed a map of the heavens—a wheel within a wheel, the stellar round, with symbols marking seasons and phases of the moon.

Fernando was in the pavilion, talking to someone on a battered field radio. He was attended by three armed Taoscal who, when I appeared, quickly moved toward me. Fernando glanced at me, but didn't speak up to stop the men forming their cordon around me. I was pushed back against a pillar. The men commenced a search. But before they touched me, they looked to Fernando, and I saw him give them a faint nod. I was patted down, and when they had finished two of the men still retained their grip.

Whoever was on the radio was making Fernando laugh. His face was lit by mirth, without its usual component of malice. He was staring at me, talking and laughing, while his bodyguards held my arms and kept my shoulders firmly pushed back against the stone.

Fernando signed off, flipped the toggle, stood up. He flicked an eyebrow at his guards and they let me go. He made a downward stirring motion with one hand till all three turned their backs to us and went to lean on the outer edge of the pavilion's pillars. Fernando came closer to me, so that I could smell the ketones on his breath.

"What was that?" I said, indicating the guards. "Some sort of surrogacy?"

"They warned me you were on your way up. They said, 'Boyfriend of Press Corps.' " Fernando pointed at Francis, below, pacing back and forth behind his tripod.

I told Fernando he should eat something. "Your breath stinks. You're ketotic."

He put back his hand to find the wall, then inclined against it, unbuttoned a pocket, and took out cigarettes. Lighting one, he scorched a third away on his first puff, the flame wavering as he sucked it in—but he kept his hands in motion to hide their tremor as he flipped his Zippo shut and put it away.

Food was pollution, he explained, while smoke wasn't—counter to the received medical opinions. He looked into my eyes, his own a feverish leached yellow. "Are you worried about me, Ido?" He blew out a thick bubble of the smoke, then swallowed it again and redirected it from his nostrils in two hard streams. "Would you like to do me a favor?" He was exhausted, so stripped of vitality that he was calm.

I turned away to regard the view. Two mules and six people were heading away from the village along a jungle trail. On either side of the trail were clearings, fields of corn and beans. The cloud cover had thinned a little above the nearest hill; its white was diaphanous there, with blue behind it. There was a faint sunset tinge to the light, and the greens were greener. The color and angle of the light were weirdly mismatched, its red from overhead, not the horizon.

I asked Fernando what kind of favor.

"Our hostages, the men from the U.S. International Military Education Training Program—we've been stonewalling them for the past weeks. They were allowed to go about the village—were fed by all the families, shared between the houses, but I have everybody speaking only Taoscal in their presence." Fernando was watching me carefully as he spoke. The state he was in, soothed by exhaustion, made him show vigilance by slowing down. He considered my expression, my reaction. "We caught these two with some Contras. Back along their trail was a gully full of bodies—all men—but none of them soldiers."

I asked him why he'd taken so long to decide what to do with his prisoners.

Others were involved in the decision, he said. He was just speaking to Maria Godshalk. *He* wanted to swap the prisoners for the U.S. Embassy's record of Democracy Wall, just to get *something* in exchange, though he would like to see me encounter my earlier self. Maria, on the other hand, would cheerfully shoot them, but knew they should be given back. Fernando said that the way everyone felt, he knew it would be difficult to keep the men alive. Fernando's people had wanted to kill the prisoners, but he'd made the village responsible for their well-being. However, several days ago one of the Americans had tried to make a break for it—and had injured a woman with her hoe. Since then the men had been kept in one of the dark rooms inside the main pyramid. "I want you to go in and talk to them, Ido." Fernando, warming to his plot, forgot himself and wrapped a hand around one of my wrists. He held my wrist as he talked, lifted it to watch his own thumb rubbing the taut white tendons on its inside. "They'll *pounce* on you. You'll be the first person in seven weeks they've understood."

"Do you want me to *ask* for the Wall?"

"Not yet. No one's mentioned it to them—or, for that matter, to the embassy. It hasn't been mentioned. I want you to gain their confidence—be their savior. I want you to seem to talk me into freeing them. Then get them to do you a favor in return—tell them you're researching the Black Room."

"The Black Room mass hysteria."

"Good, be anthropological." He dropped my arm, abrupt. I realized that, like me, he had a habit of managing people by touching them. He was poorly focused though, and I was being rather shoddily managed. Fernando was no altruist; if he wanted the Wall he must want it for himself.

We climbed down the pyramid. There were no guide ropes. It was a precipitous climb, and we went sideways. Fernando, pacified, walked ahead of me—his bodyguards followed, their steel gun butts sometimes clanging against the steps. We reached the ground. As we went by Frank, I asked him, "How long?"

"Under thirty minutes."

Before I followed Fernando into a black oblong opening in one side of the pyramid, I looked up and caught sight of a celestial body through the thick filter of intermittent cloud—a bright white crescent, but not the moon. We went down a stone ramp into darkness.

I was afraid I'd find the Americans in the dark, but they had a lamp, an antique storm lamp with a sooty chimney, the soot casting horrible shadows on the huge hewn stones of the walls. There was a round tray on the floor between them, made of braided banana leaves, and on it were fresh banana-leaf plates that held the remains of sticky cooked cornmeal and squash. My shadow swung behind me as I approached them, and I looked back to see Fernando stopped at the door to the chamber. He'd placed the lamp he carried at his feet, and its light only climbed as far as his chest. Above that this face was vague, a collection of faintly lustrous planes and angles. Beyond him his armed men were shadows, only their eyes and gun steel giving back any light.

I took a good long look at the captives, then went back a little toward Fernando. "Men not see black sky. Bad," I said in Taoscal. "Men dirty, eat with dirty." I wriggled my fingers.

Fernando signaled me closer, so I went right up to him. Looked up—those extra six or so inches his eyes were above mine. He was as sober as he'd been all day. He asked *when* I'd learned Taoscal. I picked up a little last night, listening to the stories, I told him. "What I was *trying* to say was that it's wrong to make them miss the eclipse. How often do those things happen? The normal order of business—war, torture, intimidation—should stop for rare astronomical events, don't you think? And those guys shouldn't be eating with such dirty hands. They'll catch something." All this was said in Spanish and in a low voice.

Fernando made an impatient movement. I waited, then I said, "Are you really *ready* to let me do this?"

I saw that the bodyguards were now giving me their full still attention.

Fernando warned me not to screw up.

I crossed the room again, put myself in the light of the prisoners' lamp, still standing, and lit from below. They looked up at me with grim anticipation—two clever, callous faces. The men were in their thirties, tall and spare, having shed some pounds over the period of their captivity. I asked them their names.

They responded to my different accent—gave their names. One was a major and the other a mister, one black and the other white. The white mister began, in a dreary and exacting tone, to tell me what kind of trouble "we" were all in as a consequence of this kidnapping. I remained still, listening. When he'd finished I dropped into a crouch and, looking at the ground, I put my palms together and said a brief, audible prayer for guidance. Then I raised my face into the full light of the lamp and received their gaze like sunshine.

"Are you from one of those *duped* church groups?" the white man asked.

"Let us not deceive one another—or imagine one another deceived," I said.

The talker gave a snort of disgust.

"I'm going to try to get you out of here."

The talker gave a slow skeptical nod.

"Get up," I told them.

When they got to their feet the bodyguards came forward to handcuff them. Both men took a few steps back, glaring between me and the Taoscal, then with an exchange of looks submitted, held out their arms. When the cuffs were locked I put myself between the captives and captors, I waved the Taoscal away and led the two men out.

When we passed Fernando I saw he had moved beyond the limit of the light. He was invisible, but I could feel him, a palpable aura of dangerous attention.

The most striking thing about the prisoners was that they were neither demoralized nor expecting rescue. They weren't depressed or unresponsive or cowed—but neither were they particularly indignant. I saw them take note of Frank as we passed him—his blond hair, neat denim jacket, and cargo pants—but they didn't attempt to speak to him.

I asked at a hut for some soap. A woman cut a sliver off a yellow soap bar, using one of the ubiquitous machetes. We walked down to the stream. I had the prisoners stop on its banks and stooped to unlace the shoes of the first man—the quiet one.

"What are you doing?" the talker said.

I lifted the foot and removed the shoe and sock. Did the same with the other foot; showed the shoes to the talker and said: "I hold these shoes to be self-evident."

The quiet one gave an abrupt cough—some sort of unwilling laughter.

"Well—shit," said the talker. Then he got down to remove his own shoes, couldn't use his hands properly so jarred his knees on the way down. His wince of pain was like a fissure in his sarcasm, through which I had a glimpse of anxiety and exhaustion. The quiet one had rolled up his trouser legs and walked into the water. I helped the other man up and led him in too. The quiet one put out his hand for the soap and squatted down to wash his hands and arms.

The talker seemed to need help. Needed his shirt cuffs unbuttoned and rolled, needed an arm to steady him. I asked, "Are you ill?"

"Fuck you," he said.

The quiet one gave me the soap—and a sober, sidelong look.

I dipped my hands, made lather, and began to wash the talker's forearms and hands, my palms running over the steel manacles, hairy knuckles, calluses. I rubbed his fingertips with my palms, clearing the grime that defined every whorl of fingerprint. When I'd finished he washed his face, then I helped him up. The other one was waiting, standing in the shallows with his face dripping and shirt wet. He was squinting at the sun. Then the cloud covering it moved, and he looked away. Uncovered, the sun was cool and starlike. The air had grown chilly, and the jungle's green foliage had a weird yellow cast.

"Jesus," said the quiet one.

I led them out of the water, across the muddy plaza, through a gray dusk with noon shadows. Every object was sitting directly on its own diluted shadow. It was uncanny—that disparity between the intensity of the light and the placement of the shadows.

I led the men back to the biggest pyramid, then gestured for them to climb.

"I'll just get you out from underfoot," I explained. We began up the steps. After a moment I said, "What I'm hoping is that Frank can take you out tomorrow. As a favor to me." I pointed down at Frank, who was now busy taking photographs.

"How are you going to do that? Take us out—what crap!" The talker began shouting at me. Then he missed a step and tumbled forward. I caught his arm, broke his fall.

"Justin," said the quiet one. "Chill."

The talker was trembling, shocked by his fall. I tried to assist him, get him up, but he swung his shackled hands at me—struck my chest a solid blow. To avoid stumbling I was obliged to jump backward, down several steps, catching myself on my feet and hands.

The talker had perched, all that was possible on those steps. "I don't want to hear," he said, "how *you're* what we've got—our best hope. Don't insult us, please. You've been set onto us by these Indians. You *smell* like a fucking Indian."

"That'll be last night's goat meat."

"We don't deal with armed thugs," he said.

"Excuse *me*," I said, "I thought you guys were training Contras. Armed thugs. Of course, you mean 'we' the U.S. government. In which case—it's not like your arrest and detention are acts of terror. Were you on U.S. soil? No. Were you in the U.S. Embassy? I don't think so."

"You're another benighted—" the talker began.

But the black major interrupted, speaking to me. "Justin and I were caught eight weeks ago, and no charges have been made."

I looked at him. "Are you the one who injured the woman with the hoe?"

"Yes. That was unfortunate." He put out a hand to his associate—who rejected it and got up unassisted.

"Go on," I said, then kept behind them for the remainder of the climb. At the top they sprawled on the mosaic floor. The talker's sandy hair was stuck to his forehead and sweat was running from his temples to his jaw.

The clear patches in the sky were dark blue. The sun was a bright ring. A jet was crossing the sky, very high, but as clearly visible as a fish in a rock pool, not a silhouette, veiled by glare—the normally diffuse light in the sky—but solid and independent, moving through thin light, thin air.

"Look at our shadows," said the quiet one.

Mine was so sharp that I could detect the tufts of my hair, even the texture of my shirt.

For the next five minutes we looked about us at the strange light. After a time the talker asked what I was going to do with them.

"Feed and water you first. Food should arrive soon, but those—

Indians—are playing with their shadows, just like us. We'll spend the night up here—you'll tell me your life stories, maybe—and in the morning we'll walk out, and I'll get Frank to deliver you to the U.S. Embassy in La Host."

"Is Frank like you? A 'progressive,' a 'liberal'?" the talker asked.

The other guy said, "Frank's an Australian, Justin. He's wearing those Australian bush boots. This guy is a mercenary, English, ex-SAS."

I flopped over onto my back to laugh. How the hell was I supposed to take that? Fit that with Madlena's "poetic," or Aramantha's "mindless" and "stuporous." I laughed and stamped my feet.

"I guess I got that wrong," said the quiet one.

"Keep talking. *Please* keep talking," I said. Then I sat up. "Tell me something else—Major—about myself."

The talker had made a fist of his face, it was clenched with scorn. But the major just stared at me, bland. There was a silence, which I broke. "Frank *isn't* like me. And to show you he's not like *you* either, Frank would say to you: 'Don't think of me as a gringo, think of me as a photographer. Or—better still—as a photograph. A photograph of a pile of dirty laundry that on closer inspection turns out to be the mutilated bodies of three women and eight children.' Frank has photographed a Pola Pastrez body dump. It made a big impression."

Our food and drink arrived—with two young girls and one armed man. The girls set it out, dallied, but didn't look at the prisoners. They looked at me, curious. I thanked them in Taoscal and they giggled. One corrected me. I'd mistaken "good" for "pretty." I'd said, "Thank pretty you." They schooled me till I could say, "Good. Thank you." Then they left us.

"Who *are* you?" the major asked.

I decided to tell them the truth. "I don't know who I am. I'm an amnesiac. Fernando Sola set me onto you because he knows he has to let you go, but he wants you to feel you owe me a favor. He wants a copy of the microfilm the U.S. Embassy made of Democracy Wall between November '83 and March '84." I took a deep breath, told them to eat. I watched them begin and took a little myself—tortilla, bell pepper, mashed peas with spice.

"But what does Commander Sola want it for?" the talker, the civilian, asked.

"Me. He says that when I was here then, I wrote on the Wall. He wants me to see for myself. *See myself*. There—my cards are on the table."

They exchanged a look. The civilian poured the major some coffee. After a time the major asked me if I thought they were bad people. He thought he'd figured out a way in which I was weak—and maybe meant to work on me. I said, without much consideration, yes, I thought they were bad people.

"And you're comfortable dealing with bad people?" His eyes were steady. But I tried to gauge the depth of the vertical lines above his tense top lip. I said to him that if I was him, I wouldn't start jumping to conclusions. Amnesia didn't equal suggestibility.

The major had stopped eating—had surrendered to a stronger urge and was biting the ball of his thumb. "So," he said. "We're to be released?"

"Yes."

"And all this—talk—is supposed to make us want to help you?"

"I'm doing what Commander Sola suggested. Doing it my way, I guess. He's already saved your lives—probably—by having these people look after you for a couple of months. It's hard to want to kill people you've taken care of—that's why the jailers on death row aren't also executioners."

"For all *we* know you could be an executioner. You're a new warder, a warder we haven't seen before. Isn't that how it works on death row? A new team takes over the prisoner three days before he dies."

"That's a bit convoluted and wicked, even for Commander Sola."

"You might not know yet. This could be a test of your loyalty. Could be that your Commander Sola's going to get you and me and Justin out on that trail tomorrow, then put a gun in your hand. After all, he's famously unpredictable."

I didn't respond to this. For a time I watched the scudding afternoon light slowly restore itself, and the roosting black chickens take their heads out from under their wings and resume their pecking about. Frank saw me looking his way and gave me a double thumbs-up. "I like him," I said to the prisoners. "I like that Australian photographer. He's the only one so far of whom I can say 'I like.' Who knows, maybe it's just not *me*—simple liking."

The civilian muttered "Christ."

I told them, "Commander Sola is pissed off that the government won't press charges. They said to Colonel Maria Godshalk, then to him, that you should be kept in the jungle and out of the way of journalists, till they had looked at all their options. Maybe they hoped the Taoscal would do their autonomous thing—would remember what happened to Battalion Nuevo in '85—the incendiary bombs dropped by U.S.-made helicopter gunships. Someone said—in my hearing—something about getting the war with the Contras back in the international press. Maybe there are people in the government hoping to scale up the whole war again—since they have thousands of evacuees agitating to get back to their border towns or be permanently resettled; and the Ministry of Planning has all its big programs on the back burner because of lack of funds; and there is pressure on the FDR to set a date for the elections. There are real advantages to be gained from the scenario where you're put on trial, *and* from the one where you're executed. But no one wants to be responsible for the bloodshed."

"You got all this from Commander Sola?" the major asked.

"I got it by considering what I've overheard."

"If it was *your* decision what would *you* do?"

I closed my eyes. Maybe my eyes rolled back in my head because I was drifting up and up through the rosy world of my own flesh. I felt a hand on my shoulder. It shook me. I opened my eyes and looked at the major—the not-so-quiet one—who was regarding me with a sharp, faintly startled look.

"What?" I said.

"You said, 'They set fire to the river.' "

"He's fucking crazy." The civilian offered his opinion.

I apologized and, to calm myself, I went back to my explanation. "A few weeks back Commander Sola gave me that speech they all give—about murdered children and mined international waters. He said, 'This isn't a public relations exercise.' He's letting you go because he has to. And in the process he's giving me a chance to help myself to that microfilm—which apparently I'm in need of." I spread my hands. "So you see, I'm *not* your executioner. You'll live. You'll go home." I waved a fly away from the food and ate something more—fried eggplant, creamy and sulfurous.

Francis appeared, panting, carrying only one camera. He gave the prisoners a big, shameless grin. "I guess these guys aren't doomed if Fernando's giving them to you, Ido." He asked the prisoners if he could take a photo. "Of you guys sitting there in front of that nice spread. For Americas Watch—or some other human rights group. Bit of a change from the usual tableau—say, a still life with rubber gloves, can opener, car battery, and a body burned with battery acid."

I was surprised how close he came to my earlier characterization—but his own dig at them was more deft and hearty than mine. He took some shots, without their permission, his face cool and set as he worked. He and I had a little chat about the lens he was using. Then I told him the plan. "We're taking these guys out with us tomorrow. You, me, and Fernando. You're going to deliver them to the embassy. Okay?"

"Fine."

The civilian turned his head, spat out through the carved pillars.

"And who are *you*?" The major asked Frank.

"Francis Taylor, freelance photographer. Landscapes, wildlife, ethnographic interests, weddings and funerals." Francis tucked in his chin and pulled an undertaker face.

"And who is he, Mr. Taylor?" The major pointed at me.

"That's Ido the Idea. From the Black Room. If you keep your eye on him, you might just find out what's *possible*."

On the way out we were accompanied by guards rather than guides, four men who went before us and followed after us, carrying semi-automatics as well as machetes. Once, when I turned to converse with Francis, he silenced me by a short shake of his head. Fernando was completely silent throughout the whole long walk. If he couldn't finish off his prisoners, at least he could round out their experience of imprisonment with some hours of intense exclusion and uncertainty.

We found Morgan waiting for us in the small settlement at the start of the trail. She was sipping bitter cola in the shade of an awning pitched before the wide doorway of a shed stuffed with rusting oil drums and machine parts. She sprang up to greet Francis, and he went forward quickly to walk her aside. They stopped beside a water tank stained with bright green algae. Francis spoke to Morgan quietly, then she turned and gave the prisoners a furtive look. One of the guards retrieved our jeep. Then the guards and Fernando stood about for a time, smoked, and joked in Taoscal, slitting their eyes and laughing without making a sound—which Francis had explained to me was a Taoscal mannerism. Then Fernando parted from his guards, gathered us up, and drove us out onto that slick, potholed, inferior road, which wound through a further eight kilometers of jungle before joining up with the main road east.

At that intersection we were met by a single soldier from Battalion Nuevo. Fernando parked, we got out, and we all performed another minimalist ballet of rearrangement. By pointing and little shoves the soldier got the prisoners into the backseat of his jeep. He gave Francis the keys. Then, after a long look into his commander's face, and without any exchange, either question or instruction, the soldier turned and walked away by himself along the superior road in the direction we were to travel. He left the six of us standing about, listening to the engines ticking cool.

Fernando took off his dark glasses, stretched his arms up over his head until his tendons creaked. He said, "Ah," and before he began to speak I knew he was going to speak English. To Morgan. He asked her what she liked best about the initiation rites.

"Fernando—it's *women only*."

"So, you enjoyed the secrecy."

"What am I hearing? The chief of the Taoscal encouraging a gringa to transgress against Taoscal tradition?"

"Transgression *is* a Taoscal tradition—says the Church."

"So is *lying*—what do you call it—the 'game of falsehood.' "

"That's Jon Scott's translation, his little bit of flattery."

"Why is it flattery to call you all liars?"

"*Playful* liars. So—did you have that hot dish with the frilled fungi? Interesting, isn't it?"

Morgan made a sour face. "It's vile stuff!" She stopped, her eyes opened wide, and she struck Fernando in the chest with the back of her hand.

He laughed. Then he said, "I imagine it's served for its suggestive qualities, its titillating surrogacy." He looked at me. "There's a good word. Surrogacy."

Morgan was irritated. "It's not like that."

Fernando said, "I went into this conversation in complete ignorance. I've made very good progress."

Morgan shook her head and stepped away from him. "I'm not going to talk to you any more. You're too tricky for me."

Fernando grinned at her. "You and Frank should go. I've given you the car with the best suspension."

Thus dismissed, they climbed in with the prisoners, started the engine, and—with a push from us to rock them out of the mud—drove away.

Fernando turned to me and said, "Get in. I'll give you a history lesson."

The Taoscal—Fernando explained—were the least populous of Lequama's three tribes, but the largest ethnic group represented in the revolutionary army. Almost the whole of one battalion was Taoscal—Nuevo—and a good fifteen percent of Amazonia, Maria Godshalk's battalion. (There were only three battalions. The third, Mestizo, was recruited more from Lequama's cities than from its countryside, but had a large component of indigenes, mainly El Buon, since the Mneone had pretty much stayed out of the conflict. The Mneone kept to their ancestral land and their traditional subsistence lifestyle. They kept at home, fished, built boats, spoke their own tongue, practiced their old traditions. Their biggest problem was not the repressions of Nestor Galen's government but a border dispute with Colombia. They refused to recognize the border, since one-tenth of their tribal land fell on the wrong side of it. Hence the title of the anthropologist Jon Scott's book about them: *No Line in the Reef.*)

According to the usual ethos of revolutions, the most oppressed groups at least briefly become the most visible—if not the most outspoken, then, in some ways, the most heard. The Taoscal had, from the arrival of the first conquistadors, fought the Church, state, and army—fought themselves into disease, squalor, and ruin. By the mid-twentieth century very few Taoscal under thirty could speak their native language. But in the 1960s, between global counter-culture and a health and welfare program pursued by a group of stubborn old Taoscal women—the Taoscal Welfare League—things improved for the tribe. And it became apparent to anthropologists, whose only interests in the Taoscal were historical and archaeologi-cal, that one of the ancient society's two core traditions had survived in secrecy. They discovered that the "head guide" they always had to deal with on visits to the pyramids was the clandestine chief of the Taoscal.

Slowly it all came out. The line was unbroken—there had always been a chief, either a man or a woman, deemed by personal qualities or some series of incidents in their lives to be the "luckiest" person in the tribe—to translate properly, "the luck of the tribe." It was not a hereditary position; indeed, in order that no chief could use their power to rig the luck of any child of their body, chiefs were forbid-den to have children. This prohibition did not involve celibacy, as it would in many cultures, but homosexuality. The Taoscal chiefs, one anthropologist argued, were living proof of the nurture-over-nature argument in sexual orientation. The chiefs were trained, raised, and compelled only to enter into same-sex relationships. Naturally, the prerevolutionary Lequaman Church and state found this revelation to be a pretty clear proof of the *degeneracy* of the Taoscal people. A shabby people, whose ancestral lands were inconveniently close to the capital, La Host.

On our way back to La Host, Fernando told me that the city was where it was not only because of the once-navigable river, but because a church, a great folly of a cathedral, was built there by the first Jesuit mission on the foundations of a razed Taoscal temple. The Spaniard Vasco de Faenza had massacred the inhabitants of the Taoscal city on that site, and had razed the temple, with the assistance of the El Buon, who had been at war with the Taoscal empire for centuries and were happy to have some help.

"What kind of deity was the temple dedicated to?" I asked Fernando.

No deity—ancestors, the spirits of ancestors. The temple was Turoc Iddu, "Spirit-Mouth," a place people visited to speak to their ancestors. Or to learn about them, for there was a library of lives, books made of hinged shingles of tree bark. There were forty or so in the National Museum, but most were in "ethnographic" collections in Europe and North America. Turoc Iddu was a place to cross over, and the corpses of important people were taken there to lie in state.

Fernando paused, smiling strangely, not looking at me but the road, twitching the wheel to dodge potholes. "*Iddu* is Taoscal for mouth, the gateway for the spirit. El Buon and Taoscal are related languages, and the El Buon word for 'a hole in the roof where the smoke escapes' is *iddu*."

I shrugged.

He shrugged too, mocking me. "The first cathedral, La Host, was ruined when the river flooded in the mid-nineteenth century. It wasn't rebuilt. The Presidential Palace now stands on that site. The street where I live, the Avenida Bueyes Negros—'Street of Black Oxen'—was once a half-mile-long stone ramp along which sacrificial animals were led to the temple."

I asked Fernando whether he was suggesting that when I came through the Black Room I had taken my name from a Taoscal word. Hadn't I simply written on Democracy Wall "What country, friend, is this?" And Ambre had answered me: "Who wants to know?" And I'd replied, "*I* do"—thereafter signed myself "Ido."

"It was *me*," Fernando said, "who answered you. I wrote, 'Who wants to know?' "

"Ambre told me it was her."

He looked at me, then slowed down sufficiently to do more than glance. "That's why I want you to see the Wall. *I'd* like to see it. Those were crazy times, so many confused or dubious things were said or written. And things that—" he frowned "—that *escaped* me."

(Excerpt from Fernando Sola's responses to Lydia Yahanova's questionnaire. October 1983. Translated from the Spanish by Walter Risk.)

Q: What is your worst memory?

A: Do you mean a "childhood" memory? Taoscal don't have a "childhood" in any Western sense. A person isn't rightly of the tribe, isn't Taoscal, until they understand the correct grammar of our language. Which is why every Taoscal child will now attend a preschool Language Nest. When you ask me about my childhood you are asking about a time when I was, according to my culture, something like cattle, or a pet. At seven, when I was able to give correct responses without hesitation to what we call the seven questions—*how, what, why, where, which, who, when*—I joined the tribe. The questions aren't asked in a particular order, but the order is always logical as to context, and often so everyday that the child doesn't realize the test is upon them till it's over. The questioner is formal, but the child under examination isn't rehearsed, so it's not like learning your catechism—though once the test is successfully completed it *is* like a first communion in that the child is thereafter a *member*, a communicant.

So, of my childhood I must say that I don't have a worst memory. I ran about naked and nothing was expected of me till I answered *who* I lived with and *where* I was going.

Q: Do you feel in any way to blame for this event?

A: This questionnaire is about as adaptable as a talking doll with a pull cord. And I suspect you've been briefed about the events of my early life, Señora Yahanova, and you are hoping to solicit my memories about the massacre of the village Sola. I *am* the village Sola; and the dead are silent. I am not *responsible* except to

112

uphold the traditions of my people—which is quite some responsibility and I guess could open me up to all kinds of blame.

Q: Do you feel in control of your life?

A: No. None of us are. The best we can hope for is to be in reasonable control of ourselves.

Q: What do you believe controls you?

A: Chance, the traditions of my people, my own plans, my own irrepressible impatience with things.

Q: Are you superstitious?

A: Whose "superstition" am I to discuss?

Q: What makes you angry?   ·

A: Many things, but especially the oppression and persecution of my people.

Q: Do you express your anger in violence?

A: Haven't you heard there's a war on?

Q: Have you ever used violence in a way that disturbs you? Describe.

A: Yes. Sometimes I'm a little too happy in my work.

Q: Have you ever struck anyone you are attracted too? Why?

A: Yes. Sometimes it gets results.

Q: Do you equate sex with power?

A: Yes.

Q: Do you equate sex with pain? With anger?

A: With anger, yes.

Q: Are you obsessed with your appearance?

A: No. I like my appearance. And my disappearance.

Late April. Ambre over breakfast, sucking on a cigarette and exhaling a long, robust, forked stream of smoke. She had the air of someone who has just completed a difficult task. For weeks she would clear away, and fill the sink, before my cup was empty, so that I'd sit, poised for flight, wondering where to go—where to go that day and where to *live* the next. That morning she'd fetched me another cup, then reached across the table to cover my hand with her own, warm and dry like the wood of the tabletop.

She told me that she'd cleared her mortgage. Tomás *had* signed the house over to her despite the character assassinations implied in Madlena's father's will, but it turned out there was money owing. "The bank," she said, dropping her voice and leaving her lips pursed and open. She'd had title to a little house the government gave her—when it was still giving away properties. Not a real house, but an abandoned gas station along the road to Leonarda. A horrible hot place where she couldn't grow a garden. "The ground was poisonous. Greasy." She had hoped to sell it to cover the money owing—but of course it didn't sell, it was too undesirable. "That is why Señor García the banker has been calling." As she said this Ambre lifted her head, very solemn and dignified. "We came to an arrangement to clear my debt."

I nodded. I knew she was telling me the truth—with omissions—like the necessity of other visitors, the younger García, the drama student, and the captain from Mestizo. It seemed better not to challenge her—better to let her think she could fool me. (Perhaps this was my usual practice—not letting on that a lie has gone in the "lie" file.)

We sat a while, and then it was as if my thoughts had somehow seeped into her head. She shot me a wounded look. "That captain was engaged to Madlena, a long time ago. He hasn't got over her, and wants to bust up her marriage." Ambre delivered this bit of soap opera plot with utter confidence.

"I wouldn't have thought *he* was the threat to Madlena and Tomás," I said.

Ambre wasn't to be led into a discussion about Madlena, Tomás, and Fernando. She said, "You must think I'm a bad woman."

I couldn't think how to reply.

"Oh, look at you!" Ambre said. "I've wounded your feelings." She took both my hands and promised to take better care of me, said she knew she'd neglected me, had left me to drift and worry. "It's all right, Ido," she said, "I'll look after you now."

We did chores and I talked to entertain her. I told her about Fernando's history lesson and Frank's "Airans."

She made a huffing noise, perhaps of dissent, then told me that she *had* used sorcery to try to find me—after a decent interval. "A year or more. I kept thinking of you as my freedom. There was nothing more to it than that. And it was none of *their* business— those Canadians, that Peruvian. I was just fed up with all the silly young people trying to make me into their mother. A villainous mother first, then a reformed villainess. A *mother*, everyone's *mother*. You know, Ido, how they all turn up here, unless I'm nasty and discourage them. They have problems with each other, and come to cry on my shoulder."

Then she said, "I'm holding you up. Wasting your time. Don't you have to see your *psicóloga*? She said I could expect you to be very tired after today's session, and that she would drive you home." She wrung a cloth into the kitchen sink and began on a windowsill, chasing spice jars and knickknacks along the sill with her wiping. She said, "I should be doing this all by myself. You must get ready."

"Prepped," I said, thinking of Aramantha's Amytal, her promised needle.

I wanted to go and submit myself. I wanted to soak in Aramantha's bewitched tenderness. I wouldn't shield myself, or shift an inch. She'd have to touch, have to tear, press, draw me up. I wanted the little penetration of her drug. I wanted Aramantha to *want* to climb inside me. But I didn't want to go there with her.

"So much for insight therapy," Aramantha said. "How can I gain insights from a patient who can't talk about his past?" Then she promised, "I won't fail you."

She closed her office door. Her expression was one of tenderness, and the tension of congestion—though I couldn't see it all, only her lips and earlobes.

I told her she only had to get closer.

She invited me to lie down and showed me the Amytal. She said she felt we'd changed places, that I'd dug in, into her culture, her life, while she had gone over into my silence—the place of my erasures.

I'd been taking Halcion to sleep—Aramantha's prescription—

and the "place of erasures" reminded me of the place I went when the pill kicked in. Drugged, but before unconsciousness, I'd find myself in darkness like night in the open air, in a valley where a warm wind blew, my eyes open on blackness with the shining quality, the immanence, of a dark landscape before eyes adjust to darkness.

Aramantha unbuttoned my sleeve and rolled it up; praised my skin, said it seemed sinful these days, and in this place, to love the whiteness of white skin, but that mine had so many different colors. She said she was beginning to wonder about Halcion, from her patients' reports, and from taking it herself the four nights I was away. She'd begun to feel a little oversensitive, she said. She'd slept, but with a sensation of wakefulness.

She asked if I was ready. We sat hip to hip on the couch as she swabbed my arm with alcohol. She told me that she'd do what she had already tried *without* the drug—she'd hypnotize me. I wasn't an easy subject, nowhere near "trance-ready." But with the drug, she was sure it would work.

I watched her measure out the dose, flick the barrel of the hypodermic to release any air bubbles, then turn the needle up to the light and press the plunger so that one bead of fluid showed, then ran along the needle like rain on wire.

"I'll take you back to the cathedral," she said. "Then to wherever you were before the cathedral."

Aramantha told me later that I spoke about the hand on my back, about my "unknown friend." She made me turn, she said, and I turned only into the blank sun of the Plaza. She sent me out there—to *before*. I said that my head hurt—then I jolted, my whole body suddenly rigid, and I began to weep. "What is it?" she asked. "Where are you? What can you see?" Then, collecting herself, she told me to look at my hands. "Can you see them?"

I could.

"Look at your feet, what are you wearing on your feet?" She was using what she already knew—what I was wearing when I arrived in La Host—to verify what she might learn.

I wasn't looking at my feet—I said—but *his* boot prints. Just up the slope from where he was lying his boot prints were fading, the damp grass starting up again.

"Who?" Aramantha asked.

But I had collapsed. I wouldn't acknowledge her for half an hour. I just rocked and wept.

(Excerpt from Maria Maria Conchita Conchita Godshalk's responses to Lydia Yahanova's questionnaire. October 1983. Translated from the Spanish by Walter Risk.)

Q: Do you consider your childhood a happy one?

A: I spent much time nursing the younger children while Papa Godshalk was away and Mama was ill. I was friends with my chickens. When I was seven Mama was very sick and I went to stay with the Gonzáles family in the Ambella. I had fun and got my first political education. My friend Rosa Gonzáles had a very political family. Rosa and I would make wooden guns and pretend to shoot things. I was very happy. When I returned home I organized a children's militia and we drilled with wooden guns. But this turned into a real militia as our elders were arrested or forced to leave home following the hope of work and my childhood effectively ended.

Q: Do you dream about your childhood?

A: Sometimes I dream I get a locked in the chicken coop! Very scary! Other times I dream I go to war, an adult, and at the last minute I realize I have my toy gun!

Q: Are you an adult?

A: What a silly question.

Q: Why?

A: Because I am twenty-five.

Q: Have you any sexual problems? Describe.

A: Sometimes I get a cramp in my foot during sex—is this a sexual problem?

Q: Do you consider that your partner has sexual problems? If so, what?

A: She's not complaining. She's dead.

Q: What are your feelings about death?

A: Very strong. But I can see the practicality of it. If everyone was alive that should be dead there would never be any room in my kitchen.

Q: Do you ever feel persecuted?

A: Often. When I'm being persecuted.

Q: Why?

A: As I say, I am sometimes persecuted.

Q: Do you ever wish you were a child again?

A: Never.

Q: Why?

A: I couldn't shoot people and sleep around.

Q: Do you have any problems in your job?

A: Too much work and too many other stupids trying to do it.

Q: Do you enjoy pain?

A: Only when I'm unconscious.

Q: In what way?

A: Completely.

One morning in early May, Tomás and Fernando turned up at Flores Negras with a carload of small children—the twins, Carlos and Aureliano, and Juanita's daughter. Tomás had rung the night before, and again in the morning, to ask if Madlena and Juanita were there. Ambre simply told the truth. No, why? Hearing this Tomás decided Ambre was under instructions, that Madlena and Juanita were parked in Ambre's living room, their feet up, truant from mothering because of some insufficiency of his. He'd come to see for himself. "I don't remember arguing with Madlena," he said to Ambre, lifting the twins from their homemade timber-and-quilt car seat. He put them down and they made a beeline for Barabbas—I caught them just before they followed him under the steps. Tomás looked hangdog.

Ambre peered at Fernando, aimed her dauntingly sooty nostrils at him like a double-barreled shotgun. "What about you? What have you to do with this?"

"I spent last night at the hacienda, to keep Tomás company. I haven't seen either woman since returning from the pyramids."

Ambre raised one eyebrow.

"You surely can't mean to suggest Madlena and Juanita would get the *pip*—as Jon Scott would say—because I hadn't called in on them?" Fernando implied that this was a ridiculous suggestion, but his whole bearing contradicted what he'd said. He obviously thought he was the leading candidate for anyone's "significant other."

"So. Where are they?" Ambre folded her arms and looked challengingly at both men. Tomás drooped, distressed. Fernando shook his head. "If it was only Madlena I'd suspect that crazy horse of hers. But the stallion hasn't been out, the foreman says. We *did* think of that." Fernando was defensive.

Ambre turned to me. "Ido, you mind the children while we look around."

I minded the children. Sat them at the table and gave them soft-boiled eggs. Drew faces on the eggs to make them more appetizing. A smiling one for Carlos, who looked at it in suspicion, and one with a straight mouth and thick eyebrows for Aureliano, who thought I'd drawn him. The little girl's egg had full lips and spiky eyelashes and was such a hit that I had to let her keep it and cook another.

The adults returned in the late afternoon. Tomás had sought the help of Madlena's friends at Foreign Affairs who, after calling around, managed to verify that Madlena and Juanita crossed the border together at Carmen into Colombia.

Tomás looked bleak. "This can't happen again," he said.

Fernando told Tomás not to be stupid, there was no political capital for the Contras in a horse breeder and music tutor, no matter *who* they had *once* been. Neither Ambre nor Tomás seemed to register the malice in this remark. "Don Ricardo and the Contras parted ways," Fernando said. "The only thing they have in common is the villain's ecosystem—cocaine lords, the CIA, whoever is laundering money through Ricardo's casino. Why *would* Madlena and Juanita go near him? Juanita is scared of her father."

Ambre was impatient with all this talk. She went to the phone and dialed, waited a moment, dropped her voice, and asked for Ricardo Pastrez. "Tell him it's Ambre Guevara." She swiveled the speaker from her mouth and looked at Fernando, scornful. Then her attention returned to the phone. "Señor Pastrez. I want you to tell me where my daughter and your daughter are." She listened. "They went to Colombia last night. Overland." She listened, dubious, then looked up at me. "And what if he is?" she said, then, angry, "*Oh*? I'm *sure* I believe that. Do you think I'm a fool?" A moment longer, then she replaced the receiver. "Don Ricardo says he hasn't heard from them. He'll look into the matter, he says, Juanita is his daughter, after all. Vested interest, he says, wouldn't want me to think he'd do anything to oblige me. *His* words. He's after a quiet life, he says." Ambre turned her head and spat over her own shoulder, spat on her own clean floor. A twin advanced on the fizzing spit and I prevented him. "No—Grandma's just being unhygienically dramatic."

"You!" Ambre glared at me. "He knows you're here. He's very interested."

I mopped the spit with Carlos's bib, my arm around Aureliano's waist. He'd chosen to lean on me, using my ear as a handhold. I could feel the adults, their gazes concentrating on the crown of my head.

Ambre announced that she would go to Colombia. She picked up the phone again to book a seat on the next flight.

"First I think *I* should try to find them," Fernando said.

"Oh—Taoscal divination." Ambre was dubious.

"Is this a competition?" I asked.

Ambre told me to be quiet—what did I know? And Fernando reminded me that *I* didn't even know what name to answer to.

"Of course you can *try*, dear," Ambre said to Fernando. "But I'll be on that flight tonight."

When Ambre and I dropped in on Fernando's apartment on our way to the airport, we found him lying on a rucked-up rug, rigid and staring, with pink foam around his mouth.

I checked his vital signs and ascertained that the blood was from a bitten tongue, not his lungs. His skin was cool and, on one collarbone, where I'd rested my thumb as my fingers felt his pulse, the white wedge of pressure mark didn't plump up again, but stayed like a brand. *The immobility response.* I came up with the term, itself as seductive as the idea of a sleep on a beach in the sun.

I unbuttoned his shirt and wrote my name with a finger across his hairless pectoral muscles, pressed some, and the letters remained visible, bloodless.

Ambre asked me what I was doing.

"I'm not sure," I said. "Maybe communicating."

"Communicating *what?*" She was disgusted—perhaps by Fernando, perhaps by what I'd written, not my name, as I'd thought, but a charm, a conjuring word, the one everyone knows. I looked up at Ambre and noticed what I hadn't before, that every piece of paper in the room—documents from Indian Affairs, a child's drawing, letters, a speeding ticket—all were adhered to the walls, stuck fast to the room's static charge.

"I can't stay," Ambre announced. "This is sorcery. Either Pastrez is lying, or . . ." She scowled at me. "You look after him, Ido. Get your doctor, if you want, either the *real* doctor or the Visitation woman—it's up to you. Or just ring Tomás, get him to take Fernando to the hacienda." She looked at Fernando as though from a great height, then put out her hand for the car keys. I handed them over. She said, "Stupid, vain man."

I followed her down the stairs. I said did she imagine that Tomás would stay put if he thought Madlena and Fernando were in danger? On the Wall they had been referred to as "that nice young triple."

She was several steps below me, in a hurry, and not really attending, but she turned back and said, exasperated, "Do you have to drag yourself along the wall like that as you walk? Just look what you've done to your shirt!"

I stopped. I said that it wasn't proper to leave me with the children.

"Nonsense, there's the nanny, and Madlena's foreman. Three adults, three children. Easy, and plenty of propriety—even for a nervous gringo."

I went down to her, put my head against hers, my face turned into the dark angle formed by her black hair and her shadow on the wall. Her hair hadn't been washed; it was clumped together at its roots, greasy and sweet-smelling. "I'll end up in slavery," I said.

It was too difficult to explain. But I felt that if they all left me, the adults of that extended family, the diverting, troubled, articulate people among whom I'd hidden myself, then my past would find me. They would go, and *I* would join myself in the silence. *I* would arrive with duties and decisions and culpability.

Ambre said, "Looking after someone else's children—is that what you call slavery?" Then she said, "I have to get my daughter." She took my face between her hot palms. "I know you're sick, Ido— but we need your help. Please." She kissed my cheek, then went away.

Twelve hours later Tomás followed her.

I held the fort and minded the children. It was very quiet at the hacienda. The foreman came every so often, stood on the threshold with his hat in his hands, and asked if there was any news. The twins' part-time nanny was in residence too, so she dealt with him. The nanny and I watched the phone closely. Juanita's daughter, younger than the twins, slept longer than her usual twelve hours a night and two hours in the afternoon—her way of dealing with her mother's absence. Barabbas was the only livestock for which I was responsible. I kept close to the house, the phone, and away from the polo ponies—especially Madlena's wicked-tempered stallion.

My only other responsibility was Fernando, who was catatonic. I turned and cleaned him, fed him with straws full of water, mouth to mouth, since he wouldn't suck. I'd lift his arms to wash his armpits and they'd hang, apelike, suspended above his head, till I was ready to reposition them down by his sides.

A log of the phone calls I took at the hacienda:

A woman from Foreign Affairs, Wednesday, 11:20 a.m. She wanted to know if I had any news.

Don Marcos at noon, to say *he* didn't have any news. He'd made a lot of fruitless inquiries.

Aramantha, at 12:30, to tell me I'd missed an appointment.

Tomás from Bogotá at 1:40. He'd lost Ambre, he said. She went to talk to some old pusher friends of hers at a shop selling gris-gris, on a street just below where the shantytown starts. Tomás asked how Fernando was, then told me that Fernando had said, before going off to perform certain ceremonies, that if this all turned out to be about *me* he'd kill me. I thanked Tomás for sharing this with me.

I went upstairs to irrigate Fernando, fed him juice, rubbed his throat so he swallowed. His eyes were closed and crusty, his lips cracked. I bathed his eyelids and smeared a waxy salve on his mouth. Then I went back downstairs and phoned Anton Xavier to ask him if he could come out here. Could he find the time? I wasn't able to bring the patient in — I was under strict instructions.

Dr. Xavier refused to come. "Exercise your judgment," he said.

I said, "Don't do this to me. You're asking a person with traumatic memory loss to exercise his judgment. How? By walking out the fucking door? That's what I *want* to do."

"You can choose whom to obey."

At 7:30 p.m. the nanny had the children in the tub and I took a call from Ricardo Pastrez. When I answered he sighed quietly. Then, without preamble, he said he'd managed to ascertain that his former Pola Pastrez colleague, Emilio Rivera—Madlena's father—had abducted Madlena and Juanita. Rivera had lured Madlena to a meeting just over the border from Carmen. She'd taken Juanita with her for moral support.

I interrupted. "Ambre thinks Madlena's father is dead."

"Does she really? Ah—simple, saintly, frank Ido." Señor Pastrez said he thought that Rivera wanted to remove Madlena from her mother's influence. Then he asked what Fernando Sola was doing.

"He's asleep."

We were both quiet.

"So, has this anything to do with two Canadians and a Peruvian?" I finally asked.

"That sounds like the template of a joke. Do you mean Señor Pérez-Farante? What do you know about him?"

"Entomologist. Clinical sort. Asked a lot of questions about Ido."

"Is that all?"

"*Help* me," I said.

He was warily silent.

"Help me, Señor Pastrez. There are spaces all around me just waiting to be filled. Step into one of them and help me."

He interrupted. "What are you offering? Rewards? Protection? *Amnesty?*"

I didn't know how to answer. He was listening to my blankness, my lack of content, as avidly as people tune in to a good story or bad news. "Undying love?" he added.

"Something undying."

"You're weeping," he said after a while, his voice neutral.

"I don't want anything bad to happen to these people. Something bad *has* already happened. I failed. Or I forgot my duty. Something went wrong. And I've forgotten how to fix things. I fixed the Black Room—but only because you hadn't factored me into *your* plans. I didn't defeat you, Ricardo. I need the help of someone stronger than I am, and I've chosen you."

He told me I was ludicrous, and that he wasn't susceptible to flattery.

I apologized and attended to his silence, recognizing it as turmoil. I wasn't faking my distress, or my plea, but by letting go I'd landed on my feet. I felt *experienced*—at judicious self-dramatization. In a careful, articulate whisper I thanked him for sharing his information. I knew that my lips were bloodless because they were prickling.

"I expect reciprocity," he said.

"Yes."

He hung up the phone.

At nine that evening Dr. Xavier came and examined Fernando—and said he'd like to admit him.

I disagreed. "I think what is at issue here is *confidence*. He works for Indian Affairs, has some kind of hot seat, I gather, and he's been in and out of hospital already, for drug overdoses, gunshot wounds, and 'hysterical mutism.' I got all this from Tomás. And he attempted suicide in '84—then joined the Contras for a time, came back, lost his ministerial post and was disciplined. I've been *told* to keep him out of sight. Those are my instructions. Instructions that came from Tomás, but that represent the interests of the whole tribe, I guess. Fernando isn't allowed to be *seen* to be weak."

Dr. Xavier pointed out that Fernando was a mess. He couldn't believe that they—Ambre, Tomás, and so forth—had got me colluding with them after only three months.

"The nanny and I were planning to stick Fernando in the shower, or hose him down at the horse trough. That would take care of the mess." I took a deep breath. "As for colluding—*these are my people.*"

Anton Xavier replaced his pen and thin flashlight in his shirt pocket. He folded his arms, regarded me steadily. "Your *chosen* people, Señor Idea. I don't think we are discussing allegiances. You are trying to belong by an act of will. Ido—I don't believe you're a sport of nature. No mammal I know of could live with that much phosphorus in its blood. And injuries and scabies-scarring aside, you are the *soundest* person I've ever examined—from the wax in your ears to the whites of your eyes.

"I have an old medical school friend who works in Berkeley these days, reading genes. They can do that now, read 'signatures' of DNA. I would love to send him a sample, but Lequama is too poor and isolated—the nursing sisters have only three picnic coolers to bring samples from all three Cordilleras to our one laboratory."

Dr. Xavier came around the bed, took me by the shoulders and walked me to the room's only mirror, and turned me to face my reflection.

"Fine," I said. "I'm passing. I even get bought drinks in bars."

"I can't argue with that—you are clearly equipped for survival."

I stared at my reflection, my glossy ghostly skin. "It's indecent."

Dr. Xavier shut his eyes and pressed his forehead with his palm. He said we all had to adjust our ideas. World views form around facts, plain facts or otherwise. Scientific facts don't have negative or positive values, they simply *are*.

"I can't even write a decent poem," I complained. "And I have amnesia."

"Inhuman isn't superhuman." He tapped my arm. "Now, will you please help me carry the commander to my car?"

One still morning at the hacienda something frightened the horses, and the sound of their sudden drumming approach, galloping from the far end of the long corral toward the house, frightened me. The ground was hard, but the sound seemed muddy, like hoofbeats on turf. I decided to go out to look. I went to the door, and walked into a memory.

Too many horses at once, and I went out to look. It was early morning and the dew hadn't evaporated, the grass stems were silvered, the green softened, the stones of the wall glistening. I put my hand on the cold, gritty surface of the stone.

My mind tried to supply me with names for this landscape. I decided I was looking at the Cuillins in Skye, or the land near Kamloops Lake in Canada. But before I had it—wherever the hell it was—it was swallowed by the red hard-baked soil of the corral.

(I did have feelings about these incursions of my past. This account is retrospective, and I realize that I'm writing almost exclusively about what I learned when I came here, about Lequama and my Lequamans. But I *hid* from myself in my curiosity, just as, in my former life, I'd hidden from my own blankness, and behavior that disturbed me, by lying in wait for a vanishing island. Aramantha was trying to treat my amnesia. I should have told her about the memories—the wet stone wall; a ghostly handclasp; a child asleep under an open window, the rain blowing in. We should have explored the memories together. Instead, our relationship became *her feelings about me*—and I hid there too, in her feelings about me.)

Tomás rang to report. He had seen Madlena in a cantina at the head of a little street. She was with a man. Tomás was across the road from them, four busy lanes and a tram stop separating them. The man caught sight of Tomás—a nappy-haired, dark-skinned man, mid-forties, who fitted the description Tomás had of Madlena's father. Tomás began to shout his wife's name. Emilio Rivera, very collected, fished in his vest for coins to pay the bill. Madlena started to rummage intently in the bag near the leg of her chair. A woman at the adjacent table pointed, spoke to her friend, whose bag it was. The bag's owner turned around to ask Madlena what the hell was she doing? Madlena, meanwhile, had upended the bag onto the table and was sorting as desperately as someone with angina looking for their capsules of nitro. Then she stopped, her arms raised like a zombie from a monster movie, and her father took her arm, apologized to the owner of the bag, and led Madlena quickly away. Tomás, dodging traffic, saw Rivera look back at him, then his calf muscles began to cramp ferociously. He managed to make it to a traffic island, where he lay for around five minutes, incapacitated. When he recovered, Madlena and her father were nowhere in sight.

Tomás said he was coming home. He was no sorcerer, and if Rivera was going to use sorcery on him what could he be expected to do?

The day after Tomás's call Aramantha appeared, in her jeep, a dust cloud catching her up in the yard and closing over me where I stood on the porch. She unwound the scarf from her mouth, coughed, put it back and came up the steps to kiss me through the cloth, her tongue a tumor in the taut cotton.

She brushed aside the nanny's offer of a drink, and drew me along the sagging veranda. As I passed the little girl's plaited-vine crib, suspended from the rafters in the shade and beyond the reach of snakes, scorpions, and crawling insects, I pushed it lightly. Aramantha pulled back my hand, and turned me to face her.

I was being tyrannized, she said, tied up to a house and other people's children like a servant or a poor female relative in an English novel. "They've worked out that to get you where they want you they only have to make you responsible, fill your gaps with things you can *do* for them."

But I wasn't earning, I said. I owed Ambre twelve weeks of board. And I owed her anyway—she took me by the hand.

Aramantha stamped her foot. "You owe?" she seethed. "They *chose* to take responsibility. Then they noticed how apt you are to take care of others." She threw up her hands, couldn't finish her sentence, and folded her arms looking away from me. But as soon as she glanced at me again her hands unraveled and she caught me to her. "I can't take you home with me." She was starting to cry. "I live with Marguerite Millay—the head teacher at the School of Dance. Marguerite isn't possessive, but she dislikes men. And I'm afraid of making her angry. You know, she wasn't *always* a dance teacher."

I laughed at that—it was so typical of every Lequaman story I'd heard so far, all prefaced by noises about the deceptiveness of appearances. Everyone was once someone else—back in the Golden Age of chaos.

Aramantha couldn't locate her handkerchief. I wiped her tears with the backs of my hands. She watched me in slack-faced misery. Fingers bracing her neck, I stroked her throat with my thumbs, crossing and recrossing her pulse, and the seething movements of her speech beneath her soft skin.

She talked about the control I'd always exerted on the therapy, on what happened between us. She wasn't obsessed—the feelings she had for me were real, and life-enhancing.

I had plugged into her pulses, carotid, jugular, and their current moved through me till I was pulsing. I pressed against her. She stopped, shocked it seemed, then there was a moment's furious fumbling when she and I both unbuckled my belt and popped the first button on her jeans, then she drew my penis up so it lay, a warm bar against my stomach, between us. We tilted our heads to look—as if surprised by the sight of this straitjacketed thick head, blowhole flared as though gasping. Aramantha stooped and put her mouth on it, slipped the tip of her tongue into the slit.

I said no—reminded her of the kids and nanny. I moaned, "Aramantha, we'll frighten the horses."

Licks, kisses, the vibration of speech—she was still in charge, of herself as well as me, liked the constraint—she hadn't permitted herself to unfasten another button, wouldn't let me out.

I pulled away, crossed my forearms in front of me, as if to say, "This is nothing to do with me."

Aramantha was in charge, but not in control. When I moved to disengage she sprang up, slapped me, and wound one hand into my hair. I was hauled and propelled by blows back to the steps and down them. She yelled, "Get in the car!"

I got in her car.

She drove us away. About a kilometer from the hacienda's boundary fence, she swerved to the side of the road. Our dust covered us. She turned to me in the dun haze and again seized my hair, pulled back my head so that I slid down in the seat. She straddled me—nothing between me and her shaved pudenda, shaved not for me but for Marguerite, of course. She loosed those last buttons and—at length—teased, enveloped, pivoted, *pleased* herself on me, and when she was filled turned her head to close my windpipe with her teeth, biting me breathless for a long moment till the sky turned red, then scorched at its edges. She released me, nipped my shoulder and my chest, then got a grip, her teeth grinding on the gristle of muscle. I let her, left my hands slack at my sides. I wanted to be pinned down, wanted hurt as an interfering noise, or a confining shelter, a tent of pain. There was blood tacky between my body and hers. She showed me the place I hadn't gone far enough to find, the place where I *ended*. Pain gave my dimensions definition, then piled me back on my pleasure—hot corms of testicle, strong growth, then slow crimson flowering that filled and choked me. I heard her cry out.

We hid. We parked her car by the clinic and walked to Flores Negras, past Democracy Wall. My latest poem, about "the wind through the broken shutters" had been graded, four out of ten, by either the drama student or his kid brother. Aramantha speculated that my passivity was an offense to their machismo.

Is it passivity? I said. It might be patience.

Abdication, passivity, abjection, she told me—that's what it is.

If I had all the time in the world it would be patience, I said. But I didn't feel patient. I felt spent and bruised, drawn and aching.

We stopped at the top of the arching stone bridge to study the water. It had been raining in the mountains and the river was full of yellow silt, silkily opaque. On its surface a full moon wobbled without melting. Downstream something boomed, a sound like air compressed by surf in a seacoast cave. Someone passed us and Aramantha turned me away, put her hands over the brown patches on my shirtfront where the cloth had adhered to injuries.

Flores Negras was dark, blurred by vines, drowsing in a miasma of perfumed flowers. I let us in. Only in the bathroom did we put on a light, that first night, as she turned the shower on to warm and swabbed my shirt away from the bites and gouges, dried me, applied an anesthetic antiseptic, then numbed her own mouth by kissing where she'd cleaned. She helped me—all the while begging me to help her.

We were alone at Flores Negras for five days. I don't know how long Aramantha had leave to be gone from home or if she simply stayed on longer than she intended, as helpless in her way as I was. She went out only once, to her rooms, to fetch her camera. She said she wouldn't photograph me, didn't like to think of herself, in ten years' time, brooding over a photograph. She had me in her viewfinder, and sighed—or she had the room, and shuddered. Because it was Ambre's house. And I was wrapped in Ambre's sheets—bandaged, bleeding again, on a mattress bared by our thrashing. Aramantha looked at me through the lens, then turned to snap the view from the bedroom window. It was as if she'd flinched from a blow. When I saw the photograph, months later, I could feel her behind the camera, behind the view, and me behind her. It was a picture of illicit lovers, a side-on shot through an upstairs window of a neglected vegetable patch, parched earth, and dead vegetation.

For five days I let Aramantha have me and hurt me. I was dark in my mind. But *practical*. I remembered to disinfect my wounds twice daily. I gradually emptied the cupboards and cooked. I took calls, listened to the nanny complain about Barabbas: When would I come to pick him up?

The one time I did decide to go out, I managed to find something to stop me on the veranda. There were wasps nesting in the bougainvillea. I watched them come and go, then counted them all in at sunset. And once the wasps were sleeping, I stopped their holes with gasoline-soaked rags. Soon the nests were as quiet as unplugged appliances. When I excavated them from the veranda ceiling they only rustled, like dried seed heads.

All my own internal activity had stopped. I let Aramantha tie me and I sweated under her, in pain that arced like unearthed electricity. My mind was whitened by pain and pleasure. She wiped me clean.

On our last night, when I was worn out, we lay together in the dark and I listened to her talk. I was open to suggestion, as haplessly open as the teeming holes into which I stuffed the spirits that stifled the wasps. I don't know whether Aramantha spoke to manage me or to make excuses. Her voice was bleak. At times she seemed to think she'd performed a rescue, and at other times a crime. "I knew you were a masochist," she said. "Anton made the same deduction, without passing judgment and without planning to exploit you. I knew you would let me hurt you, would *want* me to. Look at the way you treat Ambre Guevara——" (in whose bed we lay) "——fawning, being demure—it made me wild. You were contaminated in my imagination. I wanted bloodshed, but confined myself to the injection. First. One bead of blood. I didn't start right away, you know, start you talking, taking you back. I put the blood on my finger and rubbed my mouth. I thought, 'I'm mad. Filthy.' But you could take it all—their talk, stories, the tasks they set you, *and* my trespasses. All of it. You were purely inductive, learning everything. I gave you Amytal and painted my lips with your blood. I loved your stupor. But I didn't love your tears—I'm not that bad. I've not forgotten that you're distressed, though I think you are using me to obliterate yourself—your encroaching, forgotten self."

I had closed my eyes and climbed inside my body. My body was a tent at the summit camp, my breathing the oxygen cylinder's intermittent hiss. The bed, and the body in the bed with me, were a minus-forty bag drawn right up around my face. I was blinded. We were on a bed of snow, in a tent, a capsule outside which everything was in cacophonous motion. Outside Flores Negras time howled, like a storm on the summit of the world's highest mountain. With my eyes closed and Aramantha's confessions in my ears, I found that, without really moving, I could put out my hand and touch something warm and dry and scaly, something above my head like the throat of a dragon, hot and brittle, a surface that chipped as my hand brushed it, and was hotter underneath.

I made a sound, a suspicious, distressing sound, because Aramantha stopped talking and asked, "What is it?"

What was it? It was wonder at something that hadn't gone according to plan. My plan. It was my certainty stopped in its tracks. It was a black stain on my bare palm, my glove off and in my other gloved hand. I was standing on a stony beach. There was ice between the stones. A crowd of people watched me, to see what I'd do next.

I opened my eyes. The phone was ringing. Aramantha said, "That will be for you."

Only phone calls had followed me. The nanny's. Tomás's and Anton Xavier's.

Tomás had been persuaded to take up an offer of protection. He was staying at Don Ricardo's casino. "I just don't believe it!" he squeaked at me over the phone. Ricardo had asked for Tomás's help. But Tomás knew he was being humored. Ricardo apparently scorned the use of sorcery; he was sending out men with photos of Juanita and Madlena. "Canvassing," said Tomás. Tomás reported examples of sinister behavior—I was to please appreciate Don Ricardo's true nature. Not hospitable, not helpful. In the casino, in addition to the analysts who watched the monitors over the gaming tables, there was a *lip reader* at the screens for the security cameras by the pool, and in the clubhouse locker rooms.

"Uh-huh," I said.

"And," Tomás whispered, "he listens to *Cole Porter*."

Anton Xavier called to say only that Fernando was now awake.

On the afternoon of our fifth day, someone knocked on the frame of the open door. There were two elderly people on the doorstep: a handsome, bowlegged, black-browed man, and a women with skin like soft fawn suede and glassy white hair in two thick braids. A dented taxi idled by the gate. The driver stood by it with a stack of luggage. When he saw me he picked up the bags and came over.

"Is my daughter at home, young man?" the woman asked.

"You mean Ambre Guevara?"

"Yes."

"No. She's away." I stepped to one side to invite them in. They entered; she looked about, glowing with self-satisfaction. She turned to the old man. "Thank you very much, Señor Frei, for sharing your taxi. And for your company."

He took her hand, held it, said it was his pleasure. She said he was very gracious. They contemplated each other with warmth. He turned to me.

I said, "You'll find it in the phone book under Guevara." He blinked. I went on, "Lequama's phone company is a paragon of speed and efficiency—the Ministry of Armed Forces has the telecommunications portfolio—naturally."

Señor Frei looked at me without expression, then abruptly laughed. "They monitor calls, you're suggesting?"

"I just put the two things together. You were going to ask for Señora Guevara's number?"

"I was going to ask for the phone book in order to write down my nephew's number for Señora Guevara."

The taxi driver exploded into a flurry of pocket patting and produced a pen and paper for the famous poet. I gave the famous poet the phone book.

"I'm sure anyone can direct me, Jules," said the Señora, who then told me that she'd made a big fool of herself when they got to talking on the plane. "After he'd introduced himself and we'd been talking for some time I asked him what he did."

Jules Frei was enjoying this.

"I'm not a reader, you see," she explained.

Frei handed her his nephew's number. She looked at the paper, folded it, and put it down on the sideboard by the phone.

Frei again took her hand, kissed it. He and the driver were turning to go when a jeep pulled up at the gate and a woman vaulted over its soldered door and came striding toward the house. She was tall, with blond hair drawn back in a scalpingly tight coil behind her head. She was wearing red lipstick that wasn't applied following the contours of her mouth but made a messy, mad smear along it. Before she'd mounted the steps she fixed me with her gaze and demanded, "Where is she?"

I got out of her way. I told her, "Upstairs." Madame Millay barged through us.

"Goodness," said the Señora, and gave me a heavy-lidded look of interest.

Marguerite reappeared, herding Aramantha, who was seminaked and looked fearful. Marguerite began to strike Aramantha's neck and shoulders to encourage her to move faster. Then, when they were on the stairs, she poked the toe of her shoe into the back of Aramantha's knee. Aramantha's leg gave way and she fell down five steps and landed sprawled against the wall.

We all reacted simultaneously. The two old people and the cab driver all crammed themselves onto the lower landing between Aramantha and Marguerite. As they were moving to do this, I had time to see a faintly shamed look appear on Marguerite's face, and I think I might have hesitated momentarily—I could feel a brake on my speed, even as my speed surprised me. Something came on-line—something adamant. I jumped at the stairs, caught the banisters in one hand and Marguerite's hard knob of bun in the other. I pulled her past me, across the banisters and across my own bent back, changing handholds and supporting her enough as she fell so that she finally fell ass- rather than headfirst. I think as I had her I changed my mind about how I wanted her to land. I jumped after her, landed astride and, just in time, moved myself away from a well-aimed kick. It hit my thigh, hard. I recognized training, and simply rewound my leap backward and up, landing with my bare heels against the outside of the stair rails and my hands on the banisters. Marguerite gawked—I could see the wet valve at the back of her throat flutter with shock—then she collected herself, rolled away, and got to her feet.

The taxi driver pulled a gun on her.

She called him a dolt.

He reddened, then extended the weapon and cocked it.

I said, "She used the *d* word. She thinks she's in a Bond movie."

Marguerite looked at Aramantha. "If you're not back in our house by the end of today then we're finished." She was fighting it, but had begun to water at the eyes. Then she shouted at me, "You've taken her over! She's out of her fucking mind over you." Marguerite put her hands to her face and ran out of the house. Aramantha struggled out of the arms of the old people, and pursued her.

The taxi driver put his gun in his jacket.

"This bloody country." Señora Guevara was bitter.

"Eh! Señora—it's the two gringos doing all the fighting." He made a big shrug of helpless innocence.

She gave him a scathing look.

Frei asked her if she was all right.

The cab driver asked the poet if *he* was all right.

In the yard Aramantha was trying to embrace Marguerite and Marguerite was pushing her away. They were both in tears. I struck my head against the door frame and for a minute attended only to a moving target of glowing circles. Then I heard the jeep start, its engine rev, wheels grind then grip. The sound receded.

Señora Guevara was tut-tutting.

Aramantha came and put her face against my neck and wept. I held her, then she struggled free and went back upstairs.

A moment later the cab driver and poet passed me. Frei asked me when Ambre was expected home. I shook my head. He breathed angrily up at me for a time till I was compelled to meet his eyes. He told me that while I could certainly look after myself, that was only the starting qualification for maturity.

"You want to know whether Ambre's mother is safe with me."

"Quick, aren't you?"

"No one is safe with me."

Frei humphed, he said he hoped that was just self-dramatization. "Yes," I said.

He humphed again, and followed the taxi driver.

Señora Guevara was standing on the lower landing with her head cocked, listening to Aramantha sob. "Do you think she needs to talk to someone, a stranger maybe?"

I didn't answer.

"Shall we make her some tea?" She came toward me, her walk a glide, graceful and energy-efficient. With a glance at the folded paper by the phone she said, "Señor Frei will have to ring me."

"Probably," I agreed. "So it isn't necessary to read it."

She nodded and gazed at me, very still and complacent. She said, "I can't think what you are doing in my daughter's house. You couldn't possibly belong to her."

"Ambre has lots of friends."

"Huh! Men are never just friendly with my daughter. Even the ones who only want a mother figure. It's her forward development—has them all saying to themselves that they need a mother."

I shook my head.

"Don't tell me you *haven't* noticed Ambre's forward development. And call me Lena."

"Lena."

She was at the swing doors to the kitchen. She looked back at me. Put a hand up to one ear. "The way you say that, your voice right at my ear so I imagine that I feel your breath. *Dios mio!* Easy to see what trouble you are."

I took Aramantha tea. She didn't drink it, but lay on her back, wept, reasoned, projected plans. She talked about how she had to give me up, go back, renegotiate the terms of her relationship.

I took her hand and laid it against my face, I prized her palm open and moved her wrist so that she struck me. But she wouldn't play, wouldn't plunge us under again.

There was no noise in my head, so I went out for a walk. I couldn't even walk properly. The silence was a callus. It formed a blister, like a heavy-hanging sky, a blister with blood in it. The blood of someone I loved.

I reached a stream in the foothills, green water moving quietly through a sandstone channel, one of the clear tributaries of La Mula. The jungle throbbed gently in the morning heat. I watched the leaves, saw, sorted out, birds and snakes, and a spindly little deer in hiding, waiting for me to leave so it could come down to the water's edge. I turned back, began to hurry.

I'd left something behind me. The fireguard was not replaced; or I'd forgotten to pull the boat up the beach and the tide had turned; or it was blowing rain and the window in the baby's room was open, she'd slipped my notice, she was in the house alone . . .

Later that evening Aramantha came downstairs and sat with Lena, caught her up on the kidnapping and the search in Colombia. I was asleep on the couch. Lena told Aramantha that I'd come in complaining of a sore stomach and had fallen asleep. When they went to bed they took off my boots and covered me with the cotton throw.

Both women were woken by my moans. Aramantha appeared as I managed to stumble outside and vomit over the porch rail.

The vomit was red with, they thought, blood.

They woke a neighbor and bundled me—cramped and retching—into his car.

I thought I'd been poisoned. My head was splitting. I couldn't feel my hands or feet, and I got the shits in the car and tried to warn the orderlies who picked me up. I was passed hand to hand up the ambulance bay and placed on a gurney.

There was a gap. I came to gagging, there was a tube in my mouth. I could taste rubber. An alarmed bustle broke out around me. I saw faces, no surgical gowns or masks. Anton Xavier appeared above me, a syringe in his gloved hands. I heard the stomach pump—made sense of the sound as one I'd heard before—made sense of the tube in my throat. I let Anton put the needle in me.

Late in May, shortly after my trip to the emergency room at La Casa de la Mujer, Ambre and Tomás, Juanita and Madlena came home. They all told their stories.

This is Juanita's—her testimony, what she remembered of her abduction.

She spent all her time in a room in a mid-market hotel, with two men she thought of as one, "the guest." "The guest" occupied all the rooms she had to clean. Each room had a guest, but really there was only one room. Mostly the guest lay on the bed, feet stinking in thin nylon socks, and watched soccer on television. Juanita cleaned the room, scrubbed the bathroom till she ran out of cleaner and had pinpoint blisters on her forearms above her gloves. Once the guest followed her into the bathroom and rubbed himself against her backside—but then the phone rang and he bolted to answer it. After a few days he replaced her disinfectant with water, saying it would have to do. Juanita's arms ached. She made and unmade the folding bed from the closet, reorganized the bottles in the minibar. The guest asked her to sit down and eat with him. She couldn't understand why she was allowed to fall asleep on the floor in the guest's room. He accepted her apologies. He was often on the phone—but expected her to sit with him and play tic-tac-toe, though she had work to do (one hundred more rooms, each just like this, the guests identical, men in gun harnesses, dirty socks, a lacquer of sweat).

Then, when she was polishing the mirror (again) the door burst off its hinges and the figure in the doorway pointed. There was a subtle *phut* and her guest fell over with a small bloody hole in his forehead. Three men came into the room. One covered Juanita's mouth with a cloth. She shrieked, took a funny breath, and went to sleep.

Madlena told us this story.

She knew something fishy was going on. She was unaccountably saggy, baggy, and breathless for fifteen. She was told that she must wait to cross the border into Panama, where she expected to join the Sandinista Carlos D'Escoto. D'Escoto would take her to Costa Rica, where she'd train with the guerrillas. She was looking forward to it—she'd read and heard about D'Escoto—he was one of her heroes.

The man D'Escoto had assigned to mind her was very mindful and gallant, and *would* have been good company if only she hadn't felt so out of sorts. Shame to say, she bent his ear about the heat, the sweet coffee, the traffic fumes. And he asked her too many irritating intimate questions about her childhood. Had she been happy? What did she think of her mother? No, not Mama Guevara, who was her mother's second cousin—her *real* mother, Hambre. Madlena thought this Señor was clearly just another one of Ambre's conquests, still sniffing around. She wanted to talk about Che, her inspiration, whose name she shared, or about Sandino, the Sandinistas and Zapatistas, about Castonoles in Lequama, about the people's struggle. She wanted to play with the Señor's gun. "Madlena, Madlena," he was apt to mourn, shaking his head. Every night she slept badly and had terrible dreams. Not only was her body oddly ugly and loose, but her two breasts had turned into the heads of babies, of twin boys.

Relationships—her minder wanted to talk about relationships—how in any marriage there were two sides to the story and what a shame it was when only one side prevailed. Didn't Madlena think that people who always painted themselves as victims were casting everyone else as villains? Had she ever noticed that? And had she noticed how Ambre never offered to teach her? Madlena should understand that sorcery was her birthright. She was entitled to it—more so than her fraudulent friend, the so-called chief of the Taoscal.

In the cafes everyone was drinking faintly foamy dark red juice, freshly squeezed from blood oranges. The old men lined up along the bar at mid-morning for their aperitif—a shot of liquor, grappa or amaro, or coffee liqueur. The espresso machines gurgled, spat, and flourished steam. One morning Madlena ate all the sugar cubes in the bowl on their table. Her head cleared a little, and she looked at her minder. He seemed terribly familiar somehow—his dark skin, straight eyebrows, and coarse curly hair. He was asking her about religious instruction and communion dresses—which she'd clearly had in lieu of a good education.

Madlena said she was looking forward to an education in drill, guns, grenades, jungle trails, and political thought.

"You could have been *killed*," her minder said—and she saw that he had tears in his eyes. "With those guerrillas. You were pregnant by Carlos D'Escoto at *fifteen*. You were captured and interrogated by the Pola Pastrez and no one ever thought to call *me*. You had a miscarriage. Oh yes, I've read it—all the glory and triumph in your official biography—it tells only half of what really happened to you."

At this Madlena panicked. She got up, upsetting her glass of orange juice in a red flood across the table. She hurried into the street, ran away from her minder. And the more distance she put between herself and him the more she seemed to notice. Before, she saw the cafes, the decorated facades of buildings, with their griffins and winged lions, sheep weighed in slings, wheat sheaves, and doves bearing olive branches; she had peered into shop windows at shoes and handbags and belts. Now she saw the ragged children dodging among the traffic and the brown tidemark of fumes in the sky.

She heard her minder shout her name above the car horns. She ducked down an alley, went deep into a maze of streets. Half an hour later, furious, her head remarkably clear, she understood at last that she had been drugged and mesmerized. She had no money, no coins for a phone call, and so asked directions to the Nicaraguan Embassy—Lequama hadn't one in Colombia since that country had chosen to grant the criminal Ricardo Pastrez the status of a resident. The two women in reception at the embassy did a double take at the sight of Madlena's famous face, and within half an hour she was ushered into the office of the embassy undersecretary.

Ambre told *her* story in poorly organized fragments, and without regard to any differences between her world view and mine. She didn't explain anything.

"Pusher friends?" She was indignant. "Before the revolution people had that useful term 'counterculture.' You young people are just a bunch of dreary moralists."

Her friends provided a bed and roof over her head. She hadn't ditched Tomás—she hadn't *asked* him to follow her, didn't want or need his help, refused to be held responsible for him. Besides, her friend's invitation didn't extend to Tomás. She made no progress, so after five days she went to Ricardo Pastrez—went to beard him in his den.

The casino was very pleasant actually, if rather heavy on the chrome and black leather. "And heavy on the *heavies*." Ricardo was still "Don" to his men in suits. He was very formal, and impossible to provoke. Yes—they put their heads together. Looked for the young women together. She was scornful about his "Western-pattern magic"—his silver bowls of blood and salt, his chalk symbols. "It's sorcery with a condom on, if you ask me. Safe, but numbed."

She and Ricardo located Juanita—discovered where to send his heavies. One magical attack was directed their way by Emilio Rivera, but he was really too *puny* to take on Señor Pastrez. Ambre was a bit knocked about, but used her dead twin as a "mask," a misdirection.

Tomás was crabbed with anxiety. He said to us, "Don Ricardo is very sinister. Do you know he wears black shiny robes?"

Ambre hooted. "Tomás is talking about a black silk Yves Saint Laurent robe that Ricardo wore to breakfast."

"You had *breakfast* with him?" Madlena was reproachful.

"A woman has to eat." Ambre then turned her attention to me, smiled, told me Ricardo had reported my "please please please."

This provoked Madlena into a little lecture on what an evil man Ricardo Pastrez was. He wasn't someone to whom I should put myself in debt. She quickly grew impatient with her illustrations and referred me to Frank Taylor's photographs of the body dump. We were talking *crimes against humanity.*

"That's sobered him," said Tomás, faintly sanctimonious.

I asked Ambre if the crisis was over. She shrugged, then said she thought Madlena's father only wanted to have Madlena long enough to *deprogram* her. "He made her think she was fifteen—he took her back before her political education and her first love affair. He thinks they are life *events*, not life choices." Ambre said that she thought we'd all hear from Emilio again. "He wanted to remind me how strong he was. He was more interested in reminding me of his strength than persuading Madlena to consider his side of things."

The Ministry of Indian Affairs had an official line: Commander Sola, the chief, the troubleshooter, was in bed at home with a "post-viral syndrome."

Anton Xavier said Fernando had discharged himself as soon as he regained consciousness. Anton had recommended that the commander stay put, but had let him be wheeled to the phone at the nurses' station. Half an hour later a nurse reported that Fernando had left with his friend, the Minister of Indian Affairs, the Taoscal woman who'd taken over his portfolio in 1984 when he'd joined the Contras.

Madlena took me with her to visit him at his apartment on the Avenida Bueyes Negros. We found him huddled in a blanket on his couch. Madlena questioned him gently about his health. He was drained and monosyllabic. She hovered. I put the Lucozade we'd brought in his fridge, cleared out some wilted salad vegetables, and wiped green water from the vegetable bins.

Madlena kept her fingers hooked in her belt, her elbows sticking out, awkward and aggressive. She had to tie herself up to stop herself from touching him.

· I decanted one bottle into a glass and brought it to Fernando.

He fumbled free of the blanket, reached for my wrist, not the glass of Lucozade. His palm was hot and dry. "Before the hospital you had me, didn't you?"

I looked down into his flushed, bright-eyed face and considered saying that I'd written what I thought was my name on his skin, that I'd fed him mouth to mouth, washed him, oiled his lips with a salve, bathed his eyes, combed his hair. But Madlena was there. I told him I handed him over to Anton Xavier. "Too difficult for me," I said.

He let go my wrist and took the glass. He asked us to please leave.

In early June I went to see Anton Xavier. I'd thought what to do about one of his patients, a man who'd arrived on the ward when I was there after my stomach was pumped. Anton seemed very surprised to see me—but of course I wasn't a Latino, I couldn't be expected to be creeping about shamefaced after having "attempted my own life." He told me this.

I asked him was he trying to annoy me.

"Ms. Visistation said you missed your latest appointment."

"Uh-huh."

He drummed his pen on the desk, then pushed it behind his ear and folded his arms.

I asked, "How is the man with the necrotizing infection in his ear?"

"What is in the honey jar?" Anton asked. I didn't answer, and after a moment he said, "I'm not going to discuss my patients with you."

"Not even to answer polite inquiries about the health of one?"

Anton blushed.

"So, you lost him?"

Anton got up and came around the desk. "The Cubans offered to fly him to Havana where they have one of those Soviet barometric chambers. Then the U.S. Embassy got wind of it and came through with the right antibiotics." He shrugged. His eyes were very tired, the light was leaving them as he stared at me.

"What I have here," I offered the jar, "are some nice, clean maggots—I shook them off the meat before they hatched. I've been poised over it for more than a day. Ambre is disgusted. I even put them in a sieve and gave them a little rinse. They're still pretty lively."

Dr. Xavier had closed his eyes. When he opened them again he said, "Yes. It's a good idea."

We went to find the patient. Anton removed the man's dressing, had him roll onto his side, tapped the honey jar, and poured gobs of maggots into the inflamed, stinking earhole. Then he applied a fresh pad of gauze. He warned the patient that this treatment might drive him a little wild, but he mustn't touch the dressing. He turned to the ward nurse. "I'll change it myself."

I was led back into his office. "Armed Forces tells me I'm to anticipate some trauma work up in Leonarda, at the Army Field Hospital. They think the Contras are planning a push." Anton was looking through a file box lid of lab samples on his desk. "I could find work for you—if you can run an autoclave."

"I can."

"Why am I not surprised?"

"Anton—Dr. Xavier—I got a notice to report for an interview

at Armed Forces. About my CMT. On Friday. Can you requisition me before they think of something to do with me?"

"I can try. But Armed Forces is an immovable object. Ah, here it is." He'd located a Ziploc bag containing a wet brownish berry. He held it up before me. "This is what was in your stomach. These, a quarter kilo of them. The hospital laboratory had to send it out to the Botany Department at the university. Where—luckily—there is a man from Nova Scotia."

I waited for him to tell me. He waited for me to guess, or confess.

"Whiteberry," he said. "You must have really gone out of your way."

"I don't recall taking anything, Dr. Xavier, I told you that."

"It didn't just appear in your digestive tract."

"Maybe it did."

Anton sighed, sagged—and lowered himself into his chair. He gave his face a vigorous rubbing. "I had Commander Sola claiming he exhausted himself wrestling with a creature from another dimension—convincingly described as 'a horrible, suede-skinned, resilient thing.' And you're having toxic plant matter *wished* on you."

"I didn't say that. I don't believe anyone attacked me."

"All right, I'll humor you. How did it happen that I pumped a couple of liters of poorly chewed Nova Scotian whiteberries out of you?"

I looked at the floor.

"Hmmm?"

"I'm not refusing to tell you. I don't want to think about it."

"*Madre de Dios!*" he said. "Go visit your therapist."

Ambre wanted her house back in order. Its full complement now included Lena, whom Ambre accommodated but to whom she'd made it clear that she didn't intend to "dance attention." Lena then surprised Ambre by seeming to make her little room only a base for her operations. (On Ambre's first night home, as we heard everyone's stories, Lena had stood at the table ironing a lace-laden white cotton shirt. She was going out to dinner with Jules Frei. She'd been smirking to herself as she'd plied her iron to smooth the lace.)

Ambre finally remembered to fetch Barabbas from the hacienda. "You go get him, Ido. We might as well have him too," she said, then went on to complain how Marguerite, that fanciful Frenchwoman, had been trying to impress her when she turned up one day in May '84 with Barabbas—an eight-week-old clumsy puppy with a nervous wetting habit. "The whole house was carpeted with newspaper—not that it much mattered—it was that horrible little house on the highway." Between the damp patches Ambre would find her eye snagged by photos of Fernando and Ricardo Pastrez in Miami, standing side by side and flanked by gringos in dark glasses. In the biggest national daily, *La Voz de la Host*, the photo had been sectioned by black bands representing the crosshairs of a gunsight—centered on Commander Sola's treacherous heart. "I cannot express how miserable it was, stepping over puddles of piss, and thinking about my poor daughter's broken heart, and having to be properly grateful to Marguerite, who kept saying she was troubled to think of me in my house on the highway alone, but always insisted on getting up out of my bed afterward to drive back to the city."

"Your bed?"

Ambre waved a hand, airily.

I translated: "Water under the bridge."

"Don't 'water under the bridge' me! I had far too much at that time of the water under the bridge. People jumping into La Mula every other day. Never—mind you—from any of the nasty rusty things up- or downstream, always from the handsome stone bridge. Don Marcos, of course, poor boy, threw in his favorite poetry books first. Morgan too—over Frank or perhaps even Marguerite, who knows—*she* said she slipped." Ambre clicked her tongue, made a shooing motion, then came up to me to help me get a second arm into my jacket. "Honestly, Ido, can't you talk and dress at the same time?"

"Morgan and Marguerite?"

"Madame Millay is a very attractive woman."

"Uh-huh."

She pursed her lips and asked me what that meant.

"Kiss anyone around here and you close a circuit."

I could see she didn't understand me beyond "kiss anyone." She said, "Well, you're safe, you're not kissing anyone."

"How would you know?"

"I'd know. A man who is *getting it* looks sleek, pleased with himself. You look sick and neglected. You've been fretting while I've been away, haven't you? I'm flattered. You have a kind heart, Ido."

She was about to herd me out the door, but I'd decided to take advantage of her confiding mood. I set my back against the door frame. "Can you tell me something?" I said. "Can you tell me about Jiron Pérez-Farante? You visited him in Lima."

Once she had established that my question had no connection to her earlier remarks about her lovers, Ambre was quite forthcoming. She said she'd noticed how I'd got the others to tell me their stories. I mustn't expect much from her. She wasn't a talker. Her father was Mexican and spoke Spanish, her mother El Buon and spoke English. "They scarcely spoke to each other. It made me tongue-tied. And one thing I remember about my drowned sister was that I could hear her thoughts. Or perhaps it was my own thoughts I heard, but I knew we shared them."

Ambre assessed me—wondering if she'd sufficiently lowered my expectations. Then she shrugged and began. Jiron had reminded her of Ricardo Pastrez—whom she'd met several times in the 1970s with Emilio Rivera. She didn't remark on her attraction to Jiron, since it could imply a possible attraction to Don Ricardo.

Ambre said that Jiron was like a priest. Priests were soldiers for Christ, and Jiron was a soldier for *someone*. He talked about the McIndoes as if they stood for *something*—and not Canada.

"They were representative?"

"Yes, that's a better word." Ambre said. "When we spoke on the Wall, Ido, and argued, it was because I was trying to tell you that your being in Lequama—if only in spirit—wasn't a magical mystery tour. You seemed to think it had all happened to perfect your soul."

I pulled a face. She put her hands on my shoulders and said fondly, "Bighead. I wanted to make you see that maybe you were there for us. For Lequama. We weren't to answer your needs, you were to answer ours. And you *did* fix the Black Room. But when the McIndoes and Jiron turned up, they only wanted to know about you. I realized you were right. We weren't considered important. That made me unhappy. And so did Jiron's manner when I visited him. He seemed to think we—myself, my daughter, and her friends were all dangerous, like kerosene kept in a rusted can."

I put my hands over hers. I wanted to comfort her, but she shook me off. She said she had no idea now which of her ideas about me was true. Her unhappiness might have tricked her into seeing what was straight as crooked. I *had* fixed the Black Room. Ricardo and Emilio and those other Pola Pastrez first set it going, but they didn't make it, and they didn't *mean* it. "It was a place without rules," she said. "I was once a free-love hippie and I didn't think much of rules. But Señor García the banker has been telling me that there is no freedom without them. He lies there talking about 'fiscal responsibility,' trade and tariffs, and how 'free market economies' aren't free. You know how men talk! He talks and I think about the Black Room."

I asked if she had any idea why the Pola Pastrez set it in motion. What *did* they mean?

She asked me to imagine that I was pushing a needle through a cloth screen, and that someone on the other side and invisible to me took the needle and pulled my thread through. "I think the Pola Pastrez were doing something bad in their black-painted room, but what happened was a *by-product*. Pastrez's ally's mischief, the murders and disappearances, the cold, the strange sounds, blackouts, palace residents' nightmares and sleepwalking—all only a by-product. What the Pola Pastrez meant to do they did *before* the revolution, before they fled the country. I think it involved a Taoscal sorcerer who, rumor has it, was killed in that room." She nodded at me to encourage my assent.

I thanked her. She was very candid. Everyone else was rather evasive.

"They're only afraid you'll think they're talking down to you, Ido. We all know you're very clever."

There was no one at the hacienda, so I sat on the veranda and considered our conversation. Tried to sort out what I felt. I didn't want Ambre to think I was sick and sexless. I believed she *considered* every man. But why should it matter if she decided to make an exception of me? She was my friend and my protector.

Before I went off on my errand I'd asked her if she was worried about me now that she was home. She wasn't really—I did seem my usual eager self, just needed some attention, some "building up." I said something about my big righting-arm, and she looked baffled. I explained. A "righting-arm" is the degree to which a vessel can roll in heavy seas and still right itself. I could go a long way down, I said, mast flat to the waves, without capsizing.

"You must know about boats, Ido," Ambre said.

And I remembered. Remembered—or saw—that the hot, scaly surface I had touched in one of my mirages of memory was not, naturally, the neck of a dragon, but the charred stave of a large wooden ship. I saw a strip of shingle beach, stones embedded in icy slime, a beach sectioned by stone and wood slipways; beyond that an embankment, a sharp rise to a road along a long stone wharf, warehouses, a city climbing above them, a city with muddy streets, frozen and striped by snow in wheel ruts. The hull was still smoking—a burned ship, beached, on a frosty day. I touched the iridescent charcoal skin of burned timber. My hand came away warmed and blackened.

And then I was seeing the scene in print—like an old book—the notched letters of cold type; a broadsheet, *Sketches by T'reon*: "He touched the hull and his hand came away black. He seemed mystified by his reverses, not angry, only puzzled . . ."

It was so strange. As soon as I saw the print I lost the city, I remembered my self-disgust and forgot everything else. I didn't want to be *him*, the puzzled, powerful "he" of the sketch—a miserable Johnson observed by a scrupulous Boswell.

Madlena's foreman appeared, on horseback, followed by the parched and limping Barabbas. The foreman said he had been searching for Madlena's stallion, who had bolted after throwing her. She'd gone off to La Casa de la Mujer with Tomás, her shoulder out of joint.

The old man was tired, his hardness taxed by worry rather than his trek. "I have work to do," he said. "I don't want to chase that devil. When the colonel comes back she can catch him herself."

I was about to collar Barabbas and leave when Fernando arrived. He wanted me to help him find Madlena's horse. He had a gun, a semiautomatic rifle. He strapped on a belt, which held a spare clip for the gun, a canteen, binoculars. He was swift, almost incandescent with purpose, even though he looked a little unhealthy, lips fissured and his eyes a bleached, lemony yellow above dark purple circles.

I told him to wait a moment. If he hoped to get away with killing Madlena's horse . . .

"That animal is a fucking menace. She loves it, but it will kill her." He sneered at me. "I might have guessed you'd be no help. Too many nice scruples." He stood tapping the gun muzzle on his boot and lectured me. "I am not going to let Madlena have her dangerous indulgence. That animal is vicious, and I will save her from it."

I'd heard Ambre say similar things about him and Madlena. "What I was going to suggest," I told him, "was that if you *are* going to kill her horse—or take a hand in her destiny, as you'd put it— then try not to get caught. Let's take a pickax and shovel and dispose of the corpse."

"Oh. Excuse me. You are very practical," Fernando said, and we went to find the tools.

The foreman discovered us in the barn, testing the edge of a spade. Fernando reminded him that what he didn't know he wouldn't feel obliged to confess.

"Commander Sola . . . ," the old man said, and was stopped by a look, plainly implacable. Fernando went out to his jeep. I paused to ask the foreman if he'd tracked the horse in any particular direction. It had gone upstream a little way, then turned out onto the salt flats—the crazy animal.

"Has a vet looked at it recently?" I asked.

"Not for months. I tried to get Colonel Guevara to have the devil cut, to improve his temper. She wouldn't hear of it. The vet last looked at him just before she put him to two of the mares."

I thanked the foreman and followed Fernando. Later, in the flat dirty white of the plains, crisscrossed by tire tracks, we intercepted an army truck. A company of recruits from Mestizo on their way back to a boot camp near La Host. As we came up on them, Fernando placed his gun and the tools down behind the seats. We stopped and he stood up, his hands on the top of the windshield, to speak to the captain. Had they seen a black horse?

The canopy on the truck was rolled up, and the soldiers all crowded to one side to peer out and give Fernando their starstruck attention. So, said the captain, that nervous brute was one of Colonel Guevara's? It had run from them, circled ahead of the truck with its tail up. Last seen, it was headed back toward La Mula and the foothills. The captain pointed.

Behind us, white cumulus cloud had piled up in an anvil-head plateau over the mountains. Fernando thanked the captain. No one saluted, but a few of the young recruits, moved by the proximity of a revolutionary hero, gave a shy, half-mast raised fist. Fernando grinned at this, which seemed to make them very happy.

Fernando set off at a tangent to the truck, back toward the foothills. "It's heading home. We'll intercept it," he said. "But out of sight of these men."

I asked him if he was still in the army. Had he resigned? Was he "Mr. Sola" and only "Commander" out of sentiment?

"No. What makes you think that? I'm a commander of Nuevo, seconded to Indian Affairs. I was glad at the time to give it up—especially the complication of my responsibility for Tomás. The long-suffering man who took my place had to put up with hand-delivered twenty-page love letters from Madlena—to Tomás—and hysterical phone calls, and threats of bodily harm. If only Tomás had been able to *answer* the letters Madlena wouldn't have been quite so anxious. But Tomás was semiliterate. He went back to school after leaving the army. There was a government-funded literacy drive. Tomás is one of fourteen kids. His mother is so narrow and pigheaded it's practically heroic. Tomás's sisters only ever had shoes for their first communion, but they weren't allowed to wear them afterward— Señora Juiliano still has the whole eight pairs lined up on a trophy shelf and she dusts them proudly every day." He glanced at me. "She hates Madlena. Calls her a Godless communist."

"You're not a communist?"

Fernando thought for a while. "No. I put my people first, 'the people' second. Of course, the interests of my tribe and Lequama aren't mutually exclusive." He thought some more, then said, "But the prosperity of my people isn't all I want, it's not my *aim*."

There was a quote I'd had repeated to me several times—Fernando on Democracy Wall in April 1984, shortly before he defected to join Ricardo Pastrez and the Contras. I said to him, "You described Ricardo Pastrez as 'a black torch' burning before you in 'a wilderness of light.' "

Fernando was silent. He'd slowed as the jeep dipped into a dry arroyo that wound down toward La Mula. Above the growl of the gears he asked me was I trying to make some kind of move? Insinuate myself? I'd get more than I bargained for if I tried to get next to him.

"I'm not bargaining," I said. "I might be trying to help Madlena."

"Help Madlena how?"

I didn't reply.

"You think I'm a puzzle she needs help with?"

"I don't know, Fernando. But what do you make of her latest Wall poem? The dog who sings an 'impossible starved song'?"

"Are you asking me whether I'm aware that Madlena is infatuated with me? Yes, I am. She has struggled with it for years. I honor that. And it's best not mentioned. She is my friend's wife. And she's painfully aware of the futility of her crush. Given my preferences."

The jeep had slowed to a crawl. Fernando said, "What does that mean?"—probably responding to an unconscious, eager "uh-huh" from me. I hadn't heard myself.

Fernando pulled up abruptly, but left the engine on. I looked through the inverted arched opacities the wipers had made in an otherwise totally obscured windshield—saw the way ahead, a smooth sandstone channel. Framing the coated windshield were the arroyo walls, in a strange, sober light, the sun high in the sky, but now halved by a mountain crest of cloud. The glare was gone and colors concentrated.

I said to Fernando, "Is this 'homosexuality' of yours wholly based on your relationship with Don Marcos?"

"You sound like a British barrister."

I waited for him to answer my question.

"Of course it isn't. What next? Are you going to ask me if a big, masculine guy like me *really* takes it up the ass?"

"You'd always be the fucker not the fuckee, I'm guessing."

He laughed. "I've had ambitions to be the fuckee. Didn't work out."

"The impenetrable Fernando."

He explained patiently. "I had a relationship with my teacher, the former chief of the Taoscal, Aureliano Zabe. And I had something with most of my 'flunkies.' Part of how I kept them close. *Including* Tomás. Why am I bothering to tell you this?"

"You're telling me because no one ever follows you through the maze. Even Madlena says, 'Fernando! Please come back.' "

He stopped tinkering with the keys and turned to face me. Some color had left his face so that I could see clearly the raw place at the corner of his mouth, a fissure like forked lightning. "It *is* you," he said.

I waited for the look to die away, that shocked, fateful look. It was making me angry. I said that what I wanted to know was how many of his flunkies had *partners* now? Were in relationships?

He frowned, made calculations. "Eight."

"With women." I said it as a statement. I knew I was right, particularly seeing the way his jaw went loose.

"Listen," I said. "I'm guessing that like you, your teacher was true to Taoscal customs and only permitted to have same-sex relationships. I don't count him. So—apart from *Don Ricardo's son* you've had sex with heterosexual men. What have you got against homosexuals?"

I watched him think, then decide not to. He pushed me out of the car—lunged across me to open the door and tip me out onto the ground. Then he slammed the jeep into reverse and drove skillfully away from me back the way we'd come. Around a bend in the arroyo I heard him find a wider place, a turnaround, and then I heard the kicking clatter of small stones on the jeep's mudguards as he sped away.

I got up. The heels of my hands were bloodied and fizzing with pain. I could see shadowy patches where grit had been driven in under my skin. The landscape was listening, but not to me. As I stood looking at my hands an extraordinary impediment of cloud shut out the sun, and the temperature dropped from hot to heavily warm.

I went on toward the river. La Mula wasn't muddy here, but all clear trouble. There were bushes on the far bank, thick with yellow blossom that, with the sun gone, gave out light so like gorse that I anticipated gorse's sharp cultured-butter scent. I took a deep breath, smelled the aromatic in mountain wine, and realized that this was yagga, which I'd thought grew in the jungle.

I lowered myself onto my stomach on the bank and put my hands in the river. With my thumbnail I began to push the grit out of pockets in my skin. I wasn't thinking about Fernando—our conversation. If I'd known myself better I might have known what that meant— my sudden emotional bluntness. I lay on the riverbank with my arms dangling in the water, looking at and through its surface. I waited, as a crocodile waits for the vibrations that indicate the arrival of some animal big enough to eat.

I heard the engine approach, stop. Heard Fernando, droll: "I don't dare face the wrath of Ambre." I got up, my arms cold and dripping. He was leaning, both arms on the wheel. He'd opened the door on my side. "Get in, will you," he said. Said it again, exasperated, and put out a hand. I went to him, calmly took his hand, fixed my grip on his wrist and applied pressure, a sharp pecking blow with my fingertips. I broke a bone in his hand.

He yelled in shock, snatched his hand back.

"Don't you ever . . . ," I began. But neither of us understood who we were dealing with—who we had taken on. I was doubly benighted, in the dark about myself as well as him.

I think that this is what followed.

He was out of the jeep with his gun before I saw him move—so quick. I went down under his weight, his alarming, concentrated more-than-strength, more-than-training—it was *everything*, his life force throwing me over like the concussion of an explosion. My instincts took over. I went limp as the gunsight scored my temple, and the muzzle moved to grind in against my neck under my ear. I waited for him to respond to my collapse, my acquiescence. But then I heard him cursing me in Taoscal, and realized that if he didn't care whether I understood what he had to say, then *he was going to do it*. I revised my plan. I moved myself, made a great effort, flexed my spine. There was a burst of noise beside my head and a hot blow made of several separate impacts—chips of stone. I reared up, the collar of my shirt already wet and warm, and bit Fernando's arm at the crook of his elbow. A sharp tug at the gun stock and his hand slipped. The muzzle moved up, till it was pointing out under his arm. There was another burst of gunfire, ricocheting on rock, and a deep, inhuman squeal from something nearby. I pushed once, hard, with both arms and head, and Fernando toppled, his legs doubled back under him. I threw myself across him, shoved the gun up under his jaw, and put my finger into the trigger guard, over his finger. I saw his mouth and eyes opened wide.

I'd throw everything in where the water was deepest; I wanted all this gone.

I pressed his finger against the trigger.

Nothing happened. The gun had jammed. Shocked, I relaxed my grip. Fernando pulled the gun from between us and extended his arm out from his side so that the gun lay in his slack hand. Though he moved very deliberately his heart was going hard. Very softly, reverent and sad at once, he said, "It's my luck. The luck of the chief."

I was looking into his eyes, at his curious and compassionate expression. I felt his injured hand touch me, his arm a firm bar across the small of my back. He held me.

Because the gun had jammed it was only my will to kill that I threw in where the water was deepest. But that was enough. The deep water was displaced, and a drowned horror dislodged. *I saw the bloodied ruin of a shot-away face. I saw a hand open in death, upturned and relenting. I saw his body shaking. I saw his boot prints fade.*

I tried to stop. I wanted to speak, or for Fernando to tell me a story, to make a breakwater of words. I wanted to go back to sleep, to keep to my bed on the cold winter morning, to lie down again, drawing up the covers. *We should have. But he got up, tore the end off the new loaf, and walked down to the springhouse to help his mother turn the cheeses. I wrote a letter:"I'm returning the title deed to that land you got me. My plans have changed. . . ."*

I believe I got up off Fernando, stumbling like a drunk, stooped, lozenges of blood dropping on the ground before me. I scooped the gun up and stepped back, out of arm's reach—yanked the clip out, racked it to clear the chamber, pushed the clip back into place, and let off a round to test it. Fernando jumped at the gunfire. And I turned the gun's muzzle up under my chin and tried to stop whatever came next, stop myself finding a face in the electric haze of a remembered embrace, in its moist and dry warmth, its sweat fresh and up-to-the-minute, its familiar terrain thoroughly mapped by my touch.

Fernando stood. I took another step back, I could hear him talking, casting out the first filaments of that gauzy breakwater. I lowered the gun and let it dangle. I listened to him.

"You tried to kill me. So? I tried to kill you," Fernando said. "We're both lucky to be alive."

This was engaging. I said, "The difference between us is that I *mind* that I'm a murderous shit."

"Right." He laughed. "Whereas I'm reconciled." He was pale. He'd tucked his injured hand under his other arm. "I do, I never forgave you for frightening me. That's *my* problem. Or—maybe it wasn't the fear I minded, maybe it was because I was so *moved*. That's what I couldn't say. I couldn't utter a word because I wouldn't say it. Ricardo Pastrez's magical ally came after me, in the New Year of '84, two landings from the blood-covered bottom of a stairwell in the East Wing of the Presidential Palace. It had already killed someone there—horribly. Its face was Ricardo's but up close, depthless somehow, like an object in focus through a telephoto lens. Wherever it came from must have been unendurable for humans— less hospitable than hell. *You* were just the smart-mouthed know-it-all who wrote on the Wall. Who kept telling everyone off—even Ambre. Do you know what you called her? 'A woman always dry at her center for having sought too soon an end to passion.' How fucking grandiose—and just because she was being practical while you wanted to be poetic. She's had that quoted at her on and off for

155

years. No wonder she's been so busy lately racking up conquests, proving her passion."

Fernando's repertoire of remembered abuses was at the front of his memory—and egalitarian, his memory as clear on insults to others as to himself.

"You were offensive to me. But you saved me," Fernando said. "Ricardo's ally was dragging me off, and you intervened. You came down the hallway between all the helpless exorcist priests as if you were walking up a church aisle during a wedding, and they were the flowers and the ribbons tied to the end of each pew. First you were wearing Tomás's stolen uniform—were the 'unidentified soldier' of Jesús Mendoza's photo—serene and exultant, about to do battle; then you were in a different light, weak winter sunshine, and in different clothes. You put your hand down to me. You looked cheerful, and smug, and so avid that I imagined you might want to put *the whole world* into your mouth. Yes—since then I've felt you saved me by putting me in your mouth."

Now that he had my attention Fernando approached me, smooth and deliberate, and removed the gun from my hand. He placed a palm against my shoulder and I heard it squelch on my blood-soaked shirt. He dipped his head to regard my throat. "You'll live," he said. "The world is full of surprises." Then he turned me around.

Five meters away stood Madlena's horse. Its front legs were splayed, back legs quaking. Its forehead was nearly touching the ground, its nose between its front hooves. There was a large chunk of flesh missing from its neck at its shoulder, and it was wearing a wreath of its own blood, a thick, flowing scarf of red against its black hide. Its distressed, grunting breaths had been masked by the river.

"It caught a stray shot. When I haven't had my eye on you, I've watched it, bleeding out, but still on its feet." He stepped up to the horse, placed the gun against its glossy cheek and let off one shot—jumped back as it fell over, folding onto its forehead and knees. Then it collapsed onto its side, kicking. After a moment it only shivered.

"See how lucky we are?" Fernando said. "Death did respond to our invitation."

I went to the animal, knelt, and touched it. Its skin was swarming with shivers, as though it already felt the cloud of flies that would come and settle once it was still. I felt a net of fire, fizzing out, no pain, but ruin, and—right under my hand—some old problem. Suddenly I knew that the horse had a growth on one of its kidneys, right where the saddle pressed. I could still *feel* the animal's vitality, a moment back in baffling, impassable time. It was the same sensation I'd had touching the sick dog on the day I met Francis Taylor. It was as if I'd fitted the wrong key to a lock.

To begin with, Fernando did most of the digging, breaking up the earth with the pickax. I sat doing nothing till I noticed that his wrist had begun to swell above the nylon webbing belt with which he had braced his hand. I took up the shovel and shouldered him aside. He took off his shirt, squatted, and hung his head. Sweat cut new channels through the dust on his naked back.

Between us we succeeded in chopping out a wide, shallow pit with sloping sides. We stood back to measure it. Fernando shook his head. He went to the jeep's toolbox and produced a machete. "Take off all your clothes," he advised. "Blood will wash off your skin." He stood over me while I unlaced my boots and removed them, unbuttoned and shucked my shirt, stepped out of my pants. He handed me the machete, handle up. I felt unhappy about the blade and my bare feet, but set to work, curled one foot over the horse's sinewy foreleg and began to hack at its shoulder joint. It was hard, jarring work, dangerous too—when my aim was off and I cut through the film of gristle coating the bone of its ball joint, and the blade bounced back at me.

In fifteen minutes I had all four legs off. I was blood-splattered and plastered in gobs of meat from feet to crotch. I stopped, stepped back, let the machete dangle, its handle tacky in my palm. I considered the hole and the torso. I'd moved the legs during the performance of my task, just to get them out of the way. They lay, bloody lumber on blood-soaked sand, in imitation of panicked flight.

"Yes, it'll do," Fernando said. He hooked the pickax behind the horse's spine and began to pull. I pushed. The torso slid across the sand, making a big clear swipe in the blood patch, and the crust of blood-soaked sand broke up into plate-sized pieces. The torso slithered into the pit. We tucked its legs in around it, then began together, me on my knees and bulldozing with my arms, and Fernando with the shovel and his boots, to cover the body with sand. Then I rested while Fernando flicked the red paving stones of sand into the river. They dissolved, the sand sinking and blood briefly pinking the water. Fernando sprinkled a few shovels full of clean sand over the place. It looked churned up, but innocent of gore.

Fernando gave me some water, offered a cigarette, lit up himself. "I'll be another half hour," he said. "It won't take long." He took his sunglasses out of his top pocket, put them on, squinted at me through the side missing a lens—it had broken during our struggle. "You'll get a sunburn," he said. "Don't put your clothes back on, but do find some shade."

I said I thought I'd go in the river, wash up, then get dressed.

"Not here." He shook his head.

"Is it dangerous here?"

"Yes—dangerous." Saying this he unbuttoned another pocket and produced a length of cord. He made a slipknot in one end, then walked away swinging it. He passed out of sight back along the arroyo.

I moved into a patch of shade beside a rock, leaned on the rock and shut my eyes. The blood had stiffened my skin, and when I moved I could feel it pull every place it lay, then loosen and craze.

I don't think I slept, but I saw two dreamlike things. I saw a wet road, sun scintillating in dewdrops on the grass, men on horseback, one with a rifle, its stock to his shoulder, muzzle pointed out above my head.

And I saw, out on a harbor, on water that at night was a black hole between hills, a ship, afire, spinning slowly in the convection current of flames. A group of people, all in their nightclothes, were crowded at the windows. The candles they held reflected in the panes and obscured the view. When they did move aside they moved in clean halves, like theater curtains. The burning ship turned on the water. It was its own disturbed compass.

I opened my eyes to see that Fernando was back and had tethered a large and angry snake to the ground above the horse. He explained that this was what the Taoscal did—didn't pile up stones above a corpse, but loose earth and then a staked bronze rattlesnake to discourage other animals from digging. "It's part of the obsequies of a funeral—a fresh snake every few days, and after a month the honor of, say, ten snakes."

"If Madlena comes along and sees it, won't she know what it means?"

"Madlena is resolutely ignorant about Taoscal traditions." He adjusted the noose under the snake's jaw, then released its head and stepped quickly back. We watched it thrash, lunge to the limit of the tether, then retract into a sulky coil.

Fernando picked up my clothes and summoned me. "We'll go on a bit upriver to wash. There's a deeper pool."

I followed him. The cloud was closer to the ground now; its far edge had perhaps begun to make an ascent of the foothills and the rest of the mass followed, tilted, like a mattress being carried upstairs. It was hotter yet, and my sweat reliquified the blood, so that it was running when we reached Fernando's pool.

He dropped my clothes, turned his back and began to remove his own. I realized that I'd been lied to. The river at the other place wasn't dangerous; he hadn't wanted me to wash until he could watch.

I walked into the water, reached the edge of a shelf, and dropped, hung suspended, my feet a couple of meters above the obscure green river bottom. I watched blood stream blackly from my body.

Fernando swam toward me one-handed, with his injured hand curled against his chest. As he came near to me soft fists of pushed water hit my body. I backed away against the far, sheer bank, caught a handhold, and stopped—not looking at him. He touched my stomach. "You'd be easy," he said.

My head was down so that my chin was underwater. I shrugged. I couldn't understand why his proximity made me feel ill. I asked, "But then what?"

"Then you'd be *hard*." He moved closer; his good hand rested on my ribs and a knee touched mine. "Come on, look at me," he prompted.

I did——his handsome, adamant face.

"But what with your lacerated palms and my hurt hand . . ."

"I'm off the hook."

"I was about to suggest that we confine ourselves to . . ." He put his hand to my mouth, his own lips darker, but unmoved. He was in control, negotiating, setting out our options——all a kind of cold bait to which I felt myself rise. There was a moment when I felt him draw me toward him through the water, his warm muscled chest and stomach pressed on mine——then everything was obliterated by sorrow so acute it was like physical pain.

He said, "Stop struggling, I'm just stopping you from drowning."

I'd thrust myself back against the stone, grazing my shoulders. I was howling, not at him, but at something happening inside me.

Fernando was worried, but he laughed and said to himself, "What a deterrent."

I was trying to stop. I attempted an explanation. What I said was, "You're not him." Then I was spinning, turning around, looking for comfort, for the warm palms of huge hands that must hold me still, that I must still be able to find at some point of the compass.

I gave Fernando the slip. Wanting to escape the whole topside world, daytime, consciousness, I raised my arms over my head, and went down under the surface of the river. Below me on the sandstone I saw sunlight, a web of gentle electricity. A safety net; there was no descending farther. I liked the pressure, being held, but not by flesh and bones, more pressure here, less there, variable temperatures, movement, the proximity of another personality.

The next thing that happened was that Fernando pulled me out onto the riverbank and pumped the water out of me. I coughed and retched and felt with satisfaction the wet incipience of a future lung infection.

Then Madlena arrived, on one of her polo ponies, a bay with wrapped hocks. Her arm was in a sling. She'd ridden upriver in search of her horse. When she appeared Fernando was pulling his pants up over his hips——with difficulty, since he was still wet. I sat, slumped, with his shirt draped over me.

Madlena reined in, stared at Fernando, blushed, looked away, swallowed, looked back, from him to me, gradually developed a pinched sulky expression. She asked what we were doing.

Fernando said, "Generally, recently, or right this minute?"

"All of that."

"Looking for your horse—without any success. I was trying to seduce Ido and he was trying to drown himself. And right now, I'm closing my fly." He did, his back arched.

Madlena's horse gave a shiver and began to fidget. Fernando whipped his shirt off me, put it on, then dropped my bundled clothes between my feet. He said, to himself, "I really must do something about my penchant for hysterics."

"You're horrible," Madlena said.

I got up and began to dress. Madlena asked if I was okay—rather stiffly—and she didn't dismount.

My clothes smelled of sweat and gunpowder. I was a bit mystified by the blood on the neck of my T-shirt, till I remembered the stone chips that had cut my face. I put my boots on without doing up the laces, and began to walk, past Madlena and downstream.

"My jeep is this way," Fernando called out.

"Well—I'm going to keep looking for my horse," said Madlena. "I haven't got time for you guys and your sleazy scene."

"Go ahead, that's right, use your imagination."

I turned a corner. I could hear their voices for a minute more, Madlena's piping, aggrieved tone and Fernando's low, snide replies.

Hatless and with around twenty kilometers to walk, I was glad of the change in the weather. The sun was in the threatening part of the sky, and behind cloud. After a time I noticed that the salt flats had turned a gorgeous pink and, looking at my hands and arms, I found the same color there, like the blush on bodies in Tiepolo. My ears popped—hurt—as the air pressure dropped. I looked behind me at a pall of rain on the mountains, as dark and thick as a fall of volcanic ash. A long bright crack of lightning appeared, yellow, then burned out, leaving momentarily dots and dashes of green flame along its course. The thunder came five seconds later. I stopped, inclined against a warm rock, and abruptly fell asleep. I dozed, lost bits of myself, my curled hands, the position of the sun and my place in the day.

I woke perhaps only minutes later, turned my cheek against the stone to see a tarantula near my face, close up, bristly black legs with red knees, and eyes like the windows of an airport control tower, two turned my way. I watched it move its palps, thoughtfully it seemed, like a man stroking his beard. We watched each other, the spider and I. Time stopped and started, then a raindrop hit the rock between us and the spider scuttled away.

I pushed off the rock and began to walk again. More big ripe drops fell, making pockmarks in the sand. Then, in under a minute, the sand was ruined, was *mud*, mud under a film of water, and I was fighting through thick filaments of rain. Beside me the clear water of La Mula was now marbled by curled tendrils of pale silt, drifting downstream. Soon more came, like hair, flowing thicker until the water was opaque and the color of caramel milk.

I ran for a long time, till I was quite breathless. Then, rounding one formation of rocks, I ran into a barrier, a long straight stick. Ambre had put it out to stop me. She was wedged in the shelter of two rocks. She was shouting at me, but I couldn't hear her words over the sizzle of the rain. I'd crowded in on her, my soaked clothes against her damp dress and hair. First she said she was looking for Madlena, whom she'd escorted home from the hospital. Madlena was one bruise from throat to armpit, but had still gone out search-ing for that bloody horse. Had *I* seen her? But before I could reply, Ambre shot me a woeful look and said, "Why didn't you *tell* me, Ido?"

My hair was conducting water in several thin streams onto the front of her dress. So that the cotton grew transparent and its same-colored embroidery showed up like a tattoo of scarification. The ties at her neck were pasted to her skin, coiled on her damp breastbone. Ambre wanted me to meet her eyes. She took my head in her hands and raised my face.

"I had to learn about the poison from your doctor. But I suppose you told *her*, La Visisation. I didn't know you were so unhappy."

Then, "Oh," she cried, a mix of shame and sorrow and surprise. I put my hands on her ribcage, then ran them up under her ribs and each weighty breast. I pushed her breasts up, the neck of the dress opened, ties uncoiled and slithering across her throat. I bent my head again, for a moment had a hold, of a sort: a nipple, covered with cold cotton, hooked against the inside of my lower lip. Ambre pulled my head up. "That useless woman," she said. "That Miz—that skinny, plucked, painted Miz Visistation."

"You gave me to her, Ambre." I said. "Like you wanted her to use me, run me, find the faults in my program. Like I was some kind of software you had in development."

Ambre complained that she didn't understand me when I spoke like that, and she was sick of just smiling and trying to pretend to be clever. Anyway—she said—what use to me was my intelligence? *She* had never tried to take her own life.

Because we were face-to-face and the same height, I started kissing her. Her lips were cold, but her breath hot. Ambre's usual core temperature is hotter than other people's, like a low-grade fever. She didn't like my kisses. She was resisting me. She asked, "Why are you doing this?"—very unhappy—then put her face against my neck and began to take deep breaths, sobs I thought till I realized that she was moving her head from spot to spot and, mouth shut, was sucking in the air, smelling me, then letting out each breath in a hard gasp. "Ah!" She held and turned my head. I was being touched, *taken in*, like a child by its mother, a mother who suffered a separation, and fear of loss. It was daunting, unfamiliar. I moved back a little and she said, "Ido," then kissed my jaw.

This was all rather irritating—I didn't want her to take my touch this way. But even so, *my* body wasn't responding properly either. Only the hairs on my arms were lifting, against the rain, drawn by the electricity in the air. I couldn't stop thinking. I was thinking about forgetting my past, or reinforcing forgetfulness, about drowning it all again. And I was thinking about Fernando's body, his— excuse me—appetizing *cockiness*, my obvious homosexuality, about how to *change* it, about the taste of Ambre's spit, a new life, crossing over.

The river water was nearer our feet, and the stream fattened in small pulses, as tiny as waves against the shore of a glassy lake.

Ambre was paying attention to other things now—not to me. Her face was turned to gaze upriver, and it was the direction of her gaze more than the anxious suspicion of her expression that maddened me. I pressed my mouth under her ear, determined, set the tip of my tongue against the long slit in her brown earlobe, a hole stretched by years of wearing heavy earrings.

Then, abruptly, my habitual calculation reasserted itself, and it shook my mind off Fernando, my worries about my own sexuality, *and* the figure of my murdered lover standing like a migrainous black aura at one corner of my field of vision. I suddenly selected some words from earlier thoughts. "Drowning," I thought, "cross over." Because it was in my nature, because even in the midst of turmoil I was able to notice the things I *had* to notice. I looked at the river and saw a long streamer of black silt in its center, then that the water's surface had assumed an unwatery texture. There was debris in the river so coated in mud that leaves and small branches were only distinguishable by their shapes. This mass in the middle of the stream made it possible to judge how fast it was moving. Our feet were underwater, and we were on the *wrong side* of the river. The island of rocks where we stood was on a slope up from the old water level, above the flatland that lay at our backs, a mile-wide sweep of smooth river-worn pebbles and occasional boulders behind which countless dry winds had piled up salty sand. These boulders were thicker toward the middle of the field of pebbles, a considerable distance away. We were between this floodplain and a flooding river.

I grabbed Ambre by her wrist and dragged her into the shallows. She fought me. Buoyant vegetable matter, lubricated by mud, parted around our bodies. I hauled at her. I tried to explain. Then her slippery wrist slid out of my grasp and I fell forward into the current and swam.

It was like swimming in tepid stew. A smooth branch struck me, I blocked it with my arm and found Ambre's wrist in my hand again, her body downstream in the shelter of mine. For long minutes I struggled to make forward progress, to retain Ambre's arm, and to fend off debris. Then I was near the far bank, one arm around Ambre's back, fighting a current that doubled in strength every minute, it seemed.

On the far side of the river was a scoured cliff face, with several levels—horizontal, slightly tilted—where centuries of floods had scooped out the softer rock, leaving layers of harder mineral to make paths up the cliff face. I grabbed hold of a shelf and hauled Ambre around me, watched her fumble for a handhold and struggle out of the river. I was picked up by the next vomiting increment of flood, rolled along the cliff face beyond Ambre then onto the path, safe. Ambre crawled past me. The rain had already cleared the mud from the black crown of her head, but it was everywhere else on her body, as slick as jelly. I got up and gave her a hard shove. Too tired to say it: "We have to move."

Behind us came sound so solid it was like the thing that made it. We looked back to see a wall of muddy water in the river's channel, like loose earth pushed before the blade of a big earth-moving machine.

Full of great trees, foaming yellow, the crest of the flash flood rolled toward us.

In the seconds before it arrived I braced my feet and forearms against the rock below and above me. I pressed Ambre against the far wall, took a deep breath and put my lips to hers.

Just in time. The floodwater reached the cliff face, which forced it to turn as the river turned. Then water was slammed into the slit in the rock where we knelt. It simply prized us loose. I wrapped my arms around Ambre and we were rolled along the rock channel. It was dark. I kept my lips against hers and pushed air from my lungs into her mouth.

Then we were still. I let go of Ambre, knocked the mud from one ear and scooped it out of my eye sockets. The wave of the flood had passed and we had been deposited on the streaming summit of the escarpment. Together we crept away from the drop, water draining away around our hands and knees.

Ambre was muttering and moving sluggishly. I pulled at her, but after a minute she stopped and shuffled about to face the river.

Below us Fernando's jeep slid past in the flood, followed by something—I glimpsed black hair and bloody ruin and was appalled. Ambre shrieked, and began to sob. But it *wasn't* her daughter's wrecked head we had seen—or Fernando's—it was the gory stump of a hacked-off leg, part of the horse's corpse, disinterred by floodwater.

I tried to tell her. I shouted into her face, "They're not dead! No one is dead!" But her hands tore at my shirt, she flailed and screamed and dragged us back toward the edge.

For a moment we struggled above the bulky brown water. Then between the thunder and above the rain I heard gunfire. I made Ambre look where, dimly, through the sheets and sparks of rain, out on the salt flat, a horse plunged and turned and its riders, Madlena and Fernando, kept their seats despite the thunder and his gunfire signal.

Ambre sank against me, gasping. In my shock and the resolution of my shock, I nearly fell asleep again. And I saw that *one of the mounted men had a gun. I saw my lover walking up from the springhouse where he'd been turning his mother's cheeses. I saw that he would try to stop these strangers who seemed to want to take me, and I knew that he wouldn't expect the gun. When had either of us last seen a gun?*

There was a weapon pointing at me.

I tried to hide, I pressed my forehead against the rock at the top of the cliff, its lip a streaming waterfall. The world left me. I flattened my*self*—my recent self—a high-density accumulation of memories and impressions, everything I'd carefully put together since early February, when I'd first stood in the cathedral doorway. I gathered it all to me—Flores Negras, the hacienda, jokes and poems on Democracy Wall, an image of the jungle trail to Taosclan, the flash of a camera, and voices on the phone.

The lightning rubbed my eyelids with the balls of its thumbs. I couldn't hear or feel or see anymore. I retreated from knowledge by wrapping myself in what I wanted to know. But it was still there, the *other* knowledge, right beside me. It meant to crush me. It forced me inward until, finally, my recent time was propelled, *plunged* into a payload, my past, and my whole history reached critical mass.

Fusion.

And I came out again to face the world. *All* of me came out.

Transference

(A therapist's rooms, Northern California, a Sunday in 2022)

During the weeks it had taken us to discuss Carme Risk's father's memoir, each time we met I added another book to the pile on the table between us. I'd been doing my homework. I had *No Line in the Reef: Life and Customs of the Mneone* by Dr. Jon Scott. I had a monograph on the wrecked Taoscal temple, Turoc Iddu, by an archaeologist at an institute of the antiquities in Cologne. I had *Make No Noise, Francis Taylor, Photographs, 1984 to 1994*. I had a general history of Lequama; Jules Frei's *Collected Poems*; and the poet's great-niece Bella Frei's *The Culture of Torture*, Berkeley, 2003. I'd even placed an order for Carme's friend Bella's latest book, which had an intriguing title: *The Black Room*.

At our third long Sunday session, Carme arrived wearing a clinging sleeveless shirt and mother-of-pearl bracelets clasped around the compact muscles of her wiry upper arms, and I asked, to cover my long, inappropriate appraisal, "Do you work out?"

"Yes, ultimately," she said, bringing me back to her story.

We had talked about the journal as I read through it. We discussed amnesia as abdication. We discussed it as the ultimate form of rehabilitation, a chance to start afresh. For example: Carme's father, though skeptical about the enforced homosexuality of the chief of the Taoscal, seemed to *choose* to become heterosexual himself. But when, on that Sunday, I suggested to Carme that she seemed again to be demonizing homosexuality in the form of Fernando Sola, she reminded me that her father was the author of his own memoir. Any demons in "Pérdida Total" were his.

How did she want me to distinguish between his facts and hers? I asked.

She opened her bag and presented me with the original manuscript, deckle-edged, with marbled endpapers and a ribbon. She sat quietly while I compared the thirty-four-year-old manuscript with her transcription, and found that her only corrections were to her father's spelling of Taoscal words and the odd proper name.

I asked her where she was when her father wrote this. She said that she was in Dev Hughes's parents' dairy in the highlands of Eden.

For some time I just sat and stared at her.

"He came and got me." Carme said. "He played dice and cards in the bars around the Plaza. He cheated. He paid for his airfare to London, a train ticket to Dumfries, and a taxi out to the Cadaver place on the River Nith."

I suggested we put all that aside for the moment and just deal with the journal. We talked about Fernando's thought, as "read" by the mind-reading Lee McIndoe, that Ido was the same kind of creature as Lee.

"An Airan," said Carme. "We always called them 'Airans' after Tomás's mistake."

"A foundling can turn out to be anyone," I said. "In *Wuthering Heights* Nelly Dean says to Heathcliff: 'Who knows but your father was Emperor of China, and your mother an Indian queen.' She's telling him how he can put a positive spin on his bastardy. It *can* be seen as a freedom. It can also be seen as a carte blanche, an open invitation to fantasy and self-aggrandizement. Your father, finding himself with no kin, apparently decided to do without a *species* as well—though how the hospitals of his vagrant childhood missed the phosphorus I can't imagine."

Carme said that she realized that it was my job to look for inconsistencies, but wasn't it possible that the phosphorus appeared later, like a hormonal surge in adolescence?

"What for?"

"You'll see," she said, annoyingly.

I told Carme that I'd like to encounter her before much longer in her own story as more than a "ghostly handclasp" or a twinkle in her father's eye. "And I do hope I won't meet any more corrupt therapists."

Carme asked me whether I'd encountered any, when I was being treated for my own amnesia.

I blushed, but she had looked away. She said, "I think my father was an open invitation to corruption."

I decided to pursue this. Perhaps she was ready to talk about it. I quoted Ido on Aramantha: "She was looking to meet something she was equipped to treat. She could see herself taking me by the hand, a good mother, and helping me to confront the monsters of my dark closet. My black room." I said, "Ido's 'good mother' becomes a sadistic lover. He's not having any of these mothers, is he? He won't accept Ambre's protective affection as affection. So far I see this man only in a familial relationship with Carlin Cadaver, and a ghostly handclasp—with *death*."

"Perhaps we should just read on," she said. She pushed her second manuscript across the table, tapped its plastic-protected coversheet. I read: "Anesthesia Dolorosa (pain felt in a place that is normally anesthetic)."

I asked her was I helping her to help herself? And, in the silence of her thinking, I heard a car drive into the almost empty lot below my rooms. The car was Carme's ride. Bella Frei—on time, at the end of our time.

Carme got up and went out onto the terrace to sign "five" to her friend. The terrace was tiled with slate, great blocks with worn edges, taken from a demolished church. The garages below it were built like a fortress to float the slate. It was a lovely space, but I scarcely used it. I watched Carme, her pale profile against the churning purple of a jacaranda that grew hard up against the garage wall. I went out and broke a piece off the flowering shrub that grew in a pot by the door, a plant that blossomed purple, pink, and white, all on the same bush. I gave it to my client, waved at her friend, who only stared up at me through her tinted windshield, baleful, her breathing suspended. I put a hand on Carme's forearm and told her that she needed to have a character in her story—her own character—a character she could cooperate with or struggle against.

"I do," she said. "Read on."

"So far you're only the daughter of a dangerous freak." I hoped to get a rise.

"Or a beautiful, perfected freak." She tucked the broken stem into her top at her cleavage.

"Perfected is an interesting word, Carme. It suggests an outside agency—someone or something at work on him." I could see the stem and each leaf in relief between the thin cloth and her flesh. It would be making an impression there, red marks in the shape of stem, leaf, crushed blossom.

"You mean a conspiracy?" said Carme Risk.

PART THREE

Anesthesia Dolorosa

(pain felt in a place that is normally anesthetic)

*Carme Risk's journal and memoir, begun in
a transit lounge at Miami airport,
late July 2003*

"I wish I were a foreigner, so that I could go home."
—Ernesto Cardenal, *Nicaraguan Canto*

Memoir: Eden, late 1987

My father returned to us in the autumn ten months after he'd disappeared. On that day our whole household was out in the home paddock, looking for mustard weed. One of the horses had got sick, and mustard weed was the deemed cause. I had a seed bag slung over my shoulder as a receptacle for the weeds. I had a knife, its six-inch blade coated with dirt. There were eight of us in the paddock. Cassandra and her children scanned the ground on one side of me. On the other was my half-sister Astrella, who had arrived the day before to collect me, to take me back to the capital where she hoped to enroll me in the day school where her ward had already spent two terms. "*She* loves it," Astrella said to me, as she stooped and pulled weeds. "The other girls are a real mix of town and country, gentry and nobility. *You* know how undereducated all the women are here, Carme. You could be in on the beginning of a great tradition." She kept her head down, hands busy, and didn't meet my eyes. "I know I'm intruding on your grief. But it's my responsibility to think about your future." Beyond Astrella and a little apart from us were Dev's mother and father. They were working steadily, but Dev's father seemed a little stiff, and Dev's mother, always a spry woman, moved across the field in a slow, tentative way.

Carlin was out in front, setting an example I think, examining every foot of ground with a kind of comic intensity. I saw him straighten to unkink his back. He put a hand up to shade his eyes. Then he grew still.

My father was leading his horse through the orchard, through blocks of sunlight and clouds of midges. As he walked he put one boot on a wrinkly-skinned windfall apple and made mush of it. We could see that he was wearing thick blue cotton pants—jeans, I know now—and a short-sleeved shirt, white cotton washed thin, on which was pictured the matched ratchets of a cog and wheel and the legend "Highwall Engine Lubricants." He seemed relieved to see us, but his relief was only momentary. I saw him take a deep breath and brace himself.

Carlin had begun to tremble.

Dad dropped the reins and the horse put its head down to graze. Astrella, showing her usual presence of mind, recaptured the halter and led the horse behind our line, to where the paddock was cleared of mustard weed.

My father looked at Dev's parents. Dev's father had begun to weep, his handsome, too-thin face crumpled and congested. Dev's mother gave her husband a blank look, then my father a wild one. "I can't do this," she said. "I can't *take* this." And she threw down her own weeding tool and ran for the cottage, headlong and stumbling.

Dad inhaled, held his breath. "I'm sorry," he said to Dev's father. Then again, "I'm sorry." He waited, facing us all, then asked, "Can we go in? Must I stand here?"

"No, Abra. I don't think you should go in. Not till my wife has had time to recover," Devlin's father said—gently. Tears were dripping off his chin.

I put down my knife and went to Dad. I pushed my face against his ribs—inhaled deeply, his scent a whole sustaining atmosphere of air I'd thought I'd never have in my lungs again. He put an arm around me, loose, and kissed the crown of my head. "Carme," he whispered, and my name unrolled like a screen around me, shielding me from everything.

"You escaped," Carlin said, and his tone accused.

My father released me, stepped around me, and advanced on Carlin, carefully as though not to startle a nervous horse. He began to explain, his tone patient; but behind the patience I could hear exhausted deliberation.

There was a dream he'd had that he'd told Carlin about, apparently, because it was Carlin he spoke to. "Remember?" he said. He'd dreamed he was in a hot Spanish-speaking country at Christmastime. He did something bad there, in his dream—something he wasn't allowed to do. The strangers who came here to "arrest" him seemed to want to stop him doing worse. "Waking up and doing worse," he said. "They *reset* me. You know, Carlin? Like a computer: 'You'll lose any information not saved.'" They made him forget, they pushed reset. Then they put him with magic practitioners as if they wanted to improve the gene stock. That was all he knew. But he believed they shot Dev only because Dev came up behind them suddenly. Dev frightened them, and it was a mistake. "I'd have come back sooner," my father said. "But I had amnesia. And I had to earn my airfare."

Carlin stared at him. The only sound was a thump as Dad's horse stamped its hoof to shake off a few flies, then the swish-snap of its muddy tail.

"I don't want to go into it," my father said. "I'm trying to segregate here and there. Trying not to contaminate—" he looked about him, "this little orchard, this morning, with foreign names."

"Amnesia?" Carlin said, his top lip drawn up under his nose as if to block a bad smell.

My father didn't reply.

Dev's mother kept to her bed. Dad sent Astrella's groom off to the capital with a message for our accountant. Dad asked him for all the documents of our cooperative company—whose chattels were three ships, three coffeehouses, one hotel, twelve percent of the public issue of stock in the only shipbuilders at the great southern port. Before they came he sat at the long kitchen table in the farmhouse and wrote out everything he knew about our investments.

About coffee planters, and excise men at the seven ports we traded in. "No one else has bothered to take this information on board," he said.

When the documents arrived he set to making changes. And while he worked he and Astrella argued about which of them was best qualified to keep me. Astrella was the first to guess he was going—that he wasn't just catching up, doing the books, but settling his affairs. She sat opposite him one morning and watched him break the seal on his will and read it through, set it aside, take a fresh sheet of paper, and dip his pen. He paused, looking at the pen. "Rubber—from the empire," he said. "Pens with ink reservoirs. There's something to patent."

Astrella waved a hand; she'd just patented postage stamps, which was quite enough for one lifetime. She asked when he planned to come back. He was going again, wasn't he? Was he going for good?

I sat down beside him and slipped under his arm. I pressed my ear against his heartbeat. I heard it change a little as Astrella reminded him that I had been with her for two years, on and off. Because he hadn't wanted me endangered. Would I now be safe with him?

I looked at the pages by my father's elbow and saw that he'd left me his books and jewelry, and Astrella his dog—a beagle that had been killed in a mudslide nearly two years before. His will was *that* much out of date. I turned the page—found a list of tips about people we knew.

Dad said to Astrella that he'd thought he could manage his risks. But our ship, the *Thresher*, burned. And our sympathetic princess died of lockjaw. People behaved predictably, but circumstances misbehaved, he said. And someone turned up with a gun.

Astrella flushed deep red at his mention of the *Thresher*, but recovered well. She wasn't about to tell him what we had done.

I turned another page. Last wishes. A long list—all the obvious names. My own name. "Carme, I'm sorry for being impossible, dear," I read.

My father put his hand over the page and looked at me. He shook his head.

Astrella struck the table with her fist. She shouted, "Abra! I want your full attention!"

My father put his pen down and leaned back in his chair.

Astrella said, "I felt I had to *breathe* for this child when she came to me. Practically breathe for her. She'd begged to stay with you, and you sent her away. You'd made her feel sidelined—like Dev. I mean—what did you think when Dev started publishing those poems in which he imagined you martyred?" Then she muttered something about Dad encouraging Dev's necrophiliac tendencies.

"It was mourning that excited Dev, not death," my father said, softly and harmlessly. It was the first hint I had of how much distance he'd managed to put between himself and his murdered lover.

My father said that when he was in prison, and our city was under siege, Astrella had let me get mixed up in the fighting. He was mild, but beginning to build his case against her.

"She poked her little nose in. She was supposed to be in the infirmary with Cassandra."

"She fell off a roof."

"I could swim," I said. I'd fallen into a canal.

"When I saw her, six weeks later, her whole left shoulder was still yellow with bruises." He was reproachful.

Astrella bared her teeth, leaned forward. "We were calling it 'Abra's war.' The first battle of *your* war. And you weren't even there."

Dad said that it wasn't his fight—he'd sailed back from the coffee run and ended up in a prison cell below the level of the river. Then he returned the argument to its more specific subject: who was the best parent. He reminded Astrella that she'd smuggled her ward out of our hotel when it was under quarantine during the diphtheria. But she kept *me* with her.

"I didn't think she'd get it. She's your daughter."

"Yes. She's my daughter." The clincher, he thought.

"But she *did* get sick. So much for your special hardihood. She's my mother's daughter too. Besides—I have a household, family life, financial resources, her schooling planned."

"Needlework and deportment?"

"Music and drawing and history."

He moved his hand—so I read: "Dev—I don't like what I've done to you. I want you to survive me to mind Carme. I'm trying to make sensible plans and provisions, but I'm only thinking of you. Writing this in the study in late winter I know that in a minute I'll get up and go to you where you are reading by the fire in the library. And I'll put my arms around you. Abra."

I asked Dad if he was writing another will.

There was a long moment before he and Astrella disengaged and looked at me. He said, "I'm giving Carlin my power of attorney."

"Shouldn't you ask him first?" Astrella said. "You do need to talk to Carlin."

Dad put the paper aside for a moment and unfolded his copies of the plans for the two new barks, the first of which was already under way in the southern shipyards. He crossed out the names *Maelstrom* and *Flying Cloud* and wrote on one plan *Ambre Guevara* and on the other *Madlena Guevara*. Or, at least, he translated those sounds into Esindu.

"He smiles," Astrella said, telling him off.

"I'm not happy," he answered, as if reassuring her.

Astrella asked, "Do *you* have any plans for Carme?"

He looked at me, then at her. "Carme is going to attend Harvard Medical School," he said.

Journal: Miami International Airport, 2003

I began this journal in a transit lounge at the Miami airport. I'd missed my connecting flight to Bogotá. Beyond Bogotá, and a short stay with my husband at Spa Spice Island, I had another flight to La Host. It was three weeks since my finals—my last big push. I'd been told I wouldn't be expected to work quite so heroically in my post-doctoral studies. I could take a break. I wanted to be in Lequama for the big celebrations—it was twenty years since the revolution. I was going home.

But home has to pass muster. And I plan to ask a few questions about the mysterious deaths and disappearances with which my

Lequaman family were involved, and keep track of what I learn in this innocuous Word document named "Anesthesia Dolorosa." I'd like to write in imitation of my father's "Pérdida Total de la Memoria," but I'm no amnesiac, and my journal must be memoir too. Also, I want it to be a kind of guidebook, for friends and family members my age and younger, for all the young Lequamans with professional ambitions who had no choice but to leave.

When we write a memoir, we say, "he said, she said." We try to make one thing seem to lead to another, we try to reproduce what motivated us, or *must have*, in hindsight. I haven't been able to remember exactly what they said, my father and half-sister, during their intimate custody battle. But I remembered the gist of their arguments, and a few phrases that sank in. What I've said that my father said sounds likely. But it's sixteen years since I saw Astrella, and I'm guessing at her.

When my flight was announced, I boarded. But we were on the ground for hours yet, stalled at a T-junction by runway eight. It was dusk. Plane after plane came down on either side of ours, their headlights like holes poked through into a purer world.

Memoir: Eden, late 1987

Eventually I put an end to their argument. Perhaps I should have prefaced what I said with "Why don't you ask me what *I* want?" Astrella, particularly, required guidance. I told Astrella and Dad that in the autumn after Dev died I tried to poison myself.

Astrella's face crumpled.

No one had known, I said. I'd gone down through the Feln, near the cave where they had put Dev's bones, and I'd eaten a plant I knew to be poisonous. I was too scared to go in the cave. But the poison hadn't worked.

Dad spread a hand over the crown of my head. His breathing had changed, was slow and deep. Astrella's bright blue eyes were filling with tears.

I looked up at my father, and his hand slipped from my hair.

I asked him whether he remembered the note Dev sent me enclosed in a letter to him—the letter in which Dev wrote to say he wanted Dad to come up to his parents' dairy to fetch him.

My father nodded.

"In his note to me Dev wrote, 'Write to me if you'd like to.' After the funeral I tried writing him a letter."

Dad asked was it whiteberries I'd eaten.

They were white, and *dusty*. They were growing in the moss.

"What a time to get botanical." We had offended Astrella somehow.

I told my father that if I'd really been thinking of Dev I *could* have written him a letter. "But I was thinking of you."

"You're coming with me," he said. "I won't leave you."

I snuggled closer, closed my eyes, and dissolved into that aura that was almost entirely his lovely healthy scent. A strange smell, a strange vitality, and a strange retardation of time. Leaning against him I had a good long rest of several minutes' duration. I heard them each say more—caught fragments.

She reminded him that everyone he loved was here. What made him think he'd be any less dangerous to these new people?

"I promised to go back there."

"Carlin will forgive you soon—suddenly and completely—you know he will."

"I'm not sure he should. I thought I'd get myself killed—that's a pretty profound betrayal. I meant to leave you. I meant to leave *me*. Dev was the only one who noticed. It broke his heart."

What about all the stuff he'd set up? The new printing press. The weapons cache. The renegade priests' settlement? "You gambled *our house* against that muddy piece of land."

"Yes, I did. You don't need my cavalier attitude."

"What about Carlin?"

"I have to go."

"You're suddenly full of odd scruples."

"I promised Ambre."

Astrella made a list of menacing facts—and names, the names of enemies and dubious allies. The names of people my father and his supporters had ferried only halfway across a veritable river of upheaval—and were about to leave unpiloted.

"Politics," Dad said. "The anointed and self-appointed." Self-hating. "*This* country is the best bet for a parliamentary democracy. You should give up on those priests. I was wrong."

Names—the one that sounded like "algae" with a glottal stop. I've forgotten them all. An atlas full of names. A biographical dictionary full. Astrella was trying to interest my father in his life—the life that, as immigrants from Earth (he, her mother), they'd committed themselves to, sunk themselves in. Here, Astrella switched from continental Esindu to English to argue with him. Until, in English, my father said, "I have to. I promised."

"Maybe I'm getting the scale wrong, Abra," Astrella said. "Forget all that. You're necessary to a few people. Completely necessary. What's that worth?"

"I promised Ambre. She's pregnant."

Journal: Spa Spice Island, off the coast of Colombia, July 2003

Early in the morning I stood at the big picture window in our Spice Island suite, looking across the golf links. There was a ground mist, and the cedar trunks were obscured. Their dark crowns, afloat in whiteness, were like hills in a classical Chinese painting—the earth unearthed.

My husband once lived in his casino at the other end of the island, but six years ago he developed the spa and after we married he moved there.

There's a sentence you'd expect to contain two "we"s. After *we* married *we* moved. But I have never lived with him. I've been a guest, with a room of my own in which my most precious possessions are stored. For the past three years I've lived in a sorority house at Harvard, the house of a newish, modestly endowed sorority full of other Latinas—and packed with conversation, music, the long round of howling hair dryers on weekday mornings and weekend evenings.

On the island, my room and "our" suite had an atmosphere like the two things I enjoyed most on each visit—sleep and snorkeling over the reef. Night or day the suite was filled with a clear silence, all noise muffled as though by weight of limpid water. The furnishings were fine and spare, the floors marble and softened by a number of my stepmother's large woven alpaca rugs. My husband had bought them from a dealer in Paris, the gallery that showed Ambre's work—her designs finished by other weavers, usually retrained prostitutes from the Prostitutes Collective whose drop-in center was at the rear of Flores Negras. All my husband's furniture was tropical hardwood and leather, either gold or a deep cinnamon shade. The windows were wide, but shaded by deep eaves, so that the sun only peered in when it was low in the sky.

As I stood looking out over the misty golf links, Ricardo came down the stairs from his room. He was wearing one of his silk robes—black, and monogrammed with black. He looked like a sorcerer. He asked me whether I'd ordered breakfast. Then he told me off for being too embarrassed to do it. He picked up the phone and, rather than asking me what I wanted, ordered too much of everything. He said, "You should learn how to be waited on, Carme, as well as to wait. The two useful poles of passivity." He'd obviously been mulling over our previous night's talk, because he went on to say that he'd never been above *convention* himself, only above the law. Then he stated that the ruling classes were scarcely ever adaptable.

I decided that he was using that old label—"ruling classes"—out of respect for my many years in the post-revolutionary Lequaman school system. Respect, or maybe mockery for everything *but* me, for the "ruler" he once was, for the moral certainty his violence had generated in his enemies, for the expedience of labels—a venal expedience in comparison to his violence, which was also expedient. He said that he hadn't understood anything about *real* lordliness until he had seen how the big dogs could be ruled by the little one on its back with its feet in the air and ears in the dust.

"While you're here, Carme, you should practice saying, 'Do this and do that,' as you won't be *able* to in the normal course of your life." He paused, then said, "Since you are *not* going to be a surgeon—an occasional autocrat of scalpel, swabs, and suction."

I stared at him. I wondered whom he'd been talking to. Then I set out to see if I could circumnavigate his interest. "I bet this routine of yours used to terrify the junior officers—beginning each briefing with a lesson in etiquette."

My husband was imperturbable. He told me that he'd called Anton Xavier after talking to me in June. Dr. Xavier *did* need to know I had a chest infection. During my call, Ricardo said, there had been more coughing than conversation.

My doctor and my husband—it made me blush to imagine the cold, formal exchange they'd no doubt had. In the 1970s Anton Xavier had been an intern at La Casa de la Mujer in La Host. One day he had signed a petition against the dismissal of the staff supervisor of the hospital's day-care center. The supervisor had been trying to ratify a charter on the rights, duties, and responsibilities of day-care workers. She'd had consultations with a number of the city's other early childhood education workers. To the Security Forces these activities had the appearance of "the organization of labor." First she was dismissed—and her friends got up a petition. Then she was arrested. A week after he put his name on the petition, Anton received a tip-off—he'd best leave the country. And so he did, settling in Venezuela for the next four years, then the States for another four—only coming home when Nestor Galen's government was overthrown.

The last time I'd spoken to Anton Xavier I'd told him that I had decided not to be a surgeon, though I'd already completed some studies in cryogenic cardiovascular surgery. I wanted to be a general practitioner, part of a community, not just medical communities of hospital or clinic, or of a specialty with no locale or habitation, with my closest colleagues at the far end of the phone or e-mail. And, I told Anton, I thought I might do some specialist study in multi-drug-resistant TB—as a branch of chronic care. Anton was pleased, he said he thought I'd make a fine GP, and there was, sadly, a real future in TB.

Our breakfast arrived and we fell silent till the help left. And I thought of my first family—with whom I'd lived till I was two—my real mother Genevieve and her husband Ulaw and their household. I still had clear memories of the strange silences that would fall upon the entry of servants, when the family were scheming, as they often did, against other people's authority or fortune, good name, or life. A servant would enter and there would be an abrupt cessation of talk, or a deft switch from one language to another followed by frustrated yelps from some of the children, those first-generation settlers less adept in English.

The door closed behind the maid. Ricardo poured our coffee. He said that he hoped I wouldn't regret my decision. Then he changed the subject. *Closed* it. He asked me whether I'd ever seen the video of his daughter Juanita's wedding. He'd been doing a little therapeutic incineration the other day and had found it.

I said I remembered several cameras. One of the groom's brothers had one he'd borrowed from the university. He'd gone around the wedding breakfast collecting shots of accessories, ties and shoes and bags and hats, with sound bites of replies to his question: "How long have you known the happy couple?" (And I said: "I work in the office of the groom's furniture factory. I sometimes baby-sit the bride's daughter. I've known Juanita since I came here.")

Ricardo had the tape already set up in the video player, but it took him a while to find the button on the remote that opened the doors over the monitor. I watched him fumble; felt uneasy watching him.

"I don't know how to watch videos," he said. "Except diagnostically. I stand at the monitors in the casino's control room to watch the playback of some troublesome lucky gambler. And I watch for things that need my input, a dealer who needs smartening up, security that needs tightening. It's all very businesslike. I don't buy tapes or disks or tune into the film channels. As for cinema—I think I'm averaging a film a decade. I saw that adventure film made on location in Lequama in the late 1980s. I went to it out of nostalgia for the landscape. And I do recall a private showing of *The Exorcist* in the Presidential Palace in 1975."

Ricardo poured me another cup of coffee. He pushed the plate of melon across the table toward me. For a moment we made eye contact and I saw the same thing I always did—a benign, watchful look with something underneath it, something *alive*, in a burrow with no aperture, like a clam in wet sand.

He pointed the remote.

A title sequence. An arrangement on a wooden tabletop of different sorts of beans, spelling "A Lequaman Production." Next shot, words made of peas, lentils, and other pulses: "Juanita and Enrico's Wedding, September 1994." Shot three: the veranda of Flores Negras, midafternoon light, the sound of domestic animals, insects, and wind. The camera was in a static position, someone walked into the frame and squatted to speak. My father tucked his hair behind his ears and said, "I've had this tape reserved for some time, Ricardo, as soon as I heard about the wedding, but before you asked me to make one. The Garcías have hired a professional wedding video 'directeur,' so I'm going to have to be unobtrusive. Some people will guess this is for you, so you can expect a few *performances*. I did the titles a couple of weeks back when I was feeling whimsical. Uh——" For a moment my father was at a loss for words; he looked down at his hands.

I took the remote out of Ricardo's hand and pushed pause. "There was a tape of one of his hand-to-hand combat tutorials at the Castel Mirabella," I said. "Someone stole it. Some obsessive."

My husband was amused. "Any obsessive we know?"

I shook my head.

"So—is this the only tape of him?"

"Ambre has all the takes, the *rushes*, of my little sister's segment on *Entertainment This Week*. Dad's in that, turning his shoulder to the camera."

I pushed play. Dad looked up again. "Now I'm feeling a little pushed for time. So if this is a little bit thin or"—in a rush—"you don't get enough Ambre cleavage shots, it's just that I don't feel cocky enough to stick the lens in everywhere." Dad gave a quick, tired, mirthless smile, then got up, moved out of the shot to push the fade button.

Fade in. La Host Cathedral on a sunny morning, shot from the Plaza. Various guests in finery milled on the steps. They were waiting to be shown indoors by the ushers, Madlena's ten-year-old twins, Carlos and Aureliano, who were wearing black pants, white shirts, yellow waistcoats, and black ties. The camera was walked slowly toward the cathedral.

I recognized Ambre's turned back. She was dressed in one of the formal frocks she bought in Los Angeles after her visit to a fertility clinic. I remembered that Ricardo had bought her that dress. I remembered that they had walked along Rodeo Drive arm in arm, Dad a pace behind. The camera operator walked around one side of Ambre, filming. She had her usual self-satisfied, droopy-eyelid indolence. Her skin was dewy, with hormone replacement therapy rather than cosmetics. Her earrings were too heavy for her already elongated earlobes. "Look at that hairstyle," Ricardo said. "Women's hairstyles—an unexplored continent."

Ambre looked better than the García matron she was speaking to. Each woman was trying to outdo the other in good-humored condescension. Ambre, with her height, elegant dress, and dauntingly sooty nostrils, was getting the upper hand. There were a number of other Garcías of the older generation with the matron—all trying to persuade her to hurry along a little. Ambre looked into the camera, haughty and irritated, and said, "Ido!" The camera operator stepped back, then zoomed in on Ambre's cleavage (we heard his pretty laugh over the murmured conversation).

A few more familiar faces. Some spruce FDR uniforms. Minister of Health Guido Hernández and his wife, hugely pregnant and at the bloated oily-skinned stage. The camera panned over the Plaza, which I saw was only recently repaved. "They renovated the Plaza for a VIP's visit in '93," I said. "Gore. He was a guest at the tenth National Day celebrations."

The camera was making adjustments to the light inside the cathedral, the light coming through the rose window—its rosiness still pending—the pierced stone pattern filled with clear glass. There was never enough money to finish it. White and yellow flowers were tied with white ribbons to the pew ends—FDR colors. Similar floral arrangements decorated the altar. The camera tracked down the aisle, aimed at faces on the groom's side, panned over the priest and altar boys, and stopped on the two men at the altar. They were dressed in dove-gray suits; the groom and one of his brothers.

Beside me Ricardo said, "That booby."

Enrico García glanced sidelong at the camera, bristled, and his eyes flashed.

"He heard you," I said. I pressed pause. Enrico froze, glaring.

Ricardo looked at me. Then he discovered a crumb on his satin lapel and brushed at it. He said softly, "I suppose many people would consider it admirable that my daughter was so persistent in her regard for that man. But he hurt her so badly that there were years during which they never spoke. Or, at least, that's my understanding." If there was an *opposite* to gullible, then Enrico was it, Ricardo said. Enrico was steadily incredulous by nature—Enrico *doubted*, tried to jolly people out of their fears, manias, their sober introspection, even their sense of mystery. "What that booby believes in is a kind of domesticated seriousness, and attention to what he'd term *practical matters . . .*" Ricardo waved a hand impatiently. "I'm afraid I can't appreciate Enrico."

"Your daughter's husband of nine years. The father of two of your three grandchildren."

"Well—we haven't been introduced," Ricardo said, and smiled at himself. "But Carme, look at those relatives of his. Those Garcías. They think he's marrying down. But his grandfather would have had to appear before mine with his hat in his hand."

"Ah," I said, "*Patrone*." I pressed play. The bride's side were more interesting. There was Jules Frei—the venerated Lequaman poet. Beside him his lover, Lena, Ambre's mother, who looked a little transparent and frail. It was easy to see now, but we failed to notice at the time. Just two months later she died, quietly in her sleep. There was my younger half-sister, Fidela, in her brief remorseful stage then—I recalled—and not wearing anything attention-grabbing *or* looking at the camera. Only a month before Juanita's wedding Fidela had tried to "divorce" her parents—Ambre and Ido—at the instigation of her agent and the producer of *Starting Over*, the American sitcom in which she played a cute Latina tot. There was Ambre again, looking pointedly composed, and casting the odd quelling look at the crucifix, saints, candles, as if warning them not to give her any trouble. Tomás sat alone in a pew reserved for his usher sons. He was craning around to keep an eye out for the bride and her retinue. Tomás looked prosperous. He caught sight of the camera and made some signs of inquiry; answered, he abruptly frowned, shuddered, and turned his eyes away.

"If you had seen this, would you still have married me?" Ricardo asked.

"For all you know this might be just the result I was looking for—this fury, this revulsion."

"That's what Ambre thought," Ricardo said. After we married, he had her on the phone—in the first call that wasn't just a foaming cornucopia of abuse—with pop psychology. "She said, 'Carme is trying to make us hate her because she hates herself. Because her father left her.' " Ricardo did a very good mournful Ambre.

"You don't think that."

"No. You told me you needed a powerful protector. Because your father had gone."

"*He* wasn't powerful." I closed my eyes and touched my neck, in imitation of my father in the video nervously touching his windpipe. "I think they got him. The Airans."

"Carme, your father was a bar of plutonium in a locked lead box." Ricardo, in making this remark, seemed as smooth and undisturbed as ever.

The video continued to show us the guests. Marguerite Millay, hair in a tight bun to achieve a "French face-lift." Marguerite's partner, the psychotherapist Aramantha Visistation, smiled at the camera—no, at the cameraman, a small warm look. There was the music faculty from the university, Juanita's employers.

Ricardo said, "I recognize a lot of faces from before the revolution. People who disappeared and then reappeared." He shrugged.

The camera swooped to focus on the door. Zoomed in and tracked back. We heard the Wedding March. Haloed shadows appeared in the doorway. We saw sunlight bright on finery. Juanita's daughter, Xenia, appeared, hesitant, self-conscious—holding a basket from which she scooped and scattered yellow and white petals. The bride came in on her brother's arm. Don Marcos, in dove gray, was traditionally elegant. He turned his head this way and that as he walked, smiling at the guests.

"A politician bestowing benedictions," Ricardo said.

"Actually, it's a Parkinsonian strategy to conceal tremors—the shaking is worse when you're still. He's keeping his head in motion."

Juanita looked like an art nouveau print of a spring month, decorative and delicate. Following her were four bridesmaids, all in voluminous skirts of soft gold dupion silk. Their hair was arranged in different styles according to personal taste, and Madlena's practically had a sign on it saying, "Don't fuck with me." Madlena saw the camera and started; her face grew red, and only respect for Juanita's feelings—rather than the order of service—kept her from breaking ranks and beating up the camera operator.

"And here you are," Ricardo said.

The girl on the video was eighteen, stainless and self-effacing. She came into the church and looked down. (I hadn't yet learned to look away. Looking down modestly only encourages attention. A look away is taken as coldness.) The eighteen-year-old glanced up and saw the camera operator. She gave a confiding smile, a smile of pleasure and affection.

The wedding party pulled up at the altar. There were prayers, hymns, and someone sang a revolutionary poem set to music. Vows were exchanged. The camera operator backed out before the wedding party, into the sunshine. The sound system played Gram Parsons's "Juanita." Rice rained, and fluttering lozenges of colored tissue paper. The camera watched the wedding party pass by and bunch up into two cars and a very clean if elderly jeep. Fernando came into shot, as dark as an eclipsing planet, and the camera pointed down. It swung slightly between their feet.

Fernando's voice: "Who is that for?"

"Ricardo."

"Aren't you afraid that by including him you'll jinx the whole thing?"

"It's safer to include him. Otherwise, like the Groke, he might just shuffle over mournfully and sit on the lamp."

"What?" Fernando almost squawked.

I looked at my husband, who was laughing soundlessly, delighted.

My husband once wrote this to me about my father—I'll transcribe it here: "In a way it seemed he was never fully conscious. He always had an ear turned to his own body. He gave the impression of a preoccupation with the physical—which some people found enormously seductive. It was as if, no matter how else he was engaged, he was anticipating touches, was always conscious of possible impending *contact*. Of course, he was also *intellectually* moving, quick and unconventional. He enlarged life. He took things seriously. These were all causes for admiration. But what *I* loved about him was his marvelous intransigent levity." Ricardo said all this in a letter. I've never heard him *say* the word "love."

Memoir: The Feln to Ulaw, the Shuttling Wood, and Beyond, 1987

After Dev's funeral, the people of the highlands took charge of his body. They wrapped it in a shroud—linen smeared with mutton fat and as stiff and transparent as buttered paper—and placed it on a crag above the spring where the river began. For weeks, on clear days, I would watch the ravens glide in from mountain to mountain to congregate on the crag. Dev's hands were gloved and feet shod, and when the highlanders brought his gnawed, improperly cleaned bones down from the crag to wash them again in hot ashes, his hands and feet were swollen clubs inside the leather—its seams seeped and stank. After the ashes, the skeleton was wrapped again and carried away to a cave in a gorge called the Feln. "Small creatures will finish cleaning him," the people's leader explained to Dev's parents. "And after a long, long time the water in the cave will change his bones to stone. You can sleep easy now—everything has been properly done."

I was sleeping already—ashamed of my smooth dreams, of the deep creases the pillow made on my face by morning.

Carlin didn't sleep. He often sat by the fire all night, till his eyes were dull and smudged. In the daytime he moved at half his usual speed, and spoke at a fraction of his normal volume.

After Dad reappeared Carlin went to bed at night, and began to look a little better for it. It was clear he'd been waiting up for my father, not keeping a vigil for Dev. But my father and he seemed to avoid each other. And although it was to Carlin I heard my father speak about the people he'd been living with—Ambre, Fernando, Madlena: the principals—Carlin never responded, commented, or questioned. Dad would tender information in a quiet but slightly eager way, and Carlin would say nothing in return.

But the day we left, Carlin had his say.

It was frosty, before dawn, but everyone was there, even Dev's mother, hunched under a thick mohair shawl.

Dad poked his knee into my horse's ribs—it let out its held breath as he tightened the girth strap. He said to Astrella, "You can collect your horse from the stables at Ulaw." Her dead father's house. "I borrowed my horse from Twarky when I came through." Twarky was the chief groom at Ulaw.

Dad lifted me into my saddle. "After Ambre's baby is born——" he began.

"He has another plan," Carlin said, bitterly.

Dad turned to face him. I could see he'd been waiting for this.

Carlin said, "When you first came to this world all you could think of was how to *improve* it. In just the same way you used to reconfigure the motherboard on your PC, or write code to speed up its processes. *Here* you were the same kind of mind-blind nerd, pleased with your ship designs, and the coffee monopoly, and the Probity Press even after its printer was arrested and sent off to hard labor in the mines. You're just a troublemaker, Abra, a troublemaker who *fucks around* with things that just happen to have people attached to them."

My father closed his eyes. "You're not supposed to blame me like that."

Carlin threw up his hands and shouted that he didn't want to hear any more that *the problem is the problem and the person isn't the problem*. "That self-excusing psychological crap! Whatever happened to ethics?"

"You're the one who's talking in terms of pathology," my father said. "How can I be fatally flawed and still make the right choices?"

"There's no point talking to you. You're so fucking clever and full of good excuses. It's always been like that—I want reasons, and you offer excuses."

Dad turned back to his horse and caught its halter. He muttered, "Fuck you."

"I think you shouldn't come back, Abra."

Several people objected—told Carlin to just hang on a minute or to shut up.

Dad swung up into the saddle and turned his horse. He walked it to Carlin's side. He looked down into Carlin's face, his own face stiff and angry, but I could see he was searching Carlin's eyes, trying to work out what to believe.

"You're not worth it," Carlin said. "You're not worth all this worry and pain."

My horse sensed my agitation, and, already dubious of my authority, it began to misbehave, dancing off sideways so that I didn't hear the next few things they said. When I reined it in and returned to Dad's side Carlin had gone into the house. My father was telling Cassandra that he'd leave all our contact details with Carlin's cousin and with the cook at Ulaw.

"I have them too," Astrella said. "Not that they make any sense to me." She repeated them: "Care of Ambre Guevara, Flores Negras, Avenida Paolo Caravas, La Host, Lequama."

We crossed the mountains through that long dark gorge called the Feln. I took my father to the cave where Dev's bones were hidden. Dad ducked his head and vanished into the dripping cave mouth. I waited for him on the path with our horses. The river was deafening there, just beyond its highest stepped falls and where the sides of the gorge were so steeply pitched and close together that two tall fallen pines on either bank had tangled falling and were inclined upright, making a gate like an inverted V. The river was fed by a glacier, and the still water beyond the falls was a milky turquoise, less like water than pooled heavy gas.

My father emerged from the cave with his shirt off. He had tied its neck to form a bag. The bag's contents made a dull rattle, and I could see the ball joints of two long thigh bones emerging from its end. I watched Dad distribute the bones into his saddle bags. His horse fidgeted and wrinkled its top lip. Dad left the holed skull in his shirt, fastening its open end to his saddlebag straps. He was shivering with cold but didn't think to cover up till I reminded him. The spare shirt he found was one of Dev's. He'd packed our bags—and had chosen to take a few of Dev's clothes rather than his own. Dev's shirt gaped at his neck, hung off the ends of his hands, and dangled to his knees. He rolled up its sleeves.

We rode on. And my father told me what had happened when he'd remembered who he was and how his lover was killed.

It was raining, he said. He sat in the rain and howled. Then he got up and tried to go after Dev. "Where are you? Where have you gone?" he called, turning in a streaming, muddy circle—mad with the immediacy of his memory of Dev's body. It was as if they were still lying warm in bed on the morning when one of them got up to write a letter and the other to help his mother turn the cheeses. It was as if he could claw through into his past, to climb between the covers and displace himself in his own warm body like some lonely demon. It was as if, in order to lie down again beside Dev, he'd be able to lift away *time*, as easy as raising a blanket from a body—a living body.

My father stopped talking. He put his hand back to touch the skull in its sack, which rolled against the horse's flank as it walked "But I found I was still sitting in the rain above a flooding river. And Ambre was holding me."

We made camp at the three leaning stones where the shepherds stored dried wood. While Dad built the fire he sent me off to gather wet wood to replace what we'd taken. (He was leaving the world, but wouldn't leave the wood store empty.)

I came back to the fire—walked for three minutes through which it brightened, gained color as the sun began to set. Dad took the bundled sticks from me and pulled the front of my dress—damp now—away from my chest. He sat me between his legs, facing the fire, and pressed my palms together between his own. After a long time he said, "Listen to that." Another long time, then, "Where we're going there's always something, always engines, even inaudible, like the contrail of a jet dividing the sky."

We were out of the wind but faced a great gulf, the long fall of folded slopes down to the lowlands. As the sun went down a dazzle lifted from the sea, and the sea vanished. Other distinguishing features below—a square plantation of timber; a field of plowed earth, bare between others of last summer's rusted stubble; a road; the stony jumble of a village—all were swallowed. The hills floated, bronze up close, blue far away, above a vagueness. A hawk banked and slid along the wind coating the side of the nearest hill. A few small birds started up, singing in renewed hope, in the compressed warmth of the last light. The wind died. Gold briefly enriched the thin upland air.

I didn't take my own last look. I leaned against one firm shoulder that hemmed me in and turned to watch him, his closed lips, his downward, backward look on what he faced. A wintry shadow climbed on past us, to the highest place, the pinhole of a first star.

I asked him what he'd said to Carlin when we left.

My father reminded me how Carlin would yell, "Ten good reasons!" when he was incensed by a person's stated plans, or by the way they explained things. "That's what he said to me." In the fire a stick popped and threw off sparks.

Dad told me what he had told Carlin. He had explained why he was going and, somehow, on the spot, he'd managed to divide his explanation by ten, into bullet points. As my father repeated these points I was reminded of a parlor game, like the one where the object of the game is to evolve a word by changing one letter at each step—for example: body, bony, bond, bend, send, seed, seer, sear, soar, sour, soul. I thought how infuriated Carlin would have been by the glib shapeliness of Dad's ten reasons, which included having been "invited" by Airans, the inconsolability of Dev's parents, and Carlin's having blamed him. It was a list, and each reason seemed roughly equivalent. Six—our sympathetic princess died of lockjaw. Seven—the *Thresher* burned. Eight—he missed a place he'd only dreamed about, whose people buried him in a cool, dry grave of daily detail. Nine— . . . He finished by saying that he was dead already.

I was puzzled and distressed. I remember that the view I had of my father's face, sadness percolating through its calm surface, began to strobe. I was falling asleep. I made an effort—asked him if he felt that our princess dying of lockjaw and the *Thresher* burning were the same kind of bad luck.

"Both were setbacks to my plans—but the first, at least, wasn't something that happened to *me*."

"You changed your plans when the *Thresher* burned. You went to get Dev."

His face was firelit, diffuse, nearer mine.

With difficulty I added, "But you wouldn't have if it hadn't burned."

He didn't respond, or I didn't hear him.

My father didn't stop at Ulaw, because when we came around the lakeshore we could see an island of trees in the hot summer haze over the swamp. Trees that looked tired, yellowing, burned by early frosts, while those on Ulaw's timber plantation were freshly green.

Dad led our horses in over the cobbles and to the stable door, where Twarky appeared to greet us. Twarky said that his mother would want to speak to Abra. Dad told him that we'd rest and eat on the other side. Twarky went to fetch his mother while Dad unbuckled our saddlebags and gave me my share of the load.

The cook came, hovered, and said, "Carme looks very tired," and "You'll be back, won't you?"

"Astrella says Carlin will forgive me," Dad said. And then he gave the cook a piece of paper on which was written that nonsensical address. "And a phone number," he said.

"Touch-tone," said the cook. "Touch-tone phones, Twarky says."

"Not where I am. The government is still doing its business through a 1960s plug-in switchboard. Any nostalgia I might feel either way is completely confounded." My father tied the bagged skull onto his belt, where it rolled against his leg like a gourd. He took up the bulk of my luggage and bent to kiss the cook's cheek.

"You'll be back," she said.

"When I can learn not to be such a fiddle-fingers."

"That would be good," she said good-naturedly.

We left our address with Carlin's cousin. We slept there. The bed was far too soft, my pillows stuffed with some fiber without grain or—it seemed to me—any real structure. Water boiled and rooms warmed without fire. Light appeared without combustion. At breakfast the next day Dad fed me my first tranquillizers, then Carlin's cousin drove us into "town" to pick up "a rental." I was ten, but I wet my pants. Dad showed me how to flush the toilet. My silk drawers dried in the back window of the rented "hatchback" as we drove through Gatelawbridge and Closeburn. I inclined in my blanket and seat belt and stared out the window.

I now know those first roads were very quiet. I couldn't look at the other cars, but watched the world go by—fields and stone walls, not unfamiliar, but too much at once, too many angles on one scene within each minute. For instance, we weirdly kept abreast of a stellar cloud of gulls that flew in to settle on a meadow in the low sun.

The A75 through Gretna Green. The A74, then the M6 bypassing Carlisle. I got very frightened. Dad carried me out into a pub in a village off the main road, fed, toileted, and washed me before dosing me up with sleeping tablets.

Once I struggled out of sleep on the M1. Our little vessel was in a Niagara of traffic. I was only able to express my terror in a moan.

Dad checked us into a hotel near Heathrow and kept me awake to eat. He sat me in the bath and shampooed my hair. He toweled it dry, combed it, and took delivery of a big meal—my first curry. Then he fed me more pills. He had to go out to see a man about a fake birth certificate—I had to have one to travel on his passport. He had to take Astrella's rubies to "a fence." "All this takes money," he explained. I fought sleep. I begged him not to go out and leave me alone.

Dad was liberal with his dosages and managed to keep me asleep when he was out. Several times I woke when he climbed in beside me, or when I heard him talking to room service at the door. Once he came back and lay next to me trembling uncontrollably. I never knew if it was with fear or the shock of some great exertion.

I woke up once when he wasn't there. I was groggy, leaden-limbed. I pulled the thick thermal drapes open a little and looked through the double glazing at what I'd been able to hear the whole time—a pounding appalling roar. Beyond a gauzy fence, at some distance from me, whole *houses* were on the move. Houses like long white barrels. I watched one, rapid as a landslide, as a disaster, race away from me, then tip up, back end down. Air appeared underneath it, thick and charged with fumes like a spirit roiling in water. It climbed a wedge of invisible solidity, climbed the air out of sight. I craned to look after it, my cheek and palms against the unknit miracle of squeaky plate glass.

Four days later I was in one myself. My first plane, following my first official border. He'd given my age as eight. He carried me; I carried a soft toy. We boarded at 7:00 a.m. The noise frightened me, but I liked the aircraft's soft jostling. My ragged toenails caught in the airline blanket. I saw the aqua sea over an ice shelf in Greenland. I saw the swamps of the Canadian tundra, flashing like a thousand heliotropes.

Throughout the whole journey my father never once said, as he always had before, "Trust me." Instead his silence seemed to say: "I'm not to be trusted."

Journal: Spa Spice Island to Vela Bay, Lequama, August 1, 2003

Ricardo insisted on sending me directly to Lequama, instead of flying me out to Bogotá and on from there. We said good-bye on the wharf of Spa Spice Island. He stopped me before I stepped down onto the pontoon of the seaplane and kissed my cheek, minding our sunglasses. In steadying myself, my hands rested against his ribs— warm under his shirt, the shifty flesh of an over-fifty. Ricardo's aftershave was delicious, and so was the brief abrasive touch of his cheek. We disengaged and I focused on the step from the motionless jetty onto the pontoon; then I looked back to say, "I'll call tomorrow." Friendly.

To impress his employer the pilot made a point of settling me. He checked my belt and offered me earplugs. I shook my head. We coasted back into the lagoon beside the marina, then turned and took off past the jetty. Ricardo was standing by the candy-striped golf cart that had brought us out from the hotel—sunglasses off now—waving.

We were over the sea almost all the way. And once we were above Península de Guajira and the coal mine, miles of earthworks, bare subsoil under its own pall of pinkish dust.

We put down in Vela Bay, where there is a customs post. There was no water traffic at the wharf, and the pilot took his time on the turnaround, got out to unload my little pile of luggage, flexed his back, swung his arms, swiveled the bill of his cap backward and swatted imaginary chaff from his white slacks—all the time keeping an eye on the armed customs agents, who had come out of their shelter at the head of the pier but hadn't advanced. The pilot helped me shoulder my pack and supported its weight while I clipped its belt around my waist. I picked up my smaller bags and went along the pier toward the waiting agents—two men in buff-colored uniforms and shades, hands on hips. As I came up one directed me into their tin-walled customs post. Behind me I heard the seaplane turn, its engine chuckling, then I heard it taxi away.

Though the louvers were open it was hot in the shack, and the piles of paperwork were damp and dimpled. I gave the customs agents my passport. Then I came clean—said, "I'm going to do this in as open and businesslike a way as possible. Okay?" They gave me a go-ahead nod.

I put my makeup case on the table. "This has come through to Colombia in a diplomatic bag—courtesy of some friends of my husband—but all it is is a collection of prescription drugs. I've had some of my graduate friends in the U.S. writing prescriptions. The drugs are for Dr. Anton Xavier at La Casa de la Mujer."

The men inspected the bottles, the Ativan, Zoloft, and Prozac, my selection of serotonin uptake inhibitors; the Ritalin and the Xenical—just a few of the luxurious life-enhancing drugs of the first world.

"Give him a call," I suggested.

The one sorting through the pill bottles suddenly giggled, held up the bottle for his friend to read. "Viagrissimo," he said.

"Do you want some?" I took the bottle from him, poured perhaps a fourth into my palm and began dividing the capsules into two piles. Then I set to packing all the other bottles away. As I did the men palmed their piles, clipping the pills into their outside jacket pockets.

"One at a time," I said, "if you want to live to enjoy it."

"One at a time?" one asked, pointing to himself, his colleague, then me —but his insinuating finger stopped well short.

"I'm a married woman," I said.

The one who hadn't made any suggestions took off his shades and gave me a *look*, as though I were real and mattered, and it wasn't just a dull morning in a hot shed in a quiet port. He asked, "Why did you marry him, Señora?"

"Most men respect a wedding ring."

"Surely there could have been other rings, Señora."

I picked up my bags and walked out of the shed. Behind me I heard the chair legs scrape as the seated man got up, and the boots of each on the boards behind me for a short way. The one who'd asked called out after me, "But few so effective, eh?"

The road ran around the bay to a small town with a street of hotels where, for decades, men of modest means have sent their families in the hot season. There was always a taxi outside the hotels.

The taxi driver was very glad of a fare to the capital He'd meant to go there for the celebration. We struck a bargain, and he took me by the longer route, avoiding the cane fields. There was no glass in the window on my side; still, I happily inhaled the miles of dust, fetid ditches, flowering trees, pastures in the pass that wound through the Cordillera Occidental, river mud, and the scents of three little towns. Then finally, shortly before La Host, a small wedge of the *sucrellanos*, the plains of sugarcane.

Memoir: La Host, Lequama, October to December 1987

On my first night in La Host I woke up in my father's room under the roof. He'd lit a kerosene lamp; its flame was mantled low, and I found myself looking at what I thought were strangely unsteady shadows in the steady light—a cluster of small bats. I could see their eyes, or perhaps skin, gleaming through their sparse, upstanding fur. Dad was beside me, asleep, but he had my hand folded in his own. The skin under his eyes was smudged, and there was a little blood crusted around one nostril.

I lay still and listened—to his breathing and the minute shuffles and squeaks of the bats. Outside something growled, something with capacious breath, the growl rolled nearer, altered, and moved away again.

Dad's eyes were open; I was crushing his hand. "What was that?" I asked.

He frowned, considered, then said, "Only a badly tuned car, Carme. Get some sleep. You have a big day ahead. Meeting people. The household, just for a start."

I did sleep. I was jolted awake more frequently as morning approached and more motor vehicles passed along that—as I later understood—very quiet street. Later I heard a radio, and a shower running.

My father carried me downstairs and I was faced with them—a crowd of all those who had a vested interest—staring at me with curious surprise. The woman with the thick springy curls (Madlena) was sensitive enough to speak English *before* Dad delivered his little lecture on not treating me like a tourist. She said, "She's a big girl. When Mama said you'd gone to fetch your daughter I thought she'd be only a baby."

"I was seventeen," Dad said—his age at my birth.

"Madlena," said the very dark-skinned woman who was nearest me (it was Ambre), "perhaps you should speak *to* the girl."

The big man with pale eyes said something to my father, in Spanish. And then Dad delivered his little lecture. I wasn't a tourist, no one must imagine they should throw me in at the deep end for my edification and improvement.

"If you say so," said Fernando, in English. Then he turned to me, gave me his full, solemn attention. He said welcome. And I could see him *seeing*, not simply assessing me.

I didn't like Ambre, and resented her manner, which was at once anxious and managing. I hated the way she'd smirk at Dad as he flattered her, and the way he was guided by her, tamed by need. Ambre was pregnant, apparently, and Dad was responsible. But in those first weeks I never once saw them touch each other.

Of course I know now that they wouldn't have *dared* with me looking at them in resentful accusation. Whenever I spoke I invoked Dev's name—said it as often as possible. But I never spoke to Dad about Dev when we were alone, for I was a little afraid of what I sensed—the stark, mute intensity of his grief. I talked about Dev for maximum effect—what Dev would do for my father, how Dev understood my father's needs. I inserted Dev's name like a chisel blow at any weak place, in any weak moment. Dad never mentioned Dev or Carlin, the two people I'd always thought—with no sense of an injustice done me—he loved most. Their names never passed his lips. He'd given up his living friend with his dead lover.

In moments free from minding me, from providing for Ambre a buffer against my campaign of stalking complaint, Dad spent his time in the workshop the García brothers were building behind Flores Negras. He was making a cabinet, a large chest. He finished assembling it one morning in his room under the roof. The chest was seven feet in length and shaped like a narrow bed. It had a heavy hinged lid and another fitted lid inside that closed the container off in two levels like the layers in a chocolate box. Once the chest was assembled, Dad knelt beside it and laid out within, in correct order, his lover's bones. The little bones of finger and toe and fanned fine bones of feet and hands were still held together by dry tendons. I watched my father lay that skeleton out to its full six foot nine, fold the huge rattling hands on its sternum, and set the skull sideways, bullet hole hidden. Then my father shut the false floor of the chest and put our folded clothes in on top of it. Ambre had never seen the skeleton—she didn't know he had it.

When the nights in which I woke alone in the bed under the roof became more frequent, I made my disapproval felt by withdrawal.

I stopped speaking English—reverted to Esindu—used strange phrases in that language to name the shower stall, television, refrigerator, car, all things for which I had no nouns. I spoke Esindu, a rich, hearty, pointed language to all these puzzled or pitying or disapproving dark faces—till I began to feel as though my words were gobbledygook, and I was a gibbering ghost.

I made Ambre's life miserable.

How can I say this? How can I strike a balance between blame and excuse?

Children are uncivilized, so have a staggering power to harm, especially those people whose hearts need mending. In that house an unhappy child was too much rain on a high water table. I poured it on and the terrain liquefied. Ambre was in the fourth month of pregnancy, her blood volume had increased and her blood was poor in oxygen-bearing hemoglobin. She was stifled by tiredness. I was his child—so she was looking at me to see her own future. Ambre looked at me and saw a meter and a half of self-righteous hatred. But Ambre was an adult and should have been patient. I'll say that. I was showing not just my worst side, but signs of family temperament—all those qualities that would help make my younger sister the intolerant creature she became—quick-witted competence, ruthlessness, self-discipline. But Ambre should have weathered it all, continued firm, put her foot down.

Instead, she cut me out. It wasn't between me and her, but her and him. There came a night she told him—I was present—that she couldn't live with me. If he wanted to stay with her he had to "make other arrangements" for me.

So Dad took me upstairs, packed my few things, and carried me and my bag out of the house.

It was late in the evening, past my bedtime. We were both worn out. We turned the corner into a wider street. It was—after the rains—encroached on by vines, some as thick as my wrist, ribbed, with translucent hydroponic hairs and great flowers like faces turned toward us.

I thought he'd walk me all the way wherever we were going without speaking to me. But he did speak. "Dev's dead," he said, "and it's nothing to do with Ambre. She didn't kill him. She didn't conspire against him. She never met him."

"But you won't talk about him in her house."

I had him there. He was silent for long time. But then he said, "What I'm thinking—apart from what can't be said, not even by *my body* without *his* to answer it—is all too adult for your ears."

"Are you going to share it with her?"

My father pressed us against the wall to avoid a truck that failed to slow at the corner, climbed the curb and left it again with a bang. I was afraid of the truck and didn't yet understand traffic, that the vehicles in Lequama were made to make do, were often unable to stop for fear of finally stalling. My father stood still for a moment and held me hard. I felt that perhaps he was resisting tears. He answered me. "No." In that one word his despair was dazzling. He said, "I'm not going to start. They're the same—Ambre and Dev—they can't be filled up." He laughed. "He was too deep. And she has holes."

At that time Fernando was living on the Avenida Bueyes Negros, the "Street of Black Oxen," two streets from the Plaza. His apartment was on the first floor and had one bedroom and a living room-cum-kitchen. The building was mud brick and had an external staircase and open landings like balconies. Fernando shared a bathroom with the family across the landing. His accommodations were unusually humble for a former minister of government. Three years earlier he'd been compelled to give up his bodyguard—his entourage of ten Taoscal men—when there were claims that these men were intimidating other residents of the Presidential Palace. It was this allegation that precipitated the clash between Fernando and Madlena, the clash that many people said was the main contributing cause of Fernando's later defection to Ricardo and the Contras. After his three months with the Contras, Fernando returned secretly to Lequama and holed up at Taosclan, till Don Marcos persuaded him to turn himself in. Fernando was "re-educated" in Cuba and, on his return to La Host, no longer in command of his male entourage, he found accommodation in rooms too small to miss their company.

It was to this apartment that Dad carried me that night. Fernando answered the door, tousled but wide awake, wearing only boxer shorts, but with an automatic pistol held behind his right thigh. Seeing who it was he seemed to swell with interest, to take up more space, like light growing in the room. He let us in, tossed the gun through his bedroom door onto the bed and went to the fridge for filtered water, filled two glasses, put one in front of me and kept one himself.

Dad repeated what Ambre had said. Then he said, "I'll visit every day," either making a promise or offering an incentive.

"And if she needs you in more than daily doses?"

"Teach her to use the phone."

Fernando took a sip of water. There was mist on the sides of the glass and trickles of condensation from the clear patches around each hot fingertip. "All right," he said.

"Ambre will come around eventually."

Fernando grunted.

Dad bent to kiss me. I whispered, "Are you really going to do this to me again?"

"Yes," he said. And then he left.

Fernando put me in school. He was working and—after all—it was time I signed on somewhere. "Carme. Her mark," he said—then handed me the iron, so that I could do his shirt cuffs and collar while he shaved. Then he gave me his key and said he'd rather I didn't lie around the house for hours before he came home. Tomorrow he'd give me money so I could do the shopping. But for now, I'd best make a friend. He buttoned his shirt, pulled a face, flexed his shoulders inside it so the muscles showed momentarily in each quadrant of his torso, his nipples like the studs of snap fasteners. He asked me, "What's that name you call your father that makes him so angry?"

This was one of a series of questions Fernando asked to coax my father's story from me, one of the more personal ones. For the most part he posed questions that demanded answers in the form of eyewitness history. Tales, around the edges of which I mused about what motivated the people I'd lived with.

Fernando attended, and his attention was an act of entrapment. I gave him all sorts of insights, then saw him talking to my father and pretending not to know. Of course, he was waiting to see what Dad would say about himself, waiting to see if he'd lie, minimize, show himself in a better light. Dad did none of these—and I watched Fernando slowly succumb to my father's restrained power, his pain and shame.

My father and his friends for years just snapped at the heels of authority—I said. They wrote pamphlets pointing out the rigid division of rights and responsibilities between the priests and the populace. Then, when I was two, my stepfather, Ulaw, died. And my father—with Carlin, Cassandra, and a group of Ulaw's relatives—left his house. Ulaw's house, and his protection. They settled in the country to the south and had a ship built to Dad's design, the *Thresher*.

The whole move was Dad's design. Carlin thought my father wasn't planning, but acting on his old compulsion to run away, remove himself from stress, supervision, and social demands. I remembered Carlin saying to me, when I was old enough to understand him: "Every time your father does this now he's looking for a firmer footing. He becomes a more public person, a person with *ideas* who *interferes*." I can remember telling Carlin that if I was eight, then Dad was twenty-five, and it was only *adults* who could expect to have public lives. If Dad's behavior had changed it was because he'd grown up.

I told Fernando this. And I told him about why my father didn't like me to call him K'Adonatia.

The lord of the city in which we'd settled had wanted to establish a second garrison to the west of the city. He planned to build a fort near the river on wasteland occupied by refugees from the highlands of the continent's northernmost country. These highlanders were peaceful people and, after a few objections, said yes, they'd decamp—but could they please bring in the harvest first—the carrots and potatoes and beets they'd planted. The lord said no. And one evening he sent soldiers to enforce the eviction. A child was trampled, a woman burned by spilled coals. The people's emissar—their religious leader—went to the lord to complain. He wasn't admitted, and got into a fight. A courtier was injured, fatally, with his own weapon. The emissar was arrested for murder. My father persuaded our lawyer—who worked for a foreign bank as well as managing our investments, so wasn't as easily intimidated as the local legal establishment—to represent the emissar. No one else would; there were religious prejudices involved. The country was one of the two run by a secular *sect*—it was hard to explain. My father got the lawyer to make him his assistant. He persuaded the lawyer to develop laryngitis and then argued the case himself. Eloquently. There were disturbances in the courtroom. The public was barred from the trial. But before the public was barred the emissar gave his testimony. Throughout his testimony he addressed my father as K'Adonatia—an affectionate form of the name of the highlander's bleeding god-who-is-to-be-reborn. Presumably the emissar did this because of my father's various impressive personal qualities. At the conclusion of the trial the three judges voted guilty and, ultimately, the emissar was executed. On the scaffold he referred to my father as K'Adonatia. Thereafter, all the refugees of that religion, and all the displaced highlanders in the shantytowns around the capital of their own country, looked to my father as a savior.

I told Fernando how my father befriended the Queen's eldest daughter and, when she was confirmed as heir apparent, she made a speech—a speech my father had a large hand in writing. "The world is one place . . ." and "We are responsible not only for the injustice we create, but the injustice we allow . . ." I told how the Probity Press was broken up and its printer and her landlord sent to labor in the mines in the mountains. My father made enemies, and there was at least one attempt on his life.

He was out of the country when the officers of the new garrison rebelled, and they and an army of citizens threw the lord and priests out of the city, and the city declared its independence from the crown. The *Thresher* had left Dad and Dev in the port where we bought coffee. Dev had shattered his knee and was better off laid up another week. Carlin got news of the rebellion at the empire's northern port and made decisions like the military man he'd once been. He rented warehouse space, off-loaded the coffee, bought armaments and oil, linen, salves, salt pork, ground flour, and so forth.

The *Thresher* ran the blockade around the harbor of our hometown. There was no gunpowder on Eden and naval battles were all about fire, archery, catapults, and rams. The *Thresher* was a clipper, and fast; it tacked through the blockading ships while they maneuvered sluggishly by sail or oar.

What with its extra days unloading coffee and taking on a new cargo, the *Thresher* was only three days ahead of the vessel that carried my father and Dev. That ship was diverted to the capital. Dad was arrested. Dev was handed over to the care of the crown princess and her husband.

Our fortunes turned. Everybody changed. It was as though, after that time, I lived in the world colored and chilled by a permanent partial eclipse. Our city was under siege. Many of the ships in the harbor were holed and scuttled to close the channel so that the crown's navy couldn't come at us. When the battle came, the rebel garrison held off the Queen's cavalry in the west, and the citizens held the city at the river from the armies that came from the east. They held the city for six hours at its eight bridges. Astrella was in command of the barricade at the bridge on Market Street. I saw her fighting from the castle's roof. I saw a wall of furniture stopping up its holes with corpses. I saw the oil the *Thresher* had brought used to set the river on fire when the Market Street barricade had fallen. I didn't see anything else—the man who was carrying me off the roof was hit in the throat by an arrow and dropped me, and I went over the battlements, snatching at the stonework with one arm, dislocating my shoulder. I fell twenty meters into a canal. I spent the remainder of the battle on a slimy stone landing stage with my back to a locked door.

Astrella and her husband escaped. Cassandra was arrested in the infirmary, where she'd not been able to do much more than give water to the wounded and dying. Carlin was arrested and tried, and eventually sent to a low-lying, malarious prison island from which he and a number of others later managed to escape. Dad bribed his way out of his prison cell and entered the city five days after the battle. He was left at liberty, but wasn't allowed to be in a room with more than four people and wasn't allowed to open his mouth in public, which meant he had thereafter to do all his business through our lawyer.

Some months after the prison, his cell-below-the-level-of-the-river—a phrase that had some kind of magical significance for him—my father had *dreams*. Not bad dreams, but dreams that he said seemed just as real to him as his waking life. In his dreams he was back on Earth, in an equatorial country at Christmas. "I can't have invented the people I dream about," he told me. "They make me feel like a sad monster—the way *real* people always have." He said, "It started in the cell, with a strange old man who somehow showed me that I was heartless."

Dad was afraid for me and sent me north to Astrella. I lived with her first in a hotel—which was quarantined during an outbreak of diphtheria. Then Astrella took me to live in the stiflingly polite ladies' quarters at the castle. Dad joined us months later, with Dev, who was greatly changed, subdued, his knee always giving him pain. Carlin escaped and arrived in the northern country. We were all briefly together again—and Dad began to work to raise money for our cause. Then Dev went off to the highlands to live with his parents. We got news that our sympathetic princess had died of lockjaw, and one night the *Thresher* caught fire and burned in the harbor.

Dad, seeing enemies everywhere, sent me to the highlands to join Dev, who was sad and gray and no company for a child.

After some time—I told Fernando—after what seemed like a long time, my father joined us. He sat in Dev's parents' low-ceilinged kitchen and wrote letters. His industry made *sense*, because we were sitting with him. Leaning on him—Dev and I.

Then one fine, frosty spring morning, I woke up to hear horses approaching. I looked over the edge of the loft where my bed was to see my father on the bench by the door pulling on his boots. He went out without fastening their laces, so that they flapped and clumped. I climbed down the ladder and stood, one foot on top of the other, on the cold threshold. The riders were four men and one woman. All sat badly on their horses, loose-kneed and slump-backed. They spoke English, so clearly weren't agents of our enemies. The sound of their English brought Dev and his mother—in a rush—out of the springhouse on the slope above the cottage. Dev looked hostile—he often did. Then one of the mounted men—a boy really—began to shout, "Mom! That man kills people!" He sounded terrified. The horses grew restive, began to back, spin, and bump together. The woman slipped in her saddle so that she was standing on her stirrup. The boy's voice altered, not just in tone, pitch, and volume, but its whole acoustical quality—as if it was a different voice, from a different body, in a different space, not the open air. He didn't shout, but said in a kind of magnified whisper, harsh with terror or terrible pain: "*Mercy. Mercy. I'm saying 'mercy.'* "

Dev yelled, "No!" His face was white.

Then the slight, dark-skinned, smooth-haired man shot Dev. I didn't see a gun. I heard a sharp sound and saw Dev knocked back, his head turned right around in a pink cloud. He was on the ground, with a hemisphere of his head gone.

People screamed and shouted. I just let sound out of me and looked about—but I couldn't get anyone to notice me. Dad was beside Dev. But he wasn't looking at him—he was looking at the turf just up the slope from where Dev lay. I saw that he was looking at Dev's boot prints darkening the dew, looking not at Dev's body, but at the last place his life had been and made its impression.

Then the man with the gun kicked his horse over to Dad and struck him on the back of the head with the gun butt.

And they took him away, I told Fernando. From Dev's mother and father and me. We were the only people there. An old man and woman and a nine-year-old girl. We couldn't stop them. But as they were going, and it was quieter, I heard the yelling boy say quite calmly to the others: "He doesn't know how; but he wants to end the world."

Fernando stood holding the door as if hurrying me with my story, not just out of the house. It was another morning on which I was talking to him and we were running late. He had asked more questions.

"Perhaps you shouldn't remind your father of those things," Fernando said. "Perhaps it is kinder to let him forget all that pain and defeat; and a senseless end to all his—what did you call it?—*industry*."

When I neither answered nor moved he smiled, then hooked an arm at me. "Come on, girl. I'll deliver you to the sisters at San Miscere."

Bella Frei was the girl at the head of the class who wore a pretty silk headscarf, purple-threaded gold, with tassels like a long ponytail. She came up to me in the lunch hour and wanted to practice her English. She didn't need any practice—she'd been living for two years in Arizona, where her father had a postdoctoral fellowship. The family had lived in a small house on a new and uniform housing estate two hours' drive from the campus. All they could afford—because of Lequama's "soft currency," the "exchange rate."

By the end of the week Bella was sitting beside me in class and we were being told off for talking. She didn't ask me about myself— she ventured out once into the riptide of my evasiveness, felt its pull, the places it might take and overwhelm anyone asking to be taken. Instead I got to know *her*. She got me asking questions, took me into her own difficulties. We walked home together. In the small downhill stand of vanilla trees behind the school she took off her scarf and shook her hair out of it, today's windfall. "This is alopecia," she explained. "My therapist, Aramantha Visistation, tells me I'm having a grief reaction."

Bella's mother had begun chemotherapy around this time the year before—a painful postponement of the inevitable. Bella said, "I wore a hat at Mama's funeral. When I took it off, its inside looked like a grass-lined bird's nest. I've been shedding hair ever since." Bella retied her scarf. She asked me whether I thought she'd ever get over it.

"Of course," I said, to be kind.

She pursed her lips. She had her hands behind her head, and her plump pectoral muscles stood out against her blouse. "If it was *you*, would you get over it?"

I didn't say anything.

She looked at me shrewdly. "If it was your *hair* I'm sure you'd get over it. My great-uncle Jules wrote this poem that says, in one part, 'God give me the strength to will away all pains that aren't picturesque.'"

On another day Bella observed my father delivering me—after our fifteen-minute daily debrief—at the gates to the school. She hurried over. She stood before him, inches under his nose, and rocked back and forth like a pantomime policeman. She said, "You're Señor Idea. Ido the Idea. You're teaching hand-to-hand combat to soldiers out at Castel Mirabella."

"Bella," Dad said. I'd told him a little about her, had given him her name. "Bella," he said, and her face flushed, leaving a mask of pallor around her eyes. He smiled at her for a moment longer, waiting to see if she'd remember to say hello, then he bid us both goodbye. Bella watched him walk away and reported what her brother the cadet had said of my father's class in unarmed combat. That my father was full of tricks like a dirty street fighter—and "head games." He'd show the cadets how they could be hurt; then, if that wasn't enough, he'd hurt them. He'd say, "Close your ears, open your eyes"—they wouldn't get it, would be attending, then mesmerized by his instruction, as if by some kindly phenomenon like evening light. Then, wham! Some poor sucker would be on his back.

After school that day Bella took me to the Wall to show me an English translation of one of her great-uncle's poems. The translator's name was Walter Risk.

> My father's work clothes
> hung up in the wind
> were a young man dancing barefoot
> in the cool of the day.
>
> This greasy evening,
> above the street,
> my neighbor's overalls
> fat with wind, and
> inconsistently jointed,
> recall bullets
> or good rope put to a bad use.

While he was teaching at Castel Mirabella, Dad would come sometimes before supper, in his ill-fitting, sweaty fatigues, to have a beer with Fernando and talk to me. Dad said that it had made better sense to volunteer himself as an instructor when Armed Forces wouldn't defer his CMT. He had to stay in La Host, at Flores Negras, with Ambre—for the baby. When he said this he sounded both smug and fatalistic. "Anton's still writing letters. But Armed Forces can't get their heads around my talent for disabling people, and my desire to be a nurse's aide."

"Anton?" Fernando said. "Are you on a first-name basis now?"

"Why not?" Dad said. "Anton. Fernando. Madlena. Ambre."

"Aramantha," Fernando said.

Dad glanced at me, frowned, gave a small shake of his head.

Madlena took to holding big Saturday lunches in an effort to bring us all together. I avoided sitting down except over the meal itself. I offered to help exercise the horses—Madlena was short of skilled hands and I qualified—I had been around horses all my life. Madlena would pad out a riding hat with a headscarf and take me to her foreman, who would choose a horse. Lunches came and went in this way and I never had to sit in the same room with Ambre for more than an hour. I only ever turned my eyes her way when she was at a distance on the veranda and I was at the far side of the corral. She disgusted me, sitting there, perspiring, pouched, sprawling—and nothing to do with me.

Fernando and I would go out to the hacienda late in the morning. He always had people around on Friday nights.

I was sleeping in his room—he'd taken the couch. I'd wake at 2:00 or 3:00 a.m. to hear voices, maybe music, and would look through the crack in the door at perhaps six or ten Indians sitting around a table covered with plastic flagons of beer and bottles of mountain wine. They would be talking, usually fairly sober, in Taoscal thick with proper names I came later to recognize from newspapers as belonging to other civil servants and members of government. On Saturday morning I took our clothes down to the laundry in the Plaza, then shopped, then came home to work around Fernando. I'd bag the bottles and carry them out onto the landing. Fernando might grunt and pull the quilt up over his head. I'd wipe down the surfaces in the kitchen, then the living room, emptying ashtrays. I'd cut a mango in half, scoop out the pip and its fibrous envelope, then I'd leave the mango and a spoon near Fernando's covered head. I'd go tidy the bedroom, come back to find him sitting up, smoking, and eating—preverbal—maybe pointing at the coffeepot with spoon or cigarette. As I pushed my broom around the kitchen tiles I scolded Fernando: "I've never lived with anyone who drank as much as you do."

He said I'd led a sheltered existence. Then, provokingly, "Apart from your eavesdropping, I guess."

"I can't understand Taoscal."

"*You* can't understand Spanish, Carme."

I could—though I wasn't about to let on. Afternoons, after school, Bella took me to visit with her grandmother—her Nona. At first she'd leave me at the corner of the Avenida Paolo Caravas and go on by herself. Bella's grandmother never went out, couldn't cross her own threshold. Bella shopped for her and sat with her. Bella thought her grandmother should see Aramantha Visistation. But Nona only wanted the priest, who didn't do much more than pray and pat her hand.

The poet Frei had been living with Bella's Nona, his sister-in-law, when, before the revolution, the Pola Pastrez came to take him. Her own daughter, the wife of a newspaper editor, had already been arrested, taken from the house of a friend. The daughter, seven months pregnant, was bundled into the back of a van on a midnight street, shouting out her mother's phone number to anyone up and listening. Over and over, at the top of her voice, her mother's number. A stranger called—once to say the daughter was arrested, again to say she was in Los Muertos, finally, weeks later, to report what name the daughter could be found under at La Casa de la Mujer. (She was there, delirious, septicemic, her belly deflated, the baby nowhere to be found. She lived, but they never did find the child.)

Then they came for the poet. The Security Forces in their monochrome uniforms, black and trimmed with gray. The officer had horned moons, in silver, fastening his collar—a Pastrez family crest become military insignia. When he stood before the old woman the officer's moons were at the level of her eyes, two gleaming, spiteful smiles. The Pola Pastrez took the poet, then returned the following night for his papers, searched the house, struck his sister-in-law, knocked her down. They were back again the next night to conduct a more thorough search for "evidence." This time the old woman met them on her knees and they took the trouble to pick her up so that, beaten, she'd have farther to fall. Frei disappeared into Los Muertos, and Bella's Nona believed she would never see him again. But on August 8, after days of riots and firefights, the lights went out in La Host. The old woman, already afraid of the street, afraid to leave her house despite the fact that her house was where most of it happened, sat in the dark, her hands warming her knees, listening to gunfire, shouts, flight, breakage—till, in the small hours, after clearing its throat all night, the radio came alive, and it was Colonel Maria Godshalk speaking in her low-pitched, commanding voice to "*compañeros* and *compañeras*," electrified by victory.

Three years later Bella's grandmother was still afraid of the street, or the windows opposite her own, and of any shadow blackening the crack under her door. Bella never knocked. She was expected at the same time every afternoon. "Nona, it's Bella," she'd say, stroking the door with her nails. And later: "I've brought Carme, my friend from school."

Bella's Nona couldn't speak English, so out of politeness I practiced my Spanish. She showed me family photos—of her Jesuit brother, and the poet brother-in-law reading at a rally in Washington Square, New York City, in 1979. She pointed out her mechanic father, reclining on the cowcatcher of a steam engine, and her pharmacist husband in his white coat, behind him a shelf studded with bright bottles. There were photos of her clever sons and daughters—in pride of place her daughter-in-law, Bella's mother, as a student, in beret, beads, bomber jacket, and the bloom of health.

She had me peer through the shades at the opposite house. Could I see that poor child who was griping night and day? A niggly wheedling cry Bella's Nona recognized as hard teething. She cut a circle out of cotton muslin and filled it with shredded apple, tied the whole thing into a tight white cherry and had us girls cross the street to offer that poor child's mother this "chewing poppet." It was gratefully accepted, as was the teething powder the old woman concocted on another day. Several days later the neighbor arrived, carrying the child, to show Bella's Nona the new tooth. Mother and child were admitted. The toddler edged around the dark furniture, lifted the lid on ceramic cigarette boxes, sucked the Bakelite dials of the old radio–record player, and sat on the floor to play with the dog-headed draft stopper. Bella's Nona sat at the edge of her seat and watched, smiling. Later in the week Bella and I saw her Nona raise the blinds to wave to this same child.

We were all making progress. Bella had stopped "babying" her scalp by wearing a scarf. I sat behind her in the orchard and brushed her hair—it was thin, but no longer falling out. To improve my pronunciation Bella taught me several revolutionary songs and explained their cast of characters. There were songs about love, about the very poor at last waking up able to wish, and falling asleep able to dream. There were savage songs, one about the man I was staying with, Commander Sola, walking out of the darkness of the jungle with 200 Taoscal at his back, all bearing arms stamped "Made in the USA," but with no prisoners, and the trees closing behind them like silent green water.

One day in December, after Sunday school, I was asked over to help Bella's Nona make a high tea for a few family members. I'd been going to Sunday school for Bella's company and to absorb certain mythologies which I'd only heard explained before as mythologies. At last I was able to understand Carlin's "Jesus wept" and his "Get thee behind me." (Fernando always delivered me to Sunday school. The first time, he escorted me into the chapel and, on seeing him, the children spontaneously raised their arms above their heads, in a silent version of the two-armed Lequaman victory wave I'd seen in pictures of a rally on National Day. They looked like babies begging Fernando to pick them up and carry them.)

At her Nona's tea Bella and I found that the English breakfast had rusted in its tin. Bella's Nona was distressed. We brewed maté, to go with the coffee. There was coffee blossom in the centerpiece, and flowering yagga, yellow and white flowers in honor of all the patriots present. For tea there were corn cakes, German pepper cookies dusted with bakers' sugar, Florentines made of almonds and Brazil nuts with preserved ginger instead of cherries. There were sesame crackers and a wax-encased goat's milk cheese so soft that it could be spread.

When I'd finished serving, Jules Frei summoned me to the footstool by his chair. Lena, Ambre's mother, whom he was "seeing," had told him how I came, then went, at Flores Negras. He asked what Ambre and I argued about, and even as I began my stiff little speech I knew that *he* knew no words were exchanged. I explained that I wasn't an exhibitionist or looking for sympathy, I didn't want to "go into all that." The poet pulled a sad face. "What is a tear behind the eye?" he asked. "What is it on the ground? The only place a tear has any force is between here——" he touched the corner of my eye "——and here," the angle of my jaw.

"I'm *angry*, not sad. Dad has a life he won't go back to. He's avoiding grief—he thinks his actions caused a death." I hesitated, then added, "His actions did cause a death or two. But what makes him imagine the same thing won't happen here? That it's okay to be here? He *pretends* he's making a commitment, being responsible—to Ambre's pregnancy, a pregnancy she's planned with half a dozen *other* candidates, or so I hear."

The poet regarded me, his glance idled across the speed-bump swellings under his eyes. "I'm poorly qualified to judge Ambre Guevara—Lena is rather hard on her, I think—so I'll let your accusations of entrapment go by. I don't believe your father is avoiding anything. He's resilient, and resilience sometimes looks like hardheartedness. He has engaged with the world." Frei broke off and waved his bitten pepper cookie. "Did you make these?"

I nodded.

"They're very good."

"It's your sister-in-law's recipe."

"You've mastered it."

I saw what he was getting at, that if I was mastering recipes, helping out, then I must approve of recovery, and engagement with life. Perhaps I made some sign of concession, for the poet went on to say, "Your father has turned over a new leaf—as they say." He said it in English—we were speaking English. "And, though I have heard the magnificently belligerent Commander Sola tell Ambre Guevara that she has your father 'wallowing in domesticity like a pig in its shit'—though what business is it of *his*—I can see that your father is cheerfully, from the inside out, from household to neighborhood and, one day, to nation, reconstructing himself as a good husband, loyal *compañero*, and productive citizen. And—" the poet leaned down to me, warm orbs of reflected light rising over the fleshy horizon of his lower lids "—because he sent you away from him you are doing something very similar here, with Bella. You are making friends, and joining a family."

"You'll make me cry," I said, dry-eyed.

He patted the four perfect peaks of a handkerchief in his breast pocket. "I'm equipped."

Then Bella's eldest brother said, "Uncle Jules, tell us about . . ." and they were off, about heroes, rousing speeches, night flights, a house after a raid, blood-soaked bread slices scattered on a kitchen floor. *In front of the children*—just like my real mother's family, talking the talk—as pitiless as the more savage psalms, their reminiscences hardening into sacred testimony. I heard only some of it. I was in and out from the kitchen, collecting and stacking dishes for Bella. I did hear about Don Ricardo himself—the devil—with pliers, or seen from a dark chamber, standing in the doorway, in yellow electric light, stripping off a blood-stained shirt, a junior officer ready and waiting with a clean one, still wrapped in blue tissue paper.

I remember hearing that.

It was around this time that Fernando finally went too far with Madlena. I was a ten-year-old know-nothing, and I'd noticed nothing. I believed what everyone believed, that Madlena and Fernando had some kind of truce, that he had conceded Tomás, her husband, as a piece of territory. Tomás and Madlena were comfortable together. Madlena had once been close to Fernando. From August '83 till mid-'84 Madlena and Fernando were confidants and rivals, locked in some configuration of Mutually Assured Destruction. By the end of '84 they had nearly ruined one another. She resigned from the government and married Tomás, Fernando was rehabilitated and succeeded to his chiefdom. They turned away from each other and became calmer people. Everyone said that they had given themselves and each other a good scare. They had disengaged—from their own and each other's wildness—and had domesticated their mutual fascination into a friendship. But Dad knew, and Ambre knew, and Juanita *may* have known, that Madlena was in love with Fernando.

He knew it.

He was restless, I registered that much.

One evening I was doing homework and Fernando was using his Dictaphone to answer letters. He put down the microphone and asked not me, but the air, "Why is life so small? Why is it so stifled?" Here he gestured at the little window by the door, which overlooked the external stairway and was covered by a pierced hardwood screen. No one was on the landing, there was nothing to be seen.

I said, as an experiment, "Yes, wouldn't a visitor be nice. Who would you like to see?"

He looked at me and raised an eyebrow. Fernando seemed to dislike locating the source of his discontent. Perhaps he thought it *coarse* to be unhappy about a relationship or a situation. His complaints were always against the universal and entrenched arrangements of society, but in howling at his neighbors he lifted his muzzle to the moon.

He went to the fridge for a beer, first scraping a handful of frost from the freezer and crushing it, dripping, in his fist. He shook his hand over the sink, opened the beer, and took a swig. "Maybe it's the city—perhaps it's city life that's small," he mused. "Everyone is so wary, careful not to drag their cuffs in their soup—whatever. They would all rather have a civil conversation than an emotional adventure." He looked at me and said to himself, "I'm talking to a ten-year-old."

My life might be small, but it had strange and enlarging perspectives, I thought. But I didn't say it. My heart was beating hard; I was afraid, not exactly for myself, but I wouldn't have dared then to feel afraid for Fernando.

"Being stifled by politeness *isn't* inevitable, like age, like my fucked wrist." He was working his wrist with the wet, cold hand. "Politeness isn't death and taxes," he added. "So why does everybody persist in being—choked, shallow. For instance, Don Marcos is trying to set the record for consecutive days sober; and Juanita won't admit it, but she's pulled in her head to impress Mr. Maturity Lequama 1987, Enrico García—I guess she thinks she can get him back. Even Ambre is behaving."

"You'd be behaving if you were in the third trimester."

"Carme defends her enemy."

"You should encourage me."

He shrugged. "I can't help you."

"You do help me. I've been happy here with you."

He stopped moving and stared at me, then said, "Thank you." His face couldn't do sincerity or insincerity, his stillness was only surprise, but his tone was affectionate.

I ventured further. "I think you are mixing up 'civilized' and 'shallow.' There must be people who are *deeply* and privately civilized."

He didn't respond to this, except to tell me we were going out to the hacienda tomorrow.

"But Dad won't be there, he said he was thinking of going to Leonarda. To Dr. Xavier's surgery."

Fernando was looking down now, at his wrist wrapped in the steaming stream from a hot tap. He muttered something. It took me a moment to decipher. He was going so I'd have to go with him. I could ride the horses. It wouldn't take more than a few hours, he said. He wanted to talk to Tomás.

Journal: National Archives Building, La Host, August 5, 2003

I ran the microfilm of May 1987 on through conversations in daily or twice-daily increments, till I had it all, a section of the Wall, full, before rain or whitewash made more space. I turned the focus knob and the texture became visible, the words legible.

Fernando, Madlena, Don Marcos had said that they had always had stains from marking pens leaking in their pockets. Fernando wrote small, but in indelible ink, even after things he'd written on the Wall were used against him in hearings of the Disciplinary Committee.

In one corner of my screen someone clarified something about Madlena and Juanita's stay in Colombia. Madlena was reported to have been a prisoner of her father Emilio—correctly. My father had, it said, "fallen into the hands of Don Ricardo Pastrez"—incorrectly. Underneath, Fernando had written in pencil—I recognized his hand—"Give me back my pen, Timo, you little limp slug."

Someone had written: "Francis Taylor sucks." Appended to this, in Fernando's pen but not his hand: "And swallows!—Sola, overwhelmed." Then my father, facetious: "One swallow does not a Sumter make."

Near the center of the page was a little prose poem. Ambre: "When I first thought: I love him, I wonder no one noticed. While they were all talking I'd died and died and died."

Then I found what I was after, the salient bit of graffiti. "Tomás Madlena Fernando. A nice young triple." Under that, Fernando: "Smart-assed so-and-so." Someone answered him: "Fernando is getting mild in his old age." Under this Madlena, in haste, and in English, "Lev hem alon!" Again the unknown hand, a comeback: "Everyone *is* leaving him alone by the look of things, eh Madlena? That's why he's hanging around you and your husband."

I don't know who wrote the first and last remarks. I don't know if this person had noticed what was happening, or if what they wrote somehow determined what *did* happen.

I'd just put my pencil and notebook back in my satchel and switched off the machine when an archivist arrived at my elbow. He dropped into a crouch to talk to me. He reminded me that we had been at high school together, then asked after Bella. I told him she had completed her doctorate at Berkeley and she had a contract already, from the university press, for a book on torture narratives.

Naturally, the archivist said, with her famous great-uncle famously saved from the sacked Los Muertos, comatose, then for months epileptic and incontinent—all his ordeal documented in his poems. The archivist told me he'd seen my sister Fidela in that film about the incestuous brother and sister. *Ada*. Was Fidela home again?

"Yes, my stepmother hates L.A., she's still rationing Fidela. When my sister turns eighteen she'll be off like a shot."

He picked up the cartridge from the side of the machine. "I see you've been looking at the Wall. Would you like to look at November '83 to February '84—we do have that too, you know."

I followed him back to his desk. Explained that while I didn't have time today to look at any more, I would like to know for how long the archive had had the earliest Democracy Wall. He found it for me. The cartridge was in a box, with its full cataloguing details and documentation, including a slip of letterhead paper. The letterhead read "From the office of Colonel Warren Munro"—in the Pentagon. "With my compliments," the note read, and was signed, "W. S. Munro, Colonel." The date was July 25, 1995—six weeks *after* my father disappeared in Washington, D.C.

"Did Munro give the tape to the archives?" I asked.

The archivist deciphered the cataloguing card. "No. It says here that Ambre Guevara handed it over to the archives in December 1995. Would you like to book the machine for tomorrow or the next day to take a look at it? We're closed for the celebrations."

Then he asked me if I'd like to have a drink with him.

Journal: Flores Negras, La Host, August 6, 2003

The following day I was fortunate, I had Fernando and Madlena together at Flores Negras. It took me some time to get them on to what I wanted them to talk about. I first had to hear a brief, heated argument on the subject of their daughter's schooling. Madlena wanted to enroll Rosa in a Taoscal Language Nest, and was floored when Fernando said no. Didn't Madlena remember what a bad time Fidela had had in *her* Language Nest? Madlena was astonished. When she collected herself sufficiently, she asked him why he had made such a big thing all those years ago, to her and Tomás, about the *twins* learning Taoscal, and now was being lax when it came to his own child? By mentioning Fidela's experience was he finally owning up to the innate *sexism* of all Taoscal institutions? (Madlena was in fine form, her head thrust forward and hair alive with static.) Fernando didn't explain himself, just said, weakly, that Rosa was still too young and not yet fully immunized, and they could think about it again in a week or two.

Ambre was in the kitchen making lunch and carrying on a sustained argument with Fidela about, I think, some script Fidela was considering. It wasn't the script's content Ambre disliked, but how many weeks' shooting it would take, weeks in which Ambre would be obliged to sit by the pool of some North American hotel. While Fidela and Ambre niggled away and Fernando regained his composure I somehow got Madlena talking about 1983. I believe she had been composing her speeches for National Day, and that year was at the top of her mind.

It was the most exciting period, in the most exciting place in recent history, she said. It was the best of times, the worst of times. Books by journalists who were there said so and, with less sentiment and more subterfuge, so did those memoirs, weirdly itemized and abstracted, of U.S. State Department "fixers." Only Don Marcos ever had the sense to say, "Who needs that kind of excitement?"

It wasn't just that the revolutionaries were young, Madlena said. What I had to understand was that they'd been fighting a war or had been in exile, then had come out of the jungle or the cellars of safe houses or flown in at night to captured airfields behind the advancing army of the FDR. They all converged—*history* converged—on La Host. And they found themselves on a stage. The Plaza—packed with soldiers, flags, fires in oil drums—was a stage. The press was watching—they all seemed to be blond, said Madlena, like that ratty Australian correspondent who photographed her first meeting with Fernando, which he wrote up as "Fearsome Indian Commander meets the Little Colonel with the Big Hair."

Fernando took over her story. He said yes, the Plaza was a stage, but there were stages in their *heads* too. The FDR's leader, Castonoles—whom the Contras killed with a car bomb in early '84—

asked Fernando to take some soldiers from Nuevo over to the Presidential Palace. They were to go in first and spring the booby traps.

There had been firefights in the palace, Fernando said, and there were bullet holes in the wood-paneled halls, rows of spiny splinters like raised hackles, and chipped stonework. But there was very little blood, and only a few bodies. And there were no power leads. What Fernando guessed was that some energy-efficient saboteur had unplugged everything, so that the FDR couldn't use it. The saboteurs hadn't smashed the telexes or phones—which would have taken more time—just removed their cords. The soldiers found melted piles of gasoline-soaked cords in the light wells.

The palace was Fernando's first big indoor space. His men were simply stunned by the size of the rooms. Tomás kept saying: "Oh, this is like La Host railway station," resolutely unimpressed; but he eventually started mocking himself: "Uh-huh—*another* railway station." They crept along the corridors sideways, guns pointed one way, heads the other. Most of the offices were furnished with stuff salvaged from Dewhurst Mining and the foreign-owned fruit companies, after those businesses had decamped in the 1950s. The rest of the decor was 1970s—carpet with brown-and-orange medallions laid in nineteenth-century rooms, rooms with mahogany panels, high ceilings, and marble fireplaces. It seemed wrong, even to Fernando, who knew nothing, it looked tin-pot and demoralized. The President, Nestor Galen, had lived and worked in the palace, but hadn't really run the country. Lequama's *real* rulers were in the shadows—like the shadowy open door to a room with its walls painted black, or shadows in alcoves where the phones sat, their cords cut. Shadows like black Pola Pastrez uniforms.

"If I'd been less impressionable," Fernando said, "less ripe for the *romance* of the place, I'd have seen that the shadows were booby traps. When those traps were finally sprung it became clear that the cords were incinerated not just to stop the FDR doing business with the world, but to stop the energy of a *spell* working its way out of the palace."

I had heard about the piles of melted cords. My father had written about it in his journal. I was familiar with the vaunted causes of the Black Room. For years I'd organized my data, like an epidemiologist dating and documenting the early cases of an epidemic. But listening to Fernando, I found my data reorganizing itself. I imagined those junior officers of the Security Forces—going to work on the walls of a room with wide-bristled brushes dipped in creosote the color of burned arabica coffee. I saw the imprisoned Taoscal sorcerer, an old man left alone in a chair ringed with splattered blood, his arms wreathed with slackened rope, and rope marks yellow in his dark flesh. I saw, by the light of a different hour, the empty, the *locked* room, then, at its opened door, the astonished faces of his torturers.

Although there had been decades of disappearances, of arrests without trial, this is the first in *my* chronicle of disappearances. This was the version I liked. In which the Black Room was the site of a magical escape. In which the old sorcerer magicked himself to safety. An alternative version said that the old man was sacrificed and that under a second coat of black creosote was a cartoon portal painted in his blood. There was a poem, an anonymous ditty, that went: "*Había un preso en el cuarto oscuro. Había un sacrificio en el cuarto oscuro. Había un banquete en el cuarto oscuro.*" Which is to say: "There was a prisoner in the Black Room. There was a sacrifice in the Black Room. There was a banquet in the Black Room." Either way, metaphorically, the old man went out and left a door open.

Madlena pulled a face at Fernando, a face intended to deflate, and made a deflating noise. Perhaps she thought he was exaggerating. "Everyone says those were wild times," she said. "But 'wild' wasn't really the word."

Madlena had a Northwestern Lequaman accent, from the Ambella, a region named for a string of mountain villages that gave the nation its national beverage, mountain wine. Madlena's accent was the Ambella's other great contribution to the culture, an accent that produced the most *disarming* delivery of English heard anywhere. The Northwest had a sizable population of English speakers, due— in three separate centuries—to an influx of ship-jumping pirates from the motley crews of Cartagena; early-nineteenth-century alternative lifestylers from a model society of the sort Coleridge had planned to settle in; and the employees of a vast British-owned sugar plantation. After nine years in the States I still had a touch of the Ambella.

Madlena said that for years the revolutionaries had thought only of overthrowing Galen's government. *Justicia y paz.* "I was in the army at fifteen. Carlos D'Escoto, the Sandinista who trained me, tried to make me look at the whole world—and at the revolutionary process. But he was so bossy and bigheaded. I didn't want to be *improved* and *improved.* I wanted to do my job, just to push and push till Galen's government was pushed over. There wasn't any *one* job for Carlos. He was a perpetual revolutionary."

"Anyway," she said, "we won." She said she could remember sitting on the beach in Vela Bay, watching her soldiers make a pile of captured weapons. Her second-in-command, Guido Hernández, came over and said that Castonoles wanted Madlena in La Host. The capital was captured and Castonoles wanted her to meet Pico Hermano, their undercover ally, a member of the old regime who had undertaken to capture the power station and airport. Madlena went straight to Castonoles at the TV station and found herself on camera, shaking hands with Don Marcos Pastrez—the sports-car-driving playboy son of Don Ricardo.

I said that I thought Ricardo was perversely pleased that Don Marcos had tricked him. "Better to father a conscientious traitor than a ninny and fop." I had a sudden distracting image of Ricardo as Don Diego's father in the Tyrone Power film *Mark of Zorro.*

Madlena and Fernando exchanged a look. I was telling them what Ricardo Pastrez felt, giving them insights into his inner life, reminding them of an association that, for the moment, they were choosing to politely ignore.

Madlena shrugged and said, "Oh, really?" Then she continued her account. "Then I went to the Plaza. Maria Godshalk pulled me up onto a platform, between two blazing oil drums, and called out to the crowd that here was El Dora—which was my code name. Then she shoved me at Fernando, who was standing to one side of the platform with his flunkies . . ."

"Bodyguards."

"Oh, *sí, bodyguards*—ten big belligerent Taoscal men."

And then—Madlena said—Fernando greeted her in this deep, *insinuating* tone. I watched Madlena blush as she said this and Fernando's smile, his self-satisfied relaxation. He put his hands behind his head and leaned back. All he'd ever submit to was homage.

But then he surprised me by saying, "I was embarrassed. I thought she was a little crazy. She stood there under my nose with her eyes popping."

Madlena said she hadn't very clear memories of the weeks after that night. Some gringo journalists interviewed her, and provoked her to say all sorts of stupid things. And there were meetings to organize a government. There *had* been a shadow government for years of course; FDR leaders—this imprisoned union official, that sacked newspaper editor, this exiled priest. Madlena had been out of the country often, lobbying for the cause, but she was nevertheless amazed to be made Minister of Foreign Affairs. "Someone decided Lequama needed some youthful figureheads, revolutionary heroes. That's why Don Marcos and I were nominated. Then there was Maria—a great soldier at twenty-five. And Fernando, the heir of the chief of the Taoscal, and commander of the force Galen's army had most feared. We were all chosen to sell the FDR to the world. We all spoke good English. We were exports, the *idea* of revolution."

"Glamorous," Fernando said. "Revolutionary types, an Amazon, a girl soldier, an indigene, and an idealistic defector from his class."

"All under thirty," Madlena said.

"You were under twenty, Madlena," Fernando reminded her, his tone caressing. They stared at each other, as though looking back with longing and pity on the people they'd been.

Madlena said, "We had won the battles but we thought *surely* there were people who could do the rest of it for us—the tidying up afterward. We knew that governing the country, rebuilding it, was the real work. But we felt unequal to it."

"We *were*," Fernando said. He hadn't even known how to try. He crashed. "I fought for the Taoscal. I wasn't able to think about nationhood, about national interests."

They were still at war—were at war till the Berlin Wall came

down, or there were military budget cuts during the Bush Administration—whatever it was that finally decided the Americans against
backing the Contras. "The Ministry of Armed Forces comprised the
heart of the FDR," Fernando said. "For years they had the biggest
voice. When Maria headed Armed Forces you could get a good long
hearing about health and welfare and education and Indian affairs—
but once she was gone—" he broke off. "How to explain. Sometimes, at plenary sessions, the Armed Forces types would have looks
on their faces like adults in a room full of children. We hadn't even
finished mopping up Galen's army and the Pola Pastrez before we
found ourselves fighting a defensive border war against Contras
with prefabricated airstrips and stacks of high-tech weapons surplus
from every fucking place. So they were right—Armed Forces was
right. Everything they asked of us was necessary, and reasonable."

The country had filled up with gringos looking for the latest
utopia, or a scoop, or to make a quick buck. Hustlers, fixers, spies,
men and women of the press, American malcontents from Alaska to
Panama. People were sleeping in the corridors of the Plaza Hotel.
There was a black market in Budweiser and bottled water. The city
was under siege by people keen to *support* the revolution. La Host
was like a tiny room, bursting with people and talk. There were
only two working telex machines left in the city—one in the García
bank and one in the Plaza Hotel. Nothing worked at the palace. But
Maria Godshalk found a *kitchen* that worked, and the other young
government members set up house around that kitchen. Maria went
to the markets, sent her supply sergeant out to forage, and she
cooked. She fed them all.

"If you came anywhere *near* her kitchen she'd run at you with
food," Fernando said.

Madlena cocked a thumb at him. "He'd be looming and Maria
would rush out of her kitchen with a light in her eyes, saying, 'You
look like a man who enjoys a good square meal!' She was so *civilized*.
People made pilgrimages to see Maria—they came to her for intercessions, as if she was a saint. For instance, there was an old man
who wanted to work in the cathedral gardens. Maria sent him off to
the Archbishop, one of those right-wing Catholic shits who sailed

through the revolution because of the protection of the Church and superstitious citizens. Maria wrote a polite note and said to the old man, 'If the Archbishop doesn't give you a job come back to me for another note and A BIG GUN!' "

They laughed. Fernando said, "Maria was straightforward, that was her style. Whereas Madlena was a real hard-on."

I quoted Madlena on the Wall: "*Americans out of Grenada! Don Marcos out of my way or I'll slap your face!*"

But, Fernando said, when her lover Rosa was killed, Maria resigned her Armed Forces portfolio. She said, "*I'm simply a soldier, I need to get to grips with the enemy.*" After that, whenever she was back in La Host Maria wouldn't come to see them, wouldn't go anywhere near her kitchen. She only wrote on the Wall. "Like your father in December '83. Maria became as ghostly as your father."

Madlena said, "She avoided us. She was so unhappy. Her little boy died of dehydration up in her village in the Ambella, and she didn't even make it to the funeral. She wrote that on the Wall." Madlena's eyes were huge. "Imagine reading that. What could we say? How could we help?"

"Do you remember his name?" Fernando asked Madlena. She said no and for a long moment they stared bleakly at each other. Then he went on. "Maria was being straight-up heartbroken. She didn't want us to answer her. That was the thing—we all kept writing unanswerable stuff on the Wall. We were all wildly incautious. These days e-mailphobes will tell you that our private communications can be read in transit—which is true. Imagine planning a coup or a terrible crime by unencrypted e-mail. We were like that when we wrote on the Wall. When Madlena and I quarreled it took place almost entirely on the Wall. We could see eye to eye only so long as we saw each other's eyes."

He'd talk for hours, Madlena told me. They'd hang out, she'd go through three packets of cigarettes, and he'd go through a crate of mountain wine. It was a wonder he didn't have a liver the size of a doorstep.

"I was having a futile affair with Don Marcos," said Fernando. "He worked all the time, I thought to avoid me, but after we broke up he was the same. The world is purgatory to Don Marcos, and work is prayer. I wouldn't sleep because—I told myself—I was waiting for Don Marcos. Madlena only ever slept during the day—she was afraid of the dark, and of the power failures at night."

Madlena nodded.

"We sat up all night, and she heard nothing but madness from me. I felt walled in, like fire locked in some kind of inflammable box. I let her so far into my life, but she acted like some poor lame horse way back in the field of my affections, filled with a sense of privilege, but mousily silent." He glanced at her. "I couldn't believe she'd turn on me. But she started on my bodyguards. On the Wall." He quoted: "*A bunch of boyish sexists who can't see past the bottles or cocks they were sucking.*"

Madlena put her hands against her cheeks, as if to hold her face together. She moaned. "I can't read that stuff."

"After a couple of days of character-blackening free-for-all the Disciplinary Committee gagged us. They put on a ban—no government members were to write on the Wall. It lasted only for the three weeks Madlena was in Syria."

Madlena told Fernando shut up.

"We both tried to resign," said Fernando.

"That's not true! You know it and I can prove it." Madlena was outraged. "After Brad Powers and Norton Lawrence were killed—"

"Disappeared," Fernando reminded her, and smiled at me. "No one found Lawrence's body."

"—Enrico García started bugging various rooms in the palace. He wasn't going to have palace security humiliated again. I've *read* the transcript of your meeting in Indian Affairs. You were grandstanding, saying, 'Either she goes or I do.' You claimed that my remarks were racist. You said that if I wasn't disciplined then you had to conclude that racism was as acceptable to *this* government as it had been to Nestor Galen's. You said you were going to resign, and your Taoscal deputy said *she'd* resign if you did, and the President suddenly saw the likelihood of a mass defection by the Taoscal. *I* did what I thought was the best thing for the FDR. I resigned. And you wrote me a letter saying: '*Come back, I don't want to be the craziest per-*

son in the government.' Then, two months later, you went to Don Ricardo."

Madlena had flushed; her neck and the tops of her breasts were mottled. Fernando had his look, a kind of condensed inexpressiveness, that told those who knew him well that he was annoyed.

Ambre appeared in the kitchen doorway to tell us that lunch was on the table and that we were to stop fighting and come and eat it. "All this happened twenty years ago. The soup's hot this minute." As I came toward her she put her hand on my shoulder. "Carlos tells me he's put in an extra big red chili for the little gringa. I think he's flirting, dear." Her eyes were big and liquid in their webs of dry wrinkles. Carlos and my sister Fidela rolled their eyes. Aureliano, Carlos's twin—once a wild headlong child whom, in a desperate moment of baby-sitting, I'd tied to a table leg, now a silent nineteen-year-old—shot me an intense, unreadable glance, then pulled out my chair for me.

"Oh, *Mama!*" Madlena was saying, her anger downgraded to irritation.

I said, "Nonsense. No one flirts with me. I'm a married woman." That shut them all up.

Over coffee I asked about Colonel Munro, and was looked at blankly. I reminded Ambre of her donation to the archives. Ambre's face softened and became animated. She said that the North American colonel had sent Ido the microfilm, but that it had arrived after Ido had disappeared in Washington, D.C. Fernando had phoned the North American colonel. They knew each other slightly, since Munro had been held hostage by the Taoscal in 1987. Munro was a major then.

Fernando said that apparently Colonel Munro had bumped into my father in the lobby of the Washington Grand Hyatt. Quite by chance.

My father was in Washington with Jules Frei in June 1995. The family had sent him to mind Jules, who had lost a lot of ground after Lena died. Several of my father's translations had made it into Frei's

Collected Poems, which was being published in New York. Jules asked my father to go with him on the little book tour his publishers had arranged and to a conference to which he'd been invited. The conference was on "Literary Perspectives for the Twenty-first Century," which sounded quite high-minded, but it was hosted by a foundation managed by—as it turned out—a right-wing Washington newspaper.

Fernando could see I was getting excited about this Colonel Munro, as an avenue of inquiry I hadn't explored. He reminded me that Fidela and he were still the last people to see Ido. "I managed to establish that Munro saw Ido the evening *before* we arrived to take charge of Jules."

Fidela, her face down toward her soup and spooning delicately, said, "I was the last one Dad spoke to."

Fernando nodded to acknowledge this, then went on. My father had phoned him in New York on the night of June 16 to say Jules was ill and depressed, and he thought Jules needed "the family."

"I was busy at the UN," Madlena said, "so Fernando went down to Washington by train the next morning. Fidela went with him because I was busy. Fidela was staying with us then. Why was she staying with us? Did she have auditions for something?"

"Yes. Something I had to pull out of when Dad disappeared," Fidela said, and shifted her plate to one side. The bread she'd toyed with till it was a heap of crumbs. She leaned into the table, into the talk, which she scarcely ever did. "I have to say this. I thought it was pretty weird that Dad called for help. I mean—it was *inconvenient*, and that didn't make any sense. Dad didn't inconvenience people. If Jules was ill, Dad was a doctor. And if Jules was depressed—well— since when was Dad ever out of his depth with unhappiness?"

Ambre was perplexed. Fernando narrowed his eyes at my sister, then began making excuses. "Ido made it sound as if our rushing down to Washington to help Jules was *natural*, a matter of course. Ido met us at a coffee kiosk in the main hall of the station to brief us about Jules's state of mind. If his *own* mind was on anything else it didn't show."

Fidela said that when she played Lucette in *Ada*, there was a scene she'd had to do, the scene shortly before Lucette jumps overboard. Rehearsing it, she'd realized that her father had given her a way into her character. "The shipboard bores come up to Lucette—they *sidle* up and *plump* down—and she turns to them with, Nabokov writes, '*her last, last, last free gift of staunch courtesy that was stronger than failure or death.*' " Fidela stopped speaking and looked around the table. "Am I upsetting anyone?"

"Yes!" we all said.

"I can never tell. Anyway—I was there when Dad filled Fernando in on Jules. And in hindsight it looked to me like *staunch courtesy*."

There was an uncomfortable silence. Fidela finally responded to it. "I'm not saying he killed himself."

"No. You're saying he *jumped ship*." Fernando was acid.

Fidela pursed her lips, looked dubious, and sat back in her chair. "We all give different words different weights." She was drawing on the tabletop with a fingertip. "We talk about a 'disappearance' or a 'desertion.' We ask was he taken or did he go?"

I realized that my sister was *writing* on the table. I said to her, "What's the big secret?"

She laughed. And I saw that she was only making a doodle—an invisible heart.

Fernando said that when he phoned Munro, the colonel told him that when they met in the lobby of the Grand Hyatt, he and Ido scarcely spoke. "He said your father did seem upset—but he'd imagined that was because he'd broken his camera. It was a good automatic Olympus, and its back gate was open and cracked, the film hanging out of it like a hernia. This was the evening before your father called us. I established that. The colonel consulted his diary for me. He'd given a speech at an awards banquet, held in the Hyatt, on the evening of the sixteenth. The evening your father called us. I remember this, Carme, because I examined everything as evidence."

There was a cry from the next room. Rosa was awake. Madlena went to her, stood above the Portacrib with her elbows cocked, fastening a faded yellow-and-white scarf around the thick sheaf of her long, frizzy hair. Rosa kicked, and I saw her pale, wrinkled soles.

Fernando went to the kettle. The twins were stacking dishes at the bench, but moved out of his way, as though they were all magnetized and he was surrounded by a force field of reversed polarity. They rolled off him without touching him. Fernando put the kettle on to boil, then decanted the hot water into a tumbler and put a bottle of formula in to warm.

Rosa had seen the bottle and was straining toward it, almost sliding out of her mother's arms. "Wait just a minute, darling," Madlena said. Stillness, then a detonation: Rosa began to howl. Madlena smirked and passed her to me. "Papa and Tía Carme will show you the garden."

Fernando tested the milk on the inside of his arm, gave it to his daughter, plugged her leaking noise. We went out with her, walked through the gap in the head-high hedge of agaves.

We found Enrico outside the García furniture factory, washing his truck. He turned down the pressure on his hose so that he could be heard. He wanted to know which parties Fernando was thinking of attending on National Day. The García women would be up at the cemetery till noon, changing the flowers in the family crypt, and he and Juanita had an invitation to Marguerite Millay's barbecue lunch. They would watch the fireworks in the Plaza, then would look in early on the party at Indian Affairs. "Before it melts down," Enrico said. Then to me, "I think a pretty young woman like you should keep well away from that filthy melee."

Fernando said he hadn't any plans past his official duties, but of course he was going to the Indian Affairs party—the only reliable annual filthy melee. "Carme will be with all the young people," Fernando added, as if passing sentence on me.

We walked on and Rosa wriggled around, swiveled like a gimbal joint, her mouth never parting from the teat, to wave at Enrico over her father's shoulder. We found some shade and stopped, Fernando rocking from foot to foot, his head bent to his daughter's face as her eyelids drooped a little. Then he looked at me. It was like being harpooned. I suppose he thought he needed to make that—demonstration—so that I wouldn't smile, not even for a second, at what he said next. "I thought I was irresistible," he said. "That was my main mistake regarding Don Ricardo. I imagined us in bed together. Imagined the same thing my friends in the FDR were imagining once I'd gone to him—the thing that most revolted them."

The baby let her head loll back against his crooked arm, her mouth parting from the bottle. She looked at him, then she hooked her small fingers over his lower lip and teeth, found a handhold on his face. He said to me, scarcely distinct, "I thought that that was how he'd like me to express my loyalty."

I changed the subject. I behaved like a coward—here he was speaking to me as an equal, as one compromised person to another, and my nerve failed me. I found myself talking about irresistibil-ity—talking about my father. How Dad *hadn't* thought he was. Ir-resistible. Fernando watched me with his nonexpression of great attention.

"Considering the power he had over people's imaginations, still he never thought he was irresistible," I said. "His friend Carlin had kept some mementos of Dad's youth—Carlin was Dad's guardian. Carlin showed me a book of memos Dad had made to himself about how to behave, all written the year after Carlin took Dad in. Dad had been something between feral child and street kid—like one of those foxes that forage in suburban backyards. Carlin described him as silent, sly, and hyper-alert. Carlin had to train Dad in the basics, like washing his hands and sleeping in a bed. Dad would get up out of bed and sleep on the floor. The bed was too soft, too unfamil-iar—Dad would wake up before the alarm and get back into bed so no one would catch him and think him ungrateful. Carlin said he got into the habit, before retiring himself, of going into Dad's room, picking him up, and putting him back in the bed. You have to imagine this undernourished thirteen-year-old. Anyway, one of the memos read: 'I'm funny-looking. Must remember to wear ordinary clothes.' "

"As I was saying," Fernando said, "I thought I was irresistible. Does this embarrass you, Carme?" He stared at me, pale-eyed, and his daughter began to pat his neck, already attuned to his moodi-ness, his latent mayhem, and doing what a girl should to soothe a man. He waited for me to take his cue, to finally make my own excuses. When I failed to speak he turned his shoulder to me, re-arranging his daughter so that she'd take her bottle again. He gave me another chance. "But of course you know what I discovered. What Ambre later also discovered and made more public."

I began to say something about Ricardo's very strict, religious mother, who had one day caught Ricardo and a cousin playing "doctors" and didn't explode but talked about it very calmly as a matter of poor hygiene. Then she took Ricardo to a doctor and had him circumcised, at twelve, then sent him off to live with some uncles who—I surmised—had abused him.

"You're *explaining* your husband's impotence."

"He's a celibate, Fernando. He managed—with difficulty—to father Don Marcos and Juanita, then gave it up. He doesn't try and shame himself. Why do you think Ambre was so disappointed when she failed to seduce him? She lamented that he was so handsome and composed and courtly and that it must be possible to *move* him. But I think his impotence is an extension of his composure."

Fernando gave me a slow smile. "Or rather, his composure is round and regular and has no hydraulic extensions."

I laughed. Fernando didn't.

"You *married* him, Carme. Ambre says you did it because your father left you and you felt unloved—you wanted to prove you were unlovable by making us all hate you. Madlena, on the other hand, thought you didn't want to be comforted, so you put yourself beyond the pale, and out of the reach of any of our efforts to comfort you."

I told Fernando that while those were two very good guesses, perhaps I had married Ricardo because, with Dad gone, I felt I needed the most powerful protector I could find. Ambre wasn't strong enough. I told Fernando that Ricardo had other ideas about why I'd chosen to go to him. "He thinks Dad was his salvation. He thinks I chose to continue Dad's good work."

Fernando turned his head toward the house. He'd caught a glimpse of Madlena through the spiny blades of the agaves. "Listen," he said, "I don't want to hear anyone else's opinions on your motivations—I want to know why you married him. *Married*, for God's sake, didn't just climb into bed with him and try sadly to stir him up."

"You're wasting your time with this little visualization, Fernando."

The agaves rustled and leaned together where Madlena was coming through—not because she was pushing them. I heard her yelp.

The hairs on my forearms were standing up; the air in my mouth tasted of metal. "Perhaps I fell in love with Ricardo when I first met him—when I was ten. Do you think it's possible for a ten-year-old to fall in love?"

"You're insulting me with this precious little 'perhaps.' Your father would have *said*. Or he would have lied." Fernando was disgusted.

"I'm not my father."

"No—you're not."

Journal: National Archives, La Host, August 7, 2003

The archivist pushed two tablets out of the sheet of Paracetamol and put them in my palm, wrapping my other hand around the glass of water. "I knew it was serious when you stopped laughing."

I took the pills, swigged water. "I'm finished."

He switched off the film reader.

My face felt sunburned. I found a tissue in my bag—wiped my watering eyes. I couldn't locate my chapstick; the bottom of my bag seemed to be full of sugar and peanut skins—burst bags of airline food I'd squirreled away between Boston and Bogotá. My fingernails were full of grit.

The archivist said he used the oil in his ears to soothe his lips—a trick his mother taught him. He demonstrated and I copied him.

"I'm not crying," I said. "My eyes hurt."

"Any world-shattering discoveries?"

I told him that my father was rather more awkward than I remembered him being. "Insecure. A bit of a dickhead."

The archivist pulled up a chair, folded his arms on its back, and watched me. I told him that what really surprised me was that Ambre had taken him on. "Missed him—was pleased when she found him, took him into her home and her bed. He *lectured* her." I asked the archivist whether he could do me a very big favor. Could he find out who had looked at the microfilm since it arrived?

We went to his workstation and performed a search. A list came up. He asked me if I saw any significant names. Most were students of history. I saw that Bella had been here before me, which was no surprise.

"Commander Sola," the archivist said. He tapped the screen. "Before anyone else, but then he would have known about the film as soon as your stepmother took delivery."

I asked, "If you were to read on the Wall 'Ricardo Pastrez ate the chief of the Taoscal,' what would you make of it?"

"Sexual innuendo," he said. "When Sola went to join Señor Pastrez and the Contras in April of '84 it was rumored that there was some kind of sexual seduction as well the political."

"But what if it was written in November '83, before Fernando went to join Ricardo. Before Fernando *was* chief?"

"Was it?" The archivist ignited with curiosity. "Was there anything more?"

"About that, no. But if you were looking for conspiracies to commit murder, you'd have to arrest everyone. With Brad Powers, Norton Lawrence, Pablito Masolan, so many people are implicated that it's like *Murder on the Orient Express*—everyone did it."

We mused. Then I noticed that because I'd been staring into his eyes, looking for the light of understanding as *I* tried to understand, he'd begun to flush.

"I have to go," I said.

Memoir: Lequama, early 1988

On a Saturday in Ambre's third trimester Fernando and I went, as usual, to the hacienda—to find neither my father nor Ambre present. Apparently, on Friday afternoon Dad had caught a ride with some soldiers up to Leonarda and the emergency surgical station. He had decided to volunteer his weekends—to hurry along the Armed Forces manpower office. Without my father to drive her, Ambre had declined Madlena's usual invitation to lunch.

Later, Ambre tended to talk about that day along the lines of "when the cat's away . . . ," as though her presence till then had somehow held things in check. This was Ambre's revised view of herself, a view she had thought it best to develop in middle age, when it no longer seemed *seemly* being a petty criminal, a mule for drug smugglers, an existential adventurer, an adept sorcerer. From her forty-third birthday, when Ambre became a propertied woman, she began to present herself as a practical person often required to respond to the needs of a group of wild, childish younger adults. In my opinion Ambre chose to take my father as her lover in part because doing so prevented her further evolution into everyone's *mother*.

That afternoon I was quite satisfied with the whole Saturday lunch arrangement. Ambre was absent, and Madlena, Tomás, and Fernando were all in a lively mood. They talked and joked over their beers and Tomás's fine paella. The twins crawled up and down the veranda by the table, pushing their wooden horses on wheels and making engine noises. There was a warmth between the adults that made the kids easy and me happy. Juanita was there for lunch—as I recall—but left her daughter in Madlena's care and walked out to the road to wave down the 1:30 bus. She had a round of music lessons in La Host that afternoon.

The three remaining adults grew quieter over coffee. I saw Madlena's foreman come to stand in the stable doorway, tilt his hat, and unkink his back—and I excused myself and went out to him. He saddled up one of the mares and let me into the big corral so I could put her through her paces. I held the reins tight, thrusting thumbs into the hard crown of hair where her neck joined her back, and for the next hour softly spoke into her swiveling, curious ears the language I've now all but forgotten.

On my umpteenth turn back toward the house I saw Madlena

running—the erect, desperate sprint of someone who knows how to run. But she wasn't going anywhere. When she came to the rail of the corral she slowed a fraction, but still slammed into it, and hung there, the rail under her armpits, limp and crying. I kicked the horse into a trot and hurried over to her, but was too frightened to dismount when I got there. She wasn't aware of me anyway, her eyes were shut fast and she was shaking her head, slowly, like someone making a careful comparison between two very similar things lying side by side. I thought of the twins and looked at the house—found them, in the black oblong of the doorway, arms around one another. Fernando and Tomás were standing too, face-to-face, either side of the table. There was a fallen chair. Tomás seemed distressed. Fernando looked uncharacteristically awkward, his chin up and shoulders back as bold as ever, but he was tugging at the lobe of one ear, his thick hair fountaining behind his hand as though his hand had a static charge.

"No," Madlena moaned. "I've been so careful to *paper over* all that."

I asked her what was wrong. She looked at me squinting, as if I was something indecipherable—then she bolted across the yard.

Tomás tried to intercept her. He jumped over the veranda rail and ran calling her name, but she reached Fernando's "new" car, hauled herself through the window of its soldered-shut driver's door, and turned the keys. I heard a shouted sentence before the engine noise overwhelmed her voice. She yelled that Tomás could do whatever he liked, and then she drove off.

Fernando came out to Tomás, who lost his temper. Fernando froze with surprise as Tomás turned on him. Tomás said that Fernando thought he could ask for whatever suited *him*. As if Madlena and he were a job lot!

Fernando said he didn't have to listen to this. Tomás grabbed at Fernando's arm, caught the edge of a sleeve as it was pulled away— a cuff button flashed as it fell. "What *do* you want if you don't want to listen?" Tomás yelled. "What do you think you're asking for?"

Fernando strode off—toward the house at first, then changing direction and heading straight out to the road, missing the gate, the driveway with its culvert, and jumping the dry drainage ditch instead.

"We're happy!" Tomás shouted after him. "You can't just *ask* to be included in other people's happiness." He subsided and I barely caught his mutter: "Fine. Don't take a hat. Go fry your brains, see if I care!"

Tomás didn't look at me; he went inside and the twins pursued him, Carlos piping questions and Aureliano making loud yapping sounds. My horse stamped. I turned her into the dark path her own hooves had made and began another circuit. I could hear the foreman's radio; a moment later I caught sight of him through the window of his rooms behind the stable. He was tilting a bottle of the local cloudy corn liquor into his coffee. It was his day off and I wouldn't disturb him.

Ten minutes later I turned again from the far side of the corral to see Tomás driving away, the twins strapped in their quilt-covered seats.

I rode my horse back into the shadowy stables, unsaddled her, rubbed her down, gave her water, and led her into her stall.

I went back up to the hacienda to find the house door closed and locked. The ground-level windows were covered with a curved, ornate iron grill, but open, so that I was able to look in at the telephone, there on the mahogany sideboard in the living room, but I couldn't get in to make a call. There were birds pecking the crumbs on the lunch table, one dipping its beak into the yellow oil pooled in the butter dish.

I sat on the steps.

Perhaps an hour passed, and I resolved to disturb the foreman. Saturday or not, he could drive me back to La Host.

I found him on his back on the bed, feet still on the floor. The liquor bottle was empty and his snore ominously loud and loose. I couldn't wake him, so I helped myself to bread, his acacia honey, and some of the coffee, still hot on his wood range. And then went back to my post on the steps.

As I waited, looking out on the white dust of the yard, my adult life began to take shape before my eyes. I would live alone. I would wear the key to my house on a chain around my neck. I would have my own car and would always carry its keys in my pocket. No one would ever tell me it was time to go, make me put the book down before the end of a chapter. I would never wait on someone or be left behind.

Sometime later, when the house shadow was long and outlined in gold, I began to feel watched. I turned to see a face peering at me from between the bars on the nearest window. Juanita's daughter, Xenia, hadn't recognized me with my head turned, but she smiled and called out "May" as I came up the steps. "May, where's 'Nia's Mama?" she inquired, her wet forefingers still raised to her wet mouth and her grubby blanket pressed to the side of her face.

"Mama will be home soon," I said to her, and she toddled contentedly away, her diaper a darkened pouch hanging between her knees. She switched the TV on and lay in front of it, half on and half wrapped in the white cotton blanket. I turned my back on her and sat down again.

A long time after that, when the house shadow turned blue and that shadow's membrane had collapsed, its shade flooding out in a dilute form across the yard, I heard a truck on the road slow near the gate, and looked up to see my father jump down from its back. The truck idled while Dad looked at the dark house. I got up and he saw me, waved to the soldiers in the truck and came on. The truck switched its headlamps on and drove on toward La Host.

As he came up Dad said, "I thought I could detect TV light."

That was Xenia, I explained. She was locked inside and she and I were alone, our caregivers having had some emotional crisis that made them all take off. "Xenia was asleep in her mother's bed, so Tomás forgot her."

"Oh for Christ's sake!" Dad went around me and peered in at Xenia, sucking her fingers patiently in front the television. Then he went to the door, placed his fingertips lightly on the latch and looked momentarily abstracted. I heard the lock unlocking. Dad went in, switched on the light, and immediately put me to work mixing formula for Xenia while he changed her diaper.

Five minutes later, as the little girl was sitting up in her high chair with mashed banana and warm formula in her training cup, we heard the bus from La Host stop at the gate. Juanita climbed down from it clutching her satchelful of sheet music. She came in, was pleased to see us all, kissed her daughter, got herself a handful of crackers, then went to run Xenia's bath. She did ask where everyone else was. Dad said they'd gone out, but didn't explain that he'd only just arrived or tell any tales on Tomás. Juanita said, rather helplessly, that she supposed she could make us some dinner if one of us would watch Xenia in her bath, and Dad said no, he and I would go out to the road and catch a ride into town. Juanita was very tired—I could see that—and was slowed by it. Also, she was being misled by my father's vague and casual manner.

She stood frowning at us, a bit baffled, then said, all right, she supposed Dad must be keen to get home to Ambre. "Take some fruit, though," she said to me. "You look hungry." Then to him, "Are you sure you should be hurrying Carme off? She looks worn out."

He made his usual soft noncommittal noise and took my hand, led me from the house, and walked me out to the road. On the way he asked, "What happened?"

"Fernando did something that upset Madlena. I was out in the corral."

Dad said, after just a beat of my silence, "Describe what happened."

"Madlena was crying. She ran to the fence. Then she got in Fernando's car and drove away. Fernando walked—Oh, I don't know!—he just took off walking. And then Tomás went away later in his car with the twins." I shut my mouth.

We had reached the road. It was empty in either direction, its rutted route fading into two fine parallel brushstrokes only a little way from where we stood. The only light was in the house, the only movement a horse in the corral, a warm shadow in the thick darkness. I could see my father's face though.

"Is that the best you can do?" he asked.

"I'm not involving myself," I said.

He stayed still, face turned down to me for some time, till I felt he could see me better than I could see him. He said, "Involvement is a bit strong perhaps, for you." He sounded cold and lofty, and a little immature.

We didn't talk. We both sulked till he relented, sighed, picked me up and held me, my arms around his neck and legs around his waist.

By the time a car came he'd decided I was asleep. It suited me to pretend. He knew the woman, she was pleased to see him, eager to make me comfortable in the back. Dad laid me down and they covered me with a perfumed, satin-lined, wool coat. Dad got in the front with her and we drove off.

She told him that she'd been visiting a colleague. Actually she was seeing someone herself. It didn't sound to me as though she was talking about a relationship. "Partly a professional debriefing," she explained. "But of course a therapist can never assume they are themselves—uh—*finished*."

My father was, I supposed, politely silent.

The woman went on. "It is my belief that it wasn't your own decision to terminate your therapy. You were influenced in that decision, or it was decided for you. Forgive me—*querido*—but do you think Señora Guevara is at all interested in who you really are?"

"Possibly not," my father said. "It doesn't matter."

The car slowed to a crawl.

"Ambre has influenced you to become this obliging and dutiful 'husband.' I've seen you following her though the market, carrying her bags."

"Oh come on, Aramantha! She's hugely pregnant and I shouldn't carry her bags?"

"You've constructed a new personality, *querido*. A bag-carrying personality. A drudge. It is a refuge *you* have chosen but that *she's* shaping to suit herself."

"You're wrong, Aramantha."

"You're not *well, mi hermoso*."

My father said, oddly polite and timid, that he was afraid to say it, but she had *misdiagnosed* him. Yes, his amnesia had been in part post-traumatic and yes, perhaps he'd been in a "disassociative state," but—

—then he told the story of his childhood. He told it in a new way, as if he'd found himself equipped with a whole new language. As usual he gave no pedigree or date and place of birth—but he'd apparently found some answers to what had been lifelong mysteries. Answers, and an argument. He'd been misdiagnosed.

"I toilet-trained early because I hated to be touched," he said. "And I suppose I used to score well in tests of manual dexterity because I was buttoning my own clothes even as a tot. And I walked, climbed, reached for things, wasn't bothered by locks. I remember that. And I remember that as soon as I understood what people were saying, as soon as words gained meaningful content beyond instructions and the names of objects—'pick up your spoon'—I began to scramble the speech I heard. I wouldn't look anyone in the eye. Even now I can only recall their clothes, their *hands* weren't sufficiently impersonal. I was my own encryption machine, and there came a day when, surrounded by talk, all I heard was noise—talk had turned to nonsense. The hugs they offered me were horrible to me and, touched in too many places, I'd shut down.

"When I was barely big enough, I ran away. I lived wild. I could deal with the streets, I couldn't deal with acculturation. So that later, when I was a teenager living with Carlin—the man who adopted me—and I was having trouble shedding my defenses, the psychologist I was seeing listened to my story and found my few records and decided in the light of both that I'd had a developmental disorder that had relented or 'reached equilibrium' as I grew. Some form of autism, he said. I *had* had an autistic's love of systems. I told my psychologist about how I'd begun to understand signage—shop fronts and billboards and dropped newspapers—how at times the clouds would seem to try to form words, a mirror writing I'd rush down to the dawn river to read. My poor brain, forced to invent information it was adapted to learn and wasn't getting. Because, you see, if I'd listened to people—to the world—I'd have ended up like some tea-party chimp, unable to live with the rest of my zoo fellows.

"My psychologist listened to all this and said that like many autistic children, I had reported improper perceptions, almost schizophrenic, of the size and shape of my extremities. I'd said that my hands seemed not to end where they appeared to. I'd told him that I could put my hands on a locked lock, for instance, and feel muscles moving, or sap flowing, or some indescribable vitality there at work—like fingers beyond my visible finger's ends, *fingering* inside the lock, moving solid metal without even feeling it as metal or solidity. I only discussed these sensations with my psychologist to try to show how poorly equipped I was to explain how I felt about my body having suddenly *condensed* itself completely within my thirteen-year-old skin—a gas turned liquid—and how I now needed that skin touched, needed touch like a mapmaker to map me, hard, real hands. I trustingly told my psychologist all this, and he reported to Carlin. He said that it appeared that my developmental disorder more or less resolved itself at puberty—it was one of those mysterious things. I'd always be a little out of step though, and must be guided vigilantly to respond to people in socially acceptable ways.

"Carlin got on my case, gentle, like a good parent. And I forgot how it felt to resist everything human for the sake of my own survival. I forgot the strange immanence in my body, forgot how to open locked doors. Between them, Carlin and my psychologist made a *myth* of me, where my disorder was on one end of a scale weighed against my 'genius'—the point of pivot was what Carlin called my 'grit' and my psychologist characterized as 'shrewdness.' For, you see, I'd lived wild, but when it was too cold I'd turned up at child welfare, or at outpatients when the itchy rash on my neck and armpits and in my groin had begun to ooze pus and bleed. I was too *shrewd* to reject the world completely. My psychologist wrote in his notes that, at thirteen, my poor deceived brain had finally begun to change its mind. That when I'd been caught leaving Carlin's kitchen after raiding the fridge, and Carlin appeared waving a shoe and shouted, 'Hey, you!' I heard not nonsense, but 'Hey, you,' and decided to stop to hear more. The psychologist said my stopping then, my 'giving myself up,' was due to the coincidence of Carlin's firm kindness and my emergence from childhood autism."

There was a long pause. Aramantha Visitation preserved a silence as inviting as a taut, white-sheeted bed.

My father sighed. "But *this* is what happened. I saw Carlin standing there looking inquisitive and trying to look indignant and brandishing his shoe, and I decided to join the human race."

"Did you say that to your psychologist? Or was he a psychotherapist?"

"He was a developmental psychologist. No, I didn't say it—I didn't think that then. He had horribly offended me, saying what he did about my feelings about my body. He was rewarded for his insights—which is to say I seduced him. Would that be countertransference?" I heard my father shift, make some abrupt violent gesture perhaps. "But that's beside the point. It *wasn't* autism. What happened to me as a small child was this: when all little humans are meant to be learning language—as their Chomskyan 'deep structures' dictate—*I* was supposed to be learning something else. I refused to accept the data, because it was the wrong data for my program.

"I wouldn't have thought of any of this if it wasn't for Anton Xavier's blood test. I'm revising my past in the light of his blood test."

Aramantha was puzzled.

I heard my father move, slide across the seat. I heard Aramantha Visitation draw one sharp gasping breath. Then she said, faintly muffled, "Your heart is pounding. Is this your way of trying to calm yourself?" Then, "Please, oh, I love your hands. I love to feel them!"

"I was thwarted in my growth," my father said, sounding quite calm. "But I'm not done growing yet." He laughed, seeing the possibility of a double meaning. "Calm me," he said, which sounded weirdly like my name. Then it was my name. He reminded Aramantha that I was asleep in the back, and they got out of the car. She made a moan like a whimper. I heard the whisper of cloth, footfalls receding, a laugh like a bark.

A formal decision was made to receive me back into the household at Flores Negras. My father had carried me into the house late that

Saturday night, and I was put to sleep in his narrow bed under the roof tiles. The following morning, while I sat on the veranda, dipping cinnamon bread in milky coffee, Ambre and Dad strolled out to a patch of turned earth that looked like an open grave, and stood with the sun shining hot on their black crowns, discussing me. Ambre talked while looking at the ground, or over his shoulder, or at her own hands, and he watched her with an expression so attentive and expectant that I began to think I'd imagined my moments alone, dozing in the back of Aramantha Visistation's car, while, some way off, two shadows breathed and whispered warmly into each other. Dad attended on Ambre till she finally came to a close and looked at him, her eyes wide and frightened. He gave her a tender smile—then said some things that made her blush and soften. They came back to the house, his hand in the small of her back, and he helped her as she lowered herself into the wicker chair beside me. He went indoors.

I was told that it was time for me to come back. Ambre had taken me on, at first, in sympathy but without understanding the adjustments I was going to have to make, or how great a change it would all be for me. She had only thought to give me a safe home with my father. She said I must realize now that it had been better for me to live somewhere else, to see that my original difficulties hadn't had to do with life at Flores Negras but with life in Lequama, in this whole new place. My father had told her I was doing very well at school, and had made at least one fast friendship. "And I find that reassuring, Carme. You must know now that I love your father. You must be able to see our attachment. Up until now I have had a very patchy life, and have often been treated badly by men. Now at last this man comes to me, so kind and thoughtful and handsome, a man who makes me feel beautiful and worthy, and whom I know I am helping to happiness. We have both led difficult lives, and now we deserve some peace."

Ambre's voice was low and leaden, and she kept her eyes on me as she spoke. "Can you be kind to us?" she said. Then, "No. Don't answer that. I don't want you to think I'm asking you to promise anything. I'm taking you back into my house and I hope you'll be a little easier, as we need you to be, but I am not giving you any conditions.

We'll see how we do. Your father says he needs you with him—so you must come to live here."

In the siesta hour, between 1:00 and 2:00, when all the shops and offices closed and everyone either went out or home for lunch, and we guessed Fernando might be back from Indian Affairs, Dad and I were dispatched to fetch my clothes.

"I'd rather not take her," my father complained to Ambre as he was kneeling on the steps tying my shoelaces.

"Carme will know where everything is, and I want nothing left behind."

"But we can easily go back for anything we forget."

"I don't want any of us going back there."

"Uh-huh," Dad said.

From her look of satisfaction I knew Ambre hadn't worked out yet that Dad's "uh-huh" was almost always a signal of dissent, very mild, because it didn't often matter to him that his opinions were at variance with someone else's.

"Can't she do that for herself?" Ambre said, about the laces.

"Yes. But she's gone all droopy and passive this morning. Carme's version of compliance." He gave me a quick, shrewd, amused look.

"What's yours?" I said.

He got up, took my hand and pulled me to my feet, and gave a casual one-shouldered shrug. Then he led me out the gate. As we went along I told him that I thought his version of total compliance was to let people impose on him, lean a little too hard, then *fall in* after their imposition.

Fernando seemed determined not to move out of the doorway and I wondered what he was hiding. Then I saw my father lever him aside with his elbow, and Fernando stoop and inhale deeply as Dad passed under his nose. My father was speaking as he came in. He crossed the living room and vanished into the bedroom. His voice came to us regardless—he had a way with it—it carried, not sharp, but insinuating and many-shaded. "I'm under strict instructions to, if necessary, move the furniture to make sure I get every little thing of

Carme's, so that no one from our house will have any excuse to come back to yours. You're not to be provided with passports like socks or sparkle clips which you might feel obliged to return. Ambre isn't just determined to ostracize you, but to act as if she thinks you're so diabolical that you might decide to work magic on us, using Carme's his-pants-for-her." Drawers were opened in the bedroom and plastic bags rustled.

Fernando put out his hand to me. I went to him and took it. It was rough, dry, and warm. He bent to pick me up and I told him that I didn't need to be held.

"Yes, yes—your sorrows are always more cerebral," he said. "But I want to hold you." He pulled me close and said quietly in my ear that he was sorry he'd forgotten me.

Dad emerged with my clothes, glanced at us, and began to gather together my scattered schoolbooks. He continued to talk. "When Carme and I got home late last night the ground in the front yard was hiccuping and sobbing. I put Carme to bed and went to talk to Madlena, who was lying in an earth coffin in the front yard. I got the story from her."

"How is she?" Fernando seemed concerned, but embarrassed.

"She says you did the one thing you must have known you shouldn't do. You and she had a civil friendship, and that was best for everyone, and now you've ruined it." Dad squatted to reorganize a bag. He wasn't looking at Fernando any longer as he went from giving Madlena's opinions on the situation to his own on Fernando's behavior. "I gather you offered to have an affair with both of them— a compromise was this?—so that you wouldn't break them up."

"You are a prig, after all," Fernando said. "Squeamish about what I guess you'd call—in your British way—an irregular arrangement."

Dad finished what he was doing and stood wiping his hands on his pants legs. "Fernando, saying 'I think we should form a threesome' isn't a declaration of love."

"I don't make declarations," Fernando said. "Of course, *you're* promiscuous—you love this one and that one, the living and the dead."

Dad flushed.

Fernando put me down. I hovered beside him a moment, my head inclined against his midriff, breathing the below-sea-level, hot, enriched air I often imagined surrounded him. Then I went to help my father pack my things.

"Madlena can't believe you love her," Dad said. "And Tomás deserves better than this tepid interference."

Fernando said that he gathered none of this came from Ambre. And Dad told him that Ambre wanted his head on a stick. "Ambre is removing Carme so you'll know that she thinks you are an irresponsible and immoral man."

I said, "And here I was thinking I was being welcomed into her family."

They both frowned at me. Then Fernando asked whether Dad wasn't just being tidy-minded. "Ambre and Ido, Fernando and Madlena, and perhaps another lease on Juanita and Enrico. How far does your tidy-mindedness run? Have you finished screwing La Visistation?"

"Yes," Dad said, lying without effort.

". . . or thinking about what's-his-name, the murdered lover?" Fernando went on in his snide lecturing tone, well past the point where he should never have ventured.

My father grew perceptibly more beautiful as his rage began to show—a slow radiation. When Fernando was quiet again Dad said, "You have *all* already shown me that you don't want my past to count. If I do say anything about Carlin or Dev, whenever I'm brave enough, or when my forbidden terms of reference foam up, solid, against the back of my tongue and I have to talk or choke. In the dark—say—when I can't see Ambre's face, I might stumble into an explanation that includes them: Carlin and Dev. I'm never unprovoked, for she'll have said wistfully something like 'I wish you weren't so unhappy, Ido.' And so I try to explain why my unhappiness might be *reasonable*. And she lies there, silent. And her silence says: 'What am I to do with that?' So, since you won't trouble yourself to use Dev's name, don't talk about him at all."

Dad picked up my bags and opened the door. He pushed me out onto the landing—he wasn't rough or impatient—he just wanted me out of the house and he wouldn't take his eyes off Fernando. Once we were out the door Dad turned back to Fernando and said that he could, of course, see why Fernando would want his proposal to Madlena and Tomás to look like bargaining, rather than a declaration. It would be clear, then, to all onlookers that Fernando was playing, and that there were stakes, and that his *luck* was involved. Dad said, "Everyone will know that you're staking your rare, magnificent self—at long odds—against sense, and social outrage. And everyone will know—chief of the Taoscal—what a show of *will* it is, to trust to luck." Dad slammed the door and hustled me ahead of him down the stairs.

Journal: La Host, morning, National Day, August 8, 2003

We were up early. Like Easter, National Day was a day to remember the dead. I drove Ambre and Fidela around the flank of the cooling hill that rose behind our street, around and up into the morning sun. I parked at the end of a long line of cars and we walked to the cemetery gates, where the usual road—red clay corrugated by runoff—gave way to paths of pinkish gravel. Fidela and I carried two potted plants, Ambre a bucket and scrubbing brush.

Around many graves families were at work. They detached and wound up skeins of vine from the stones. They freed old memorials of silk flowers in pots, bleached plastic flowers in bell jars, and glossy wreaths of glazed ceramic roses, once white and red, now faded to bone and mauve. On the cemetery's second terrace we went past the group of García females, at work around a marble tomb with the approximate dimensions of a bus shelter. Two of the women were scrubbing black mildew from the "García" legend with ammonia and toothbrushes. We greeted them, then went up one level. The gravel near Lena's grave was full of the fibrous pits of palm nuts, in various stages, ripe to rotten to fleshless. Our feet made a paste of the fresh windfalls and a sweet scent came up around us.

Lena's narrow grave lay beside Jules's plainer but more commodious one. Lena's grave was, in fact, within the Frei family plot. Jules had instructed his family to set him and his lover aside, and the graves were enclosed together within a low iron fence. Directly on the other side of the fence were the poet's first and second wives, top to tail in the same grave (they were sisters).

When Lena came back to Lequama in 1987 and decided to settle, one of her first purchases—after a new queen-sized bed, quilt, pillows, valence, bolsters, the equipment of a very feminine nest—was her own headstone. She had kept it at Flores Negras, propped behind the door to her room, a thick marble lozenge about the size of a welcome mat and decorated with a heart, flame fountaining out of its cleft top and wearing a bandolier of fruiting grapevine. Only her name was inscribed on the stone—Madlena Guevara—no date or place of birth; these remained a strict secret. When the headstone was put on her grave, Jules omitted also the date of her death for, he said, reasons of symmetry. His own grave had no headstone, was just sealed, level, by a sheet of marble, crystalline white but barely visible under a compost of tributes. There were new flowers heaped on the old; there were yellow-and-white scarves knotted on the iron fence; there were photos, postcards, notes on yellow Post-its, and keys.

I filled Ambre's bucket at the nearest tap. Fidela and Ambre stepped over the fence and set to work with the scrubbing brush on Lena's headstone. I hesitated, then started sorting out Jules's grave.

"There's a trailer load here," Fidela complained. "And we haven't got a trailer." Then, "Never mind, here they are anyway."

And they were—the Freis—Bella, who had told me she'd be unable to come back to Lequama for National Day, her father, her oldest brother, several cousins, and an assortment of nieces and nephews. Bella saw me, thrust the armload of orchids she was carrying at her brother, and ran down the path. I jumped the fence and we hugged.

She'd got in at eight last night, she said. "It's still the same drill—smack!—your suitcase goes on the tarmac beside the trolley and one baggage handler curses the other one and they pick it up and throw it on again, and it falls off the other side—crash! And so on, like a comedy. I rang you from the airport and Ambre said you were deep in conversation with Fernando Sola and wouldn't want to be disturbed."

Ambre overheard and defended herself. "I meant to tell you Bella was here, dear, but I went up to bed before you. I believe I told Fidela to tell you."

"Not me!" Fidela said, busy, her back turned.

"Hello Fidela," Bella said.

"*Sí, sí,*" said Fidela.

Bella's brother had a wheelbarrow. He took an armload of dried foliage from Ambre and packed it down. On Lena's grave Fidela had uncovered the marble book, Lena's and Jules's pictures on its facing pages. His portrait was the dark-haired Jules, *before* Los Muertos, a man none of us had really known. She was pictured at seventy, a mother-of-pearl comb in her glassy white hair, and wearing her usual sunny self-satisfied expression.

Ambre and Bella's cousins had excavated "Jules Frei, poet, *compañero*, great Lequaman," and his dates, "1919–1998." The nieces and nephews climbed the fence and knelt to try to pick out whole the moss that filled each letter. One girl extracted a complete *s*, and carried it about, wet, on the pale inside of her arm. She showed it to two gringo tourists, who had stopped to fill their drink bottles at the tap. "Is that a birthmark," one said, "or a big mossy mole?" He looked at me, as if to share the joke, and blushed. He was one of those thin-skinned white blonds whose consciousness shows in their flesh like red mercury rising behind glass.

The girl showed the gringos where she'd got her *s*. She pointed out the tiny red mites taking shelter in the shade of each deeply carved letter. The white-blond gringo said that where he came from, red mites were called "money spiders." She asked where, and he said, "New Zealand."

Again he glanced at me, looking for attention or approval.

I turned my back and read aloud the legend under Jules's name and dates: "The years like great black oxen tread the world."

Bella said that people thought the lines referred to how, in his years of exile, her great-uncle carried his homeland—his birth-place—with him. The people thought the "black oxen" referred to the street where he was born, the Avenida Bueyes Negros. Actually, it was a line from a Yeats play, *The Countess Cathleen*. "Jules loved Yeats. The whole quote appeared in his funeral service—but Papa and the aunts wouldn't put all of it on his grave. You see, in the play, when the Countess dies her old nurse says to an angel: '*Tell them who walk upon the floor of peace, that I would die and go to her I love; the years like great black oxen tread the world, and God the herdsman goads them on behind, and I am broken by their passing feet.*' " Bella sighed.

Bella's father said, "He was happiest with Lena. So that was fine at the funeral. Appropriate. But not here—not the whole thing—that would be a slight on his wives." He added, "Besides, what the people think, about his exile and his homesickness for the street where he was born, that's good. Uncle Jules enjoyed ambiguity."

Ambre snorted. "People never mind so much being made fools of by the dead. Even clever people."

"Señora Guevara, do you suppose Jules's admirers are only clever people?" Bella's father said.

"I do admired Jules," Ambre said, decisive. Then, as though she were doing propositional calculus, "I do was clever."

"Lena admired Jules," Bella's father said, "and she couldn't read."

"Grandma didn't 'admire' people," Fidela said, "though she was very *sensitive to* admiration. Jules was a gentleman and attentive."

"She loved him," Bella and I said together.

Bella's father stepped across the path to ask the gringos whether his granddaughter was bothering them.

"Not at all," said the New Zealander, not taking the hint.

His friend said, in murky, accented, atonal English: "Oliver, it *is* them."

Bella's father caught the child in a firm hold and encouraged her back across the path and away from the tourists.

The New Zealander was doing something similar. Though he tried to make it look friendly, he was bullying his friend away down the slope. The friend—an ugly customer—craned his spotty neck to peer back at our group. I heard him say: "The older one is approachable. But neither is ovulating."

"Ga-ga," said Bella. She nudged me with her shoulder. "With yagga."

We knelt together to scrub Jules's grave and talked about Bella's supervisor and the size of her advance on her book. Bella told me her trip home had been paid for by a British production company that was doing a documentary on Lequama, including the twenty years celebration. "It's mainly battle soundtracks over grisly scenes from the Taoscal bark books in the British Museum, and pyramids by torchlight, I suspect. I'm supposed to be a talking head—a talking head taking a walk through the museum at Los Muertos and giving a potted version of my thesis from *The Culture of Torture*, occasionally quoting Jules Frei. The film also involves that anthropologist—Jon Scott—who did the big ethnographic study of the Mneone back in the mid-1980s. *No Line in the Reef*. I have questions I want to ask Scott, relating to things I need for the foreword of my book."

"Can I be there when you ask your questions?"

Bella stopped, straddling the fence, and frowned at me. "Sure," she said. Her need for a cigarette was so immediate she didn't finish dismounting the fence before shaking one out of its packet and lighting up. "Why do you want to be there?"

"You're going to ask Scott about Turoc Iddu, the temple that stood where the Presidential Palace now stands—the Miniseries Building, as everyone now calls it."

"I have to make sure I get that stuff right. I didn't know you knew about it, Carme. Turoc Iddu. I'm talking to Scott and to Fernando, but I don't have high hopes, since the Taoscal do tend to go, 'These things are very esoteric . . .' and fob you off."

"You sent me a draft of your foreword," I reminded her. "I'm not reading your mind. And Dad mentions Turoc Iddu in his journal—at least, he reports what Fernando said about it."

"I forgot I sent it to you!" Bella looked relieved. She hadn't even an air of someone politely waiting to hear a verdict. She was very autonomous. She went on to say that the production team had invited everyone involved in the documentary to a cocktail party at that conference center in the old Pastrez mansion. "Five-thirty tonight. Basically, between the big official ceremonies and the bacchanalia, both of which they plan to shoot. I'm going to the cocktails to buttonhole Scott. It might matter that you don't have an invitation—but you could always tell them that your *husband* used to live in the mansion."

All the sound around those two graves was momentarily suspended as every busy action and conversation missed a beat. And from the upper level, above the fifteen-foot mortared wall, came a gasp and then a furious cry. A woman there, well-dressed, middle-aged, stooped over the spike-topped iron fence and spat at me. A spray of foamy spit hit my face. She shouted, "Whore! You whore!"

Bella's father raised his hat against the sun and squinted up at the woman, while the children backed off, and one caught the fence of Lena's grave at the back of her knees and took a tumble. I wiped my face with my sleeve, but didn't move. I tried to understand what the woman was shouting but made no sense of it. I waited to hear Ricardo's name, and didn't, so I couldn't hear anything.

People at graves on the upper terrace rushed to restrain the woman. "Señora! Señora!" they pleaded, as she raged and towed them after her.

Ambre seized my arm and began to hurry me away. She told me that of course I couldn't expect to return to Lequama "without incident."

Bella picked up a stone and hefted it at the woman, and was grabbed at by her own relatives. She shook them off and followed me.

Then the woman fell back with a sharp cry into the arms of those holding her, and I saw blood trickle down from her hairline, though it wasn't clear who had thrown a stone—none of us, apart from Bella's father, had a raised hand, and his held his hat. I didn't see any more. Bella caught up with us, and she helped me with Ambre, who was breathless after only a minute hurrying. By the time we got to the lower terrace they were both coughing—Ambre a confined, asthmatic bark and Bella throatily. Fidela, as imperturbable as ever, told them they both smoked too much.

Ambre scowled at my sister. Then she drew herself up and informed me that *that* was what it meant to be Ricardo Pastrez's wife—I was a pariah in my own country. "Here you can only go among your friends."

Bella coughed and shook her head.

I said, "I'm not sure that was it."

Ambre was frowning with distaste at the ferrous stain on her palms from where she had gripped the iron gates. Though she wouldn't meet my eye I was sure I had her attention, so I told her, "I think that was *his* wife." I found I had forgotten a name. I insisted: "My *art teacher's* wife."

My high school art teacher. I've avoided thinking about him for so long that his name has settled in one of those places hard to access— brains are forests full of trails, kept clear only by the passage of feet.

My art teacher had kept turning up. He'd said, "You won't ignore me. I'll make sure you can't ignore me." I picture him still, his yearning attention, as clearly as I can picture the formidable family meeting in which his fate was discussed. I can see the people at the meeting, the council of war. There was Dad; my unofficial García uncles (I'd been doing clerical work on weekends in the office of a furniture factory the García brothers had built at the back of my stepmother's property); Ambre and Madlena and Fernando; and Don Marcos, the most *officially* powerful person of our acquaintance. All the people who had already "had a word" with my art teacher—excluding the high school principal and a detective of the La Host police. I can remember my father saying that the problem shouldn't be solved by murder. He said, "You can't keep *doing* that." And he counted off on his fingers—"Norton Lawrence, Brad Powers, Pablito Masolan." Enrico García, head of security at the Presidential Palace when the men on Dad's list disappeared or died, sat with his face in his hands—made complicitous by listening, and finally supplied with answers to every mystery he'd once been blocked and bullied from investigating.

But I have to tell my story in the right order.

Memoir: Lequama, 1988 to 1994

I returned to Flores Negras. My father spent the evening hanging head-down in Madlena's earth coffin and whispering. Ambre went out several times to watch this but didn't venture near. (I suppose that it was then that Ambre relinquished some of her responsibility for Madlena to Dad—in later years she'd say, all too easily, "Ido, you talk to her, she listens to you." This was never strictly true. What Madlena did, from that time on, was talk to Dad. It wasn't unusual for them to spend an hour on the phone—which rather intruded on my long conversations with Bella.)

That night I opened the window in the attic room and listened to the voices at the earth coffin—Madlena's muffled, aggrieved tones and Dad, reassuring and persuasive.

The following day Madlena decided to disinter herself, and instead sat bundled up in a rug on a wicker settee at the purple-shaded end of the veranda.

Juanita came and begged Madlena to come back to the hacienda. She was very sorry, she said, that she'd always treated her own situation there as temporary, because it *had* been a real home to her and Xenia, the first she'd ever had in a way. Tomás came with the boys and sat with his wife, tight-lipped and wounded. He had always known Madlena was "carrying a torch" for Fernando. Tomás had known, but had felt secure in his knowledge of Fernando's homosexuality, and in Madlena's sexual pride—could she *really* love someone who wasn't attracted to her? Tomás gave the impression of a man who had faced everything at once—more than Madlena and Fernando themselves were able to. Madlena still maintained that Fernando was just playing a cruel trick and didn't really want her. Didn't, *couldn't*. And—as my father had divined—Fernando was still telling himself stories about what kind of love was suitable for him, and how much of himself he was willing to offer to anyone he loved.

Ambre, Dad, and I walked Tomás to the gate—sending him off for an evening at Plaza Bar One while we minded the twins. Tomás said to us gloomily, "I used to wonder why they always picked fights with each other, when she'd get so upset and he'd be so offended. But our marriage was doomed once they *stopped* fighting. Not because they learned to like each other better, but because then they just had to get to grips some other way."

It was at this point, when everybody was occupied, if only by their thoughts, that the Contras made a big push in the Ambella at Las Maravillosas, and the whole country was plunged into a state of emergency. It was the last effort in a war that fizzled out, not coincidentally, around the same time that it became impossible to sell the protection of U.S. financial interests by military means as "the struggle to prevent the spread of communism." The Contras were well trained, well equipped, and sufficiently motivated to provide one final week of bloodshed on Lequaman soil. Most of this went over my head at the time. I do remember the night I stood barefoot on the chilly tiled floor of the kitchen brewing coffee for Madlena, and following her with the cup to the door, where a jeep waited. I believe she was called in to write copy, to face the press, as a spin doctor for the government. When Madlena had gone, Ambre turned on the television and we listened to Radio Venceremos broadcasting over the test pattern, then a still shot of the President. There was an announcement from the President, then we heard Colonel God-shalk, speaking from the front.

Dad left at dawn following a call from Anton Xavier, who was taking his trauma team up to Leonarda and the army surgery. Two U.S. medical students picked Dad up—they were interning in the holidays through an arrangement with an East German group called "Student Friends of Lequama and Nicaragua."

Bella wasn't at school the next day, and in the evening her father brought her around to Flores Negras. Very awkward and reluctant, he asked if she could stay for a while. He had managed to get three tickets from a standby list on a flight from La Host to Lima, and had decided to take his older son and his mother—who couldn't be left again to, as he put it, "the vicissitudes of fate." He would have left Bella in Jules's care, but if everything did "go bad," she'd not be safe with Jules. Could Lena? Would Ambre?

Ambre was happy to take Bella in, but only once she'd shamed him by saying he couldn't possibly be suggesting the Contras would advance as far as La Host.

School was suspended—it was impossible to enforce the attendance of the bigger boys, who, having endured years of their older brothers' and sisters' brave tales of stoning Galen's soldiers from street corners, began to build up their own arsenals. Two boys from our class suffered burns when they mishandled Molotov cocktails while smoking.

An American television crew flew into La Host and, of course, wanted Madlena Guevara. She told them what the government would like reported—that this attack was an invasion of a sovereign state by a foreign power, or at least a foreign-backed power, "but let's not make too fine a distinction." She talked about the mobile airstrips directly across the border, shipped, assembled, and attended by U.S. military personnel. She talked about the U.S. Army major, Munro, who was captured on Lequaman soil in the company of Contras. She talked about the mined waters two miles off Porto Barrara—mined *international* waters. This is all great, said the TV journalist, but would Colonel Guevara—La Dora—like to take them into the Ambella so they could film her saying all these salient things on the hot spot, as it were.

And so they went where the war was, or five kilometers shy of it, and Madlena shouted her commentary into the camera against the backdrop of army trucks that fumed and fishtailed along a churned-up red mud road. The cameraman shot wobbly, flinching footage of a swift-flowering foliage of fire growing above the tallest trees in the forest canopy. They moved on farther against the slight current of wounded—filmed themselves arguing with a corporal from Amazonia who wanted to commandeer their jeep to help carry the wounded survivors of her platoon back to Leonarda. She threatened and the TV journalist resisted while simultaneously trying to interview her. She spoke English well, but still misunderstood. "Was it a rout?" he asked. "No, it was a trackless jungle you stupid man," she answered.

Madlena asked the film crew if they wanted to go back—didn't they have enough? She said to the corporal that she hoped these TV people were going to deliver to their network very very soon. The crew did turn back, taking the wounded on board and behaving solicitously on camera and off. The journalist was disappointed. He was, for Christ's sake, still *clean*. A little dirt would be more credible.

They were at a bend in the road, tall trees on one side and a crescent-shaped crop of coca on the other, when the road was shelled. The camera recorded the great displacement of earth ahead—as if an invisible stone had been dropped into dark water that shredded dryly. The camera jumped and a truck leaped out of its viewfinder, its tires burning. The cameraman recorded the journalist's rush toward the burning truck. And his abrupt halt, and the way he stood flapping his hands, as though they were wet, before a tangled pink cordage stretched between a pair of legs and pelvis, and a torso, sans head, its arms still briefly stiff and defensive, then limp enough to fall. Then Madlena was suddenly on camera. She grabbed the journalist and ran off, the cameraman following them.

Madlena ran low, the journalist after her, trampling through the traces of his own vomit. There was a three-minute-long period of shouts, panting, jostling darkness. Then the journalist was glimpsed scrambling across a stony streambed, urgently beckoned into shelter by a group of dark-faced soldiers. Minutes later the cameraman put the camera down on a trestle table in a jungle clearing. For a short time nothing was visible but small squares of light that billowed—camouflage netting. Then the cameraman found his camera still running and turned it, with no vanity or self-consciousness, to record his own white, drawn face, then the journalist, sitting on an empty ammunition box, scraping his hair back over and over. The audio picked up his repeated "Jesus . . . Jesus . . ." There were some distant crumping explosions. The camera jolted, then it found a group of officers with maps and radio. The autofocus adjusted and their figures swam out of the tearing green murk.

Maria Godshalk's second-in-command sat wrapped and upright in a seat pulled from the back of a car. The major could be heard asking, "What news? What news?" like a dying king in a Spanish translation of a Shakespeare history play. She *was* dying—but did it several hours later and off camera. There was a soldier standing very erect beside her, holding up a bag of plasma. The cameraman filmed Madlena making makeshift repairs to Maria's ear, fastening one earring to a higher one with a shoelace, to help a torn lobe stay temporarily in place. Then Madlena wrapped Maria's head, and wiped the blood from Maria's glasses on the only clean item of her own clothing, her little Adidas stretch top. Fernando was in the background with the map talking to the commander of Battalion Nuevo. They were both tapping the nails of one forefinger against their top teeth as they considered decisions—turning now and then to the radio operator. They were taking reports on the ground held, by how many and against how many. The cameraman recovered his professional distance enough to pan between the discussion and the waning major, cocooned, still upright, but white-lipped now. The last thing he filmed for hours was a medic and Maria gently unraveling the blanket. It was clear to me—when I saw the footage in full years later—looking at the major, with her shirt off, her skin and clothes relatively unbloodied but darkly bruised, and her abdomen visibly distended, that the plasma would do very little good. One of the blood vessels near her spleen had torn and she was bleeding out into her own abdominal cavity.

Eight hours later, after a montage of running and smoke from distant gunfire, most shots partly obscured by cover, the cameraman decided to do something with the final four minutes on his tape. He set up a "hero shot." He might perhaps have preferred the commander of Nuevo or Maria Godshalk, who were on active duty and in uniform, but he had lost them along the way. He was in a little village—one of the Ambella villages that lie along the saddle of the Andean foothills. It was dark, near dawn, and in the confused light of several fires, handheld torches, headlamps, and one friendly patch of radiance coming from a little cantina, the cameraman managed to persuade Fernando Sola to face him as the commander paused to ask a Mestizo captain about a row of prisoners who were sitting along the coping of the kind of town fountain where women usually gathered to wash clothes. Fernando turned to the camera operator who was wheedling away: "Commander Sola, Commander Sola . . ." Then the cameraman made sounds of encouragement—the camera went out of focus as he stepped forward to pull someone into shot—then it came back and there were Madlena and Fernando, her shoulder wedged awkwardly under his arm. She looked stunned and was blushing. He looked sated, dazed, like a man interrupted after several hours of doing what delighted him most. He seemed to come to after a moment and take note who was beside him. In the same moment that his mouth fell loose, she glanced at him—and he put a hand up, touched her throat, and, by lip-reading, he can be seen to say her name.

That was one thing that happened during the Contras' last offensive—or, as Tomás called it on the radio, "to date their most offensive offensive." Bella and I, sitting on the veranda at Flores Negras, listening to the radio and painting our nails, laughed at that, Tomás on the News of the Day, either our national crisis or the international scene. For instance, he wanted to know why, since he'd signed up for Amnesty International, he hadn't received *his* free Nelson Mandela.

The other important event during the offensive was less public than Fernando's televised claiming touch. I didn't know about it till later, let alone understand its implications.

A week before Fidela was born I went with Ambre and Dad for a full physical. It was the first time I met Anton Xavier, and I liked him, his perfect mix of curiosity and practicality and compassion. It was hot—April— and the air was full of the farthest-borne fumes from the burning cane fields, some eighty kilometers southeast of La Host. Ambre was wearing a cotton shift and rubber thongs; she was braless, pendulous, weary. There was a rectangle of striped shadow on the wall by her head from the sun through the cane blind, and, paler beside it, her own panting shadow. Dr. Xavier had attempted to reassure Ambre, who was afraid her child would be a monster. He said, "Carme isn't a monster, is she?"

Without thinking about it, Ambre answered, "No, Carme is beautiful."

"Your baby will be too—healthy and beautiful." There was a kind of exultation behind the doctor's calm.

Dad rolled his sleeve up. He was looking at Ambre, reflecting her fear as shame. Dr. Xavier turned from Ambre to Dad to draw blood—swabbed the place, pumped up the cuff around Dad's arm, inserted the needle, let the cuff loose and watched the blood fill the tube behind the needle. He decanted a drop of blood onto a slide. The blood was silky and mercurial.

Dr. Xavier said, "In my opinion, one of the finest things in life is a repeatable proof." He slipped the slide under the spotlight of his microscope, where it remained as discrete and radiant as arterial blood though it came from a vein, lit not by recent oxygenation but by phosphorus, poisonously too much.

My father glowed like Garbo or the young Gary Cooper. "We thought it was his *soul*," Fernando said, when he heard about the phosphorus.

When I was in medical school and could be expected to follow his thinking, Anton Xavier aired this theory. He speculated that the phosphorus was there, at a low constant level, to produce phosphoramidites. By the time Anton came up with his theory my father was no longer on hand and Anton couldn't verify anything—wouldn't have been able to anyway, in his poorly resourced hospital laboratory. The process by which my father's body manufactured and used phosphoramidites was never discovered. The thing that was observed was probably a distant consequence of the process. A miraculous thing.

I now subscribe to Anton's theory. I know, for instance, that the life sciences conglomerate Perkins Elmer sells "Masterpiece Phosphoramidites" for the manufacture of DNA that is "chemically authentic." And I understand that what my father's body made from its surfeit of phosphorus was one of the reagents elsewhere used in recombinant DNA technology. The phosphoramidites in my father's body were ingredient and fuel, like coal in the production of steel.

It was during our physical that Ambre and I first heard from Anton that Dad had, during the Contras' push, graduated from sweeping floors and running the autoclave at the army hospital in Leonarda to holding retractors and suction hoses and closing up wounds after the surgeons had finished making their repairs. Anton Xavier said, "We were in the theater for hours, when one of my young American doctors got a cramp and Ido asked if he could lend a hand."

My father was silent. I remembered that he'd come home two days after the Contras were pushed back. Of course the efforts of the surgeons had had to outlast those of the soldiers. I'd found Dad sitting on the steps up to the veranda, in the early morning, someone else's coat pulled on over surgical greens, the front of which was stiff and brown with blood. There was blood dried on his boots too, on the leather an iridescence softer than a gasoline slick, and there was blood, thick as mud, on his trouser cuffs. When he saw me he said, "Good. The house is up now," and went upstairs to wash and rest. Weeks went by, but he remained subdued—as ghostly and silent as he'd seemed that morning.

On the evening of our physical, after dinner, when Ambre had retired, worn out, to try and sift a little sleep out of sweatiness and sore hips and heartburn—I went up to my bed and discovered that my father had taken the false bottom out of the clothes chest and was leaning over its side, his fingers interlaced with Dev's skeleton's bony digits.

I retreated from the room.

A week later my sister was born. A big, loud baby, sallow, waxy with vernix and a redhead, which came from no one in Ambre's family, so gave my father the only imaginable picture he ever had of his parents, one of them a redhead.

Flores Negras became, for the next few weeks, the twilight zone. There was no night and day for us, the baby was either awake or sleeping, and that set our clocks. I'd come home from school to find Ambre asleep with Fidela beside her in the big bed and Dad dozing on the couch. There was always food, because when Dad was home and conscious, he cooked, cleaned, and did laundry. Several days a week Dad still got on the old Honda trail bike he'd inherited from a García brother and had nursed back to health, and drove off to Leonarda. Bella's father was back in the country—a bit shamefaced. Bella was at her house, I was expected at mine, so we'd sit for an hour on the phone each night. I was suffering a dearth of news—I'd been involved in other lives and was now cloistered with one exhausted adult, one depressed one, and a tiny baby. It was like missing several key episodes in a television serial. Ambre was doing what she had to do first, devoting herself to her own health and the health of her child. When Guido Hernández's wife dropped by with a bundle of hand-me-down baby clothes and asked how Madlena was, Ambre said: "I don't know. She's not my priority."

Tomás turned up one day and asked, proud, whether Ambre could have the twins for a few hours. Madlena would collect them shortly, he promised. He had to inspect a couple of apartments. I could see Ambre mustering her sense of entitlement and whatever words would come with that. "Oh, Tomás. You're not really thinking of leaving . . . ?" she began. Then she shut her eyes, heaved a sigh, and said, "I don't have time for this."

"I don't want to trouble you." Tomás was rather brittle. He put down the twins, who had been hanging under either arm, their bright black eyes aimed at Ambre, and left.

"Carme, could you mind them?" Ambre said. Carlos and Aureliano looked at me, then at each other, and then ran off in different directions. "And keep them quiet!" Ambre begged, as I charged after Aureliano, knowing that if I caught and tortured one twin the other would probably come to his aid.

Dad eventually came home. He was wearing his threadbare surgical greens again—it was easier to wash them at home than at Leonarda. He pulled his shirt off and put it in with Fidela's diapers to disinfect, then he untied Aureliano from the table leg and went into the kitchen to cook the beans he had soaking. Aureliano went out into the living room and started pounding on the floor with a shoe. Dad removed the shoe. He kissed Ambre, sat beside her, and folded a pile of fresh diapers I'd just fetched in from the line into a stack ready for use. Ambre told him about Tomás. She was upset and Fidela became agitated. Ambre's milk was still coming in faster than Fidela could drink it and Ambre's breasts were tight, their nipples distended and difficult for the baby to manage.

Ambre was still struggling to get Fidela comfortably and effectively latched on when Fernando walked in. Madlena had sent him to retrieve the twins. She was still at the hacienda, and he was at his place in the Avenida Bueyes Negros, he said, when Ambre asked if they were now living together. Actually, she stated it "So—you are together," in a cold, unimpressed tone.

Fernando was standing, very still and erect, his head up, looking a challenge at Ambre. "Was there ever any doubt, once I'd spoken?" he said, his tone thick with pride. "All I had to do was put out my hand."

My father was looking over the swing doors in the kitchen. Ambre had forgotten everything but the infuriating man in front of her. She hadn't covered herself, still held one naked nipple between two fingers; Fidela, unlatched again, wobbled her head in front of the nipple like a kitten mesmerized by movement. Ambre said to Fernando, "You're very lucky that she has always loved you so much."

"Luck isn't involved. If anything, this runs completely contrary to my luck," Fernando said, still haughty but warming, as though intrigued by his own thought.

My father gasped, strode into the living room. He scooped up one twin around his waist and the other dangled by the back of his shirt. They went limp and round-eyed. Dad deposited the twins at Fernando's feet. "Take the children, asshole," Dad said. Then, "We love Madlena."

"I love her too,"

Aureliano, who was impossible to subdue, said, "*I* love Mama." The angry men looked at him and blinked. Fernando took the twins by their grubby hands and helped them to their feet.

Ambre raised her voice to say Fernando wasn't to come around again until he had learned to speak properly of her daughter.

"He's crazy." Fernando jerked his chin at Dad. "And you're a pious cow, and I can do without both of you." He walked out.

This is how I found out about my father's gift. We were at La Casa de la Mujer, an hour after Fidela's uncomplicated birth, and I left the room for a minute—the room where my father stood above his new partner admiring his new daughter. I got a soda and sat down near the room, so that when Anton Xavier left he saw me and came to sit beside me.

"If I tell you a little story, perhaps you can help me understand a few things about it," he said.

I nodded. I stared at him, trying to work out what kind of interest his was—never having witnessed interest so civilized and pure—at least, never directed at my father.

He told me that during the Contras' push, they had been overwhelmed by the casualties—most of them from Amazonia, which had first met the invading force. Hours into hours of operations, Anton Xavier said, they were working in a surgery that was literally awash with blood, bloody dressings, and discarded human offal. He wasn't particularly aware of my father, who had been alternating some heavy sweeping and carrying work with tending the autoclave, till, at one point, he appeared at the head surgeon's side, gloved and sterile, with a fresh batch of instruments. Then after depositing them in their tray, he stood a moment watching. The young volunteer who was assisting Xavier got a cramp in her hand and couldn't close up. Dr. Xavier told me that my father stepped up to the table and held his hands out over the wound, to show he was gloved, the doctor assumed, and said, "Can I help?"

"He meant to show, too, how still his hands were," said Anton Xavier. "And when his hands stilled so did the blood—the small oozing blood vessels stopped oozing, locally, under his hands." The doctor looked at me hard, then said, "What do you think of that?"

I didn't know what to say, and I shrugged, probably giving the impression of reticence or stubbornness, because the doctor began to push some. He asked me who Dev was, then he said, "I recommended psychotherapy for your father because he had amnesia when he first came here—with no signs of cerebral trauma. Eventually his memory was restored to him, but he never *introduced himself*. Do you see what I mean? He never told me who he was."

"Dev was his lover who was murdered," I said. "What did he say about Dev?"

"When the casualties thinned out some and we were able to rest I sat down with your father on a felled tree outside the surgery and he said to me that Dev was dead. I wondered which of our patients Dev was, and was about to ask when he told me what happened when he offered to help. He said that he looked down at the wound and saw the whole stomach, as it was several hours back, the healthy body rising up through the injured one. He said he had nearly left the surgery then, because surely it's better to be human and live with grief, than outgrow your humanity and learn to raise the dead too late to raise your own. Then he said, 'But I understood that it's easier for all of us to clench our muscles than to flex them—so that we make fists even in our sleep—and I put out my hands.' " The doctor continued to peer at me.

"What?" I said.

The doctor said he thought maybe my father could heal. As for the other, perhaps my father had some sense of a trajectory to his talent.

"No," I said.

"I wonder what it's like to *be* him," said Dr. Xavier.

I shook my head. "It's too late now." I thought of Dad's fingers linked with Dev's finger bones.

The doctor sighed and got up, the bench creaking, to fetch me a tissue.

Dad's gift had consequences, it took us places—and that was related also to where my sister's gifts were able to take us.

Fidela, from her first year, was clearly a prodigy. She was the deftest, most coordinated child I've ever known. At two and out of diapers, she was as slender and poised as a child of nine, but tiny. Very early on she began to sing and dance, for herself or anyone who cared to watch. She was a sprightly, weightless thing. She loved not clothes, but costumes, and I remember that Dad, who was always "handy," took up sewing to supply her with apparel. He bought Lycra and made leggings, he dyed and hand-painted stretch cotton. He knitted lace gloves when she was in her Madonna phase and lace gloves were impossible to come by in Lequama. He sat up late sewing, onto a skirt, sequins salvaged from an evening gown belonging to Juanita's mother, which Juanita had found in the attic of the old Pastrez mansion after the revolution and had waited patiently to grow into herself, but never did.

We all doted on Fidela, Ambre most of all. She'd been a baffled and embattled mother to Madlena many years before. *This* time she was determined to get it right. She wouldn't provoke her child, or blow hot and cold. Instead she'd show unstinting love and latitude and approval. Dad followed Ambre's lead, was indulgent and affectionate. Fidela only had to ask for something—a tape deck, a keyboard, a Walkman—and he'd contrive to get it for her.

It was because of Fidela's material needs that Dad first went looking for more money than he could reasonably expect to get working at La Casa de la Mujer or playing the dice games with tourists in the bars around the Plaza.

I hope I don't sound envious. I wasn't. I aided and abetted the overindulgent adults. I admired my little sister. And while she was growing, a stealthy happiness came over me. I made friends at school. I found myself part of a big, busy, needy family (because, of course, Madlena did bring Fernando back into Ambre's house and Ambre and he continued to have their flattering—to Madlena—tussles of influence). Dad got a job at outpatients in La Casa de la Mujer and was known thereafter as Dr. Risk—although he had no qualifications. And in his job he did more than any of us knew till—after he'd gone—various people turned up one by one at Flores Negras and, as if obliged to bear witness somehow, told Ambre that "Dr. Risk, Ido the Idea, he *cured* me." They were all alike, as cases: they were never at death's door, or seriously injured, or affected congenitally; they were people with chronic complaints or persistent pain from old injuries. They were the bad backs and bum knees and arthritic hands; people with asthma following pneumonia, or liver damage following hepatitis. There were some children with leukemia five years in remission whose parents came—somewhat dismayed—to Ambre to say that they'd heard Dr. Risk had gone, had been *taken*, and they hoped it wasn't true. But there was nothing obviously impossible or world-shattering. There were no clear miracles.

Life was sweet. I infiltrated my stepmother's kitchen—she let me stand with her at the counter prizing fava beans out of their cushiony pods, peeling garlic, and scraping the seeds and spines from jalapeños. She got into the habit of talking to me, first about

Fidela, then about everyone else in the family. There was a day when I realized that she always smiled at me when I arrived home from school, and that this wasn't kindness on her part, she was simply pleased to see me.

Ambre flourished. Apart from "the family"—which included Juanita and Enrico García when they were courting; and, for a time, Enrico's sister, who moved in with Tomás; and Fernando, Madlena, and the twins, who lived half the week with their father and the other half with "Mama" and "Uncle Fando"—there were Lena and Jules, who lived in Lena's long room at the side of the house, a room that had its own door and its own veranda, a "granny flat" with superannuated lovers. Ambre had Fidela, her little rosy apple, and she had a business. She began mapping out original designs on graph paper and making up big bright alpaca rugs on her loom. Soon there was a workshop with three looms and apprentices from the Prostitutes Collective—then Marguerite Millay found a friend who wanted to sell Ambre's rugs in her gallery in Paris. The García brothers enlarged their furniture factory at the back of the property—and Bella and I, doing homework at the window of my attic room, were treated to the constant spectacle of handsome García men in shirtsleeves with brown forearms and halos of sawdust caught in their sun-bleached arm hairs.

When the weather got hot we would all pack up and go camp on the beach at Vela Bay. Except the workers—who would run back to La Host during the week, Tomás to the radio station and Madlena to her consultancy at Foreign Affairs. She had sold all the horses in 1989—the market for polo ponies evaporated after Black Tuesday. Fernando was "troubleshooting" at Indian Affairs—he hated the word "consultancy" and said he felt more comfortable with a job that included the word "shooting." And Dad went back to his steady supply of people with soluble problems.

I have never been happier than I was then, during those days of intolerable heat when we camped in the breezes on the beach at Vela. Bella and I and her school-age brother would tread water for hours in the big swells far from shore, keeping a cautious eye out to sea for sharks, and with no duty to watch the younger children in the shallows, the twins, and Fidela sitting between Ambre's legs in the long stretch of foaming water.

Friday evenings would arrive, and we'd be there, our land legs quite gone and salt dried in shingles on our cheeks, when suddenly we'd be swamped and upturned by the adults—Tomás, Fernando, Madlena, Dad—newly arrived from the city, hot and elated and untrammeled, splashing and whooping and dunking each other. Streaking around us, stronger, paler, more charged than we were.

During the rainy season in '92, Ambre had a fit of impatience with our latest batch of dramas. I was pining painfully over the callow, skateboarding son of some American Jehovah's Witnesses. Fernando and Madlena had recently caught each other out cheating—and with the same man, an inertly handsome French baritone who was in Lequama giving master classes at the university. Dad's advice was sought (by both parties) and Ambre was either piqued at this or fed up with the whole thing, and declared she needed a break. She took Fidela and went to spend two weeks at Ricardo's spa. (It was her third visit to Ricardo, but more on the second one later.) Everyone except Dad was floored.

Anyway—during their visit Fidela entered a talent show at the spa's Kids' Club. Some other parent—with connections to entertainment in Las Vegas—was impressed. He videoed her number. Fidela walked off with the trophy, the money, the free turns at minigolf—whatever they were offering. Two weeks after Ambre came back from the spa a studio executive rang from Los Angeles to ask whether, *by any chance*, Fidela Guevara would like to do a screen test for a part in a planned series. They could send a camera crew, it could all be done through Lequaman TV, *as easy as can be*. Wouldn't Ambre like to see just what was possible for her daughter?

Ambre distrusted Americans, and declined. But she told Fidela; after all, it was praise the child had earned. And Fidela declared that she wanted to be on TV.

Ambre and Dad had no peace. Fidela reasoned with them. I can remember her following first one then the other parent around the house and talking in this keen, clear voice, with its touch of the Ambella. "It's what I've wanted to do all my life," she'd say, a phrase

272

that, in the mouth of a four-year-old, shouldn't have had much weight. But they let her have her way. The camera crew arrived, she tested, and she shone—she shone like a star. The studio paid all our fares up to L.A. and wooed us. Fidela helped them woo us. She was sensitive to the tiniest cues about how to proceed with people. Her task with Ambre was simple—many under-fives would be equal to it. She pleaded, persistent and firm and gracious. Whereas to Dad she said that there was no reason to suppose that a child, too, didn't have *a right to work*.

The studio certainly knew what they were doing. (They knew what they wanted—Madlena Guevara's little half-sister. So when they pitched their sale to Dad and Ambre they also addressed, through them, the other member of the family who, although she wasn't there, they hoped might have a say.) The show, *Starting Over*, was a family comedy. The "Dad" in the show is a law graduate, who some years before has had what his family—East Coast old money—refers to as "a foolish youthful fling" with a Lequaman lawyer when they were working on some UN-sponsored human rights project. (When we heard this pitch it was '92, not even a whole decade from '83, but somehow *light-years* away from the revolution, with '89 intervening, and the pulverized cement rubble of the Berlin Wall.) The show's "backstory" had the Lequaman lawyer return to her country, pregnant—without having told her boyfriend. Four years later and he has shelved his humanitarian interests for a high-flying job in his father's law firm. Then one day, the day of his big engagement party—he's marrying an anal-retentive interior decorator—he gets a phone call from LAX. It is the Lequaman girl's mother, who tells him that her daughter is dead—"of something heart-wrenching and sudden," the producer explained to Dad and Ambre. "We haven't got that figured yet, but the upshot is that the old lady is bringing the lawyer his daughter." Enter little Rosalita, a lovable, feisty, bilingual, politicized kid—Fidela's character. (Later, in the entertainment magazines, Rosalita, and Fidela herself, were always written up as "cute Latina tot.")

"*Starting Over* is a story about family," the producer said, earnest, his elbows on his knees and his head deferentially below Ambre's, his tie hanging out over the table like the rescue slide from a disabled plane. "And it's a story about contrasting values."

His pitch was punctuated by Fidela's "I *want* to do this. I want to *do* this. I want to do *this*."

They gave in. Or at least Ambre gave in. Dad said, "Thou mayst"—like God. He'd looked about him at the freeways, the automatic teller machines, the plate glass, at whatever the hell it was that made his gaze grow opaque and excited.

How to explain?

Ambre went with Fidela to the Mall of the Americas to shop; I went to the Getty Museum; and Dad came back from browsing in the periodical section of the library at UCLA with news about what someone in Osaka was doing with superconductors and someone in Perth with holograms and someone in Portland with cryogenic surgery.

It was my memory of Dad's gradual, magma-like passion that first misdirected me to cryogenics. Talking about the new techniques, Dad described thoracic surgery as "a competition between tasks and finite portions of time." He said, "With the same skill, but more time, just think what a surgeon could do." My father was always attracted to the limits of what was possible. Lequama had hope, hard work, and wonders; it was full of magic lore and mended things. My father knew his instinct for excellence was being warped by Lequama; he saw his salvation in the States, in big money and hard science.

I've sat for several minutes trying to find an alternative to my phrase "instinct for excellence." I know it's not right, that it's like something from the publicity department of a large corporation. "Mastery" is a better word than "excellence." Given time, my father might have found some brilliant pioneer—introduced himself, struck up a conversation, seduced some other genius. He might have returned, finally, to medical research—his original trajectory, the course he was on before his collision with the vanishing island of Carlin's "bloody Brigadoon." Given time. But when Fidela's pilot was shooting he and Ambre both sat, anxious, and watched their wonderful daughter perform. And in the first season of *Starting Over* the star's parents took turns being there for her to climb up into a lap and snuggle while she listened to the instructions of her director. Fidela raised her capital doing this, she was so clearly adored, and by such singular, self-possessed, exotic people. Dad didn't have time to do more than dabble in ideas—attend a few lectures, read books. He did go so far as to insinuate himself into a couple of graduate seminars. The professor who admitted him, compelled by Dad's outrageous, intense *"Please* let me listen," did so on the proviso that my father didn't ask questions. Dad took it as a very good sign that the professor hadn't called campus security.

But my father couldn't find a foothold in the future. Instead, Edwin Money found him.

Edwin Money's fortune was founded in the 1960s in telecommunications—satellite dishes, military contracts. In the 1980s his business boomed and he bought his first satellite, part of the payload in one of those Columbia shuttle missions. By the mid-'90s he had four satellites. In *Forbes* he's quoted as saying that he was selling time to the networks who could then sell *life* to the world—a paraphrase of Shelley's "O World! O Life! O Time!/On whose last steps I climb, . . ." Money liked to be called "Old Father Time." He saw himself as a primogenitor, didn't like to owe his existence to anyone. When he had an initial share float in Chronos, his company, newly incorporated in '93, the prospectus boasted that Chronos's growth was such that the company hoped soon to attain independence from "federally funded space programs." In private I heard Money's right-hand man, Nathan Wrytower, refer to the United States as "federal America"—Money had that in common with the militias of the Northwest. He resented all federal controls as "hobbles" on business. He believed in "fiscal responsibility" as he believed in the tooth fairy—which is to say, not at all.

In '93 Old Father Time was eighty-nine. He was no Howard Hughes, mad and abject. He was a recluse, however, due to failing health. Edwin Money suffered from the diseases of old age: arteriosclerotic weakness, an enlarged heart, angina pains, emphysema.

Money was enjoying his second fortune. The first, earned manufacturing pressed steel plates and cutlery for the army during the war, he had played away in the '50s and '60s. He had been married three times and had one son, who was said to have retreated to an ashram in India. Money made his second fortune when the pleasures of youth had been lapped by those of maturity—power and influence. In '93, resident in his quiet house on four levels from waterline to clifftop in Santa Monica—a house with Islamic gardens, fountain courts, pierced stone screens, tessellated mosaics—Edwin Money had, as well as power and influence, what pleases the ear and eye. But, sitting in front of his sea view on a water cushion for his pressure points in a high-tech wheelchair, with its own oxygen supply sighing through transparent silicon tubing that forked in his nostrils, what was he able to enjoy? The sea? A saltless meal before him. Nothing before him.

I don't know how he heard about my father, but during the shooting of Fidela's second season, Dad was approached by Nathan Wrytower—the self-described "secretary of a very wealthy and private individual." Wrytower didn't love his employer and there was probably some disgust, rather than any concern about nonsexist language, expressed in that "individual" substituted for "man." Money *was* a sexless, desiccated invalid. Wrytower told my father that his employer had—for some time—been experimenting with various alternative medicines, with some good results. Dad pretended interest, asking *which* alternative medicines had this "individual" found helpful? And what exactly was this "individual's" complaint? My father, without any particular hostility, reflected back at Wrytower the secretary's attitude to his employer. The man had been given a task, for Christ's sake—he should either do it honestly, without signaling that he felt he'd been sent pimping, or he should refuse to do it. Wrytower changed tack and for about forty minutes of his precious time my father had this secretary "chatting on" about reiki and acupressure, acupuncture and barometrics, aloe vera and wheatgrass juice. My father was enthusiastic about some of the time-honored indigenous medicines of Lequama, and Ambre's herb lore. He told me that Wrytower tried very hard not to give the appearance of humoring him. "The fool," Dad said. "He thought I was being coy."

Wrytower became impatient—and said that his employer wanted to consult Dr. Risk, as a healer. And then he backtracked, said, "I have been screening healers."

"How many so far?" Dad asked, with polite interest.

"We have developed a rigorous process—we don't chase rumors. The evidence must be quite substantial before I make any approach."

"I've passed tests? Would I have noticed these tests?"

"Yes, you've passed tests. Or rather, some rumors concerning your talents have been substantiated."

"Does that happen often?"

"It happens occasionally. But thus far all effective healers we've investigated achieve their results with forms of hypnotism, or with 'faith.' These people are of no use to my employer, who is an incredulous and unimpressionable man."

"He has no faith," Dad said, baiting the secretary.

"He has hope—and he has money," said Wrytower.

My father told me this when we were at home in Lequama, sitting on the steps one morning, damp and tired after a tussle with Barabbas, whom we were trying to bathe. I wanted to know what he had done about this approach.

"Nothing. I said that it was all *most* interesting and I left the lobby, went upstairs, and fished under beds for Fidela's snow leopard slippers, then read her that babyish book she's so fond of, *Are You My Mother?*" He was very offhand, but glanced at me as if seeking approval.

Bella arrived, riding on the handlebars of her boyfriend's push bike. I told Dad, "It's my ride." Bella's boyfriend usually took us to school, Bella on the handles, me on the back. We'd all wobble along, the bike bristling with idle legs.

Ambre came out, stood beside Dad, and asked me, "Have you told Ido about your art teacher?"

I shook my head at her, but when I left, pulling one foot back from a looming gatepost, the bike squawking in protest at our combined weight, I could hear Ambre explaining about Señor Carvos. About his advances, his furtive admiration.

Felipe Carvos. That was his name.

In the months between the shooting of the second and third sea-son of *Starting Over*, there were phone calls from Wrytower. Mr. Money was considering using Fidela in promotional material for Chronos—a print and audiovisual presentation for the prospectus. Dad told Wrytower to contact Fidela's agent. Then Wrytower called to say Mr. Money was interested in sponsoring a museum of Lequa-man arts and culture in Los Angeles. Dad asked Wrytower why so coy? Who did he imagine was listening in? Then, "I'll tell you what. La Casa de la Mujer has only one X-ray machine, and one lead vest, child-size, no gauntlets, so parents who have to steady little children are getting a good dose of radiation at each exposure."

Meanwhile, my teacher continued to stare, to single me out in class and lean too close when overseeing my work. I began to wear baggy T-shirts and to hide behind my hair. I confided my further dis-comfort to Ambre and she went to have a word with Señor Carvos. His attentions were an affront to my youth, my openness, my sense of fun, she told him. How dare he imagine that any of that normal teenage liveliness was *aimed* at him. Señor Carvos was red-faced and mock-mystified. Ambre, huffy, passed all this on to Madlena and Juanita. They all agreed it was a bad idea to report this—intensifica-tion of trouble—to Ido. "Well," said Madlena, "not till he's in L.A. and will have to think before acting on anger."

Almost everyone was upset and preoccupied in the week before we went to Los Angeles for Fidela's latest stint of work. Madlena and Fernando were having a simmering quarrel about his refusal to have a child with her. Tomás wasn't speaking to Madlena. His latest girlfriend, the García sister, had left him, saying she couldn't live with the twins. Tomás thought Madlena had never done her share of child minding, enough to take the pressure off the poor beleaguered girlfriend. The twins were so *difficult*, the girlfriend so *tolerant*, after all *she* couldn't be expected to behave in any way like a parent just because she was sharing a house with him and the twins, why should anyone expect her to put up with being left alone with those boys, even for an hour? "Oh, *sí*," said Madlena. "Too much to ask of any long-legged blonde who *puts out*."

Money couldn't wait for Dad to reach L.A.—or was possibly

avoiding directional microphones aimed by "federal America." Anyway, he sent Wrytower to La Host. Wrytower rang from the airport and Dad, still performing his improvised rites of initiation, arranged to meet the secretary in Bar Two. Wrytower said, vis-à-vis the X-ray machine, that Mr. Money wasn't going to spend two hundred thousand in *good faith*. That wasn't how he did business.

My father told me that he asked Wrytower why Money would imagine he would want to do this. Dad said, "I know your employer wants to live forever. I won't insult him with reasonable expectations, like a prolonged or pain-free life. But if I can do what he hopes I can, what does Mr. Money imagine I want? What can he imagine I *need*?"

Wrytower said that Mr. Money could pay my father to *significantly* improve his health, at regular periods, at—say—$1 million per consultation. The secretary looked nervously about him at the noisy Latino and indigene patrons (most of them just civil servants and shopkeepers).

"Does Money imagine I care about increasing my spending power?" Dad said. And then he momentarily lost interest and almost swayed sideways as his ears picked up Madlena's boozed, passionate voice. She was telling Juanita to accept Enrico if he did propose—that, although their relationship had been so cautious and civil the second time around, what good was a great passion? It was better to have respect and contentment and security than to *be had* by a great passion.

"Have I lost you, Señor Risk?" said Wrytower. And my father said to talk to him tomorrow—he couldn't think with this noise.

He went home to find Fidela carping on at Ambre about something. Something being not-quite-right. Fidela was unimpressed. Fidela was articulate. Fidela was under a lot of pressure.

"What did you do?" I asked my father, when he was telling me all about it, months later, sitting on the side of my bed around midnight on the night on which—I now know, having consulted the death certificate and my own and Bella's diaries—he must have stopped my art teacher's heart. "What did you do?" I asked. I had a nagging notion that he had *done* something, that very night. But really I meant him to tell me how he felt about Fidela.

"You know your sister, Carme. She turned her complaint into a lecture on how foolish Ambre was to want another child. She'd just found out we intended to visit that fertility clinic in Los Angeles. She said she was worried about her mother's health. It was five years since her mother had last given birth. I was a doctor, why wouldn't I discourage Ambre? And so on. I could see she regarded our plans as a *slight*—thought that, by trying for another child, we were being disloyal to her, and somehow suggesting we hadn't *got it right*. And—you know how nasty she can be. She said: 'Is it worth putting Mama's health at risk just to humor her?' I thought—well—I thought here's this five-year-old, equipped with all these insights, but they're like chess moves to her. I'm ashamed to say this. I began to sense that she frightened her mother. I was finding her a little repulsive. We'd wanted her never to live with self-doubt, so we'd always celebrated that she was so *central* in her world. She never had those dreams children have, of being left behind at the bus station, or of their hand sliding out of the grasp of a mother or a father and a crowd of strangers closing in, closing out all the familiar faces. *I* didn't have those dreams either—whose face would I have imagined? But you did. You'd climb in between Dev and me talking about how you dreamed that the rope broke on the river ferry and left you drifting. And you'd go back to sleep with your little, heavy hand in mine." He thought a moment, then said, "Carme, I wasn't going to do anything about Wrytower's offer. But when we were next in L.A., and we left Fidela in your care at the Hilton and checked into the clinic for tests . . ."

Ambre and Dad checked into the clinic for tests. He conceded to a sperm count, only to seem like a "helpful partner." Ambre was to have scans, examinations, her lifestyle "interrogated." She filled out charts describing what she ate and handed in her homemade herbal supplements for analysis. Ambre had decided, if necessary, to go as far as having her remaining eggs brought on by hormone injections, and harvested, and they'd try in vitro fertilization.

The clinic was a spa too, and they had checked in for a full four days. All of this was paid for with some of Fidela's *Starting Over* money—comparatively little—and Ambre regarded having another child as, in some ways, a gift to Fidela, despite Fidela's disapproval. "She'll get over that," Ambre confidently declared.

Ambre was examined from head to toe, and had a manicure, a massage, her hair done, she even had her hands decorated with henna. A counselor spoke to Dad about the "negative signals" he was giving Ambre. By refusing the full physical himself he was signaling that any problem they had getting pregnant was wholly *her* problem. Given Ambre's age it was almost certainly true, but what harm would it do for Mr. Risk to dissemble a little?

The female clinician had a different attitude. She showed Dad the labeled straws of his semen in a stainless steel container full of foaming white liquid nitrogen. She made some remarks to the effect of how easy it was to obtain male genetic material and in what spendthrift abundance it came. At which Dad said to her, mildly, "Well, you're a woman with a white coat and a world view, aren't you?"

On the third day, when Fidela was fully occupied on the set of *Starting Over*, Ambre, Dad, and I had lunch with Ricardo, who was in town to see some of the casino's backers. It was these men with Italian names who recommended the restaurant, which had a stunning wine list and snoop-proof walls and windows. It was funny watching the three of them. Dad and Ambre censorious and flirtatious and friendly by turns, and Ricardo, dignified and thrifty with affection—but it was *real* affection. After lunch we went shopping on Rodeo Drive. I remember walking behind Ambre and Ricardo, who went arm in arm. He bought her a dress, which would have pleased no Lequaman but my sister, one of whose complaints was that, in going to the clinic, Dad and Ambre were spending *her* money—couldn't they find any money elsewhere?

This, of course, brings me to the false note in Dad's claim that he was waiting for the persistent Mr. Wrytower and his temptations to pass over. I'm sure he would never have spent Fidela's money if he hadn't been sure he could pay her back, and *not*, like Ambre, by presenting her with a sibling.

Back at the clinic my father and Ambre had an interview with their doctors to discuss test results. The doctors told Ambre that some of her homemade ground herbs in gelatin capsules contained, as well as the expected herb mix, Marvelon, the mini-pill. Dad and Ambre were mystified only momentarily—then they guessed that it was Fidela.

Ambre was devastated. How could her little daughter be so cold-blooded, so fearless about her mother's health? "She doesn't see me as a person," Ambre mourned. She also said to my father, "She gets it from *your* side!" (I have to say I was hurt by this, as the only one on my father's *side*.)

Dad wanted a confession. He went to the Hilton and got one. I was there. He kept saying to Fidela, "What's wrong with you? We've given you everything—how could you do this?" Then, hard, "Your mother doesn't want to see you right now. I'm having to reassure her—how we'll do this and that, and treat you differently to get you back in line."

Fidela asked whether "this and that" would include interfering with her career. "You shouldn't even be upsetting me like this," she said. "What I'm doing is very difficult, and I need *support*." Then she looked into our father's face—and because of what she saw there her tone changed. There was no whine, no wounded dignity. She was cool. "I'm under contract," she said, "and you and Mama don't have enough money to get into a law case with the studio."

"Litigation," Dad said, reflexively extending her vocabulary.

Sitting on my bed in Flores Negras, at midnight, three months later, my father told me, "I felt like I didn't have my daughter's respect—because I didn't have the earning power of the people surrounding her. The people who kept reminding her how, for her, the sky was the limit." He was silent and my hand sought his. He moved closer, scented by a La Host night, and the light, sour, discharged scent of his gift's use. "I don't want to put too much emphasis on that. I felt less unmanned than provoked. But the next morning I called Wry-tower. And told him what I wanted and what I might need. I got Ricardo to set up a bank account in the Cayman Islands. And I told Wrytower I would need a resuscitation team on hand, with equipment ranging from defibrillators to hot packs to a supply of good screened type O blood for transfusions. I knew that I felt knocked about if I just fixed the cartilage in someone's knee. For instance. And I couldn't gauge how far I'd have to go with Money—or how far I might want to *take* him. So I took precautions."

He took me with him. Actually he took all of us. I think he'd finally discussed Money's proposal with Ambre, and she was against it. He convinced her it would be silly not to at least investigate further, and she decided to go with him to keep him under her eye. Fidela had finished for the week, and when she launched into a complaint about being dragged off to visit her parent's "weird friends" she was told that she had no vote.

Wrytower sent a car to fetch us. When we got to the estate I could see that even Fidela was intimidated by how exclusive, how *hermetic* it all was—a show of great wealth by silence and privacy. Ambre lost her nerve, and we left her sitting on the edge of her seat, on a vast white sofa, knees together and hands in her lap, as though scared of contamination. Fidela was in an adjoining room with a hundred-inch central screen flanked by eight smaller ones; she had the remote in her hand and was grazing, her mouth wide open.

I insisted on going with my father.

Wrytower walked us into the heart of the estate, through one long room with a wall of glass, beyond which sand and waves seemed piled up. There was scarcely anyone on the beach, even near the water's edge. When Dad asked about this, Wrytower pointed up as if at heaven and said, "Cameras. Not everyone likes being watched, even in California."

As we walked, Wrytower explained what his employer hoped of the "treatment." "Let's not talk anymore about your 'alleged' talent.

We'll take it as true, just for the purposes of clarity. My employer realizes that your talent is precious and finite at any one time. At least, that is what we've learned by report. Also, you seem to have a fear of overextending yourself—I gather you want the resuscitation equipment and blood products for yourself, not Mr. Money?"

I gave Dad a horrified sidelong glance, saw him nodding.

"My employer doesn't want to draw any attention to you. He isn't a hasty man. He may want the clock turned back, but gradually. He'd like to get off the oxygen and spend maybe an hour or two a day out of his wheelchair. For a start. In two more years—say, five more visits—he'd like to get back on the golf course. He'll say it's a special diet, surgery, meditation—and grow younger, discreetly. Grow young enough to enjoy the full pleasures of life."

Wrytower spoke of his employer's wishes as the rich do of their expectations, as though all of it is utterly reasonable. They have the power to pamper themselves, and pampering is somehow *progress*—while there are people puzzling out where best to place the baby's crib so it won't get wet when the roof leaks. It occurred to me that this was why it was safe for Dad to do this, that a man who pays, and who thinks that anything he can acquire is his right, is not going to be too impressed, is not going to worship or witness or proselytize.

We were taken into Mr. Money's suite. The resuscitation team was in an adjoining room—highly trained, well equipped, and totally in the dark. Not only did they have no instructions, none of them could speak English. All were Taiwanese imports who wanted someone to sponsor their green cards.

Mr. Money was a fragile, bleached old man in a wheelchair, wearing a paisley silk dressing gown and pajamas that were as glossy and beautiful as the plumage of a jungle bird. His eyes were a peach-rimmed and marbled blue, his mouth was open, and his cheeks hollow with sucking at air. The skin over his hands was so thin and shifty it scarcely looked alive.

Wrytower directed me to a chair by the wall and took a step back himself, leaving my father looking down into the face of the man in the wheelchair.

Edwin Money spoke, his lower jaw never moving up to touch his lips together, the words all in a small breathless head voice. He said he was paying for proofs at the agreed price.

My father stepped up to Money, swooped really, eager, and went down on his knees before him. He took Money's hands.

What did we see? Wrytower and me? A kind of rapture of focus that wasn't sight or touch, although Dad was looking at and touching Money's spotted hands. Then he parted the robe and pajama jacket to discover Money's skinny, fallen chest, his high-hitched shoulders, always raised to draw breath, his mottled throat and face. We saw pale fingers with pink tips against sinewy neck and skull face, a strong thumb brush lips as lean and yielding as good schnitzel, and the pressure of the touch shift the old man's false teeth. And then we saw blossoming, a glow of better health that seemed to surface—a flush, like fury or sexual excitement. I felt that I was seeing signs of some odd and mutual joy.

Edwin Money was supporting my father in his arms. He got up out of his wheelchair and helped my father to his feet. Dad sat on the bed. Money pulled the oxygen tubes away from his nostrils and walked to the room's full-length mirror to look at himself with a placid, critical eye, like a man checking the knot in his tie.

Dad turned to Wrytower, who was standing near me, so forgetfully still that I knew he was another fatally snared imagination. Dad said, "I don't need a transfusion. I'll have a vitamin injection and fruit juice. Then you can have us delivered back to our hotel."

Wrytower rang the bank in the Cayman Islands—made the transfer of funds and had Dad check that it was done. Dad said to Money that he'd see him in three months, and we were taken back to the Hilton.

In the car Dad went to sleep, his mouth partly open so that we could see his bleeding gums and blood-smeared teeth. His head rested on Ambre's shoulder, and she stroked his hair, and told me how afraid she was for him.

The big earthquake a couple of hours later didn't even wake him.

Back in La Host Fidela went to school with the nuns and for a while came home only on the weekends. She was quiet and dutiful, helpful around the house. She went a little overboard with acts of contrition—burned her posters, wore somber clothes—but Ambre and Dad thought it was self-dramatization, never mockery.

I began to avoid school, and persuaded the García brothers to let me do their books. But I did have to confide to them *why* I was avoiding school.

And so a family meeting was called. *The* formidable family meeting.

Madlena, Fernando, and Ambre visited the school principal and then went to the police. People stopped trying to protect the feelings of my teacher's wife—and she found me in the market one day and pursued me, calling me a "little whore" and bashing me around the head with her wallet. Dad was away when it happened and I came home and cried in Ambre's arms.

Dad had escorted Fidela to Los Angeles, where the first part of a Thanksgiving special was shooting. The plot was something like this: Fidela's character and her screen father were searching for her mother's brother, who had gone all to the bad in Miami some years before. Fidela's agent and producer persuaded Dad that they could mind Fidela during the filming in Miami. They said, "She knows us so well now." Fidela pleaded—she wanted to be baby-sat by Barbara and Alicia—please Papa, please. And so off she went to Miami, while Dad improved Money's health and then flew home.

Everyone, including me, continued to protect my father from the full extent of our fears about my stalker. We didn't tell him about the wife's assault. But he was home when Señor Carvos sent me a bunch of flowers and card to "apologize for the trouble he'd caused me." Ambre tried to hide the flowers from me, but I was in the living room when the delivery boy came to the door. She said to me, "Don't touch them or look at them, Carme." She passed the card and flowers to Dad and went to the phone to call the police. Dad was having one of those strange pulses of stillness he always had when conflicted, when he was so involved in inhibiting an uncivilized action that he couldn't move at all. When I came down the stairs an hour later—Juanita had arrived to keep me company while Ambre and Dad went out to see the police again—I found the flowers, so aged they were dark and desiccated, and the paper of the card foxed as if it had been stowed away somewhere for twenty years and corroded quietly by its own acid.

Later, Fernando told me that they had all met to browbeat the La Host chief of police and threaten him with the specter of 1983-style vigilantism. "Your father was the only one who made no threats," Fernando said. "Unless you count his saying that he wouldn't be self-indulgently merciful."

The next day Ambre and Ido were informed that Fidela had brought proceedings against them to "divorce" them, on the grounds that they were threatening to sabotage her career, and that they were destructive, unsuitable, experimenting parents who practiced black magic and took drugs.

Of course they rang Miami and tried to speak to Fidela, but were only allowed to talk to a lawyer, who said that the hearing date was being set. Fidela had complained of certain unsavory practices on the part of her parents. "For instance," said the lawyer, her voice dripping fastidious disapproval, "your practice of *burying* family members when they're ill or unhappy. Very distressing for my client." The lawyer said that Ambre and Dad could arrange a conference before the hearing—they were to get *their* lawyer to work with her on that.

That week diphtheria broke out in La Host. Not among the under-sevens, who for some years had been part of a government-sponsored vaccination program, but among unvaccinated adults. Dad was busy at the hospital—and I volunteered my help, since I'd already had diphtheria. Anton Xavier and my father had the first of only two quarrels they had during their friendship, because Dad wouldn't follow procedure and act in an unselfinterested fashion. He insisted on taking some of the small supply of vaccine that was already in the country in excess of normal needs and using it to vaccinate friends and family. He and Fernando had to hold down Madlena, who yelled that she'd rather die than act in a way that was against the people's interests. Then, vaccinated, she went off fuming to throw her weight around with the World Health Organization and other aid agencies—and soon there was vaccine shipment in sufficient quantities for a campaign of mass vaccinations that temporarily closed the high schools and meant I was *legitimately* able to avoid my art teacher.

Señor Carvos had appealed successfully against his suspension by the school. The principal argued that if there was improper behavior it wasn't unprovoked. Hadn't Bella and I been caught lying on the school copier making photocopies of our breasts? (We had.) Weren't we part of that group who swam in La Mula off the stone bridge without bothering to wear swimming costumes? (We were.)

At La Casa de la Mujer Anton Xavier showed me how to perform emergency tracheotomies. I catnapped in the hospital corridor while my father worked for seventy-two hours straight, then went home when it was all over to see how Ambre was doing with the lawyers.

When the diphtheria was under control, Ambre and Dad flew to Miami for the conference at which Dad said very little—apart from the obvious "You're our daughter. We love you. Please come home." But he said it all in a stony, implacable tone. Fidela spent only thirteen minutes in the room with her parents. She said, as if speaking to two immature people, that she believed she knew what was best for her, and hoped, if they loved her as they claimed, that one day they'd be able to see that too.

My father and stepmother came home—Ambre weeping helplessly most of the way. The next morning I heard her howl of despair and a stifled flurry of movement in the room. Dad spoke to reassure her, very tender. He came out carrying her in his arms and wrapped in a blood-soaked sheet. He put her in her car and drove her to the hospital where, it was confirmed, she'd had a miscarriage. She stayed that night and he stayed with her.

The next day I kept an appointment to have a dress fitted, the dress of gold dupion silk I was to wear at Juanita and Enrico's wedding. While we bridesmaids were at the dressmaker's, talking, laughing, flouncing about or holding still, my art teacher barged into the fitting room. Señor Carvos was shouting that I was cruel, how could

I send him these *letters* and yet pretend I despised him? He was waving a piece of paper. There was a hiss of fury from the other bridesmaids, then a flashing rustle as they hustled him out down the stairs. He dropped the paper and I picked it up. It was ruled, torn from a school exercise book, and it read:

I don't often think of you. I wonder if you'd recognize me now with these clumsy hips that keep connecting uncontrollably with the corners of tables and desks. I try to conjure you at times, in this hot country, perhaps when I'm coming back from delivering my friend Bella's oranges to her Nona and we're carrying the pot between us, swinging it, and I try to see you in front of me, and imagine I could run to catch you up and tell you how happy I am. But I find I have trouble with your face, trouble remembering it. You are as mute as Dad once was—and you're hiding your huge hands. You look ashamed, but it's my shame you're looking with. I'm sorry to be so forgetful.

Carme, who still loves you.

The bridesmaids came back to find me weeping, with the paper balled in my hand.

I wasn't asleep that night when my father cracked my door and whispered my name. I sat up in bed, rearranged the pillow, and put out my hand for the light switch.

"No!"

I drew my hand back. He came and sat on the end of my bed. The air in the room changed—I became gradually aware of that scent, sour, metallic, like hot circuitry.

He said, "Madlena told me how upset you were. She said Carvos had a letter he claimed was yours."

"It was mine. But not to him. It was a letter to Dev."

He was silent, so I reminded him how Dev had written me a note once saying, "Write to me if you can, or would like to."

"Yes. I remember."

"I don't know where Señor Carvos found my letter. It's quite old. Two years maybe. I guess it dropped out of my bag—I don't send them."

We were both quiet, perhaps thinking how forgetting is more deathly than death.

Then Dad sort of shook himself, and said, in a cool and precise way, that although when he had come to Lequama with me he'd set out to be good, now he found he had been merely well behaved.

"What have you done?" I asked. "Have you done something?"

He was silent. And I was glad I hadn't turned on the light. I didn't want to see him, because I suddenly understood that if I looked I'd see all I had of him, all I'd ever have—a short stretch of a long, long road.

Journal: La Host, evening and night, National Day, August 8, 2003

The British documentary crew was at pains to explain the scale of their project. They were shooting in 35 millimeter, with their eyes on film festivals and general theatrical release. "And we are, as much as possible, trying to avoid *editorializing*. Of course, we do choose where to point the camera, and whom to interview, but we're shooting heaps and heaps of footage so, to a certain extent, we'll find our narrative in the editing suite."

This was the director.

On our arrival at the cocktail party Bella and I were presented with frozen margaritas in the right kind of shallow glass rimmed with salt, then introduced to the director, Bella as "Frei's granddaughter." She didn't bother to correct them. The director talked about his film, introduced Bella to the people who would walk her through Los Muertos (the prison was now the Museum of the Revolution). The director had read Bella's book in proof, and wanted her to talk about "the culture of terror" with anecdotes, ending with a reading of Frei's poem "Still Life with Severed Heads." Here he got technical, describing the script of Bella's appearance as "from 'Violence reached unprecedented levels' to 'Jules: Silence, Paralysis.' "

One of the producers touched my arm and pointed at a fair-haired young man on the far side of the room. He was a director's assistant, Oliver. Could we give him a ride when we left? Oliver was off work for the evening and was going to the party in the Plaza—naturally—where he hoped to hook up with his rather odd German friend, Hans. "We're all terribly fond of Oliver," the producer said. "He turned up in La Host a month ago when we were researching locations. Fortuitously. He's been traveling through Central America in some fairly *hairy* places, with a false press pass. He's recently finished a one-year internship at the UN. They're hard to get, you know, it's quite an honor. He has a law degree, I believe. He's a New Zealander, but quite cosmopolitan, and a very nice chap."

Oliver looked our way then, and I recognized him—one of the young tourists from the cemetery.

I was curious about Oliver and the "odd" Hans, so I said yes, of course Bella and I would give Oliver a lift, once Bella had done talking to Dr. Scott.

"Andrew!" the producer said to the director. "You're keeping Ms. Frei from Jon Scott!"

There were apologies, and Bella was taken by the arm and led out onto the terrace to meet Dr. Scott. I followed to listen. I saw Oliver crossing the room to intercept me, but there was a crowd, and he seemed to be popular, and I was out the door before he could reach me.

Jon Scott was wearing one of those rumpled cream linen suits that Englishmen seem to love to get into whenever they travel anywhere even remotely warmer than the British Isles. He was slight, balding, good-looking in a faintly pinched way.

Bella, always blind to social niceties when her interest was engaged, practically shouldered aside the person who had made the introductions and stated her business. Bella was researching, and she was using her time well. Behind her abruptness I had a sense of all the proposals she'd had to write in her academic career. *My* education in the American university system had been paid for, almost entirely, out of the fund of several hundreds of thousands of U.S. dollars my father had left for his daughters in a trust administered by

Nathan Wrytower, secretary of a man so rich his life was like the life of Stoker's Dracula: "At best mystery." *I* hadn't had to hustle.

Bella explained to Dr. Scott that she wanted to ask him some questions that would help her write the foreword to her book on the culture of terror.

"Ah, yes, Andrew has read it," Jon Scott said, guarded and conceding at once. "He says it's very good." It was as though he thought Bella was trying to catch him out.

Bella literally shook herself, to let this slide off her. She explained her great-uncle's epitaph and said that someone told her to "ask Jon" about the Avenida Bueyes Negros. Its history.

"Ah!" Jon said. "That's an interesting question, Bella—may I call you Bella? I assume you know about Turoc Iddu, the Taoscal temple that the Spaniards and their Indian allies pulled down stone by stone in 1588, the year of the Armada, actually. It was where the Presidential Palace now is. The bark books came from its library."

Jon Scott told us that Turoc Iddu was built toward the end of the Taoscal wars of conquest, to celebrate a certain great chief and his armies—posthumously—on a site already sacred as a grave or gateway. The words were interchangeable in Taoscal. "The tradition of tethering snakes on graves was known as 'putting guards on the gate.'" The temple was a four-sided pyramid with a double donjon—one atop another. It had a ramp in its eastern face, and when the temple gates were open, the light of the rising sun shone into its main underground chamber. The gates were around twenty feet high, of palm wood covered in panels of copper relief work. Two complete panels are in the Institute of Antiquities in Cologne. An archaeologist at the institute calculated the dimensions of the gates from the remaining nails and these panels—and he calculated the temple's dimensions by a comparison between these remnants and the size of gates in a picture in a bark book belonging to the British Museum.

Jon Scott said that from bark books and the archaeological record, this fellow in Cologne also ascertained that there was a slightly elevated, paved road that ran from the river to the temple—in the exact same location as the Avenida Bueyes Negros, which appeared on maps of La Host as far back as 1830. The archaeologist's thought was that the road was used for processions of captives and for the passage of sacrificial animals, latterly oxen, which, like horses, had arrived with the conquistadors. Actually, Spanish livestock reached the Taoscal before the Spaniards. There are pictures of them in the bark books. Black, ceremonially perfect animals, in a cavalcade, herded, and waylaid by priests with long-handled slashing knives.

Almost by the by, Jon Scott said that at Easter in Florence the oxen that drew the flower-covered wagon bearing the model of the Baptistry, into which the rocket-powered dove flies from the Duomo, igniting fireworks, were traditionally pure white. "There are certain almost universal aesthetic principles deriving from what, in nature, will strike human eyes as exemplary. It is unusual to find a culture that doesn't have something to say in the form of proverb or nursery rhyme on the subject of white horses, black dogs, and so forth.

"The fellow from Cologne thought that the captives were sacrificial too—but I doubt it. Bearing in mind that my area of expertise is the Mneone, who are basically of the Carib language group, while the Taoscal are Quechua. I'm no great expert on the Taoscal. But because I'm an *anthropologist*, not an archaeologist or historian, I can use my *imagination* to extrapolate a little. The Taoscal have very complicated and particular traditions around *ingestion*, not eating, which involve ideas not so much about hygiene as about power and inheritance. They have unique ideas about inheritance."

"The chief is forbidden to have children," Bella gave as an example.

"Yes. Every Lequaman knows that. And I'm sure that every Lequaman had a little giggle about Madlena and Fernando's recent birth notice! But Bella, think about this: in the Taoscal 'spider ceremony' the sorcerer who is bitten by the spider is supposed to—briefly—be taken into the spider's 'wisdom,' which means its multiple viewpoints—those eye-studded tank turrets tarantulas have. The hallucinations are part of a toxic reaction to the spider's bite, but the Taoscal don't consider that the spider's bite puts poison in their bodies—the bite is *ingestion*—the spider takes the sorcerer into its body and the sorcerer is 'spider-eyed.' "

Bella said, uncertain, guessing, "So they would never have eaten the captives because the captives weren't wise enough to have triumphed or escaped."

"More or less. And these oddities about power and ingestion do extend to humans. For example—there's a prayer of instruction, on becoming a sorcerer, that begins 'Go to a haunted place and offer up your flesh and bones.' And they have at least one cannibalistic rite. The chief's heir is required to eat the dead chief's heart before becoming chief him- or herself. That right has *always* been observed, so that the line of succession isn't one of procreation, but *ingestion*. Back in early '84 when the then chief, Aureliano Zabe, finally died—do you know about this, Bella? He basically faded away; the poor man had been tortured in Los Muertos and, like your greatuncle Frei, was found in the prison infirmary on the eighth of August, '83. He'd been beaten so badly that a section of his small bowel was twisted and had died. There was an operation that removed the dead section, but left him without enough bowel to sustain effective digestion. He died of malnutrition eight months later despite the best medical care the state could buy. Aureliano Zabe died, and Fernando Sola ate his heart."

At this point I turned around to see who else was listening. I saw Oliver, looking our way, but not near enough to overhear.

Jon Scott was saying, "It's no use asking Fernando Sola for further details. Firstly, he'll not recall the ceremony, because he was almost certainly under the influence of yagga, and secondly, the chief isn't the keeper of the law regarding the traditions and ceremonies of succession. In fact, the elders don't tell the chief's successor any detail of what he's expected to do till the time arrives. After all, the chief is supposed, while chief-apparent and after succeeding, to exhibit signs of having 'the luck of the chief.' Things have to work out for him or her by *chance* alone."

"Hang on." Bella had begun to rub the too-thin hair at her temples. "You're telling me that the elders trust to the chief's luck except where it comes to the *choice* of chief? I always thought that the chief chose his or her successor."

"Has Sola chosen his?"

Bella shrugged.

I said, "I don't think so." Then I asked Dr. Scott what having his heart eaten made of the chief's grave, if the snakes are meant to keep scavengers away, but part of the chief's body has been—well—already scavenged or salvaged for the next chief?

Jon Scott said he supposed that if other bodies were secured intact and the chief's wasn't, the intention must be to plow the chief's life force back into the tribe, as it were. He actually *said*, "As it were."

Dr. Scott saw us out to Bella's car. Bella had been so attentive to his talk that he was showing his approval by courtesy. The New Zealander followed us—after a hurried introduction at the door. Since Bella was still in conversation, Oliver became my responsibility. We stopped behind Bella and Jon Scott on the flight of wide shallow steps that went down to the old crushed-limestone circular carriageway. The lawn sprinklers were on and the grass had begun to sparkle and stand up like prickling hairs.

Oliver said he'd seen me at the cemetery. "And your sister."

I was used to this. I said, "Yes, I'm Fidela Guevara's sister."

Oliver seemed annoyed. He said, "I suppose it *is* possible to read a book upside down."

"Meaning what?"

"Meaning you're not just someone's sister."

Was this fan of Fidela's meaning to suggest I had a low self-image?

Jon Scott shook Bella's hand, wished her luck with the shooting on Friday, with the book, with the good old academic diaspora. "But *I* can't talk, who never really left Cambridge."

He shook my hand too, and went back in. Bella lit up another cigarette, then we all got into Bella's old Lada and she coaxed it back to life.

Bella wanted to know why Dr. Scott hadn't looked at me.

"I've gone native, I'm wearing my hair in barrettes like every other Lequaman girl under the age of thirty."

"I love that style!" said Oliver from the backseat, and Bella and I both turned around and, as though we'd settled between us to do so if he bothered us, gave him quelling looks. "It's so timeless," Oliver grinned at us. "You look like my aunty's photos of her days coffee-picking here in '84." Bella and I did exchange a look at this. More nostalgia. He probably thought he'd hit a jackpot—in a car with Frei's great-niece and Fidela's sister.

We didn't get near the Plaza, but drove around and around its anterior streets, through the narrow gap remaining between parked cars, looking for a space. Several times we advised Oliver to get out, if he *did* want to find his what's-his-name.

"Hans. But I'm quite comfortable here," he said.

Eventually we had to take the car to Flores Negras and park it in the front yard. There were five other cars in the yard, but the house was closed up.

Bella was in a hurry not to miss the fireworks scheduled for 9:30 but, like me, she had to make some adjustments to what she was wearing. She squatted by one wing mirror with her makeup bag at her feet and did her eyes and mouth by the car's interior light. I was wearing my Elizabeth-Taylor-in-*A-Place-in-the-Sun* dress—simple, white, finely quilted. I took off my canvas shoes and put on high-heeled sandals. I removed my barrettes, hung my head, tossed my hair forward, combed out the static, then straightened, feeling it fall, heavy and warm, against my upper arms. I borrowed Bella's lipstick.

The New Zealander was watching me with a serious, displeased look.

Bella said to him, "Come on, we're walking." She took my arm and we went out through the gate. He followed.

The fireworks began before we reached the Plaza. Bella cursed and broke into a run. We chased her. We came to a stop with several dozen other people at the top of the arch of the stone bridge as great geometrical lights expanded overhead and under us, stretched and blurred by the river water. The sounds of the explosions were sharp and out of sync. One big concussion set off all the car alarms. Around us cars began to flash and whoop and whistle. Bella hung laughing over the railing, her breasts pressed—tempting and perilous, held, it seemed, only by surface tension—at the neck of her top. While still involved in her laughter she decided she needed another smoke, got one out and looked around for a light, was lit—then came away from the obliging man with a full bottle, from which she drank off half and gave the other half to me. It was mountain wine, which they were now bottling in stubbies with twist tops as "Spiritos las Montains." I drank and was pressed against the railing by a surge of people. Oliver caught me around the waist to stop me from falling. "Are you going to drink all that yourself?" he said, and took the last bit in the bottle from me—playful, but showing me his strength—all very easy and brotherly. Galaxies were growing together on either side of us. Oliver dropped the bottle, making a momentary tear in the distorted nebula below us. He followed it with his eyes and, while the shock waves of the fireworks tamped the air around our heads, his head was against my neck, chin on my shoulder. "Let's find a bar and get one each," he said, and pulled me away from the railing. I put out my hand for Bella and collected her with a couple she seemed to have snagged.

We ran on through streets more closely packed the nearer they were to the Plaza. Then we were in the Plaza. We walked from a reverberating roar into a wide one. The front of the cathedral was lit up. Yellow-and-white banners draped the length of its two towers. Strings of light were twined about every projection in the stonework so that the cathedral bristled with light. The sound system was up too loud, playing a distorted Alberto Duarte.

Then I saw the singer, on a stage by the cathedral steps, fat and fiftyish, in a glistening lounge-lizard jacket, singing in a strong white spotlight while the crowd sang along with him: *Rosa, where are you now?* His greatest hit. Whoever Rosa was, whose whereabouts Lequama had been wondering for twenty years, it seemed Duarte still missed her acutely, for I could see that while sweat beaded his brow, there was an unblistered lacquer of tears on his wobbling cheeks.

Despite the terrific noise I could still hear a group of girls, very near to us, teasing two officers of the La Host police force who were mounted on two stonily calm, so possibly deaf and blind, police horses. "Come on, show us your nightsticks. Please do," the girls were saying.

Bella began flapping her arms over her head, then plunged forward through the crowd. I saw that she had collared a twin, and that it was Aureliano, wearing one of those soda-dispenser hats that were a gimmick for some years at U.S. sports stadiums. Bella hauled Aureliano back toward me, saying, as she came into earshot, "Honey, let us have a suck on that." She pulled the end of the plastic tubing out of the corner of Aureliano's mouth and put it in her own, took a deep draw, rolled her eyes, gasped, and kissed the surprised twin. Then she pushed him face-to-face with me and offered me "a suck on his tube." I hesitated, asked was this Aureliano's entire private supply? He nodded. I had money, five bills neatly folded in one of the little zip-locked pockets on the inside edge of my hem. I asked Aureliano if he had any money, and he answered, typically, that Carlos had their money. "Then you mustn't lose Carlos." I took a sip of the warm brew and tasted only its plastic dispenser.

Aureliano pointed out that Bella had kissed him.

"You don't want me to kiss you," I said, disbelieving. I was seeing another of those serious looks, and drunken dignity.

"Oh," Bella cried, "can I kiss Carme too?" He hadn't, but she did, a nice hard long kiss with her big soft breasts pressed against mine. I caught her around her warm, creaking, vinyl-covered waist. She broke off, gave me a dimpled smile, and moved on to Oliver. She lost no time in prizing his mouth open with her tongue. Light pooled around his fingertips where they depressed the slick black vinyl on her buttocks.

I told Aureliano to take off his silly hat. He did, and I straightened his hair and gave him one small chaste kiss. He thanked me, put his hat back on, and said he must find Carlos, who had wandered off. They would finish the booze between them before going to the party at Indian Affairs where Tomás would be bound to give them at least one more drink.

"The purpose being?"

"Getting falling-over drunk," Aureliano said, seriously and soberly. "Where do you want your evening to end up?"

We were jostled together as Oliver, deprived of air for some time, buckled at the knees and staggered.

I wanted to go back in time. I wanted to see Madlena Guevara ride her nasty black stallion into the Plaza fountain. I wanted to see Tomás, covered in Dairy Whip and dancing on a table. I wanted to see the Russian ambassador being blanket-tossed by a group of dancers from Marguerite Millay's academy. I wanted to see Fernando and the flunkies and Don Marcos and the English poet Norton Lawrence playing Russian roulette on the palace rooftop; and drama students dressed in Pola Pastrez uniforms, thinking they are terribly shocking and clever, bursting into the party at Indian Affairs and being pelted by chairs and locked in the storeroom, the key to which disappears down the gullet of a hysterical Guido Hernández. I wanted to see the doomed Brad Powers floating a foot from the pipe-covered ceiling in a basement corridor. In short, I wanted to be at the country's most famous, wild, unplanned party, New Year's Eve 1983, and not National Day 2003.

Aureliano repeated his question—my answer must really have mattered to him—just as his twin found him and, savvy as ever, immediately tuned into what was going on. "At the moment it looks like she is going to get only whatever Bella leaves for her." He pointed at Bella and Oliver, who were pushing, pelvis to pelvis.

Fidela had followed Carlos. I heard her clear, carrying, bored voice before I saw her. "Carme. There you are. Was Jon Scott very dull? I've already spotted some of those film people—three self-important pimply young men with a fluffy wind-baffle boom somehow strayed from the camera operator. Ambre is over there." She pointed. "I'm going to have to ditch her. She said she'd go home after the fireworks. Doing her 'I'm an old woman who has no use for parties' act. Now she's sniffed out old Papa García and his grade-A-beefcake sons and grandsons, and she is sticking her tongue in the old man's hairy earhole. I kid you not."

Fidela finished and looked straight into Oliver's flushed, slightly tumescent face as though it were the hairy earhole in question. Her very stagy and succinct complaint had stopped all activity in a ten-foot radius. We were all staring at her. "But I suppose," she went on, making allowances, "everybody has to do something tonight for old

299

time's sake." She looked at the group of us and, although she was ten years my junior and four years younger than the twins, she said, "Well, have fun, kids," and walked off. She made her way through the crowd using her brisk, insistent voice and tone of barely patient politeness. It worked wonders, and she quickly disappeared from sight.

"Right!" Carlos was decisive. "Let's take Carme to the bar." He stooped and put his shoulder behind my thigh so that I was forced to sit. Aureliano caught on and did the same on the other side of me, and I was lifted onto their shoulders. "Woman in need of air!" Carlos shouted, and they began to barge through the crowd, their outside arms folded across my knees, elbows out at head height. I thought I heard Oliver—not Bella—call out my name. Several people—addressing themselves always to Carlos, never Aureliano—threatened to tell their mother and Fernando Sola that they were making a nuisance of themselves.

"*Dios mio!*" Carlos yelled, to anyone in earshot. "Have a famous parent, and a famously *loco parentis*, and everyone's always on your case!"

Carlos made a sudden change of direction; I fell, but caught him about his neck. Aureliano kept hold of the leg he had and I was, briefly, a suspension bridge sagging between the two, the hem of my dress dragging across the litter of paper streamers. Carlos took us up the cathedral steps, where a very big man in a suit straight-armed him to a hard stop.

Someone said, "It's all right. It's the Juiliano-Guevara twins with a girl." The twins set me down at the foaming edge of a sea of floral wreaths, laid at the feet of a statue. I could see by the rippling border of red satin draped around its base that it was newly unveiled. The statue, in shining bronze, was of a soldier, shirt unbuttoned, leaning on a rifle. He was talking to a peasant woman who was sitting at his feet by a basket full of fruit and flowers, with a plump infant in her lap. There was a podium near the statue with a bouquet of microphones. Back from the edge of the terrace at the top of the steps stood Don Marcos Pastrez, vice-president of the republic; the Health minister, Guido Hernández; the Archbishop of La Host, in full purple regalia; and a collection of aides in suits or uniforms and clergy in white lace surplices. An electronic scoreboard above the cathedral's main door still shone with the words of the post-revolutionary prayer: *"Lord, I thank You that I am on my knees only to You. I thank You for my work, and for my sufficiency of Your world's good. . . ."*

Carlos was explaining to a bodyguard that I'd felt faint and they had brought me up out of the crowd.

"I was trying to get to the bar and they hijacked me," I said, and the bodyguards turned, frowning on the twins, who began to back away. At that moment both Don Marcos and Guido arrived by my side. The twins, seeing parent figures, were quickly reabsorbed by the crowd. Guido Hernández wanted to congratulate me on my chosen specialty. He told me that Health was running a Directly Observed Therapy program in La Host. There were fewer new cases of TB this year. He said, "We want to do the same in the provinces." He had a head start, I told him, with housing still fixed at ten percent of income. No crowding, no epidemic—that's more or less what it came down to in the end. Then, since I was still sober and we were having a conversation, I asked Guido if I could see his "lead content in the soil" file sometime.

He looked cagey and mournful, wondering if he was being mocked.

It didn't help that Don Marcos laughed.

Guido Hernández had—notoriously—insisted for years that the erratic behavior of certain government members was due to lead poisoning. All those years in the jungle living on river water cleaned only with purifying tablets. The Ambella had high levels of lead in its soil—a fact verified only recently not by tests related to soil or water but from the satellite images commissioned by a Taoscal-owned mining concern. The Council of Projects was looking for certain minerals, silver, gold, nickel, and lead. I told Guido that I'd read about the satellite's findings.

"Yes, I *did* have something," he said.

We were holding our conversation head-to-head, in shouts—the crowd was in howling high spirits. I told Guido, "I have a theory of my own."

"*Sí?*" Don Marcos was sighting along his straight nose. Guido even managed to look skeptical, difficult for someone whose normal expression is chaffing worry.

I told them that it was Maria Godshalk's cooking. A sudden change of diet caused a food allergy. An allergic reaction. I was specific. Activated immune cells released cytokines and interleukins. There would have been changes in their endocrine systems that would produce effects ranging from fever, somnolence, agitation, combativeness, belligerence—didn't all that describe Madlena and Fernando in 1983?—through a sense of impending doom and hallucinations—the Black Room phenomena—then fatigue progressing to lethargy, memory loss, and dysphasia, which meant forgetting words. Wasn't Madlena always forgetting words and substituting others? Her sexual ethics in favor of "nonmonopoly," and when she drank too much she'd take a pledge to become a "tree toeteller," to the frustration of the mountain-wine-loving "omnipotent" Tomás. And didn't they all forget *names*? Forget when they'd last seen certain people? Powers, Lawrence, and Pablito Masolan, for instance.

Guido was looking at me, slack-jawed.

Don Marcos reminded me, coolly, that dysphasia was a symptom of Parkinson's disease, linked to a difficulty swallowing.

"Ah, *bodies*, we can't forget them, can we?" I said. (After I'd talked to Madlena and Fernando about their old quarrel the other day, Ambre had taken me aside to explain that Madlena's outburst on the Wall would have been due, in part, to the fact she was around six weeks pregnant with the twins.)

"So, Maria's cooking made us crazy?" Don Marcos said. "Have you ever read Lydia Yahanova's questionnaires? Yahanova's questionnaires do show what we were like, heavy metals and—what do you call them?—*interleukins* aside. We are there in our answers—my repression, Madlena's egoism and earnestness, Fernando's sinister self-love, and Maria answering as though she misunderstands the questions, like Bertolt Brecht's testimony before the House Un-American Activities Committee. Lydia Yahanova wanted, as any self-respecting sadist would, to tie Fernando down and clip electrodes to his nipples. She was a corrupt practitioner, but the questionnaires she had us fill in do say a lot about the people we were then blindly aiming to be."

"Señor Vice-President, Minister Hernández?" an official interrupted us. He said the road had cleared a little behind the cathedral and the cars could now leave.

They were due at a banquet in the old palace, now named the Ministries Building, since it housed several ministries as well as the parliament, but popularly known as the Miniseries Building, because of its history of dramas.

I looked across the Plaza at the packed balcony of Bar Two, the seething shadows on the hotel's balustraded roof, and beside the hotel the street covered with plastic sheeting, laser lights casting green and red geometrical lozenges on the inside of its roof.

Don Marcos took my arm and turned me away from the Plaza. He said Madlena had told him I'd been asking about the murders and disappearances. He walked me into the cathedral, saying that since I was ultimately headed for the party at Indian Affairs I should catch a ride with him to the palace. The street selected for the dance party was the usual direct route; the organizers must have been hoping it would act as a catchment between the Plaza and the palace. His car was going to have to take him around by a less direct way.

He and Guido were going in different cars; too vital a pair of eggs to be put in one basket.

We walked through the cathedral. It was quiet and smelled of incense and the straw of the straw-bottomed chairs. Its choirs of candles were full, every saint appearing illuminated. Underneath the altar was a glass coffin containing the wax effigy of an obscure local saint, the Taoscal priest Miscere, whose sainthood was disputed by the Vatican. The top of his coffin was covered in fresh red roses. He looked young enough—and the people had taken him to represent whomever they had missed for twenty years.

Don Marcos said, softly, "I believe Pablito was murdered because he was offensive to our dignity. He mocked and jeered, and once appeared at the palace peddling triple-decker coffins made of timber wardrobes to the poor grieving families who were in the capital after the victory to look among the corpses for missing soldier sons and daughters. Maria and Carlos D'Escoto tried to bust Pablito's un-bustable ass. It was as if he had a death wish; I've never met anyone so compulsively offensive. But I'm not exactly sure *who* killed him. *I* shot Norton Lawrence and Madlena and I fed his body into a fur-nace in the palace basement." He paused, waiting for a reaction. When I was quiet, he went on firmly, "I'm telling you that we did these things, Carme"—he looked into my eyes—*"for no good reason.* You're asking questions—Madlena says—like you're performing surgery and you expect results. But there's no point asking about these acts because these acts were *pointless.*"

"Doing something for no reason isn't the same as having a trivial reason," I said.

Don Marcos reached out to catch the door the bodyguard ahead of us already stood holding. As he did so I noticed his Parkinson-ian hesitation tremor. He asked whether I was trying to find out how wicked they all were to mitigate his father's—my husband's—wickedness.

I opened my mouth to tell him how far off the mark he was, but he didn't give me time.

"Norton Lawrence attacked Madlena, mistaking her for another young woman. *Any other* young woman. His poems were full of Ro-salitas and Carmelitas with 'cigar-roller thighs' and 'breasts like but-ter buns.' He was a lascivious, harassing, balding boy. And he'd had his brains fried by a huge dose of yagga someone slipped him. Some-one he offended. Possibly Fernando. By New Year's Eve he was rav-ing, twitching, unwashed, and with a permanent erection. Madlena and I killed him because we were angry and repulsed. However—just to distinguish 'pointless' from 'bad'—my father used to order people he didn't like flown out over the gulf in a big helicopter and sprinkled into the sea. He'd do that, periodically emptying the pris-ons. One flight, one tank of fuel. It was very economical and showed sound fiscal sense."

"I know all this," I said.

We were walking through the vestry, where the doors of all the cupboards were open. They had long mirrors on their insides; the vestry looked like a dressing room in a theater.

"When you married him we were all upset," Don Marcos said. "But now that we've got over the shock, and some of our sense of offense, we are *worried* about you."

The Don Marcos I first met had distanced himself from the friends of his youth in order to live quietly and work hard. But recently, I guess, he'd been thinking about 1983 and had fallen back into that old loving "we." Changing tack, I asked if he had been called upon to explain the Black Room in the course of talking to journalists about the early days of the revolution.

"The Black Room is too sinister to talk about, or too silly. I can't get it *right*," he said. "I learned that years ago. It's too sinister to fit with the image of Lequama as a 'Revolutionary Romance'—that's the title of a book, you know, by a British journalist. And it's too silly to conform to ideas people have about hauntings. The Black Room wasn't plausible as a story—no one could see where it came from or how it concluded."

He asked me if I had read that interview with Francis Taylor in *Vanity Fair.* "Some odd and maddening things happened to Francis and he's *talked it all up.* He describes his time in Lequama, where he took many of his most famous photographs, as the 'storm in the still eye of my life.' This country helped him survive everything else, he says. He can't talk about how it *really* was, he has to romanticize. And since therapy is still fashionable, talking about the Black Room as if it's all personal and reducible to metaphor seems to be the proper thing to do. So Francis says: 'Strange things happened to me and I was *improved* by them.' Or he says: 'Strange things happened and I survived them.' And that's all he *has* to say. That's the influence of therapy on our stories. We have a tiny therapeutic lexicon for describing what has disturbed and hurt us, and we find it increasingly difficult to describe all the oddities of individual experience, all the silly, inexplicable stuff. Even the *mutual* inexplicable stuff. We have only the journalistic 'Black Room mass hysteria.' I can't properly articulate my experience; and so my experience doesn't enter the culture." Don Marcos made a gesture, cast something away from him. "Don't you find it disturbing that at the same time the general public has reached a consensus about what a person can expect from therapy, therapy reaches the point where it scarcely ever admits there's any *social* dimension to private pain?"

The bodyguards were watching Don Marcos closely. One spoke into a microphone—telling the driver that we'd be a minute yet. Don Marcos looked at him, irritated. "I can talk and walk at the same time," he said. The guard pushed the door to the street. Beyond, a car door opened, glistening, and we got in. It closed with a solid thump.

Though he'd left minutes ago, Guido Hernández's car was only twenty meters in front of us, its taillights flashing madly as it edged forward through thronging people.

"I went back to the Church," Don Marcos said, "so I could be surrounded by the approved mysteries and not have to feel like the Ancient Mariner." He took a deep breath and added, "And there was work to be done."

Then he turned around to me and asked, wasn't it worse for someone who had left Lequama? Like Francis, or me. After all, if *he* was feeling the burden of his precious hoard of secrets he could just go sit down with Ambre and talk about it.

"But the *world* behaves toward you as if you are a person to whom none of these things really happened," I said.

"This is Lequama, Carme, not the world. We might be socialist, but the materialism never quite took here." I could see he was searching for an illustration, a comparison; oddly, he hit on the man I'd just met. "You've heard of Jon Scott, haven't you? The British anthropologist who was here before and after the revolution researching the Mneone? Jon Scott was in La Host during the Black Room." Don Marcos told me how Jon Scott sat in that shabby salon near Maria's kitchen—where they all used to gather—and talked to him and Madlena about different "belief systems" and "hermeneutic phenomenology," which is the belief that consciousness is the home of meaning, that cultures that believe in ghosts are liable to see ghosts. Jon would be explaining in his Oxbridge accent, itself the soul of reason, that *of course* subjectivity and consciousness were not universal and transcendental in structure but thoroughly historical and cultural. And while he talked a membrane of darkness was closing the throat of the corridor three turns away from where they sat, and a shadow was winding its roots down the stairwell to the palace basement, where the huge coal-fired furnace of the water heater stood, its thick round door open—its hinges like clenched fists wearing brass knuckles—breathing a fume of cold, sooty air.

"Madlena and I listened to Jon. I remember listening like I was being talked down off a ledge. And I remember Madlena cowering in the corner of a big couch and paying desperate attention to all those words she didn't understand—a slippery lifeline. Jon was on the spot, and he talked it all away." Don Marcos sighed, the car slid forward, stopped, started, inched a little on. "How can we talk about it?" he asked again. Then: "Do you ever, in your sorority house, tell stories about your colorful South American childhood?"

I said that I could, and my sorority sisters would probably think my stories were an expression of "the operations of consciousness" in my home culture—*à la* Jon Scott. But my stories were stacked up so that under the colorful South America was *another country*. I could almost see it—in a distant perspective like the view down the funicular railway on Mount Bedim in that northern city on Eden, snow sparkling between the rails, which receded away together, a long pointer into a dark tunnel mouth. Any stories, any talk of that sort, took me there. I said to Don Marcos, "I come home every year so that my doctor can give me a physical. I'm *not* a registered organ donor, and I *don't* give blood. You have your untherapeutic memories, and I have my body."

Don Marcos nodded. As if we'd been arguing and I'd just won the argument.

A security man opened the window between the front and back seats and said he was sorry that this was all very badly planned, the only thoroughfare from the cathedral to the palace ran along the quay, beside the Wall, which appeared to have become a site of pilgrimage. "And I am not just making excuses, Don Marcos."

Don Marcos just looked interested, amused, keen. "Nothing is going to happen to me," he said to the security man.

"No, Mr. Vice-President, but the dinner will be overcooked and the other guests will have drunk up all the champagne."

"Champagne?" I said, hopeful, angling. And Don Marcos said would I please stop leaning against him in that warm, insinuating way?

I straightened up. I hadn't realized I was leaning.

There was a thick deposit of sweating people at the Wall, and peddlers in brightly colored hats selling marking pens. There was the coffee vendor whose usual spot it was, his stand quaking, his machine steaming, his white shirt smeared with the granulated brown of exhausted grounds.

Some people saw the car, came over and cupped their hands to peer through its window. Don Marcos looked at me briefly, then opened the door and got out. The security men and driver groaned. There was a roar and Don Marcos was picked up and passed over to the Wall, his jacket rucked up, tie askew, hair all out of place. Hands reached out of the crowd among the hands that held him, and offered pens. He took one, making an amusing show of fussy choosing. The people who held him then, careful and cooperative, raised him upright, so that he was standing on hands, his own hands against the Wall, above the high-tide mark of other graffiti. They were urging him to write something; there were shouted suggestions and laughter. He laughed and pushed back his hair with his wrist. I could see he had a streak of red ink on his cuff already.

I got out of the car too, and leaned on the door. A security man joined me, offering in unsuccessful succession a cigarette and gum, then, successfully, a flask from the glove compartment. "It's respectable," he said in English. It was brandy. Then he said, "The vice-president really is a most difficult charge." He sounded like a nineteenth-century governess.

A man with a clipboard shyly approached. He held his clipboard up shielding his chest, and dipped his head at me over it, using my name. After a moment I recognized him as the archivist.

He was working. There were three of them here from the archives and three from the history department at the university. They were approaching people among the pilgrims and asking them whether they knew anything about this person or that person, unidentified names from the Wall between '83 and '92—anyone whose name occurred frequently but whose identity was uncertain, or whose name appeared in intriguing or important contexts. "Intriguing" had to be a criterion because of all the falsehoods on the Wall. The archivist pointed out for me a little woman in a yellow T-shirt that said, "I'm a big bitch in a little bitch's clothing." "Señora Tropez over there is a narratologist—she's just as interested in the lies." He looked a little scornful. "Though she tends to be a little liberal in what she regards as *lies*—for instance certain slanders against her aunt, who became the Minister of Affairs after Colonel Guevara's resignation."

"Minister of Affairs," "Ministries Building," this was Wall parlance and the history professionals of the country were using it.

"Sometimes we are asking, 'Do you know what happened to this person?'" He turned his clipboard to face me and I scanned a list of names. I looked at Don Marcos who, in true form, was inscribing not a patriotic slogan but a simple memorial. There were sighs coming from the people directly behind him, who watched as he wrote, "Rosa Gonzáles, José Castonoles, Aureliano Zabe . . ."

I said to the archivist, "Xanto was the man who supplied Don Marcos with heroin in 1984, but you must know that."

He nodded. "We're trying to work out what *happened* to Xanto. But we're not playing policemen—the man's *only* documentary existence is on this wall."

"Unlike Brad Powers and Norton Lawrence, who aren't on your list."

"Too inflammatory—with all these gringo visitors."

"And who is *Raphael* Masolan?" I asked. "Don't you mean Pablito?"

"Raphael Masolan was a Taoscal elder. Dead before '83, we think, but he was cited several times in early '84, and is a bit of a mystery."

Don Marcos had finished writing and was laughing nervously as the crowd passed him back over their heads toward his car. As security from the car and the two uniforms on motorbikes behind stepped up to receive him I actually heard them say thank you as though they had been passed the salt. "*Dios*," said Don Marcos, breathless, back on his own feet. "I'm all out of statesmanship and patriotic gestures. I don't have another appropriate public action left in me."

"Señor Vice-President . . . ," the driver said, leaning across the top of the car.

"I'm going to walk back around the edge of the Plaza and try to get into Bar Two," I said to Don Marcos. "I want to find Bella."

He kissed my cheek. "Are you all right?" he asked me, holding my arms. "Are you going to do what I used to—find the drunkest person you can and tell them what's in your heart?"

"I'll see you later, maybe at IA," I said. "Thank you." He released my hands. I told the archivist to keep up the good work and that Jiron Pérez-Farante, the Peruvian entomologist, who was on his list, had been living on Spice Island with my husband for the last sixteen years—but under another name. He was floor manager at the casino. In fact, under the name of the Glenn Ford character in *Gilda*—someone's little joke. I left the archivist alternately scribbling and holding up his pen in a "just one minute" gesture.

Memoir: Casino Spice Island, 1988

When Fidela was still a baby on the breast, Ambre and my father took us to visit Ricardo Pastrez. Ambre left a note for Madlena and Fernando, first asking them to remind Lena to feed Barabbas—this in part Ambre's usual habit of slighting her mother as elderly, forgetful, and impractical, and partly a naive way of trying to remove weight from the *other* subject of the note. "*Ido and I have decided to go and speak personally and face-to-face to Señor Pastrez to find out if he thinks we have anything more to fear and expect from your father Emilio who kidnapped you and Juanita Madlena.*" All in one redundancy-laden, unpunctuated sentence, and signed, "*Your loving mother.*"

Spice Island was cool and breezy and beautiful. Ricardo hadn't yet built his spa. The golf course was being landscaped and planted, sweeping greens and concrete-lined water courses appearing around the big cedars.

Ricardo was coolly surprised to see us, and all politeness. He put us up and spoiled us. He handed the smirking Ambre into dinner in the casino's top restaurant, he arranged some tennis lessons for me—and the right outfit from one of the hotel's several boutiques. He showed gentlemanly goodwill toward us—and settled very quickly any questions Ambre had about the likelihood of any more trouble from her ex-husband.

Emilio Rivera was in Costa Rica, licking his wounds. "I believe you are now quite safe. I had a few words with him." Ricardo flattered Ambre a little further, in the guise of a reassurance. He hoped Ambre knew that the enduring confusion about which of Lena's girls had drowned—Hunger or Hungrier—and her time-honored defense of using her dead twin as a "mask," did indeed work to divert Emilio's "sending." Ricardo then favored my father with a little bow of his head. "I assume that you've made your own masks by hiding yourself behind so many different names and histories—Ido, Walter."

"Walter," Dad repeated, coldly, like an echo on a long-distance call.

Our questions were disposed of. I played tennis, and water-skied, and sailed up under a parachute behind a speedboat.

Ambre lay on the sand with Fidela asleep under her arm, her skin streaky with lazily applied sunblock.

But Dad knew there was more. He got close to Ricardo—focused his attention on him—and he made Ricardo make an offer, not as appeasement, but in friendship. Ricardo admitted that there was something he was hiding. *Someone.*

The sun had gone and I replaced my sunblock with insect repellent, but I still lounged, oily and redolent, on the sand. Fidela was on the sunbed beside me, under the umbrella, as she had been all day, and asleep, as she had been most of the day. Ambre was in the water— standing in the surf, her hands combing its flounces, at each wave her hair alternately gleaming on her back or billowing behind her in the water, a spilled ink that wouldn't disperse. I ran the sand's fine grains, retentive of warmth, through my sunburned hands. Dad came and sat beside me. He watched Ambre for a while, and touched Fidela to check her temperature, then told me that he'd just been speaking to a very frightened man. "The good soldier of my enemies. Jiron Pérez-Farante."

I waited.

"I gather that he's afraid of them. Gillian and Lee McIndoe. And all the *other* Gillian and Lee McIndoes." He looked at me, not just with an air of inquiry, but with some wonder and a lot of respect. "Do you remember that puppet master you were afraid of, Carme?"

I was startled. My scalp began to sweat. I said of course I did.

The man had a marionette theater and traveled, seasonally, between towns and villages of the southern country of Eden. We met him after the siege, and shortly before my father sent me off to live with Astrella. The man was ostensibly harmless—elderly, birdlike, and full of little conceits, like his habit of saying he carried around the world's history and the reputations of the great in the four trunks in which he kept his puppets. The puppet master was a collector of stories. As he put it to my father, a story was "the great round world" and all any human could ever hope for of "sense and recompense." He had the habit of calling other men "my dear fellow"——or its Esindu equivalent. I remembered his appetite for the stories my father did tell him—histories of this or that important event in which my father had some part. I felt, listening to the puppet master coax, that he was after *more*, not merely latching on voyeuristically, to get material, but as though he was gathering evidence for a court case. My father, much to my horror, had encouraged this man, had flattered him right back. He'd admired the puppets, for instance, the puppet of the Queen, the puppet of the dead Ulaw, my stepfather, and the dead Genevieve, my mother. Dad had said, studying them, "How *clever*, what a *craftsman* you are." While Dev—who had good instincts—looked uncertain and lifted up the puppets' clothes as children do to check for undergarments and genitals. I hated the man because I thought he wanted to make a story and puppets of Dev and my father, and take them about on his tiny stage, their bodies and voices mimicked and their stories nicely rounded into "sense and recompense."

On the beach of that island off the coast of Colombia my father said to me, "I pretended your fear was silly to fob him off. I acted complacent, and obviously disarmed. There was something about him that I didn't like. Something that made me want to avoid his eyes or echo his words, *not* just his pomposity, which maddened Dev. It was partly that boy who worked for him, behind the scenes, and did all the voices. Do you remember?"

I remembered that the boy was unprepossessing and that he was an amazingly good mimic.

"He was a *blank*. A creepy blank. He was the best mimic I've ever met—but I've since heard about another just as good. Francis Taylor told me about Lee McIndoe—who was the best mimic *Frank* ever met."

I thought about this, tried to remember the puppet master's boy, to me just a lumpish adolescent.

"Jiron Pérez-Farante has parted ways with these people," Dad said. "But he still believes in them. He believes in their cause but is uncertain about their methods. He didn't sign on for murder—though he did accept a gun."

I waited.

"He was the one who shot Dev."

I think I made a move to get up, and Dad held me down. He told me, once I was calm enough to hear him, that he wasn't going to revenge a mistake. "The man is sick with guilt—I've never felt as strongly about killing. It's beyond being respectable, Carme, and I *respect* that."

I was crying, I subsided, and Dad held me. And while he held me—while I tried to make myself stay afloat with the idea of a real person, someone who pulled the trigger, someone *startled* who pulled a trigger and changed my whole life—Dad told me this.

He'd managed to gather something of what it was he did that offended them—the people for whom he still had no true name. "I know three or four things about these Airans. I know that they make use of the powers they seem to be dedicated to suppressing. I think that something like a Black Room happened to them, with disastrous results. I know that they travel in threes or pairs, and that one is always an impressionable, formless, mimicking mind reader.

Maybe they cultivated a mind-reading gene in their population—which *would* make them 'eugenicists.' I know they recruit—because Pérez-Farante is a recruit. He *is* a Peruvian entomologist. He also comes from a family with a three-generation tradition of interest in 'sexual hygiene,' 'fertility and fitness,' and 'social engineering.'

"I know that they positively don't want me dead, because if they wanted me dead I'd *be* dead. Apart from that, I have to guess. I think that they don't approve of movement between worlds, but that they probably wouldn't make a peep of protest if someone managed to build a classic science fiction faster-than-light spaceship to travel between planetary bodies. I think 'worlds' are only roughly equivalent to planetary bodies. It's the nature of the traffic that they disapprove of—because it moves along lines of likeness, and imaginative sympathy. It follows blood, particularly mixed blood—like your mother's family, who moved from one world to another and interbred. Tomás was certainly right about the spirit of their prejudices. They think that *miscegenation*—mixing blood—causes all kinds of trouble. And they're not just police, and haven't only policy—they have a world view: a sense that some possibilities, some possible outcomes, are less desirable than others, for *all* people. They have a sense of the offensiveness of what they've set themselves against. They want weak links, discrete worlds, and unpolluted histories. They want chance and randomness and possibility, except perhaps in their own population. They track anomalous energies through wandering elementals like Ricardo's ally; or through powerful covens, like the Pola Pastrez one that originally performed rites in the Black Room; or through freaks of hapless nature, like me. They prefer to see life perform without strings visible, prefer art to magic, the 'sense and recompense' of art; they hate those who, as the Bible says, 'maketh and loveth a lie'—the conspirators and cheats—and are unforgiving to anyone who trespasses in the guise of destiny or divine rescue.

"*And*," my father said, "except that they hate me, *I am on their side.*"

Ambre was coming up the beach, tired, sated with seawater. I watched her come, the muscles of my mouth hurting as they always seemed to hurt when I had decided to say something but felt I had to be careful. "How did he manage to persuade you to spare him, and that he was justified?" I said. "Oh, Dad . . ."

"Not justified, *reasonable*. I couldn't torture Pérez-Farante to get him to tell me more. Ask Ricardo, he can tell you torture doesn't work; no one uses it to get the truth, only to manufacture terror. Do I want Pérez-Farante to fear me? Do I want the Airans to? No, I'm not going to offer any further offense. I'm going to be good." He put his hand on Fidela's plump honey-colored back.

Ambre sat beside him, dripping wet, and wrapped her arms around him. She said he and the sand were the same temperature but soon the sand would be cooler, thank goodness.

Journal: Night to morning, August 8–9, 2003, La Host

Two hundred meters on, well oiled by my own and others' sweat, I was overtaken by Marguerite Millay, Aramantha Visistation, and another woman, American, small, with sleek gray hair, who, as it turned out, was the journalist Morgan Gray. I told her I was pleased to put a face to her name.

Marguerite told me they had just gone an hour out of their way—they too were heading toward the mecca of the Miniseries Building and IA—to deliver a distraught five-year-old to the La Host police. Marguerite complained that she could have had them come to her in perhaps a third of the time if she'd assaulted someone, instead of wading politely and purposefully to their post at one corner of the Plaza.

"It's a *crèche* in there," Morgan added. "A dozen sniffling children, four harassed police, and another dozen hysterical parents looking for children who haven't yet turned up."

"The girl's parents *were* waiting," Aramantha said, and touched my arm. "In case we're worrying you." She probably had opinions about my susceptibility to separation anxiety.

Marguerite saw some people just getting up from a sidewalk table, put out her arms, and bulldozed all of us that way. "I'm sure you won't mind spending half an hour being middle-aged," she said to me, and ordered us all drinks—Pernod.

I added water to mine till it was as pale as barley water. Morgan and Marguerite began a catching-up conversation, with occasional delighted cries of "No! Really?" at bits of news. Aramantha was drinking fast, and fast becoming drunk. Before long she was telling me how she had had to tell Ambre that exorcism rituals weren't an effective therapy for disassociative identity disorder. "She *did* perform them on your father." She shook her head. She was pouting faintly and her cheeks moved, just a fraction off flapping. Her soft beauty was going over the top. She said that my father, though strong, was terribly troubled. She said that, when he disappeared again, in Washington, after his encounter with a man called Munro from *military intelligence*, it had occurred to her that *that* was what he was. A spy. And she put up a frosty-pink-nailed, beringed hand to count. "Consider his proficiency in martial arts. Consider his skill with languages and his technical knowledge. *I* think he was a member of an intelligence community, a secret agent whose divided loyalty had divided him."

I shook my head.

"It isn't my job to convince people," she said, and patted my arm. "And who am I to impose on you? Regarding your father I did almost everything wrong. Right up to the end, when I supported Ambre's wish that he go with Jules Frei to the States. I thought he needed to enjoy the rewards of one of the few positive things he hadn't *planned* or labored conscientiously toward, those twenty-four poems in Jules Frei's *Collected Poems*. Your father made the translations, over a period of years, because he was *moved*, just for pleasure, not for profit or good housekeeping. He told me his plans. He talked in the *good-husbanding* manner he'd adopted to keep peace with Ambre. But I got the feeling he wanted me to say: 'No, don't do it. Don't go there. Don't do that.' Later, when Fernando told me about the man from military intelligence, I thought that of course it was *Washington*, some old association, some forgotten phone number or meeting spot on the Georgetown towpath. There was some influence he didn't want to be near again."

I let the psychotherapist take my glass of Pernod, her own being finished. I said, "Perhaps Dad thought you might counsel him against visiting Fernando without Ambre or Madlena present."

"Ah," said Aramantha.

Marguerite said we should get on to IA—if that's where we were all going.

I leaned close to Aramantha to say I thought hers was a very good theory, a theory that *felt* true. But Dad had first met that colonel as a major, a prisoner at Taosclan in '87. With no signs then of mutual recognition.

We were walking, out in the crowd again, part of a stream that was in motion against the walls of the residences along the Avenida Bueyes Negros. Aramantha held my hand.

Bella and I came together, coincidentally, at the gates to the palace, both with passes for the "private" party at Indian Affairs. The gates were a bottleneck because of their shape, rather than any attempt by the soldiers on duty there to control the foot traffic in and out.

Bella was mauled and smeared; the shine was gone from her vinyl. She said she was pleased to see me, but she looked tearful. I anchored myself to her with both arms—and lost Aramantha Visistation.

"Oliver *did* ask after you." Bella said. "He said, 'Where has your sour friend got to?' " We were being squeezed forward slowly, as if by a process of peristalsis, but the pressure was inconsistent, the crowd a little colicky.

"He said that?"

"He hesitated a long time before the word 'sour.' I'm sure it was a second choice, after 'beautiful.' He had to wrench his whole head around to come at it." She laughed, slightly hysterical. "Anyway, I sure pulled *his* string."

"There goes my only prospect for the evening," I said.

"Jesus!" Bella pinched me hard. She was really angry. She said she knew me better than I imagined, and I should just get drunk and do what I *must*. "Stop being good! You're the only person in the world

317

who could've hit on the idea of marrying Ricardo Pastrez as a way of being *good!*"

The crowd suddenly surged forward.

"There he is!" Bella screamed. The crowd was screaming. I looked around—not for my husband, of course, despite Bella's association of ideas.

A group of uniforms and suits had appeared on the long balcony backed by the restored second-floor grand reception room. My eyes went to the spots of color. The President wore one of her yellow silk suits. The woman Minister of Indian Affairs was wearing traditional Taoscal orange and black, turquoise and white. I saw Don Marcos in his skewed tie, hand raised holding the raised hand of a woman I recognized from television as Maria Godshalk, who was holding the raised hand of Madlena Guevara, who was holding the raised hand of Fernando Sola. There were perhaps forty people on the balcony—all members of that first emergency government twenty years before. All their faces were shining and happy, buoyed up on this great molten sea of sound. Then, this being Lequama, instead of the roar organizing itself into the national anthem, which would have been beautiful, several soldiers by the wall began firing their guns into the air, not to warn the crowd but in an excess of high spirits. On the balcony various security services, bodyguards, palace security, army, began to try to get the heroes back into the ballroom. But this was Lequama, and it was virtually 1983. Madlena pulled Maria's gun out of its holster and began happily firing into the air. Then Maria had a hand-slapping tussle with a bodyguard to relieve him of *his* gun so that she could do the same. And the yellow-and-white bunting was shot away above and began to drift sedately down through a shitting, molting storm of panicked doves—all this by the light of camera and muzzle flashes.

Madlena emptied the clip and restored the pistol to Maria. She shrugged off a bodyguard and went, skipping, back into the ballroom. Don Marcos took his fingers out of his ears and clapped, then went in too. The shots died away. Fernando leaned over the balcony rail and into the haze of blue gun smoke drifting up toward the roof and security cameras. He waved to someone directly below him in the crowd, then he went in.

Inside the palace we found corridors that still looked like those in a 1950s mental hospital, with layer after layer of lumpy cream paint on the ceilings, paint in drips and dribbles, like stopped time.

I made up my mind to lose Bella when we passed the painted arrow that pointed to the East Stairs. I gave her the slip in a crowded hallway, then doubled back.

I passed through swing doors with wire-reinforced windows and found the stairs. The stairwell was wide enough to fall down; at the bottom was a gray slate floor. I went down, my hand on the bannister, staring at this floor, which seemed to beg me to mark it somehow. There was a skylight four stories above me, which let through filtered light, fitful camera flashes, spotlights with bodies swarming before them, whether human or insect it was impossible to tell. Other lights came in through the windows on the doors at every floor, the one I'd left and those above. I went down into dimness. My feet fell softly, but my footfalls sounded both in the step and as the metal plates reinforcing the stair's edges slapped the concrete beneath them, making a doubled footfall, as though someone behind me were matching their movements to the sound of my own. I turned to look back.

There *was* someone behind me: a dark shape, standing still, with its hand on the bannister and its body twisted sidelong. I stopped breathing. I tried to pull myself together enough to watch the steps before me and run. But I couldn't move. I was like a boat aground in water too shallow for its engines to draw. Then I saw that the shape was my shadow, cast on the wall of the landing by a light below me.

There had been no light below me.

I turned around. There was a young man, in uniform, at the foot of the stairs. He had his hand on one of those orange pilot-light timer switches and had turned on the light in the basement. I saw a slim figure, thick dark hair and a fair face. I saw my father in Tomás Juiliano's stolen uniform.

Then I fell down the stairs and he caught me. I smelled after-shave and cigarette smoke—and he wasn't my father. He was pale and startled. He lifted me up and began up the stairs with me, looking down into my face, concerned and very, very serious.

"No, wait," I said.

He asked me to please speak Spanish.

"Wait. I came down to look at the furnace."

He turned, sat on the steps and settled me on his lap. Our pulses went on like a squash game. He told me his name, and that he was with palace security. He'd seen me on one of his monitors and had left his post. "My supervisor went out an hour ago for a can of soda—he said."

My hand had flopped when he lifted me, and still rested with its back and knuckles against the side of his face. I made it taut and pressed a little, so he felt that it was there.

He swore and said, "Where did you come from?" Twice, as though crazed by the suddenness of something. Then he pulled himself together. "No. I watched you. I saw you leave your friend in the party clothes."

"Bella." I couldn't remember his name. He'd just told me, but I was too shaken to take it in. I got off his lap and told him I wanted to look at the furnace.

He stood up after me, his hand sliding down my arm to snag my hand. "You're married," he said heavily. His fingers had found and fondled my wedding ring.

We walked down the stairs.

"You're beautiful," he said—with an absence of expression I'd often heard, during my accident and emergency internship, in the speech of those in deep shock.

I told him that he'd caught me without my usual defenses and, without them, sometimes I was beautiful.

We found the furnace. It was large, separate, and plumbed in, like a heart, by thick vessels—a big water heater with pipes radiating from it. It was in use, veiled in wriggles of horrible heated air. Its doors were closed, its hinges like hands with brass knuckles.

I told the young man that someone tonight had told me how they fed a body in there. "But it isn't long enough." I was calculating with my eye. "They must have pushed and prodded with pokers to fold him."

"I know that story. It was Don Marcos Pastrez and Madlena Gue-vara, disposing of the body of the British poet."

He'd floored me. How could it be *known* and nothing have hap-pened to them? Seeing that I was upset, he shook his head and made an "it isn't what you think" gesture. He said, "*I* know because my *mother* told me. The British poet had assaulted her. He got drunk and . . ." His face colored, with anger, not embarrassment. "Got her in the corner on a barstool and put his fingers in her. I was about two, and she was carrying me in a sling under her breasts at the time." Then he stood straight and began to back away from me till the warm wall beside the furnace stopped him. "But look at me— *I'm* just touching you without having asked." Then he squeezed his eyes shut and slapped his own face.

It was impossible to resist this. I went to him and pressed against him, my hands on his ribs feeling the big bones and scant flesh. "But I like it." I took his hand and guided it to my thigh, where it traveled on of its own accord up under my skirt, past the elastic at my crotch. I parted my legs till he got his bearings and slipped two fin-gers into me. It felt so good I bore down and we listed, slipped down the wall. I twisted around to unbutton him while he employed his thumb, and put in four fingers, right up to his knuckles. I finished my unbuttoning. He was big. It grew and shrank and grew. But he was moaning "No." I put my mouth on him and still he moaned "No," then he lifted my head, turned my head and pointed at a security camera, sulking in the corner, its eye shrewd and agleam.

He asked me to follow him. We put our clothes back in order and returned the way he'd come, to a service lift. He was shy now, and held both the inner and outer door of the lift open for me—the fingers of one hand glistening. He pressed his body back against the doors as people politely do to keep out of one another's way.

He kept my hand from the red button in the lift, and indicated another lurking camera. They were all operative, he said, had been regularly serviced and nursed, but were old and had been here since the days of Enrico García, who'd had them installed because he'd had to account for the wash of blood at the bottom of the East Stairs. Blood and a crushed body and no clue to what happened *but* the photo of Brad Powers, floating near the ceiling with his clothes pressed against his body as though by a high wind.

The security guard told me this, no longer fending me off, but rushing me along the corridor. We were on the first floor, I decided. It was as if he was more scared of what the cameras were there to watch than of the cameras themselves, his supervisor perhaps behind the monitors again.

He wasn't. We came to a door and unlocked it, went into a long narrow room with its one window painted out. There were two chairs in a horseshoe-shaped workstation, and ranks of monitors—some newish and in sharp color, others black-and-white and encased in grimy plastic. The room smelled of beer, burning dust, and hot metal—bloody.

When I saw the beer bottles on the desk I was a little disappointed; his rapture was just a tipsy lowering of inhibitions—a party mood. *My* inhibitions had been short-circuited by a hard jolt of terror. I hadn't looked at him and been overcome by his attractions—but I expected that from him. I didn't want impaired judgment; I wanted to feel that I was irresistible.

He locked the door. He went to find something in a drawer, and in his haste pulled the whole drawer out with a crash onto the floor.

I told him that I had a condom, and produced one from a small pocket on the inside of my hem—the dress made so that its pockets, the size of a wrapped rubber or a folded bill, had the same dimensions as its quilting.

He took the rubber, closed it in his fist. He had other ideas about where to begin—helped me to step out of my panties, both of us struggling to free a catch of lace from the buckle of one of my sandals. I reached back to unzip my dress and dropped it off my shoulders—but it never reached the floor, for he was kneeling in front of me, the dress gathered up by his hands, his palms cupping my hips. I was lifted to sit by the half-emptied beer bottles on the desktop, in the amphitheater of monitors. He parted my legs and touched me with his tongue, groomed the hair to one side or the other, as a cat parts its fur around the place it means to seek after a flea. I watched him work, stooped so that his arms slipped up, trapped, inside the loose wrapper of my dress. His hands found my breasts and brushed sideways against the slight, the not-so-slight, the hard interruption on the tips of the softness of each. What his tongue touched gradually grew as unyielding as his tongue, grew muscly and pressed back.

My eyes had strayed to the monitors and—only able to take in simple information—saw only empty or sparsely inhabited corridors. Along one I saw, from a high perspective, a slender figure with a sleek blond head. I saw him first as he paused by an arrow that said "East Stairs." It was Oliver. I saw him stop and hover and swing his head to and fro, then go on down the corridor with the piped ceiling, toward the swing doors with the wire-reinforced glass. He disappeared. The sweat on my body had gone cold and my scalp was stirring—too soon for it to be only my circumstances stirring it. But I felt the tongue more exactly than ever, felt it sculpting, trying to round out the Gothic arch below the place it was best to touch. It was furious and exquisite and I was making sounds and he was using my breasts to pull me down toward him. But I wanted to see the monitors—to find again, with my eyes, the object of my terror, Oliver, hunting for me. I found him, discovered his hand on the light switch at the top of the East Stairs. My back arched. My lips were too fat to close, my tongue too swollen to stay in my mouth. I was making small, constricted grunts, my ears deaf, my scalp stiff, and a fiery thing coming alive between my legs with its wing beats making my legs quake. I found Oliver again at the foot of the stairs, and then at last at the door of the furnace, his head backlit by the flame in its single slit eye. The fire solidified inside me and I made the same deep, inhuman squeal that Madlena's horse made when a stray shot chipped its neck away and threw a bright wreath of blood against its black hide. Oliver went out of the camera's eye and I lost him.

The security guard held me while I convulsed. He kissed me and smoothed my hair. Then I watched as he released himself, with difficulty and spectacular results—and tried for some time to fit the condom on. I helped. My hands were weak and shaking. Then I laid my head on his shoulder and he worked into me and fucked me, me flopping, him greased and bony and tense, till I was building up again, exhausted, still terrified and thrilled by my terror—hunted, taken, hopeless, willing, sacrificial. It was beautiful. He wiped his teeth and tongue against my throat and we lolled backward, him still pushing but beyond it already, spasmodic. Then I put my hand down to get my balance, and a bottle toppled and rolled. My hand was sliding through the wet, there was an electric crack, and the monitors went black and the room went white.

For a moment I was in a deep and distressing pain. The agony was in me, was knocking inside my own skull, like some quick creature having raced to the dead end of a maze and demanding to be let out.

I came back to myself on the floor, with a chair leg by my head. I was crying and my hand hurt. The guard was bending over me, one nostril dripping red, touching my shoulders. There was a terrible taste in my mouth, as though I'd been drinking blood.

"Thank God!" the security guard said, and sat down heavily beside me. Then he put his penis away.

There was a cloud of bluish smoke against the ceiling—which was not, I saw, quite so thickly painted as others in this neglected, underinhabited building. Here the paint roller's strokes were visible, in big haphazard swipes of various thicknesses, white over some very dark color.

"We got an electric shock," the guard said.

The room was still alive with the electronic bristling of cooling monitors. A shock would explain the taste in my mouth—and the spurts of panic and distress that were still making me weep, despite my own cold eyes.

He was saying that with any luck, it was only the fuses in the circuit boards blown. Probably, since the current was cut and we were still alive. He'd have to wipe up all the spilled beer and see if he could get the system working.

It was a big room, long and narrow. When I sat up and looked at the locked door I saw he'd only opened one half, the other was bolted, and the doorway was wide enough to wheel in a piano.

"This is the Black Room," I said.

He nodded. "It was Enrico García's way of getting everyone over it. He filled the room with the whole rest of the palace." He gestured at the blank screens.

My tears continued to fall. I saw the guard was crying too—probably involuntarily, like me. I took his hand. We sat there together, me with my dress around my waist and wet with spilled beer.

There had been an explosion in my head and things were settling differently afterward, some ideas beside unfamiliar others, so it seemed that there were many new things in my mind.

Like this. My father and Juanita and I had once, in the early '90s, tried to work out together the chronology of the Black Room. We had calculated that Juanita would have wheeled her piano into the black-painted room and sat down to play at about the same time that my father was apparently idling away hours at the harpsichord in a rented house in the northern city where we were exiled after the rebellion in the southern port where we normally lived. Dad said that when he played the last tune he was to play—Albinoni's "Adagio"—and closed the lid on the keyboard, he was getting up to go and carry out a lot of plans that would put him and those he loved in great danger. He had a cause. Blood had been spilled, and his allies had set a river on fire as a barrier between them and the army of their enemies. That fire was, so far, the most terrible sight—slipping slowly between stone embankments, putting out its many arms to warmly embrace soldiers and horses and warehouse roofs. (He hadn't seen it. I had. I was there.) His allies had begun it, so he followed through. He sent me away. First to the northern city, then farther, to the highlands and Dev's parents' farm. Everyone acted sad for him and his decisions, but he was right. Meanwhile, Juanita wheeled her piano into the black-painted room where, it was said, the Pola Pastrez had imprisoned a great Taoscal sorcerer who subsequently vanished, it was said, from a locked room. Juanita lifted the piano's lid and sat down to play Albinoni's "Adagio," because she was sad. My father played the "Adagio" and then closed the lid of his harpsichord and got up to get on with things he thought would get him killed.

"It's irresistible," Juanita had said. "I imagine we were both in boats, Ido, making a landing, throwing out mooring lines, and our lines tangled, and our landings vanished, and we pulled in to moor against each other."

Dad told Juanita that he'd done further calculations, according to things Fernando had told him. Things Fernando had heard about the great Taoscal sorcerer; not *what* happened but *when*. It happened at the same time that in our world the rebellion was on, a river was afire, the Queen's armies had surrounded our southern port, and my father was in prison in the capital in a damp cell below the level of a different river. He'd been kept alive because the Queen's eldest daughter, her heir, who later died of lockjaw, had brought him his meals, fixed them herself—or her husband had, or his sister—they were all in my father's camp. And he'd been supplied with warm bedding and paper and ink and paints when he asked for them. He'd painted a landscape on one wall, first plastering and whitewashing it himself. His fresco showed a beach, the shore of a certain lake, and a large house owned by the family of a famous, shrewd, self-advancing man. The landscape was painted as if from the water, not from a boat, but with the water at eye level, as though the viewer were swimming in to shore. He painted the sand and, on the left, the house atop a low, timbered hill. On the right was only sky with swifts circling over the wetlands and, at the farthest point in the painting's perspective, the crowns of trees—blue with distance—on a wooded island. He painted his way out into endless possibility.

So that his jailers wouldn't suspect him, he kept busy. The capital grew still. The Queen and her armies went west. He had an escape planned, people had been bribed to leave things unlocked. "I was at that point baffled by locks," said my father, as though mentioning a temporary indisposition. "I was to go shortly before dawn, when the watch changed. Before I went, before I blew out my lamp, I painted footprints leading up the beach from the water. I wanted to give my jailers a turn. I wanted them to imagine, if only for moment, that I'd walked away into the picture.

"Anyway—I put out my lamp and lay down to rest and keep watch. But I fell asleep. I *thought* I slept. For, without a change in the light, or atmosphere, a man walked down the faintly gleaming patches of my receding footprints—the paint was still wet—and stood before me. He was old and small and dark-skinned—and he had his shirt open and was applying traction to his ribcage with his own two hands in order to show me what was missing."

"What was missing?" said Juanita.

"His heart, of course," Dad said. "And I woke up and thought, 'There's a warning to me.' But it was a bit spurious, I thought, because I'd been told for years that I had various syndromes or developmental disorders that somehow always sounded like they were meant to amount to heartlessness."

Juanita and my father seemed pleased by their "calculations." The Black Room was produced by a series of very strong and coincidentally identical gestures, between people in two worlds. "It's like that superstitious thing people do," Juanita said, "when by accident they say the same word at the same time. They have to shut their mouths tight, till they've linked their little fingers."

"Then Ricardo weighed in with some serious malice," Dad said. "And Fernando, Don Marcos, and Madlena worked themselves up into hysterical states and the whole place went nova."

I was sitting in the Black Room with a burned hand and the taste of blood in my mouth. Of course I was experiencing other electric shock–induced sensory disturbances. There were moments when I found myself imagining that light on wavelengths invisible to the human eye had become visible to me. And there was a powerful pungent smell in my head, no matter where I pointed my nose, of flowers or, at least, floral bath powder.

I got up, slipped my arms back through my sleeve holes and zipped myself up. I located my panties; they were in a puddle of beer, so I left them. "I'm going to the party at IA," I said.

"I have to stay and fix this. At least my supervisor can't blame me for any damage—since he's AWOL, and we're both earning triple time, like all our Christmases coming at once." He came to me and held me, put his nose in my hair. I was writing out my mobile number and Ambre's number.

"You're married," he said again.

I said yes, but that I'd like him to call me. I asked him to keep an eye on me, and gestured at the monitors, "If you get them up again."

He promised that he would.

I went to find Oliver.

I found Aureliano instead. He was bent across one of the building's wide marble windowsills—chipped inside and out by the revolution's gunfire. He was vomiting. He subsided gradually and slithered back indoors and onto the floor. He was panting and covered in sweat. Alcohol fumes were around him in a cloud so dense and expansive that I was sure he'd be in danger if a match was struck within five feet of his person. I said to him, "Where's Carlos?"

It seemed never to occur to Aureliano to ask, "Am I my brother's keeper?" when faced with the usual question. Never, because we all regarded Carlos as *his* keeper. Who could fathom Aureliano but Carlos? Aureliano was so headlong, opaque, accident-prone, stubborn, and silent. His first answer was a couple more dry heaves.

I said, "Have you eaten him?" Then I looked quickly around—feeling someone standing behind my shoulder. No one was there.

I took him in hand. I made him stand. The long shabby chamber we were in was unlit except by the strong spotlights around the exterior walls of the building, which, with torch flames and the lights of news cameras, still came through the window. But at the end of the dingy chamber was a small yellow-painted room whose door was ajar. I thought I could see a basin. I led Aureliano toward this promising stainless steel gleam and we found ourselves not in a bathroom, but a small kitchen.

I ordered Aureliano to take off his shirt, and while he did, his trembling slick fingers fumbling for the buttons, I ran my hand under the tap. It really was burned, the palm scalded by the spilled beer that had heated up for the seconds when the electricity jumped through it.

Aureliano shuffled over and dropped his shirt in the sink. I made him dip his head under the stream from the tap and began to slap water on his face and throat, and to rinse gobs of partly digested food out of the hair around his face. Again I felt someone behind me. I turned and there was Colonel Maria Godshalk, looking as neutral as somebody behind one in a toilet line. Then she recognized Aureliano and asked him—not me—"Is that one of the twins?"

"It's Aureliano," he said.

Maria was helpful. "When I walked out of IA, Carlos was still there."

The twin grunted. I rolled him aside and began on his shirt. For good measure I switched on the little water heater and found some detergent.

Maria Godshalk said, "That's new," about the water heater. Then, "But of course it's not *new*." The oven was the same, she went on, condemned probably. There were about three weeks in late '83 when it rained and rained and the hydro station on La Mula couldn't cope with the water. "Or at least Don Marcos had been slightly overenthusiastic when he captured the power station in La Host on August eighth, consequently several electrical engineers had absconded. They came back later with the amnesty." Maria said that there was a power cut of several weeks' duration, and it rained, and the roof leaked, and Madlena and she tried to dry their underwear in the gas oven. She opened the oven door and found clean black enamel, but for a scabbing on the oven's floor. "And that is what is left of Madlena's nylon lace panties," Maria said. She took one end of the washed shirt and we twisted it together, then she shook it out and hung it on the oven door.

Aureliano watched us, hunkered down by the wall, weak and sheepish.

Maria said she'd enjoyed my theory about her cooking. Guido Hernández had acted indignant on her behalf. "But his eyes glittered—that man just loves science." Then she put out her hand and took mine, shook it. "We've never met, you know," she said. "You're Ido's daughter, who married Don Diablo."

"She did it to punish herself for losing her father's love," said Aureliano, slurring. Then he put his head in his hands and moaned. "It hurts."

Maria found some bottled water in the fridge and I found a glass and we gave it to him. I was amazed that Aureliano subscribed to this most operatic of views. I said, to Maria, "I married Don Ricardo to stop Ambre from going to him for consolation. I could see she would. I wanted her to act like a widow." It was the first time I'd said it, even to myself.

Maria looked at me with interest and respect.

"It's rather Homeric, actually," I said. It was. It was the dark star, the heavy gravitational body of my motivation. But, having said it aloud for the first time, it began to recede, not just shrink and grow denser as it had for years.

"Oh, *Homer*, he was just one of those men, like Shakespeare, too heavily influenced by Freudian thought," Maria said. She slapped me heartily on the arm. Then, serious: "Madlena always said her mother had loose morals."

"I wasn't really thinking of her *morals*. When my father's lover was killed he went off and found Ambre. So I became the first mourner. I just wasn't going to be the first mourner again."

"It's sad to be first only with the dead. To feel you have to stay behind with them. I had a little boy I left with my cousin when I went to fight. When he died it wasn't so much that I wished I hadn't left him behind—it was just that I felt *I was* with him, in a room with the blinds closed, like a sickroom. And that I was promising to stay with him." Maria fell silent. She looked so patient, leaning in the door frame, that I suddenly saw why she was so well regarded. Patience to me was Dad's patience, which always rested on his resourceful security in his own eventual triumph over people and circumstances. This was quite different; it was patience without any certainty except perhaps the intrinsic good of patience. After a time Maria said, musing, "Part of my trouble with all these drama queens—" she gestured around the kitchen, meaning her friends of twenty years back "—was that I wanted to be *first* with someone. There was all this wild jockeying for good places in the race for affection—each other's affection, and the Lequaman people's. I adored Rosa Gonzáles but she used to say, when I showed it, 'Oh Maria! You're so full of shit!' Personal relationships are bourgeois, she'd say, and people aren't property.

"As for the *people*—I think they're sentimental about me. They respect Don Marcos, and admire Madlena. But it's Fernando who has their passion—a jealous, punitive passion. It's a starstruck thing—nothing to do with his work or his reputation as a soldier. Madlena was a better soldier. When she made rousing speeches she said what was in the air, and people would say to themselves: 'She'll take us where we already know we want to go.' But Fernando—it's impossible to take your eyes off him."

"Yes."

Behind Maria's big round shoulder I saw a sleek blond head. Oliver had appeared at the far end of the long gallery and was looking about him. I stepped sideways out of his line of sight.

"Colonel Godshalk—can you please divert that man who's coming? I don't think I'm ready for him yet."

Maria didn't hesitate, she came about in the doorway and went along toward Oliver, her hands behind her back and shoulders squared. I went toward the oven as far as I could go and listened. Aureliano, hulking and drunk but suddenly capable of stealth, shifted himself across the floor farther from the door.

"Pardon me, Colonel Godshalk," said Oliver, suitably breathless.

Then Maria—leading with her mask, because of course it was one, even though she was no sorcerer: "Maria Maria Conchita Conchita Godshalk," she said, and I heard her palm slapped into his. She began to explain, conversationally, about her parents' commemoration of her dead older sister in her name. It was a story everyone knew. Then she said she'd been "communing with her past"—talked about that, with the heavy relish of cliché. It was quite a performance. Then she asked Oliver about himself and he said he was a New Zealander—at which Maria launched herself into a reminiscence about the only other New Zealander she'd known, a man called "Whine," who was in Lequama with a trade commission and ended up marrying a cute little private from the palace motor pool, a protégé of Madlena's. "All very Foreign Affairs. Ha ha ha," said Maria, and I could hear her slapping Oliver's arm, and his feet moving so he could keep his balance.

Oliver said he was looking for me. Did Maria know Carme Risk? But it was a bit tricky, he said. He'd been kind of *set on* young Miz Risk by the director of this documentary he was working on, who told him that Carme Risk was married to Ricardo Pastrez and that they'd just love to be able to say something new about Señor Pastrez in the doco. "I'm supposed to cozy up to her and sound her out about it."

"Hmmm," Maria said, like a woman primed for advice.

"So—I'm all set to cozy, but when I saw Miz Risk I thought—oh hell—she's *gorgeous*. And I felt like a real dickhead. Which is a bit superficial of me, I know. Then I got on the wrong side of her friend Bella. We got into—you know—" I heard him swallow, hard.

"Hmmm?" Maria was a perky bee.

"In the heat of the moment," said Oliver, matching Maria cliché for cliché.

"So the *wrong* side of Bella was her *inside?*" said Maria. "Ha ha ha!"

"I have to get to Carme before Bella does. I've never seen anyone before I was so sure I wanted—a chance with."

"Okay, my advice to you is . . . ," Maria began, and I could hear that she'd turned him and was directing him back the way he'd come. "Admit to the pimping but not to the sex. Wash your face—your chin is a little crusty. Tell Carme Risk you've never seen anyone more beautiful. All roads lead to Indian Affairs. Your way lies clear." They went out of earshot.

Though I'd been trying to get to it all night, I gave up on the party at Indian Affairs. I walked back toward the main doors of the Miniseries Building. I led Aureliano by the hand. He carried his shirt, was docile; I'd told him that for him the night was over.

I still had my anticipation of the party, my excitement a mirage made out of reports of another party, the one on New Year's Eve, 1983. The La Host paper published a time line of that party based on captions for Mexican photographer Jesús Mendoza's photos. It went something like this: At midnight Madlena Guevara, her breasts wet and bare, rides her big black horse into the Plaza fountain; at 12:30 a.m. an unknown soldier of Nuevo is photographed leaving the midnight mass at La Host Cathedral (my father in Tomás's uniform); 1:00 a.m., Tomás and Madlena *share* some Dairy Whip; 1:30, Juanita Pastrez has a fire hose in the palace hallway, on full bore and aimed at lovers. At 2:00, a gringo economist punches Enrico García, Marguerite Millay attempting to intervene; 2:30, Brad Powers levitates in a hallway at the foot of the East Stairs, clothes wrung against his body and his face like that of a test pilot pressed by g forces. At 3:00 a.m. Fernando and his flunkies entice Norton Lawrence to play Russian roulette on the palace rooftop. At 3:30 drama students dressed as Pola Pastrez and thinking they are terribly clever arrive at the party and are pelted by chairs and shut in a cupboard, Guido Hernández swallows the cupboard's key. At 4:00, in her kitchen, Maria Godshalk cooks up a storm, while Marguerite's dancers blanket-toss the Russian ambassador.

The rest was the mirage that floated above the newspaper's time line, and the photos—Norton Lawrence's assault on Madlena earlier in the evening, or Madlena and Don Marcos escorting the shaken Englishman away from the rooftop, their faces turned to his in feigned concern. Or Brad Powers's body, which looked as if it had fallen from a great height, bones shattered, flesh split, as though dropped not once but a number of times and comprehensively mashed. Madlena and Don Marcos had taken Norton Lawrence— dead or alive—past the Black Room and down to the basement in the service lift. They went back the way they came. The furnace was one corner away from the bloodied stairwell and Brad Powers's body. The death and disappearance had coincided in both time and place even more closely than the closeness of coincidence that had so taunted, troubled, and embarrassed the head of palace security.

We reached the main doors and reception. Security was checking passes to the Indian Affairs party—and there was a line like the lines outside popular nightclubs. I waved to a wall-mounted camera, blew a kiss, and left the building.

Aureliano was sluggish and faltering and I saw Morgan Gray on the steps, so we sat beside her. She was looking out over the thinning crowd on the palace grounds. She'd come out for a quiet smoke. "Can you believe it, the palace is a no-smoking zone. Live long enough and you'll see darnedest things." She was waiting for Marguerite, Aramantha, and Ambre. They were all going to take a walk along the river before turning in.

I asked her if anything about tonight reminded her of the party on New Year's Eve '83. She said she'd got about a bit more tonight. "I was under treatment by Ambre then. She'd had me take a two-week vow of silence. I'm sure she was trying to educate me out of my yakking American culture, disgraceful in a reporter, and I was possibly a better reporter after those two weeks." She smiled, remembering. "I have this lovely picture of me sitting, with nunlike composure, next to Tomás Juiliano, who looks really paranoid; he thought I wasn't talking to him because I was mad at him. It's the nicest photo of me I own. Frank could never get me—I was so crazy about him I stiffened up whenever he aimed the camera at me."

"Was it a Jesús Mendoza photo? The nice one?" I asked.

"Yes. Frank thought it was a shame those photos turned into tabloid news. He thought Mendoza was a real artist. Frank met him when he was teaching a photography workshop in Tuscany a few years back. Asked him about the light effects—and made sense of some drunken testimony about a flashing apparition. Mendoza used a box brownie with an adapted flash that threw light backward, and he wore a vest covered with mirrors, like those Indian cotton skirts with mirrors in the embroidery, but these were bigger, makeup mirrors. That's why the photos have those spooky dapples and halos. Like your father's halo. Frank had a delightful time writing about Mendoza, among other things, in his introduction to his 'Flukes and Fakes' exhibition. It's traveling, you should try to see it."

We watched the lights playing on the clear plastic, hangarlike tent over the street of the dance party. From a distance it looked like one of the pods in *Invasion of the Body Snatchers*, pulsing with light, just about to hatch. It was such a good match that Morgan said: "They're coming! They're coming!"

Ambre, Marguerite, and Aramantha arrived—all far less sober than Morgan, who whispered to me, "Where's my sitter's fee?"

Ambre peered at me blearily—and even drunk, her eye was infallible. What was that all over my dress? she wanted to know. Spilled beer, I told her. She merely glowered at the drunken Aureliano, and told him that Carlos was wondering where he'd got to.

Aramantha said that Maria Godshalk had appeared with a blond young man and had trumpeted that this boy was looking for Carme Risk. "Then your friend Bella rushed up to him and slapped his face. Then Fernando Sola came and loomed over him wanting to know *why* he was looking for you."

"Poor boy," said Ambre. "Don't laugh, Carme."

I asked her please to take Aureliano off my hands so I could go to the dance party. But she wanted a nice quiet walk with her old friends. She'd been minding Madlena's boys for nineteen years.

"I've done my fair share of minding them too."

"I don't need minding." Aureliano looked hurt.

So I took him with me.

We got into the dance party without too much trouble—I as a young woman, usually in short supply at clubs, and Aureliano on the strength of his parents' celebrity. We danced for an hour, drank only water, and Aureliano managed to sweat out some more of his mountain wine. Fidela had moved on. We didn't see anyone we knew well, and kept together, winding our way up the current of the music. As well as the laser lights there were machines that occasionally blew confetti at us, even into our open mouths. There was a performance: people in harnesses danced high over the heads of the crowd, flying like trapeze artists through colored lights and dribbles of water, so that they, and we, were sopping wet.

I got a sore neck watching them and leaned against Aureliano, who put his arms around me, awkward, but with an unfolding appetite that let me know that he'd wanted to do it for some time. I made calculations, counted the years between us—six—which was rather silly for someone married to a man thirty-six years her senior. Then I thought of the family, and I thought of myself as a desperate ten-year-old baby-sitter, tying a four-year-old to a table leg while he tried to bite me. I felt his lips on the nape of my neck. It was practically incest. I ran it over in my head. He whispered my name and I imagined whispering his—an impossible name, five exhausting syllables. Aureliano—who was Hyde to his brother's Jekyll. Carlos—whom everyone liked and admired, who owned this one, his twin, shadow, and affliction.

I thought of all my missed opportunities, all the men I'd discouraged. My only defense against unrequited love was self-denial and sexlessness and a marriage that was like an act of secession from family and country.

I bent my head back against Aureliano's shoulder and gave him my throat. I wondered if he could smell the security guard's cologne.

The performers rappelled down into the crowd, which shouted, "Encore! Encore!" So did my body. I turned around into Aureliano and found his mouth, a little sour, but capable. I pressed into him, took the measure of his clumsy readiness. For all that he'd harbored repressed anticipation he was more hesitant than the security guard, a more experienced man whose imagination I think I instantly overwhelmed.

We kissed for some time, jostled by the dancers. Aureliano's hair smelled of detergent and mountain wine. His bare stomach was almost adhesive. I slipped one flat hand down the waist of his pants, through a silky thicket, till I found a handhold. A button popped. I pulled him against me, touching as much as I was able of this soft-skinned hardness, like fine kid leather with faults, its defined veins. I looked down at the coin-sized dark spot that appeared on the front of his pants, and my fingertips pulled a little preparatory slickness back into my palm.

We were pushing each other toward the darkness, the nearest darkness—it was the door, curtained with flying insects, loud in the light. Aureliano pulled me through the swarm and used his fingers to comb live insects out of my hair.

We found the first doorway occupied, door banging rhythmically against its hinges, a white ass, and her sandaled feet hitched up around his hips. The next few doorways were full too, their steps' worn surfaces interrupted by a number of matter-filled eruptions of dropped condoms. Then we found two young men fully naked against the rattling aluminum grating on a storefront. Aureliano was embarrassed; he hauled me on into the semidarkness.

None of the shadows was vacant. And there were groups of youths leaning on cars, their feet among broken and rolling bottles. Aureliano put a protective arm around me to lead me through. One young man had a snapped-off car radio aerial and flicked it at us; it whistled and cracked, but we hurried on. We took a wrong turn along a curving road, well populated, and found ourselves at another entrance to the Plaza.

I pulled Aureliano up short and began to kiss him again—I didn't want privacy—I just wanted a resolution to my congestion and wetness and my now powerful desire to see the color and consistency and volume of his come. *It had to not matter who saw us.* It had to not matter. I'd never again be as abandoned as I had been already that night—in the horseshoe work bay of the security monitors, the whole palace blazing behind me, seeing *everyone*, knowing how many rooms away *everyone* was, and seen by no one. Then, when it was already too late to talk myself out of pleasure, when I was only eyes and breasts and loins and spine—*being* sought, sought as if smelled out, which gave me pleasure to the point of extinction, and left me tenderly open to being moved by the security guard's largeness, his *largesse*, his clumsy haste, the sounds he made, the way his body bent into mine, joy hardening it, as though it had set and would stay that way forever. *It had to not matter who saw us.* I had always stopped myself, or hurried myself, feeling disloyal, not seen by others, but watching myself, my cold, private, unwanted self.

I kissed him. I pushed him back against a wall and only did one cautious thing, as I stooped I kicked at the ground with my sandals to check for broken glass— there was some. I got up again, so against my own inclination it was like trying to stand up in a waterfall. We went on. Once in a while I drew back to look at him, his bare chest with the sweat running on it as fluent as plain water. He said we should go to Flores Negras, he just wanted to lie down with me. But I wanted him in my mouth, aquiver, like the slippery muscle I'd once had a gloved hand on in an emergency room—a fibrillating heart.

Crowds were coming toward us, a sizable sluice of human bodies leaving the Plaza. A scooter appeared amid curses and screams, pushing its way through. I stepped aside and it went between Aureliano and me—the gap further filled by people in pursuit. One flung bottle bounced off the driver's back, then exploded on the street. There were more shouts and shoves. Dogged, I went on the way we'd been going. There were several people equally lost and jostled—one woman with a finger in one ear and shouting into her cell phone. She looked right at me. I read her lips. I thought I saw her lips make my name. And then she looked about to get her bearings, found the street sign, the steel plaque above the street. The Street of Black Oxen. She became excited at what she heard, then started toward me. I spun about and went the other way, in a straight line away from her. I was trying to think where I'd seen her face.

Someone grabbed my left arm and swung me about, not hard, but in a managing way. It was Oliver. "Carme Risk," he said, as if conferring a title. "You've eluded me all night." He looked at my dress. "Been rolling *in* the barrel, I see." His head was cocked, he was jocular.

There was a man beside him whom he introduced as Hans, his friend. Hans had a brush cut, coarse complexion, poor muscle tone, and was breathing through his mouth. Oliver said something to Hans in German about me and Fidela, because I heard both our names—but I couldn't understand it because, at the same time, he put out a finger to move a lock of my hair which was stuck to my jaw and throat. I felt a small pull where it clung, felt it uncoil and fall away. I said, "Keep away from me, or I'll have my husband kill you."

Oliver's brows shot up. "Will you say that again for the cameras?"

I pulled sharply away from him and felt, from behind me, a hard glancing blow. My side stung. Directly in front of me someone began to shriek, in a high falsetto and in Spanish, "You little whore! You evil little whore!"

It was Oliver's German friend, Hans, his dim-bulb eyes dimmer than ever, blind behind his round glasses. Then, still in Spanish, but in a hoarse voice with absolutely no bottom to it, he whined, "She's just a dirty-minded little girl, you mustn't listen to the dirty-minded little girl . . ." Then he began to rasp, like static, an untuned radio.

Oliver's face was still and drained; he simply stood, his hand against his side.

Aureliano yelled my name. I turned toward him, so was in time to catch the hand with the knife, raised high above my head to make a theatrical and ineffectual downward stab. I saw that there was blood already on the blade. The woman with the cell phone dropped her phone to grab the hand too, and we wrestled, Señora Carvos drunk and demented between us. Then Señora Carvos went down, flat on her face. Aureliano had burrowed through the crowd and pulled her legs out from under her. I wrenched the knife from her hand.

Oliver was slumped against the wall, blood was coming between his fingers. I crawled over to him. I moved his hand and applied more pressure. Hans had disappeared. The crowd near us had quieted considerably, I could feel them form a circle against the wall, feel their dismayed attention.

"Thou shalt not kill," Oliver said, rueful, looking right into my eyes.

"It wasn't me. It was the woman behind me, trying to stab me."

His gaze wandered—no—moved. He was trying to work it out—his face had a polite, patient look. I turned around to tell the woman with the cell phone to call for help, but she was doing it already. When she looked at me, appalled and stricken, I recognized her, because she was like him—was his sister, Carvos's sister. She, too, had been at the graveyard.

What did she think would happen when she dialed Señora Carvos's number to tell the Señora that she'd found Carme Risk in the crowd?

I felt a light touch slide along my side and looked down to find it was Oliver, his finger in the long bloody rent in my dress, tracing the blood that ran below the horizontal slash over my ribs. I didn't feel it till I saw it, then seeing it, I lost the strength in my hand—the hand I was using to apply pressure to Oliver's wound.

"You're lucky," Oliver whispered.

My wound was cleaned and stitched in a curtained cubicle in a very busy room at accident and emergency, La Casa de la Mujer. While the nurse worked I watched through the gap in the curtains as Aureliano spoke to the La Host police. Then the nurse helped me into a surgical gown so worn it was practically transparent, and wheeled me to a "quiet place," Anton Xavier's office.

"Try to sleep," the nurse said. "The way the streets are you couldn't be taken home right away even if we could locate your stepmother." She gave me a pillow and cotton coverlet. Looking at me lying there she said she almost envied me that position, what a night it had been.

The electric clock on Anton's wall said it was 7:20 a.m. The room was quiet enough for me to hear it tick. I closed my eyes. A little while later the police came and took my statement. Aureliano held my hand.

The police left and Aureliano fell asleep in a chair beside my gurney.

I dozed. Woke up at a light touch, as my hair was brushed gently back from one ear and the ear was stroked, very light but lingering. I knew who it was in the room, changing the air, its quality, making the filtered clamor of the hospital and the tick of the clock sound more momentous.

I took Fernando's arm and drew it under my head as a pillow. He was obliged to lean down, the creamy hidden skin at the crook of his elbow against my mouth and nose. I asked him how come it was *him* and he said that he always made sure there were plenty of well-placed people who would know to tell him certain things before they told anyone else. He said he'd called Ambre just before he came into my room. She'd be hard on his heels. The general consensus out there—he gestured at the door—was that Anton should look me over before I was discharged.

We both looked at Aureliano, sprawled in the chair. Fernando said, "Do you remember how he used to run about half the night no matter what we did to soothe him? Then sometimes he'd sleep so deeply that he wouldn't stir even when Carlos pulled him out of bed and onto the floor?"

I did remember. And I remembered his sleepwalking and his bed-wetting and how he'd sometimes get so angry he'd bite his own legs and arms.

When I looked back at Fernando he was watching me with that open, affectionate look I've seen turned only on me and the twins and little Rosa. All of us his children.

"How do you feel?" he asked.

340

"Lucky—like Oliver said. He died." I found I couldn't go on. A stuffy silence came in my ears and just sat there, I was deaf and alone.

But I *could* hear, because I heard Fernando say, "Poor crazy bitch," about Señora Carvos. Then he explained he'd got it all from the police—or rather, he didn't suppose for a second he'd got *all of it*. He said this with a blunt, resigned tone.

I removed his arm from under my head and kissed the back of his hand. "Fernando, if there are things I don't tell you it's only to protect you."

"What things could *I* possibly need protection from?"

I was so tired I was tranquil. The codeine helped. I felt very comfortable. I was Yu Hsuan-chi's loosed boat afloat on the thousand-mile river. I said to Fernando that I'd tell him something I'd never told my father. Just to give him some sense of my capacity for secrets.

It was early winter in the northern city and Carlin sailed the *Thresher* back from the empire with a cargo of coffee and a drug, baasera. It was an analgesic, not illegal, but habit-forming, and there had been recent improvements in methods of refinement. Our company had a coffee monopoly, but the baasera was a cash cargo.

We were in exile and buying not arms, but better favor. And *land*. The two great monasteries of the "first" and "second" missions were losing clergy at a rate of dozens a week. My father and some of his friends raised money to buy land and build a *third* mission—one for all the renegade priests and priestesses. There were all sorts of other business in hand, none of which I remember in any detail. I *did* remember my father taking his meals to eat at his desk with inkstand and papers, sand and sealing wax. He would write dozens of letters at a sitting, shifting his pen from hand to hand, consolidating our position.

On his arrival Carlin looked in on Dad, gave his report, gossiped a little, and came out complaining, "It's just *chess* to him."

There were strangers in and out of the house, and we saw we

were being treated like his *household*—not all of us, because Astrella had acquitted herself very well on the barricade on market bridge, and her husband was a prince with some schemes of his own that were regarded as tributary to our cause.

Carlin sat down to lunch with us. Footsteps passed back and forth beyond the open door behind his chair, doors opened and closed, and he said, "Who *are* all these people?" Then he asked where Dev had got to. And we told him that Dev had gone up to the highlands to stay with his parents and the goats. "Why did he do that?" Carlin wanted to know. "Was he sick?"

"He was sad," I said.

We were all quiet, our knives and forks still. We heard a door open and a voice we didn't know say they'd be back tomorrow, then, "You can lay out your scheme in detail."

Carlin put his knife and fork carefully down on the tablecloth by his plate. He went to close the door. Then he said, "He thinks he's infallible."

We thought we were losing him—his inner circle, his family and friends. We were jealous. We had been the first to follow him because we agreed with and loved him. When he was opposed, we were indignant. And when our indignation was treated as criminal we were roused. But we were loyal to him rather than his "cause." Of *that* we weren't entirely sure; we hadn't got to vote on its every clause. What we liked was our singularity—how necessary we were to the strange able person we'd had to *protect*.

And now he was in the next room, scattering sand on his handwriting and laying out schemes. In private he never seemed like a schemer—he acted as if it was all magical foresight and infallibility, as if he knew what was right and what would happen.

Sitting over our lunch that day, we began to conspire against him. What could we do to shake our all-knowing friend?

I remember that Carlin stood with his back to the room against the serene early-winter sunshine coming through the mullioned windows, his face dark in the thin purple shadows such glass makes. He was looking out over the harbor, its forest of masts. Out of the stream, and waiting for the longest berth at the main wharf, was the *Thresher*, the fastest and fairest ship on the seas, whose pattern was the *Cutty Sark*—a vessel from another world and another century. The *Thresher* was *ours*. Carlin was its captain. It contained, in its still-unloaded cargo, the capital my father required for his schemes.

So, that night, Astrella, coated in thick goose grease for warmth, swam out from the nearest point pushing a wooden washtub before her, which held the dry cotton and thick pitch, the tinderbox, coiled rope, and grappling iron. The *Thresher* was guarded, but Astrella knew by whom, and knew their habits. Carlin had made sure that there were only three, two on deck, fore and aft, and one asleep in the galley. In the hold Astrella made a ring of pitch around smoldering cotton. Then she swam back to shore, where a friend waited with his carriage, and a bed of blankets and warming pans. Thirty minutes later, when the fire was detected, the men on deck couldn't get through the smoke to open the seacocks and flood the hold. But they had already released the anchor, hoping that—hold flooded—she'd sluggishly drift with the tide into the shallows. They went over the side—and watched as, fully afloat, the *Thresher* began to turn slowly beneath a tall, twisting plume of flame. The wharves were covered with smoke rich with the scent of roasting coffee.

My father woke up to the sight of orange firelight on his ceiling—lively, but without the sound of logs burning in the hearth in his room. He could hear people talking in the long gallery. He got out of bed and went there, to find us in our white nightclothes before the long windows. We stopped talking and looked at him, then drew slowly aside "like theater curtains," his journal reads, to show the ship afire and turning in the water. "It was its own disturbed compass," my father wrote.

We had set his compass spinning.

"It's a long time ago now. Almost as long ago as Pablito Masolan, Norton Lawrence, and Brad Powers, almost as long ago as your defection to the Contras. Dad changed his plans when the *Thresher* burned. He went to get Dev. So that when the Airans came for him, they came to Dev's parents' dairy, and Dev was killed. Dev died, so Dad came to stay here in Lequama. And so did I."

Fernando put his elbow by my head again to lean closer. He was very sympathetic. He said that while he saw what I was saying, these were unforeseeable results. Why should the action that I felt guilty about necessarily be the *key* action? There was a Gaelic curse—"I wish that I had died, ere I lived to see this day"—which wishes to undo *everything* because of a bad result. I was saying—Fernando pointed out—that if Dev had never met my father, or if Astrella had cramped in the cold water and drowned, then Dev would be alive. "But you can't think like that. Think like a Taoscal. Abdicate responsibility. Say: 'A luck of great gravity was involved in these events.' "

"Not mine," I said. And I began to cry.

Fernando gently stroked my hair and brushed the tears from my face with the back of his hand.

Aureliano slept on.

Anton Xavier arrived to check me over. He'd got the whole story from the head of the last shift. He couldn't help himself, he had to have his say. It had been painful for him, a peaceable man, to accuse my father all those years ago. But he hadn't been able in all conscience to sign Felipe Carvos's death certificate, which had said: "cardiac arrest." Not after the autopsy, when he'd discovered that the heart valves were all aged and thin, while the heart muscle was otherwise in "the pink of health." Anton said, "Everything about it pointed to your father. It was impossible. And *so delicately done*. All the aged valves had been torn by the force of youthful blood pressure, in a state of high excitement—" Anton compressed his lips and lifted my dressing.

"That poor boy," he said, meaning Oliver, not Felipe Carvos. "And poor Señora Carvos. Your father had a great responsibility in his gift." He shook his head. "And this is the end result."

Fernando said no—*he* thought that this was only a result along the way.

Journal: Spice Island, late August—San Francisco, November 2003

I hung still in a shallow valley in the reef. The coral was making its own storm; beside me was what looked like a cauliflower in a high wind. A fish passed my face, eyes full of light, seemingly hollow. On a shelf at the level of my eyes were cassiopees, fanning themselves from below, clean and sturdy—it was impossible to say "delicate" of something so radiantly robust. Beside the cassiopees, oatmeal-colored filaments of coral impatiently fingered another fish as it rested, not troubling to be invisible, its livery yellow and indigo and fluorescent white.

I checked my air, and went up, not too fast, following my bubbles. I watched the sky grow a little less blue beyond the bright, scaled membrane of air on water. I didn't see the silver lookdowns until I split their school, and they were below me, visible, air in the shape of fish and suspended in the sea.

One more thing belongs here. I'd been back in the States a month, and was very busy already, studying detentive care at the University of California in San Francisco. Ricardo called me from Spice Island—he usually called me several times a week. He was telling me about the artificial reef they were building on the other side of the island, out of giant concrete "jacks" and several wrecked buses. His voice began to slur. After a few sentences he paused and said, "I'm slurring," puzzled.

"Well, *stop* it," I said, fearful.

He went on, then said, "I can't."

I said to him that *I'd* talk, he could try again in a minute. I told him about the apartment I'd found, overlooking the Castro, right under Sutro Tower. Ricardo ventured a few remarks, his voice blurry. Then he said he'd hang up and would call back later.

I sat by the phone. An hour passed. Eventually I called him. He told me he had been lying down and felt better. His voice was as clear and measured as ever. "Why did you say 'stop it,' Carme? I couldn't, you know."

"I know." I told him I wanted him to see a doctor. "Go tomorrow." I said I thought it was possible he'd just had a TIA—a transient ischemic attack. A stroke precursor. A warning.

Transference

(A therapist's rooms, Northern California, 2022)

I was, I thought, very cunning. I began to collect and display every book mentioned in Carme Risk's text. I took pains, and by the time I was near the end of her journal I had—in addition to the two Freis, Jules and Bella, Taylor's *Make No Noise*, and Scott's *No Line in the Reef*—Tove Jansson's *Moominpapa at Sea*, where the Groke trails Moomintroll around all night, threatening to sit on his lamp. I had *Lequama: A Revolutionary Romance*. I sought out and displayed every book she mentioned just so that I could place *Are You My Mother?* on top of the whole pile—where it stayed, session by session, and Carme paid it no mind.

I asked her questions. Didn't she care about her childhood? Why did she just give it up? What about her *other* half-sister Astrella? Carlin Cadaver and his wife? Eden?

She said that she'd had no power over her situation. And she just *forgot*. She gradually forgot every detail she hadn't been able to memorialize officially. Her father discouraged her from talking about it. "Look," she said, "it isn't uncommon. Something similar happened to Bella with her mother, who died of cancer when Bella was nine. Bella's father used to get drunk every night, write a letter to his dead wife, then burn it. Bella told me that she was scared

347

she'd upset her father by talking about her mother. She was afraid she'd make his pain worse. So she has all the *official* family memories, but the rest of her childhood map is moth-eaten. She can tell people stories about things she can remember her father doing when she was four—but her mother has faded from all her family pictures." Carme said to me, "You're not the only one with amnesia!"

Anyway, she said, she *did* try to go back. Twice. In 2011 and '15. The island was there—in the river—but it *stayed* there. She spent weeks camping on the island till the local landowner, a Cadaver, found her and moved her on. It was then she remembered hearing about old John Cadaver's experience, how the island had once disappeared on him for fifteen years. How he had guessed it had two types of cycle, one like a lunar cycle and one like a comet's orbit. "And that is why Carlin never came," Carme said. "My father thought he wasn't forgiven. But Carlin wasn't able to get across."

I asked Carme if she understood that because Eden was the only part of her story I was unable to check against historical records, I was tempted to generalize her experience. So—she was an immigrant or refugee making a new life for herself, letting go what she wasn't able to use, acquiring what she needed. "I have generalized positively. But you made your new life out of bits of others' lives. You were always listening in, and never looking in a mirror."

"My mirror was a platter black with flies," she said. "And I was of no known provenance. I couldn't go back to the parish records to find my people's people. What could I call my own?"

In our next session—maddened by my reading—I opened *Are You My Mother?* to its last page and left it open between us: " 'Yes, I know who you are,' said the baby bird. 'You are not a kitten. You are not a hen. You are not a dog. You are not a cow. You are not a boat, or a plane, or a Snort! You are a bird, and you are my mother.' "

Carme didn't deign to see it.

She showed no interest in discussing her marriage to the mass murderer. But we talked some more about the Airans. I asked her if she'd ever considered, since it seemed that the Airans *were* "eugenicists" of some sort, and her father was possibly an Airan, that he was a sport of nature—not lost but hidden, possibly even by his parents? And had she never thought that perhaps her father's amnesia wasn't something the Airans did to him, but that it was in his makeup? "Remember," I said, "by his own report he forgot how to understand the spoken word for a substantial period of his childhood."

She shook her head. "No. That can't be right."

"He had faults, actual faults in his functionality—you both say so."

"I suppose you think you're playing by my rules?" she said, frowning. "Okay, let's play. The Airans found my father—and began to monitor him, or perhaps to *cultivate* him. They handled him with armored gloves while watching through glass saturated with lead."

"Were the Airans *afraid* of him? Is that what you think?" I asked.

I then asked Carme if she had any idea why the Airans turned up in La Host at the twenty-year celebrations? Oliver, and Hans—who seemed to be a mind reader and a medium, operating as a receiver for the thoughts of Señora Carvos *and* her deceased husband. Did Oliver and Hans expect her *father* to be in Lequama, or were they investigating her—as his progeny, perhaps with his potential? And why was Oliver apparently so set on having sex with her?

"Everyone wanted to have sex with me that night," said Carme, calmly.

"Everyone except Fernando Sola."

Carme Risk said, "I could hit you."

I got up and went out onto my terrace, where, after a minute cooling off, she joined me. She came close, but only to ask what that plant was called—the one I'd given her a sprig of the other day—purple, pink, and white, all on the same bush.

"I grow it so that I can tell people what it is," I said. "Therapists are always filling their rooms with artful ambushes. This ambush is called a yesterday, today, tomorrow plant. It blooms purple, and its blossoms grow anemic, then ghostly over the course of three days. Yesterday, today, tomorrow—all in flower and on the same bush."

"I'm impressed," she said. "But you seem to be ashamed of your contrivances."

I didn't look at her. I said, "So. You married Ricardo Pastrez because you couldn't have Fernando Sola. Or you married Ricardo Pastrez because Fernando Sola had once tried to form a perverse alliance with him. You wanted to do something shameful to join Fernando in his shame, because you understood that *that* was why Fernando and your father were close. They thought they were more monstrous than anyone else."

Carme said that there was some truth in what I'd said, but she'd thought for some time now that she married Ricardo Pastrez because it was her destiny to do so.

"We've had *conspiracy* and now we've got *destiny*. Both suggest an outside agency." I was dogged. "This is what, as a narrative therapist, I am able to do for people. I can help them see that their apparent lack of control over their lives is really only their habit of thinking of themselves as being controlled. Controlled or doomed." I turned to face her.

"I'm sorry I threatened you," she said. "Do your clients ever hit you?"

"I've even been bitten. But many of my clients are children. I'm a little disappointed in you, Carme. I expected maturity. You've got fifteen years on me."

"I *knew* that mattered to you," she said. "And it's *seventeen* years— seventeen years between us."

I didn't think much of her arithmetic—and her a doctor.

PART FOUR

The Autokinetic Effect

(the tendency to perceive a stationary point of light

in a dark room as moving)

(Carme Risk's journal, 2010)

La Host, Lequama, December 2009

Fidela laughs at us whenever we talk about the poster campaign. She thinks we've been startled by something purely coincidental. "That's the trouble with conspiracy theories, they leave nothing to chance."

This was at Christmas, when we were all in La Host. Fidela's husband, Bob Renzi, had gone out with Tomás and the twins to "see the sights"—such as they were. Juanita and I were laying the tables on the veranda. Fernando and Madlena were lighting the barbecue, using far too much accelerant, I thought. We had waited for Bob Renzi to go in order to discuss the posters—to talk properly at all. Bob was *uninitiated*, and it was evident from his bluff, indulgent way with Ambre that he'd been well briefed about her—*our*—"eccentricities." Bob's manner infuriated Madlena, who believed that Fidela was ashamed of her family, culture, and country. It wasn't the whole story, because, if Fidela was encouraging her husband to see her family as superstitious, or subject to the typical "operations of consciousness" south of the Panama Canal, it wasn't just that she was saying to him, "I'm not like this. This isn't my world." It was also her way of protecting us from him.

Bob Renzi had invited my sister to live with him when she was nineteen and asked her to marry him on her twentieth birthday. He suggested they get together, with their lawyers, and work up a prenuptial contract. It would be in both their interests. "Seems reasonable," Fidela said to Bob (and to me). She wasn't a starry-eyed creature who required big gestures of romantic abandon. Bob was rich, an entertainment lawyer, and self-protective, but Fidela had plenty of her *own* money and meant to keep it.

She never signed. She told me that one morning she took a call, not at home but on the set on her latest show, from the man who managed our trust fund—the education fund she hadn't drawn on for years. Nathan Wrytower told her that Bob Renzi was having her background checked. Renzi had a friend in the FBI who, years before, had worked on an investigation into Edwin Money's business practices. The FBI man had been "tweaking the Money leads" for Mr. Renzi. The Money leads led to the trust. Wrytower said to my sister, "I thought you should know."

Edwin Money was long dead and beyond the reach of federal investigators. The trust was soundly legal, and any investigations would lead only to stories about how once, years before, Money had put pressure on the networks to cancel *Starting Over*. Stories about how a six-year-old star's career was sabotaged from on high, so that she was, in the end, only able to get work in ads in Japan. Stories about how the pressure on Fidela and all concerned with her career only relented when she withdrew her suit to divorce her parents and went home to Lequama. Beyond the stories there was only speculation—about Money's senile gullibility and our father's "alternative treatments."

Fidela was furious. She broke her engagement, moved out of Bob's apartment, and refused to take his calls. Bob only won her back with big romantic gestures, and they married, free of the shelter of a prenuptial contract and under the open sky of Californian marital property laws—as Fidela put it, satirically. Fidela chose Bob because he was hardheaded, because she could respect him, and because she couldn't spend all her life holding the world at arm's length. It was a solid marriage and they presented a united front, Bob being—every minute of every hour of every day—nobody's fool: shrewd, scrupulous, *intact*. And Fidela being—as she must—practical, droll, undramatic, *unlike her family*. But although for my sister Bob Renzi represented some kind of mental or moral health, she never wholly regained her confidence in him. So that when, on their Christmas visit, she made sure that Bob would be absent long enough for us to discuss the mysterious poster campaign, I knew she was not just saving herself and him from our "embarrassing carrying-on," but excluding him from parts of her life he'd tried to know, to *own*, when he'd had her investigated.

Aureliano was the first of us to see a poster. He spotted one decorating a door in the wing occupied by the faculty of beauty therapy in a technical college in California where he was struggling with an engineering degree. He removed the poster and mailed it home to Madlena. A month later Francis Taylor sent Madlena a second one, which he'd peeled from the fence around a building site in Kuala Lumpur. In the first six months of the year we had reported sightings in Bristol, Rome, New York, and Sydney (again by Frank Taylor).

The poster was thirty by twenty inches and predominantly a vivid FDR yellow. At its center, in a love heart, were three people: Juanita and Enrico García, and the bishop who officiated at their wedding. All three were identifiable—although the picture was a drawing made from a photograph. Enrico and Juanita were eye to eye, her lips parted, their hands clasped. The bishop smiled beneficently beyond them. Under the picture were two words in bold, decorated letters, mainly a fluorescent pink. "Forever Faithful." The only other information the poster contained was in nine-point Arial and on the bottom right-hand edge—a box number in San Francisco. Of course the first thing we decided to do was to stake out the post office of the box number. Aureliano watched the place—during its open hours—for three weeks. He was spelled by a scornful Fidela on one Saturday, and by me on the other two. The only result was that Aureliano's grades fell and he had to repeat a subject over the summer. Our second strategy was more open. Juanita wrote to the box number asking why her and Enrico's faces were being used on a poster, and what was it advertising?

Juanita's letter went unanswered.

Then the poster was reported in Calcutta and Oslo, Glasgow and Rio. Madlena posted a page on the Net offering a reward for information. She was deluged with crank mail, fan letters, and several proposals of marriage. Her father even wrote, tried to make contact. Emilio Rivera said he knew nothing about the poster but had answers to other questions, if she'd care to meet him and ask. Madlena didn't reply. This was only a month before Christmas.

The barbecue was lit and Madlena was hovering over it, impatient for the white ash to form on the coals so she could put the chicken kebabs on to cook.

"*Someone* must clear that box," Ambre said. "It must be possible to catch them at it." For once she had consented to sit idle while salads were tossed and the table was set. She was in Lena's wingbacked wicker chair. Her hair was now entirely white and I could see how like her mother she'd become.

"Maybe different people clear it each time," Fidela said. She began to rock back and forth, heel to toe, which was a way she had of laughing when very amused—by folly.

"We could have strangers keep a watch," Fernando said.

"We'd have to pay them," I said. "It would take a lot of organizing."

Juanita said that it was *them* trying to trap us. The Airans. *They* thought sorcerers were solipsistic. "They think that if they show us our pictures, we'll behave like ghosts trapped by a palindrome."

"What?" Madlena said. But Ambre was nodding in a sage way.

Juanita explained, "*They* think we're like caged birds bewitched by our own reflections."

"You're all nuts," Fidela said. "But since I'm in San Francisco, and I have resources, I'll organize a roster of strangers to keep watch. But if, after a week or so, we don't catch anyone, or we catch someone who just came, quite coincidentally, across a picture of Enrico and Juanita and used it to be decorative, or to advertise matrimony—"

"Yes." Fernando cut my sister off. "If you can satisfy us that it's all harmless, then we'll let it go. But if you require us to say how silly we were, Fidela, you should try to remember that our paranoia, as you put it, is an adaptation to the world we've lived in."

Fidela raised her palms, pacifying.

Aureliano arrived, parked his rust-seamed, tin-can-patched jeep.

He carried a crate of mixed bottles—orange soda and mountain wine—onto the veranda. He said, to no one in particular, "I was trying to get back before Carlos. But I just saw them—Carlos, Dad, Fidela's Mr. Renzi—at a flower stall in the Plaza."

"You did get back before them, dear," Ambre said, puzzled by Aureliano and used to being puzzled by him. She was being kind about his illogic and simplicity. It made me uncomfortable.

I walked ahead of him, holding open the swing doors to the kitchen. He put the crate down with a crash on the kitchen table, then lunged at me, bulldozed me back against the wall and burrowed his head into my neck, kissing. For a moment he sounded like any other young man, muttering that it was *weeks*, and why did I have to stay at Flores Negras, couldn't I get a hotel room, like Fidela and her gringo husband? His lips landed on mine and we made powerful competitive suction till I could feel my tongue prickling with drawn blood. I put my hands under his shirt, almost stifled with delight and by my efforts to keep quiet.

I tried to think how to say that we had to *talk* about this— our intermittent, unequal, lovely, secret six-year affair.

The swing doors flapped and Fernando came into the room, heading for the refrigerator and the marinated kebabs, I guess. We hadn't heard him coming—he'd always walked without making a sound. He stopped and looked at us. He registered no surprise, and no emotion, but was so still that I realized he was holding his breath. We turned away, as if dazzled; we actually averted our heads and froze, head-to-head, facing the wall.

"Children," Fernando said, quite kindly. "I'm not going to tell anyone."

I turned back. Aureliano wouldn't move, so I put my palm flat against his ear, the ear facing Fernando, maybe meaning to shield him from things Fernando might say. I said, "Maybe *you* were the one we didn't want to know."

A small crease appeared between Fernando's brows. "Why?" Then he saw something beyond the room and said, "Carlos is coming." He opened the refrigerator, got out the dish of kebabs, and set it down on the table.

Aureliano pushed me away from him—forceful in his panic—

and I fell against the table and bruised my tailbone. He began to unload the crated bottles and stood beside Fernando, shrinking a little. Fernando looked hurt, touched Aureliano on the arm, and said, "*Don't.*"

Aureliano took a deep, quivering breath and said, "It's okay."

"What's okay?" Carlos had appeared in the door, his arms full of flowers. Aureliano's grip slipped and a bottle of soda fell to the floor and smashed.

"I'll get a cloth," I said.

Carlos looked around, squinting, color high, as cheerful and domineering as his mother in her best moods. He went around us to the sink and began to cut flower stems. He smirked at me over his shoulder and said, in Taoscal, "Good girl—clean up after the clumsy one."

Fernando remarked—trying to find a new subject—that he was surprised Carlos knew to cut the stems, *and* at an angle.

I stooped and wiped, gathered some glass in my covered hand, worked my way across the floor past Aureliano's legs and stood up beside his brother. For a long moment we were eye to eye. I told him he shouldn't say nasty things about his brother. Then I realized I didn't have the stamina to go wherever my anger was trying to take me.

Aureliano came and took the wrapped glass shards out of my hand, then he drew my hand to the sink and turned on the cold tap. "For some strange reason, Carme, Carlos is shocked to hear I've been teaching you Taoscal. He was telling me this morning. I think he means to ask you about it." Aureliano was admirably composed.

"Have you?" Fernando asked him. "*Why* have you?"

"Carme puts me up during the breaks. She got me work on the clam beds. She edits my papers and e-mails them back to me. I have to give something back, and the only thing *I* can teach her is Taoscal."

Carlos pulled a face and left the kitchen.

Fernando moved in and examined my hand too. "You cut yourself."

I watched both sets of dark-skinned hands, Aureliano's fleshy spatulate fingers and Fernando's long and big-knuckled. The hands moved in accord, cooperative, synchronized, as if these two were also twins. They seemed absorbed by a similar sort of tenderness.

"I don't think you need to protect Aureliano from Carlos," Fernando said to me. "He can hold his own."

"What is my own?" asked Aureliano, and Fernando, after a beat of time, let my wet hand go. He dried his hands, said he'd fetch a clean towel and a dressing, and went to do it.

In March of this year Fidela presented us with a culprit—and Madlena reported how she'd questioned this culprit on the phone. He was a member of a small New Age Christian group whose mission was to teach family values in a "joy-filled and nonpaternalistic way." He'd shown Ms. Fidela Guevara some of their literature, he said. His group wanted to teach by *pleasing*, not by proselytizing. Hence the posters. He didn't know where they had found the image but he had chosen to use it because the handsome couple were Latino, like himself. Would Juanita and Enrico García be *terribly* offended if the group used up all their old stock before finding another image?

I met the man for lunch and he told me the same story—showed me some flyers and waxed enthusiastic about future "advertisements" of "the harmonious life."

Afterward I met Fidela in the park by the Exploratorium and we watched the wind push the ducks, head down and tail up, across the green water. Fidela did try not to gloat. "See, it's a coincidence," she said. "Why can't you just relax, Carme?"

I went back up north, where I live, and as I slowed for the tollgate before the bridge, I decided that I'd start another journal.

California, near Bodega Bay, a Monday in June 2010

At the beginning of this century the epidemic was making only its first alarming incursions into people's lives. So, when I finished my first degree and chose my specialty, I often had to explain that "detentive care" had nothing to do with teeth. That it was detentive as in *detention*—quarantine care in the management of multi-drug-resistant TB.

I work twenty-four hours a week in a general practice, at community medicine, with kind, civilized colleagues, and patients with often intriguing troubles. I like it. I spend another twenty hours at the Carter Isolation Unit, where I practice the specialist medicine for which I trained for three years—on top of the five of my M.D. and two of premed. At Carter I care for immune-compromised patients who can't decently ease out of the world surrounded by friends and family because they are "sputum smear positive"—persistent secretors of multi-drug-resistant strains of tuberculosis. I care for detained, noncompliant, homeless youths and intravenous drug abusers. And I care for the poor, the people from crowded houses the government has now by law to *pour* money into, resources in the form of good food, drugs in combinations of symphonic complexity, a clean bed in a single room with negative-pressure ventilation, in a hospital where none of the nurses wear white, where all white is aglow in the antibacterial ultraviolets.

I was attracted to detentive care because it involved a war on a relentless infectious disease. As a small child I experienced an outbreak of diphtheria that frightened me so thoroughly that infectious disease came thereafter to seem some awful divinity.

I'd been living with my half-sister Astrella in a hotel in the northern city she'd chosen as a home in her exile. Diphtheria broke out in the hotel and it was put under quarantine. Astrella was able to smuggle her own children out. They were small enough to be stowed in something and carried. Astrella thought I wouldn't get it, because I was my father's daughter and he was never ill. She sat by sickbeds and bathed foreheads, but kept me away from the infected people. I spent several days in a nest on a window seat, the curtains closed around me. I read in the daylight; at night I lay beneath the mullioned window's compound eyes of darkness. Then I fell sick. There was a mirror in my room that was as loud and black as a platter full of flies. I remember that the mirror grew to the size of a grave, still buzzing busily. And *grew* to take the whole wall, as though the hotel had been sliced in half, or the *world* halved at the hotel so that space shone through. Then my fever broke and I melted in my bed, and slowly recovered.

Besides being a way of making war on that darkness, I enjoy the complexity of the treatment of multi-drug-resistant TB. It's a treatment that requires strict attention and resolution, rather than the nerve and decisiveness needed for the surgical procedures over which—when I first entered medicine—I had fantasies of mastery.

Like my general practice, the work at Carter is good and rewarding, and I win many more battles than I lose.

But that Monday I'd had a particularly bad day—and I hadn't been able to contact Bella.

I stopped by Bella's house in the afternoon and tried to raise her. I buzzed for entry and waited. There was no response. Nothing was visible through the windows.

Bella's house was a fortress, a pole house. It had only one story, its patio a platform before a curved wall of glass. There were two ways to reach the house: one by riding on the platform lift sixty meters up the sheer hillside to the patio gate; the other by a back access, a path that branched from a scenic walkway along the ridge behind the house. The walkway began thirteen minutes away by foot from one end and forty from the other. You had to have time to spare to go and knock on Bella's back door.

I called her on my mobile from the bottom of the lift. I got her machine. Her message—"*Bendita día,* if you want to hear from Bella Frei . . ."—was now commemorative. Though we could speak to Bella, have her news, she'd never be *heard* again—her smoky, droll voice. She had lost her larynx to cancer.

I knew she hadn't kept her appointment with the speech therapist who was to fit her with one of those state-of-the-art, collar-mounted synthesized voices. A voice like her own, a "vocal picture" made up of data collected from taped interviews and those numerous videos of talks she'd delivered at the conferences she'd attended.

Bella at twenty-six walking through Los Muertos, reciting Jules Frei's "Silence, Paralysis"; Bella at twenty-nine on cocaine economies; Bella at thirty giving a paper on "The Gun" at Orlando; and Bella two years ago, giving a talk on her core subject, torture narratives—and reaching for the water glass ten times in a half hour, trying to check the only real catch in her career, a catch in her voice that no lubrication could finally salve.

She didn't pick up the phone. The machine beeped and I was cut off.

Bella lived about fifteen miles from me, nearer the bay and Berkeley, where she taught. Her friends knew she was still alive because she had placed her usual order with the supermarket in town, and the delivery boy had confirmed that the groceries had ascended to her pole house as soon as he stepped off the platform of her lift. Besides, the driver on the twice-daily bus run along that road, who knew Bella, reported seeing her Subaru pulled in on the white roadside dust near an old marble quarry. Bella sat fifty meters from her car, her back to the road. The bus slowed and the driver hailed her, but she didn't turn, remained as motionless, as spookily wind-stirred, as a scarecrow.

That was a week ago. A last sighting.

I stared at the window, then turned sharply away, dazzled by reflected sunlight. I got into my car and turned back onto the road to Carter.

I had an appointment, one of my twice-weekly meetings with Carter's resident, where we discuss the drug regimen of our patients and make any necessary adjustments. And I had to visit one of my patients, whose cultures had been negative for six months and who was due to leave, graduating to Directly Observed Therapy by his own doctor, who would be acting as a kind of parole officer.

I used to do the test myself, when I was at Carter full-time. I'd grow cultures of samples taken from my patients at intervals of six hours. I always had a dish ready for the next stage, like a TV chef who runs between fridge and stove top, countertop and wall oven. Nurses and lab technicians were my floor managers. The samples were taken by nurses and cultivated by technicians, and then I would add the phage, which attaches only to certain microbacterial cells and "reports" on the presence of TB. I'd turn out the light and check the samples. I'd *measure* the light. More light meant the drugs weren't working, and the patient's drug regimen needed to be changed. (The speed of results on the phage test was the key to fighting drug resistance—and to not producing further drug-resistant strains. In each patient medicine battles a population of bacteria, and has to kill the *whole* population.) Measuring the light myself was a thing I did to feel I'd confronted the disease—kept it under my eye.

It was a month before the start of the vacation season and, coming over the summit where the road met the sea again, I looked out at a series of enchanting coves, pockets of fawn sand flanked by bare rocks. The coves were unoccupied and, spring-cleaned by a spring tide, as unmarked as freshly made beds.

The parking lot of Carter was full of trucks and tire tracks in scabbed dirt. The contractors had the roof on the new wing, and the little group of patients out on the deck of the day room were no longer obliged to wear ear guards to enjoy the sun and air.

Carter Isolation Unit was undergoing extensions. The expansion of the facility was reported in the local TV news, which talked of thirty beds to fifty-five, then showed black-and-white stills of a famous old sanatorium at Calistoga, Robert Louis Stevenson in a chair on its lawn. It was an example of the kind of reportage that's part dire and part nostalgia, and seems to say: *Bring back the old disasters with all their terrible certainty.*

When I walked into the resident's office he jumped up to clear a space on his desk for my laptop. He poured me coffee and opened the cookie jar, then he bustled back into his seat—his little performance of *getting right down to it*, of not wasting his "talented colleague's" time. He went on to make seventy percent of the decisions—as is only proper, since he ranks me—but he seemed to quiver as I considered each one, his eyebrows hitched together above his nose. He couldn't forget, and wouldn't let me forget, that my M.D. was from Harvard, and that I was "underutilized" in my general practice—*rusticated*, he thought.

He was right, I wasn't at the center of things. Not where the money was or at the cutting edge of research. But I was where I wanted to be—working with a man too timid to trespass into my life. And I had the key to my house on a chain around my neck.

Bella *had* been watching me as I stood below her fortress of a house, because, when I got home, there was an e-mail waiting for me.

Can't you see that I don't want to share my affliction? I would like to be able to say what has happened to me, say it once, not necessarily in my own words, but in my own voice, and fluently—*O! you are men of stones. Had I your tongues and eyes, I'd use them so that Heaven's vault should crack!* But why be extravagant?

To put it sufficiently—I can't ever forget my laryngectomy. I get up in the morning and see the hole in my neck. I can't take a shower without my shower shield—a waterproof nylon *bib*, for want of a better word. Mine is cream with a brown trim and looks like an ecclesiastical collar. Without it I'd drown. After breakfast, which I can taste but not smell, since no air moves through my nose, I vacuum my house. I can't tolerate dust; I no longer have the usual filters of hair and mucus. In this warm weather I wear a high-necked red lace bodysuit whose mesh forms a fine grill over the hole at the base of my throat (when I do go out and encounter people I catch them staring, transfixed by that hint of deep darkness that, unlike the body's other hidden darknesses, breathes, sometimes noisily). I've been out and contrived to be surly and speechless and, if I had to speak, I've shut off my Blomfield valve and used my temporary synthesizer to make like a cyberman. Everyone stares. And when I go to bed sometimes the sheet falls across my neck and I wake up with a start because I can't breathe.

I went out into my garden and spent an hour pinching the laterals from my young tomato plants and weeding the rows between my other vegetables. I thought about Bella's e-mail—or, at least, I tried to feel my way into it. Then I went to shelter in the shade of my big open basement. My hands were fragranced by tomato leaves. It was hot, and the pile of tomato prunings had wilted already. My cat sat near it, eyes closed, his ears swiveling among the finches in a bottlebrush, a car on the road, my own movements, and the muted jackhammer noise of the pump.

The couple who owned the house before me left me the pump. It was their sprinkler chugging away between my broccoli and onions, and their black plastic hose pulsing by my foot, its snout in the stream among the reeds. From where I stood, I could see that the stream was less lively, had started to back against the pressure of the sea a mile away at its mouth.

When I bought the house I told the couple that if they wanted to keep their bits and pieces in the garage they could—for I noticed tears filming the eyes of the woman as she spoke about how much they had to move. They came now and again, from Santa Rosa, where they had retired, to pick up the things they needed seasonally—say, the deck chairs and barbecue—only if I was sure *I* wouldn't need them. The husband returned after only a month for his tools. He said he thought he'd like idleness more, in his new low-maintenance house. Beside me, on the basement wall, there was a square of pierced hardboard where his tools once hung. I found myself staring at this board. It had painted silhouettes of hammer, plane, level, chisel, and screwdrivers in ascending sizes. It had a place for everything, and *a shadow of everything in its place.*

I went indoors to call Fidela—and caught her running. She had driven her Mercedes to the top of a long flight of steps that climbed beside the wood of eucalyptus and Monterey pine behind the Presidio. The steps linked Pacific Heights to the Marina district. From their top Golden Gate Bridge and Marin Heights were obscured, but the Exploratorium and Alcatraz were visible. I knew the view, knew that every day Fidela ran up and down those steps twice—she liked it better than using the step machine parked in the amphitheater of her home entertainment center, although I'd heard her complain that she sweated off her sunblock.

I listened to my sister pant into the phone. I told her I'd be in the city the following Thursday, visiting Ricardo in his long-term care facility. Would she like to have lunch with me?

Fidela said that she didn't know why I bothered visiting Ricardo, and I told her I was keeping up appearances.

She hemmed and hawed about lunch. She and Bob had some kind of function at the yacht club in Tiburon. (Bob and Fidela had a house on Locust Street, open plan inside, with vast rooms, but on the outside mock Tudor, whitewashed plaster between black beams, and mullioned windows. There was also an apartment in L.A., where they spent half of their time.)

I asked Fidela *when* the function was.

She hesitated, then told the truth. It was at six. "Are you on your own this week? No one in the spare bed?"

"No one. And Bella isn't speaking to me."

"If we have lunch, Carme, you'll just go on all paranoid about poster campaigns, or whatever's the latest *persecution*." Fidela's tone was both impassioned and impatient. She'd patented this attitude, and I always thought that despite the bad press Fidela sometimes gave Bob, it took a man to withstand my sister's peculiar brand of bored intensity.

"I just said lunch." It seemed to me that there was something slippery under Fidela's tone, dry and slippery, like a graphite lubricant. I asked her what was wrong.

She was just a little tense. *I'd* be tense if I was taking my temperature six times a day and my husband was obliged to arrive at odd hours, by cab, and run up the front walk already loosening his tie.

"If he's in that much of a hurry you should tell him he doesn't have to loosen his tie."

Bob and Fidela were trying to get pregnant. She was young and healthy and had expected to conceive as soon as she made the decision and stopped her contraception. A year after the decision they had moved on to testing her temperature and the viscosity of her vaginal discharge.

"Bob's booked us into a fertility clinic," Fidela said. The best in the state, of course. She had seen their counselor last week. "We had to fill out forms. Our family histories. I had to mention Mama's fertility problems. It turns out it's the *same clinic*."

I waited for more.

"I didn't tell them how I fed Mama Marvelon. But I imagine they checked their records. I think they know. I imagine this smooth little gringa is looking at me and thinking that I can't get pregnant because I have some kind of guilt-induced inhibition."

Fidela was upset—a rare event. I couldn't think what to say, but did say, lamely, that I doubted that the clinic kept records that long. (But I knew they would, in this litigious nation, in the medical profession, and especially in any branch of it concerned with fertility and childbirth.)

I told Fidela that *if* she could find time for lunch that would be nice, she should think about it and let me know.

San Francisco, a Thursday in June 2010

I decontaminated myself, removed my coveralls, balled them up, and pushed them into a chute through a slit plastic membrane. I scrubbed down, which involved only a little *less* scrubbing than scrubbing up for surgery. I replaced my made-to-measure mask in its Ziploc bag and stepped out of the luminous inner corridors of the Isolation Unit through the double glass doors of the airlock. I went to my car.

Bella was waiting for me below her house, on the platform of her lift. She was wearing a summer dress, and her head and neck were loosely draped in a gauzy scarf. Bella was the only thing near the road not covered in dust. The coated roadside plants looked like ghosts of themselves.

Bella's second e-mail had asked me to do her a favor. If I was visiting the "dilapidated demon" as usual on Thursday, could I drive her into the city and deliver her to the voice clinic?

I opened the passenger door and watched Bella cross the road. Because her silence made me nervous, I began to talk before she'd even got in. I asked how high up the hillside the road dust rose. Did it get into her house and trouble her? Then I talked into the space meant for her reply—said something about how I hoped it would rain soon. Bella paused with her hand on the top of the door. She was smiling at me and her eyes were fully alive, seeming to float before her face, as the light of a torch behind a window will show in two places, at its source and on the glass. She cocked her chin at the view toward the valley, where, in the rain shadow at the back of the inlet, clouds were collecting above the forest, only there, gathered as if shyly in the corner of a too-bright room.

Bella got in beside me and closed her door.

I shut my mouth. All my life I'd been surrounded by talkers, and had been able to keep quiet and wait for contact, for a spark to jump the gap. I was finding this terribly difficult.

Bella touched my arm, smiled, then hooked a finger into the bunched filmy scarf, drew it down, slowly, almost sexily—Bella always understood the theater of such things. I looked at—into—that black flexing hole, and she moved just a little so that the sunlight hit the back of the narrow, cartiliginous shaft. She was showing me the worst of it.

The sight did steady me. I started my engine, and Bella produced a disc with a homemade label and fed it into the stereo. I waited for enlightenment. I anticipated a *statement*. But the disc was a recording of Tomás Juiliano, in a playful frame of mind, on his morning radio program. He told a story about a burst pipe in his apartment, and the plumber who stood about chatting while Tomás watched his tiles come adrift beneath two inches of plaster-clouded water. The plumber said that in a former life he had been the Roman engineer who built the Pont du Gard. "I told him," Tomás said, "that in a more recent past, when *I* was a young man, people who got too fanciful were driven out into the Cordillera Pacifica and had a gun put to the back of their heads. And the plumber said he'd have my pipe fixed by tomorrow, no, *today*, possibly even yesterday." Then, of course, Tomás played the Beatles' most lucrative ballad.

Bella's mouth was open in her soundless puppet laugh, and air hissed through the hole in her throat.

The long-term care facility was like a nursery with softer corners. There were pictures on the walls with labels as large and pleasing as the alphabets and word lists in a kindergarten. The furniture was all adult-sized, but there were wooden bars over the safety-glass windows, plus ramps, elevators, and watercoolers with paper cups the same size as those used to dispense medication—two-gulp cups. Sun came in the window from the patients' garden, where a double spiral of stepping-stones, flush to the turf, wound in to a papery, pink-leaved Chinese toon tree, so gorgeous it looked artificial.

My husband's day nurse took me to the pool. Ricardo was at aqua fitness with his physiotherapist. He was running, tilted forward and pushing the water. He moved with little steps and wore a light-weight flotation jacket. When he lost his balance the woman beside him put out an arm to steady him; every time she did, he struck at her, momentarily furious, then intent again.

"He had his medication at eleven," said his nurse, and looked at her watch. "He'll wind down soon."

The woman in the pool pumped her arms to show Ricardo what he might like to consider doing—an exercise or two. He looked around at her, fearful, then began to mimic.

There were two pink-skinned old men in the pool's far end, aqua jogging. All the other patients at the facility were Anglos, possibly all Republicans too— which is why I chose to commit my husband to its care.

As he came toward the end where I stood, Ricardo looked up at me. His eyes seemed to have grown yet another layer of thick transparent skin. They were glazed, preserved —like slices of orange in the aspic on top of a pâté—faded brown and buried, symmetrical, and only *like* eyes. The fine skin beneath them was loose and full of fluid. He turned himself around, plunged out of his minder's reach, and ran away again, on a diagonal course across the pool. Sweat was starting through the thin spot on the crown of his head.

It took ten minutes for his minder and nurse to coax him out of the water. I wrapped his robe around him, hugged it to me just before I let it go, savoring its fresh, dry, static scent. Ricardo's nurse fed his arms through its sleeves and followed them with her own, so that she stood for a moment chest to chest with my husband. Then she arrested his fists as they emerged from the sleeve ends.

"He's thinner," I said.

"He's being very difficult about food—aren't you, Señor Pastrez?" She was asking in that way they have, not expecting an answer, but at least she didn't shout. She squatted to dry him, removed his trunks, and then reached for a pair of adult diapers, already the shape of a skinny pelvis, padded and molded. He obligingly parted his legs as she put them on. All the while he looked at me, his brows down, as if squinting into the sun, and chewed his lower lip between his top and bottom gums. It was because of this habit that his nurses now only let him wear his false teeth to eat.

"But we'll see how we do today," the nurse said. "We've cooked something special for you today, Señor Pastrez." She said to me, "We'll leave him in the robe for now. Unless you would rather we dress him?" Then to him, "Shall your wife come with us to your room, Señor Pastrez?" As if he had a choice, or could make a choice. She led him away and I followed.

Ricardo had a bedroom and sitting room. He had a view of the garden and a glimpse over the wall of a small wedge of the bay, and the section of the Bay Bridge over to Yerba Buena Island. I stood looking out the window until the nurse had Ricardo installed in a chair with a tray that could be swung around in front of him to keep him "up at the table," imprisoned in one of the few necessary hours of his day. The nurse said lunch was in fifteen minutes and would I like to have some? Then, *sotto voce*, "It might encourage him. I sometimes eat with him."

I said yes.

When she'd gone from the room I drew up a chair and sat down before Ricardo. We were going to take communion together—a meal, and it would be on good flatware with silver cutlery. The facility treated its residents like the grown-up people they were—*once were*—the wealthy grown-up people. Ricardo wouldn't let me take his hands. He huffed and whined and pulled them away, kept them in peevish motion, then seemed to see the humor in it, laughed, looked up at me as though I was contriving a game for him, and made a bigger business of evading my grip. I begged him to be still.

I had preferred him after his first stroke, when he was too embarrassed to speak and get the words wrong. Silent, uncertain, but composed still. After his second stroke he turned up the television (which he'd never watched before) because he couldn't hear it, he claimed—but there was nothing wrong with his hearing. He couldn't follow much of what he heard, wasn't able to understand even one-third of the huge lexicon he'd once held in his head. It was at that time he'd taken me, shuffling, into his hidden sanctum and I finally saw all the magical apparatus Ambre had so disapproved of. He couldn't use it—would I take it? Hide it? "That part of me is— cut," he said. "Cut off. But things *move around* in here all night." After his third stroke he was in a hospital at Medellín for a long time, and they managed teach him to walk again without his feet always turn- ing in. Then he had another, maybe two in quick succession, and he lost all his orientation to the world, and I paid a lot of money to a lot of different people in order to bring him to California.

One victim of multiple small strokes is reported as having com- plained, "God is taking me in pieces." What Ricardo said, between his third and fourth stroke, was, "I am being eaten."

"Please be still," I said to my husband. I remembered him, in the hospital bed at Medellín, his gray-and-black hair combed back from his forehead, reposed, eyes closed, nose pinched, face pale. I re- membered how I'd stroked his hair and run my fingers along his warm, still mouth.

I got his hands, I held them down on his knees. He looked at me, eager and atremble, waiting for the next game.

Our lunch arrived and I let him go. I drew back.

The nurse first set his food before him and tucked a napkin into the bunched top of his robe. Then she placed a small table before my chair and gave me mine. Ricardo looked at her and said, urgent, "She's—she *is*—isn't she?" In Spanish.

"Your wife, Señor Pastrez."

"No—no—*daughter*."

"No, Señor Pastrez, this is your wife, Carme."

"*His* daughter."

"Yes, I'm his daughter," I said to Ricardo.

He nodded.

The nurse paused, pressed her hands together and looked from me to him—wanting our attention. Then she swooped forward and lifted the steel covers simultaneously from my plate and his. She refrained from a fanfare.

Ricardo peered at his food. Then he grunted and started to shout, "No! No!" He flapped one hand at the plate, at the pile of steaming meat, the pink-centered, brown-gray graininess of well-cooked kidneys.

"But this is what you wanted, Mr. Pastrez." His nurse had forgotten the "Señor." She said to me, "He managed to let us know he'd like some 'offal.' He wasn't more specific than that."

"No!" Ricardo said. "Not like *that*!" Then he threw himself back in his chair, averted his head, clamped his lips shut, and closed his eyes.

I got up and moved away from him. The papery, pink-leaved tree was like coral. There's nothing lovelier than light shining through something alive. The tree's leaves made shadows that incorporated the light. People are opaque and have bones in their bodies, which seems, in itself, to show no humility. Considering—*considering* the sounds of the senile tantrum behind me. Considering what happens to people.

I said to Ricardo's nurse, "He wants it raw." And I knew by the noise behind me, the creaking rustle, the little huffs, that my husband was now nodding, perhaps looking from her to me—the clever one—*his* daughter. Just for a moment I looked at the sun, trying to freshen the darkness inside me. "But *why* does he want it raw?" I said.

The nurse was making noise with the plates. I heard the suck of a fork in the mashed potatoes and her trying to coax him. "You realize we *can't*, Dr. Risk, not offal, it's not safe."

"What are you saving him for? I'll sign forms, whatever forms it takes."

"It's statutory, I think, not just our policy."

I thought about statutes and policies, and one of my incurables with her perpetual sore throat and, this week, scarcely able to raise her arms. The policy of detentive care was cautious, and mindful of medical ethics—very necessary in a climate of fear. Detentive care *is* a compromise of civil liberty, and therefore no persistently infectious patients confined at places like Carter could be eased out of the world no matter how terribly they suffered.

I said *of course* I understood, but how unaccommodating these institutions were—and I worked in one—toward expedient, lively, practical solutions.

"I agree with you," the nurse said. "Or—I know exactly what you mean. But there it is."

I left late, after Ricardo had fallen by stages into a jumpy sleep. It was dark, and the air was fumy, fog coming. As I unlocked my car and its sidelights flashed, the headlights of another car in the lot switched on. A car parked facing mine. I shielded my eyes and saw a thin redhead jump out from behind the wheel. My sister. Fidela called out—she was worried that she'd missed me. "I just want to clear up a misunderstanding." She stood watching me, her arms folded and shoulders stooped. "I mean, I wasn't brushing you off. Really, Carme."

I took my phone out of my jacket and held it out to her, to show that I had it.

"I lost mine. I left Tiburon before Bob."

Of course I wondered why she didn't just go home and call me, but I didn't ask, I waited to see if she'd get around to an explanation. I asked if she'd like to go somewhere for a drink. I'd already eaten with Ricardo.

"You said *lunch*," she said, as though I were the inflexible one. "Look—I just didn't want you misunderstanding me."

I asked her what was wrong and I put my hand on her arm.

"I have to go," she said. The light was behind her, her hair bright but insubstantial, thinner than it once was. I could see only her ears and jaw; her face was a shadow the shape of an Egyptian life cross, without a life cross's open keyhole. I let her go, saying Bella was waiting for me in a bar downtown.

"Drive safe," she said, and turned around into the light. She was very thin and flat-chested in profile.

It was the only time I ever saw Fidela rattled. Now I know why.

My sister always so much loved her own efforts that, correspond-
ingly, she couldn't stand accidents.

I dropped Bella off and went home.

Aureliano's beat-up car was parked outside, well off the road,
one side mirror buried in my hedge. It was straighter than he'd ever
managed to park it before, but it looked surreptitious, lurking. My
house lights were off. I found him in "his" room, just lighting up a
cigarette, which I never let him do indoors. I wagged a finger at him
and watched his eyes appear, gleaming, in the light of his first inhala-
tion—then he rolled over and stubbed it out.

I went to him, into his arms, glad I'd dressed up—for Ricardo—
and that my ceremonious, always superfluous preparations would be
used. My silk dress with the seven silver buttons, my bra with its
front catch.

The smoke in his mouth was superficial; his skin and hair smelled
of soap and shampoo. Although no one smoked in my house, I still
loved that acrid cigarette smell on people, *those* people—Ambre,
Madlena, Fernando, Enrico, Tomás, Aureliano. It was the smell of
the bars, cafes, buses, public buildings, and private houses of home,
and I missed it in his cleanliness, his preparedness. Both were unlike
him. I began to be suspicious. "Didn't you hear my car?" I asked, and
he kissed me, his breath baited with toothpaste and mouthwash.

I went from suspicion to certainty.

He sat up to pull off his own clothes. For a moment be seemed
about to direct the bundled shirt and pants to the chair by the bed,
then he dropped them on the floor, turned abruptly back to me,
gray-skinned in the light, the small muscles over his ribs catching
hard-edged shadows like scales. He unbuttoned me to my waist and
spent a moment kissing my collarbones. He was thinner than his
brother. His body seemed condensed, hard, but not insistent. My
still-covered breasts brushed his chest. I managed the catch myself,
since he wouldn't—would neither speak nor speed up. My breasts
weren't bared, but instead of uncovering them he used his hands to
cover my eyes. For a moment he lay still, then he said, "So, it's true.
But do you know Taoscal?"

I pulled his hands down from my eyes, until his fingertips rested on my cheeks. I said, "Since *I* was pretending, Carlos, the least you could do was to continue to pretend yourself."

He jumped, giggled, then said, "I'm far too fucking nervous to— well—"

"To use your obscenity as a verb and in the right place in your sentence." I relaxed, arched my back, felt the warm cloth cups slip their anchorage on either breast and cool air touch my nipples.

"I *could*," he said.

"Could fuck me? Or say 'fuck you'?"

He didn't say anything. I made a move to shake him off and he caught my wrists and pressed me back against the bed. He asked, "Do you remember how, when we were kids, you once tied up Aureliano?" Then, "How do you think I felt about that?"

I asked him what he was going to do and he asked me what I wanted him to do.

"I want you to let go, get up, hang your head, and say, 'I'm sorry, Carme.' "

He let go, got up, and said he was sorry.

And I invited him back.

Later he was showing off. I was filled, but he was immobile. I made noises, put out my tongue, touched myself, but he was still, and still held my gaze. Then he asked, in Taoscal, which one of them I loved.

"Neither," I answered, in Taoscal.

"How can you not love someone who loves you?"

"My heart was taken."

He pulsed, waxed full, but his face showed nothing at all. "Where was your heart taken?" His sentence would set up a wave of head shaking among the elders beside the oven pits of Taosclan. What the purists, the old grammarians would say was that his sentence lacked "courage."

I answered that my heart was carried away like a burr on the coat of a jaguarundi. I answered in *courageous* Taoscal, and I thrust with my hips so that he gasped, and threw his head up and clung to me, pushing back as if meaning to pass through me. "What you mean?" he gasped, scarcely articulate.

"I mean, the one who took my heart doesn't know he has it."

Carlos's back was slick to the touch and suddenly seemed cold. He whispered in my ear another question. When would my heart return to me?

"Never," I said. "It's been gone so long it no longer knows me."

"Beautiful," he whispered. "Beautiful sentence." This he said in Spanish, then again in Taoscal he asked, "*Who* do you love?" He held me close, his upper body quiet, his lips soft on my neck, but his pelvis moved, spasmodic, uncomposed.

"You know who," I said.

He tried to look at me then, but his eyes were finally full of fog. He moaned and came; then as he withdrew I came too, stifling myself against the springy muscle of his shoulder. For a minute I just stared, stupefied, at the glistening dents my teeth had made in his flesh. Then, with his first controlled breath, Carlos asked me why circumstances had to be so perverse? And I thought to say—said— the Taoscal proverb: "A luck of great gravity is involved in these events."

His look—it was dark and hard to tell. Was it one of awe or horror?

San Francisco, later in June 2010

Locust Street. Fidela's Hollywood Tudor house. I passed it looking for a parking space. All the lantana bushes along Jackson Street were in full flower, cerise and yellow and brick red, and dwarf agapanthus alternated with box in short ornamental hedges. Some of the houses had closed for the summer, but the available parking spaces were still filled with the ten-year-old cars of cleaners and gardeners. There was a mobile dog groomer pulled up in Fidela's drive and I could see her bottle-blond poodle, Miss Mansfield, sitting patiently on a stool being blow-dried.

I found a place and walked back. I was admitted by Fidela and Bob's Samoan maid. She moved her hands around me in the hall-way—as if blessing me—then realized I didn't plan to relinquish my long-sleeved top. "Perhaps you can make Mrs. Renzi take a

376

break," she said, and nodded at the door to the gym. "She's been going an hour and a half, which is half an hour longer than her old routine."

Fidela was on her step machine, her wiry legs treading down the pneumatic pedals and taking her nowhere. Her thinning hair was plastered to her head. She said hello.

"You should stop and warm down," I said.

"I'm finishing," she panted.

"I'll come back tomorrow and bring calipers to measure the flesh on your arm. Or the lack of it."

"I'm only trying to stay toned, Carme, so don't start." Fidela did finish. She picked up her towel to wipe away the sweat pooled in the shape of her hand. She dismounted and lay down on the floor to go through her stretches. She was so exhausted I could see her lips move—she had to *count* herself through them.

"You're losing muscle, Fidela. That's why you don't feel toned. You're a rational person, you know I'm right. And if the doctors at that fertility clinic are worth the money you and Bob are paying they must have pointed out to you that the second greatest cause of infertility in women *after* pelvic inflammatory disease is being underweight." How had her body deserved such punishment? I asked. To be underfed and exercised into a state of foul-tempered, knock-kneed, hairy thinness, and then be subjected to hormones and laparoscopies and fiber-optic intrusions?

Fidela said she was having a shower—was I staying for lunch? When she went I drifted toward the kitchen and found the maid paying the dog groomer. Miss Mansfield put her paws on my hips and stared into my eyes. I rubbed her long soft ears. When the dog groomer had gone I told the maid I'd had a word with Fidela about her exercising.

"Twenty-three, and worried about her hips," the maid said. "I tell her it makes it look as if Mr. Renzi can't afford to feed her."

Fidela hurried her shower and came in, superficially pink and wearing only her robe. She said to her maid, "Why don't you make us your fish with coconut cream and yams, to please Carme?"

I was led by the hand from the kitchen. We sat on the terrace over the Renzis' small, groomed backyard. It had only a lawn and a big, acidic blue spruce that cast shade on the whole back of the house much of the day but which Bob, with his Californian reverence for trees, wouldn't cut down.

Fidela said she and Bob were off to L.A. and the clinic tomorrow—to get the test results and discuss their options.

My sister had brought a magazine with her onto the terrace. She put it down on the tabletop and pushed it across to me. I saw that it wasn't a magazine, but a brochure, advertising the fertility clinic. Fidela asked me to look at the list of patrons.

I scanned the credits and my eyes lit on "Edwin Money, Jr." I said to Fidela, "I read about him in a magazine. The lost heir."

Fidela fiddled with her robe, clutched it closed, although it was a mild, Bay Area nonsummer day. She started talking, to the tabletop at first, then gradually looked up at me, as fearless and forthright as ever. She'd gone to the gathering at the yacht club in Tiburon. Bob had recently taken up sailing. At the yacht club Fidela met Edwin Money—she paused—Junior. Junior was a hale and hearty seventy. This was Edwin of the ashram, an only son who spent twenty-five years in India, then came back when he inherited Money's empire. "Every time anyone mentions Edwin Junior they mention the ashram, as if it's a title or qualification. Anyway—Bob was talking to some other people and I was alone at the buffet with Money." Fidela smiled. "Alone with the unlocked *till*. I said to him, 'So, are you Edwin Money the son or Edwin Money the father?' And he began patiently to explain that his famous father had been dead for nearly fifteen years. Then he gave me a sly look and said he knew his father had done me some harm. And I said, 'And mine did yours a great deal of good.' I said, 'I say this because I think maybe it is *you*—Edwin Money Senior. You got lucky.' "

I stared at my sister. I couldn't see why she'd do something so reckless, so socially awkward and against her own interests. Even *I* wouldn't have. (Dad might, he made daring guesses, I think he could hear truth blundering after his guesses and trying to catch its breath.) I asked, "Why did you say that? Why would you think it?"

"Dad didn't keep his promises—you know, the *extravagant* ones like 'I won't leave you.' But Edwin Money was more project than promise and Dad usually saw his projects through."

"I need evidence."

"Okay. Money's *lips*. He said, 'My father has been dead for fifteen years.' And I said that I didn't approve of what I learned as a kid in my world of witches and necromancers, but I did believe it. And he looked at me, and he didn't lick his whiskey and soda—*what* a '50s drink—off his lower lip. He wasn't nervous, so he didn't. He wasn't wondering how to give this crazy woman the slip. He was *excited*. Be cause he'd been sprung, but I couldn't prove a thing. When he didn't lick his lips I took it as a sign of what my guide, Lindy, would call *Eros*. Lindy has been working on my Eros—it's one of those things I do for myself like electrolysis and having my hair highlighted. Money left his lip wet, he *magnified* it, he went soft in his muscle as his blood detoured to his soft tissue. He *sighed*, for God's sake! I know about gesture, Carme, I understand gesture. That blood thing is one of Lindy's visualizations. 'Imagine all your blood flowing into your soft tissue,' she says. 'Who needs collagen?' That's the *Dionysian*—for want of a non-drama-school word—behavior Dad inspired in all sorts of people. In everyone he ever *took charge of*."

I said that if Edwin Money, who had been a frail eighty-nine, was now a hale seventy and holding his own, then Dad was alive.

"Alive and turning back time."

I was looking at my sister, and I was sitting down, but suddenly the world began to scroll upward, all its details like lines on the computer screen on the move, or a ladder slowly reeled up into the belly of some hovering helicopter. There was a rushing noise that drowned out everything, the birdsong above us in the blue spruce and Fidela's words. I came back to myself a minute later to find my head down on my arms and Fidela holding my shoulders. "I'm sorry, Carme," she said. "I waited outside that long-term care place for you on the day it happened, but I was too scared to tell you. It's my feel-ing that Money won't admit it. But I'm going to try to talk to him again."

"Why Money?" I said. "Why not Ambre, or the sick kids in La Casa de la Mujer where he was *needed*?"

"I know," Fidela said. "Why trust Money and not us? And how come Money's a patron of my fertility clinic?"

That night I called Fernando. I didn't mean to tell him anything—how could I let him in on a secret he'd have to keep from Madlena? Who would be unable to keep it from Ambre. Who had *not* to be told. The family was insufficiently insulated and all too easily over-heated.

I called because I needed to hear Fernando's tenderness, his un-priestly, possessive "my child." But I got Madlena, who said Fernando was out, browbeating some Taoscal elders who'd frightened Rosa. "A couple of toothless poster girls for osteoporosis, who pawed Rosa in the street. But he's blaming me! He's being a crazy bastard! Rosa is his little precious girl who is too good for his *own people*. I sent Rosa to the Taoscal Language Nest so it's *my* fault they speak to her in the street!"

"Could I speak to Rosa?"

"She's *over* it. It's Fernando who is out somewhere ripping the heads off old people." But Madlena did fetch her daughter.

Rosa was shy—unsure what to call me. The six months since Christmas were a long time for an eight-year-old.

I asked what the elders had done.

"Nothing much. I was afraid of the one who was bent right over. She walked that way, as if she was looking for something on the ground. When she held my hand and I wanted to take my hand back I was scared she'd fall over and break, and it would be *my* fault."

I listened to Rosa breathe heavily through her nose. I was about to ask something when she said, "Papa was angry, he wanted to know what they asked, and he *shook* me."

"What did they ask, Rosa?"

"They were being polite, except for grabbing me. They asked me how I was today and what I was carrying and why I was carrying it in two pieces—which was silly because it was my flute and my flute's case and if they hadn't been deaf they would have heard me playing it as I walked along. I was letting the spit drip out before I put it away. Then they asked me where I lived and I didn't want to tell them so I said the Avenida Bueyes Negros where Papa still has his apartment. Then they wanted to know which was *my* door, and I pointed to Papa's old door. And then they asked who I lived with, and I said with my mother who is Colonel Madlena Guevara and my father who is Commander Fernando Sola, just so they'd be *warned*. Then I got really nervous because they grabbed me. I was going. And the straighter one asked me when I was expected home and I shouted, 'Right now!' and I ran away."

"Are you okay now?"

"Yes, but Papa was acting strange."

"Can I speak to your mother again?"

A clunk as the receiver was dropped, Rosa calling, "Mama!" Footsteps, Madlena again.

"Look," I said. "Was this interrogation conducted entirely in Taoscal?"

"Yes. So?"

"Those were the 'seven questions.' Hasn't Fernando explained this? The 'seven questions' are an initiation rite. It's like a confirmation. A first communion. Fernando talked about it years ago to Lydia Yahanova. Rosa had to reply in perfect Taoscal, which I guess she did."

I could almost hear the clockwork of Madlena's thinking; like Rosa she breathed heavily through her nose. Ambre had this mannerism too, and was the only one who didn't sound retarded when she did it. Madlena said that Tomás had once told her that Fernando first became a candidate for the chiefdom because he made "momentous answers" to the seven questions. "He began, 'I am Fernando, who is the village Sola'— because he was the only survivor of a massacred village." Madlena paused. "Carme? What are you thinking? Why is he so upset?" Her voice was pinched and little.

We talked it over for another quarter hour, with no progress. But as soon as I put down the phone and turned around to see my kitchen, the cork tiles, my cat basking in the white, reflected radiance of the refrigerator door, I realized that I, too, had been asked the seven questions. From "Which one of us do you love?" to "Why are circumstances so perverse?" And I remembered that Carlos— who I knew didn't love me—was moved by more than the wet friction between us. "Beautiful sentence," he'd said.

Momentous sentences—evasion, analogy, confession, proverb—and all of them in perfect Taoscal.

California, near Bodega Bay, July 2010

Fidela called me from L.A. She'd learned her results. (I thought of premed, all our lonely moments at notice boards looking up newly posted grades.) My sister wasn't depressed, but reported the facts and her interpretation of them with a measured, corrosive vehemence.

She'd stayed in the clinic overnight. The place was full of females over forty being strenuously encouraged not to *blame* themselves for waiting too long. It was true that some had been in bad circumstances and some were too busy. "But one said to me, 'Why didn't my body tell me when it was time?' " Fidela said she'd never been exposed to such vanity and obscure thinking—human misery magnified by consumerism. "I can't say *I* waited too long. But I was there, in that clinic, with all the other miserable creatures, because, as far as I was concerned, there was not going to be something I *couldn't have*. I thought I could have everything, not because I'm privileged and can *pay*, but because I've always worked so hard and taken care of myself.

"Anyway—the doctors tell me I have ovaries, which produce all the right hormones, so that I'm womanly, from my hairless chin to my hairy snatch. I've got ovaries like permanent estrogen patches. But Carme, I don't have any *eggs* in my ovaries. My problem isn't fallopian tubes clogged with 'adhesions'—the doctors can't harvest my eggs and fertilize them in a petri dish and put them back in my womb, because I don't have any eggy genetic material to contribute. To my marriage. To the world. If *you* submit to the same tests I bet you'll find the same thing. Because, Carme, we're hybrids. We're *mules*, sterile mules. And for us it's like 'End of the line; everyone off!' Our *kind*, to continue, would have to be cultivated, like nectarines."

Bella has her new voice, mounted in a beautiful collar she's had made. The speaker and its mechanisms are concealed behind an oval of filigree silver. The voice is Bella's, but clear and cold—the deep roughness of her chain-smoking now only in its timbre, with no sense of a parched territory behind it, of physical conditions.

Unlike the contemporary text readers, which will render any text into speech as natural as grammar and punctuation permit, Bella's voice synthesizer is unable to *read* her sentences before she speaks them. It can't quite get them right. To compensate for this, and for the least little hesitation while it thinks and finds her words, there's a kind of mellow, modulated superpersonality the machine imposes on Bella's voice. Although the synthesizer responds to specific sorts of pressure—and Bella now has a broadcast-quality shout—generally she speaks with an un-Bellalike nonchalance.

She has begun a new book.

Let in on its subject, one of her colleagues at Berkeley remarked that Bella hadn't lost her sense of the sensational. "She's wrong," Bella told me. "I'd never have had the nerve to tackle this before I lost my larynx. *Before*, I kept thinking of my career. I thought that I had control of my public life, and that was what *mattered*. But nothing I do matters, and far from being in control, I was clearly always lost—writing the right books and smoking my stupid head off. I'm not sure books matter much, and *mine* certainly don't. I can't do the *right* thing. But that means I can't do the wrong thing either, so I'm going to take on a subject at the limit of my ability—I'm going to write about fascism and magic, beginning with the Nazi black masses. But at the heart of my book are those Pola Pastrez sorcerers in their Black Room."

She poured me a glass of Essensia, a dessert wine we both love. She was slowly feeding her friends the contents of her cellar, her taste buds no longer up to the job, unable to savor those orange muscat grapes without breath on her tongue, in her nasal cavity, and against the roof of her mouth.

Bella was fine, she was putting forth new growth. Wine was lost to her, and swimming—for fear the sea would pour into her where she was breached, where she drew breath, at her neck—but she had her courage. She might be feeling it as fearlessness and fuck-you-all, but it was still courage. And she had her trained, shrewd intelligence, so that as we talked and kept the occasional eye on the television, and I saw something inexplicable, she was able to explain it to me.

Bella had ordered a couple of busy recent action movies as a kind of background music to our talk. She said she liked to half-watch movies and wonder what was happening, that wondering about plot was good for her brain.

I stopped talking and stared at the screen. I recognized the man I'd questioned about his cult's poster "advertising matrimony." On the screen I saw the man breaking a window with the butt of his gun. I told Bella, and we turned the volume up to catch the name of the character he was playing. Then we flicked over to the film's credits and found that "Felix" was "Sam Morales." I told Bella about the strangers Fidela had hired to watch the post office box, and how she had caught, and *we* had questioned, Sam Morales. Who was an actor, it turned out.

"Have you got a copy of the poster?" Bella said. She'd seen it, but only in passing, and while preoccupied by the side effects of chemotherapy. I fetched the one I'd unwrapped from a power pole in Phoenix, where I'd been at a conference on detentive care. Bella studied it, then said, "Oh—*I'm* sorry." She looked up at me, eyes crinkled, her substitute for laughter—the voice technicians hadn't been able to reproduce her laugh because she didn't laugh during phone messages or when delivering a lecture. "We must all be dim," she said. Then she turned the poster to face me. "Think semiotics. Because this was designed to be *read*. What do you see? Forget that it's Juanita. She's a bride, what's she saying? At this moment in her life what is the bride saying?"

"I do," I said.

"That's the *address*. This poster is a *letter*. The letter's contents are the fine print, the box number. And it's signed, only the comma is missing. Think—'Yours sincerely, Carme' or 'Regards, Bella.' This says, 'Forever, Faithful.' "

"It's Fidela."

"She hired an actor to finally throw you. To stop all of you from noticing her posters. She's trying to find him without any of you knowing it."

Bella crawled across the floor and held me. "Carme, did you know that when my uncle was putting together a second edition of the Frei *Collected* I helped to make a selection from the unpublished poems? There was one—we didn't use it because it wasn't finished—called 'Fidela.' It was dated '97, when she was still nine. It begins: 'Fidela, the stone in your shoe is your country, the dust taking their shine off is the breath of mother, sister, aunt. . . .' It goes on about rows of heated iron shoes ready on the hearth for the guests at her wedding. I'm sure she never saw it. But it does *get* her. Fidela: resentful, unimpressed, regarding all her family as impediments—right?"

I nodded.

"But what is she like when she *loves* someone? She's exposing herself to all sorts of horrible possible defeats in trying to have Bob Renzi's baby."

"*A* baby."

"No. Bob's baby. A baby for their family. And she loves *you*. She's keeping her search secret because there have been searches that failed and she doesn't want to see you disappointed again. She wants to find him for *you*, Carme."

An e-mail from Bella:

Did you know that the Taoscal sorcerer murdered in the Black Room was a Masolan, like Pablito Masolan, who was also murdered but *after* the revolution? I haven't been able to establish yet whether they were related. My impression, asking questions—admittedly over the phone—is that the Taoscal (represented here by Fernando and the Minister of Indian Affairs and a professor of Taoscal language and customs at La Host University) are terribly cagey about that murdered sorcerer. What I need is a Pola Pastrez informant. Any ideas, Señora Pastrez?

My e-mail to Bella:

> Madlena has her father's address. Emilio Rivera. If you can persuade her to give it to you. Good luck.

Fidela's e-mail to me:

> I had a sympathetic talk today with Edwin Money. He was very gentlemanly, although we were standing in the parking lot at the yacht club, and I had my hair in a towel. To celebrate our talk I went to Stockton Street and bought some nectarines.

La Host, Lequama, September 2010

When the first call came, at 4:10 a.m., I had the phone in my hand before realizing I was conscious. I'd been yanked up out of a dream where I stood at a long window watching thick snow fall. Then my phone was ringing, and the snow turned to ashes. I found the phone in my hand and hissing. I couldn't hear who it was for the weather, the weather on the line, not echoes on fiber optics, but a static, a surf—someone in tears.

The second call was mine, at 7:00 a.m. to Bella. I made arrangements for my cat and garden, told her she must be sure to remember to switch the pump off as the tide turned. Having watered once with salt water I'd not like to see it happen again. I said all this to her answering machine, then she came on and asked, "What is it, Carme? What's happened?"

Juanita's daughter Xenia met me at La Host airport. She was on her scooter. Her mother had threatened to hide its keys, she said, but *someone* had to come. The phones and power were out at Flores Negras. That afternoon someone had used a tractor to pull down a power pole at the head of the street. Xenia said: "While I waited here I heard that the government has declared a state of emergency.

For the first time in twenty-three years. The newsreader sounded nostalgic."

Xenia's scooter was burdened and slow, and we were forced to take a number of detours. We used the rubbish-filled walkways along La Mula till we came to the stone quay. We heard gunfire from the direction of the Plaza and, as we passed it, I saw a cordon of soldiers and police at the head of the Avenida Bueyes Negros. The street was sealed by police tape, fluorescent plastic fencing, and parked jeeps.

There was traffic turning onto the stone bridge from the only open roads, cars moving at a crawl. Xenia's scooter crept through the foot traffic. Faces and bodies flared in its waving headlight. We were blinded for a time by the high-beam lights of cars stopped on the far side of the bridge, waiting to cross—their lane was closed. The soldiers were trying to drain the city. We found a way through the jammed traffic. We passed one prone and two leaning power poles and turned into Ambre's street.

Flores Negras was obscured behind parked cars. There were men at the gate. I recognized one of Xenia's García uncles. I'd never seen him carrying anything more warlike than an orbital sander. He held a semiautomatic. There were long leads plugged into car batteries and caged lights suspended from trees and the woodwork of the veranda. Every object had both a thick and a dilute shadow, the yard bristled with the shadows of twisted aloes and the spiked mats of agave, and the big ficus, a tree of clubs. The house was lit up and there were candles in jars, pale on the porch. Before Xenia parked and switched off her headlight I saw a last solid shadow seemingly slink back under the steps, only darkness pushed by light, but for a moment I thought it was Barabbas, till I recalled that he had been dead for many years.

The house smelled of baking and the big pots of chili and green herb gumbo on the stove top. I recognized several of Ambre's fellow weavers, and the secretary of the Prostitutes Collective. There were people everywhere, but no bustle. Ambre's kitchen and living room had become anterooms of a sort—*anti-rooms*, crowded as a party, but hushed. Too crowded for either privacy or rest. I saw no one I knew well. Xenia showed me upstairs. A twin sat, slumped, on top of one of Ambre's big linen chests in the hallway. He raised his head and I saw that it was Carlos, drained, cowered, and *unlike himself*. I put a hand on his shoulder. He said that Aureliano and Tomás were at La Casa de la Mujer. "But Mama is keeping me here."

I went into the bedroom. Ambre was in bed. The covers over her long shape were neat and smooth. She'd been put there and hadn't moved. She was facing the ceiling and didn't turn to greet me. Madlena was sitting on the floor, her back to the bed. When she saw me she said, in a normal, informative voice, that Ambre had felt light-headed and had been persuaded to lie down. When I looked back at my stepmother I found she had finally turned her head. Her look said everything—that she was tired and this was all beyond her, that sorrow had thickened and stilled and filled her like edema—the time's toxins this time too strong for her. She'd been waiting for me.

Madlena folded her bitten, bruised hands in her lap. When she spoke a scab on her lip cracked and bright blood crept to the hollow in her chin. She was wearing her glasses—but their lenses were so greasy the glass looked frosted. I asked her if I could clean them for her and she took them off, handed them up to me. Her eyes looked as if she'd been throttled—blood vessels broken in their sclera and in the tight red flesh around them.

I went into the bathroom and rubbed soap on Madlena's lenses, rinsed and dried them.

Back in the bedroom I noticed Rosa—I'd missed her before. She was sitting below the window, twisting the end of the curtain in her hands, partly hidden behind it.

Outside there was an abrupt commotion, shouting, the sound of an engine, people running out onto the street. Madlena scrambled up, stumbling over her own loose hair, and blundered across the room to Rosa, shouting at her to get away from the window. Madlena hauled her daughter by her arm and ankle across the room and into the shelter behind Ambre's big bed.

There were more yells, then we heard an engine reversing away. Ambre put her hands over her face.

Rosa was whimpering, her face pressed against her mother's belly.

I said, "Madlena, it was probably only reporters. The García brothers have seen them off. Listen—if you don't mind I'd like to give Rosa a *job*. She should go down and ask those women in the kitchen for some sweet tea for her grandma."

"Where is Carlos?" Madlena said.

"He's just outside the door."

"He mustn't leave the house," Madlena said. Her voice was a whisper, ruined by weeping. She suddenly stiffened, then set Rosa away from her and got up. She said to Ambre, "Mama, I'm going to take Carme and show her the street." And, set in motion by this plan, she marched me out the door.

Madlena was forced to stop and stand on the veranda while the Garcías made a call. We were put in a vehicle, an armored car borrowed from the García bank. We drove to the head of the street, where the police met us. Enrico, who was in the back with us, said we had better lie down under blankets. That the police were a giveaway.

I lay muffled, listening to the gears growl, and stray fleshy thumps on the car's walls. The fists of people we passed. Beside me Madlena was inert. Sometimes I shivered, because I was afraid, but she was wide awake and fearless, indifferent to the situation—*false to life*, her manner a flaw in my own bad moment through which worse times were forcing their way.

While we rode I thought of the *good* I could do. I could give Ambre a checkup, to see if she was ill, exhausted, or merely lying low and conserving herself. I could dispense medicine, give people pills to help them sleep or stay awake or manage their anxiety.

Enrico turned up the volume on his radio. A local commentator was speculating about schisms in the Taoscal nation, between traditionalists and the progressives focused around the Council of Projects. The commentator talked about a nickel mine that some said *wasn't* a nickel mine.

Madlena's head emerged from the blanket and she leaned closer to me, intent. "There's uranium in the mountains near Taosclan. But no one is mining it. No one was ever going to. The trouble is, it's the only rumor that sounds like a *reason*." Madlena looked desperate, her eyes tortured by more coming tears, lids squeezed as if to hold her eyeballs in. She was trying not to cry, simply to avoid more physical pain. "We have no reason," she said.

I didn't answer. In my head I began to recite a high school geography lesson. Lequama's exports. *Gold, silver, iron ore, salt, platinum, nickel, sugar, mahogany, lignum vitae, cedar*—I recited—*pine, balsam, rubber, cinchona, vanilla, sarsaparilla, ginger, castor beans, coffee beans (coffee is not a bean), guarana, cocaine (unofficial).* All primary produce.

People were beating on the van—dinning. I could hear shouts and reverberating gunfire.

Trout, carpon, sailfish, sea bass, tuna. The Mneone had a big factory ship—courtesy of the Council of Projects. I recalled high school history—how Aureliano Zabe, Fernando's predecessor as chief of the Taoscal, had said to Castonoles, leader of the FDR, when they were discussing socialism as a solution and socialists as saviors: "What is all this to us?" The Taoscal weren't the *peasants*, the *people* evoked in Castonoles's speeches. "Factories, farms—what are these to us? Taosclan lies between three mountains *terraced* to grow corn and amaranth—who now takes that kind of time?" The chief's famous gesture at Castonoles's wristwatch: "*You* think time is a trophy."

The Avenida Bueyes Negros. It was twilight; the sun would soon be up. We left the van, which was backed up to the barriers. Several police made a screen with our blankets and we were hurried in beyond the police tape and parked jeeps.

Directly inside the barriers several soldiers from Mestizo stood, gun butts braced against their thighs and guns muzzle up, around two soldiers from Nuevo who knelt with their hands behind their heads. Both had been beaten; one had blood still tacky on his chin and neck, the other had a swelling in his socket the size of a tennis ball, a tennis ball with a slot, from which his eye peered. I hunkered down to look them over. One of the standing soldiers yanked at my shoulder and I stood up and shoved him. My strength has always had an extra available gear, and I was pleased to see him stagger. Enrico backed me up. He had a shotgun, which he waved about, threatening indiscriminate damage. I was able to get the two Taoscal soldiers up. I made them remove their battle jackets—with their identifying insignia—then I propelled them out through the barrier. They limped away. During this the other armed men had appealed to

Colonel Guevara. But Madlena just waited for me, her back turned to all of us, in her inky dress, as faceless as a shadow.

She wasn't waiting for me, she was waiting for the light. Once it had shone along this avenue to the temple that had stood where the Presidential Palace now stands. It shone upon the palm-wood temple gates, and, if they were open, into the great burial chamber at the temple's center. As I came up beside her, the sun appeared, throwing our shadows down before us. Madlena began to walk and talk.

Fernando had kissed her on the hair. He'd said he'd had a call from a neighbor who told him that there was broken glass on the landing by his old apartment in the Avenida Bueyes Negros. He'd said he wished that Carlos and Aureliano would sort out which one of them wanted to take the lease on his old place—it had been empty too long.

It was early in the morning and a bank holiday. There was no one much about. Only the waiting car. Only the three men with machetes.

Madlena walked me through it. We stopped at the place he was set upon. The first blow, on his right shoulder, the second, on his left. He defended himself against the second. Madlena said, "They found his fingertips here." He couldn't raise his arms, so he ran. Madlena pointed at the patches of blood, the double trail of drips that veered in toward a wall.

A neighbor had looked out over her balcony. She was hanging out the day's first wash—she had four children under four. The neighbor screamed. And screamed. Fernando was silent, staggering—his slack arms swinging—away from them. They followed, their long knives *pecking* at him. The woman said that it was then that two children turned into the street.

Madlena stopped, told me, "This is where the three men paused, facing the girls, their machetes dripping."

I looked at the three spaced, paced, distinct points where the men had stood steady, wet blades hanging in their relaxed hands. One blade had made a circle of dark drips—the assassin had let his machete dangle on its strap.

Madlena walked on. She pointed at the place where the assassins had crossed the blood trail—there was a smear, half a boot print. She said that the cries of the woman on the balcony brought out two neighbors, a man and his thirteen-year-old son. They intervened. They put themselves, arms raised, between the assassins and Fernando.

Madlena followed the trail to the wall.

The assassins fled. Fernando was on his feet only a moment more. He was still gushing blood from the two crippling cuts between neck and shoulder. He fell and rolled against the wall.

Madlena crouched among the signs of melee, either the injured man's struggles or his rescuers' panicked efforts. I saw dried black blood like a burned piecrust, thick, congealed in the angle of the wall. Above the black border of blood was a whole handprint, and another with dark claws where his multilated fingers had dragged at the wall. Madlena set her own hand, with its chewed, bloody knuckles, above the whole print, and caressed the stone.

Fernando had looked at his rescuers—seemed to see them, his face showing nothing. Then he trembled for a while and died.

It began to rain. I felt big drops tap my neck, then saw the clawed handprint scored by a drop and begin in one place to melt.

Madlena let out a strangled cry. She put her shoulder to the wall above the handprints and arched her body protectively over them. Our minders ran to her. Jackets were stripped off and a makeshift tent made against the wall, in the shadow of which Madlena crouched, moaning, her hands covering the handprints, till from somewhere the soldiers of Mestizo produced a tarpaulin and masking tape and, in a further five minutes, some silicone gap filler. Madlena wouldn't consent to move until she saw the bloodstains preserved from the weather. She could scarcely walk. Enrico lifted her and carried her back to the open doors of the armored car, where the soldiers still waited, drenched and blinking the rain out of their eyes.

In our absence Carlos had gone, and had been replaced, it seemed, by his father and Aureliano. With them was a woman I recognized as the Minister of Indian Affairs. The woman was Fernando's one un-wavering ally—but as soon as she saw her Madlena looked wildly about and shouted for Rosa, who ran out of the kitchen. Her mother took her in her arms and confronted Tomás. She asked where was Carlos? She'd told Carlos to stay in the house.

"Carlos is at La Casa de la Mujer, and will go from there to Taosclan," said the Minister of Indian Affairs.

Madlena screamed at her. "I wasn't talking to you!"

"Madlena," said Tomás. He put out his hands, pleading, but didn't approach her. He began to explain. "What would *normally* happen is that the chief's body would be taken to Taosclan—"

Madlena howled in rage. She released Rosa, who ran from her and crammed herself into a corner of the couch, her knees drawn up against her chest and hands covering her ears. Madlena continued to howl, her face distorted, hoarse, and wordless. She screamed herself into breathlessness, then drew a breath and spoke. "*They can't have his body.*" She said, "I have expressed my wishes to the government and they will uphold my wishes."

"Madlena, please," Tomás begged, perhaps only asking her to be calmer.

But she continued, voice winding up in pitch and volume, shouting into his face that she'd have stood over Fernando's body herself and let no one near except she'd bargained away the right to do so—he would get a state funeral and stay in La Host only if she accepted the government's protective measures. "I want Carlos back here now!" she ordered.

"Lequama is this close—" the minister used two fingers to measure out an inch of air, "to martial law. Carlos is Fernando's heir. As you well know. Surely you can't imagine that just because *you* opposed Fernando's choice that he'd have changed his mind? Carlos must be confirmed as the next chief."

Madlena jumped at the woman and managed to land several hard blows. Aureliano and Tomás together pulled her off. The minister touched her bleeding ear. They were all in tears. The minister said that at this time it was vital to uphold tradition.

"Tradition murdered him!" Madlena screamed. "Do you think

I'm an idiot?" She sobbed. "*He* thought I was an idiot, he never explained to me about that law——" She abruptly sagged between her ex-husband and son, her neck slack, face strained, and eyes rolled up.

I looked for Rosa, but Rosa had fled upstairs, so I was able to say, to the minister, "Fernando broke the law when he fathered Rosa. Don't pretend you don't know. Rosa didn't matter, didn't *count*, till she answered the seven questions and joined the tribe. We knew there was a law—that it was a crime, but not one with a death penalty."

The woman just stared at me. She didn't recognize me.

Carlos had to go to La Casa de la Mujer before Taosclan because that was where Fernando's body—Fernando's *heart*—was. Madlena understood this—and I felt myself catch her rage in, it seemed at first, a low-grade way. "Your squalid traditions," I said to the minister, to Tomás and Aureliano. Then I shut my teeth and found I couldn't speak. My jaw, tongue, breath locked. I felt something in my mouth crack. My head filled with the smell of blood. I was called *gringa*. I wasn't even Lequaman, let alone Taoscal. This was the minister, but I could see that the others agreed with her. I said, "Squalid, unwholesome, horrible." I thought of Carlos's half-insane, sickened face. And I recalled a dissection in my first year at medical school, the yielding, impressionable flesh of an iodine-stained cadaver. I recalled an operation, a diseased heart separated from its plumbing, pulsing veins and arteries pierced by delicate catheters, and the machine beside the table, cooling the rerouted blood as it came, red with life, from the pulmonary artery. I recalled the fibrillating heart I'd held in an emergency room, slippery, quivering with stalled life. I began with horror and ended with clinical beauty. And thinking of a body without blood I remembered the tobacco-yellowed writing callus on Fernando's right hand, easy to imagine, always bloodless. I wanted to feel, just once, his inert, cold hand in mine. I didn't have the *evidence* I needed. Madlena had shown me the script of his execution, a scrawled mess on the street. But I wanted to see——

——that it wasn't true. *"Put your shoes on, Carme. I, for one, am going to be out that door in five minutes."* He picked me up and set me on the sofa,

brushed the grit from my footsoles and rolled the first sock on from my toe.
He held my toe in the cloth to roll the sock one-handed, his warm palms
warming my feet—

I had my forehead on the floor but no one came to help me. I heard Aureliano, still struggling with his mother, say, "Carme's fainted."

Then Ambre spoke, from somewhere above us—she was standing on the stairs. "Señora"—to the minister—"you have brought all your bad news, and now you can leave my house."

The plan was that the coffin containing Fernando's body would be taken from the morgue at La Casa de la Mujer to the palace, to the great reception room, where it would lie in state as people came and passed by the great staircase up and down. The undertakers would open the hinged top half of the coffin, with its mirrored lid, so that people could see him, clean-faced and smooth-haired, the bridge of his many-years-broken nose jagged and sunken into sharpness.

The hearse left La Casa de la Mujer by an ambulance bay, followed by the people who had stood in vigil around the hospital. The mourners' cortege moved slowly through the clogged streets. There were tens of thousands in and around the Plaza, the palace. I was four cars back, in the President's limousine, with Don Marcos and Juanita and Enrico and Xenia. Madlena was in the first car with her mother, Aureliano, Rosa, and a very sober, mute, dutiful Bob Renzi. He was standing in for Fidela, who was newly pregnant—at great cost—and too fragile to fly, let alone sit in a car in a crowd that surged and roared. All sound was swept about by the helicopter that hovered over the Plaza, the wide black nostrils of its guns pointed down at the crowd.

I was *there*, but it felt like history. Can one letter from a word fly up, hover, and read the other words, read the page, turn the page?

I sat in the quaking car and imagined that I, too, would take my turn up that left-hand curving staircase and into the room, among the soldiers in dress uniforms; among the yellow and white flowers and under the long banners and the portraits. A photograph of Fernando at fifty-three, with his hair graying, shorter, swept back, lines around his mouth and his very clear, amused, self-loving eyes; and Fernando at twenty-seven, on a makeshift stage, looking at the camera across the footlights of oil drum fires, glossy-skinned, packed with savagery, his power shining around him like a light in which he is caged and dazzled. I knew what was planned—the ceremonious disposition of the room. I saw myself, before his casket, unable to *prove* anything to myself, unable to take his hand, for he'd be swaddled right up to his marred neck. But I was well acquainted with corpses and would know one when I saw it, and shouldn't need to *prove* my loss by testing the temperature of his cheek.

The cortege followed the road, curving into the bullet-pocked, blackened concrete main gates of the palace. Because it curved I had a clear line of sight to the gate and saw what happened.

The hearse stopped without its brake lights illuminating. The crowd had stopped it, was on it. I didn't know what they wanted; the faces near the one-way glass of Don Marcos's car were blurred by craziness and glazed by tears. People had torn shirts—as if they had all been in a fight, I thought, till I saw one woman tear her own dress and tug at her own hair.

The hearse rocked; people climbed over it and clawed its sides. I saw a muzzle flash, and saw a gun torn out of a soldier's grasp and the group of soldiers at the gates go down under the people swarming around the hearse, now concentrated so thickly they climbed over each other like ants about a cake crumb.

From the palace grounds a big police van appeared, and its water cannon came on. When it did, Don Marcos, who'd been weeping hopelessly for some minutes, gasped and began to get out of the car. He was *concerned*. He was going to talk sense to whoever would listen. But once the door was open the noise came in, mad and solid. Juanita hauled her brother back and Enrico slammed the door closed—shouted to the driver to reverse, to get the President *out of there*. The driver swung around and put his arm over the seat back as people do to reverse and Don Marcos's limo began to creep backward. I had a glimpse, past the driver's blanched face, of churning shadows in the front car. Its backing lights were shining, but someone inside was in riot. I saw hair like smoke, threshing arms, Madlena fighting the people in the car with her.

The water cannon swung toward the gate, but it was too late. The crowd around the hearse got its back open and first the flowers, then the flag, then the coffin were taken out. Flowers and flag were torn apart and the crowd lifted the coffin up and began to pass it over their heads—and into the palace grounds. By some insane consensus they had decided that *they* would deliver Fernando to his waiting bier. As the coffin began to move inside the gates I saw the water cannon veer away from the trouble spot, a white jet that wavered, then deflated and dribbled out. The police had turned it off.

The coffin was between the gates, tilting and rocking like a boat on choppy seas. Then the crowd lost control of it, and it slipped, swung about, and bashed into a gatepost. One of the hinged lids sprung open. I saw a mirror flash, saw disclosed gleaming white satin. The people with me in the car moaned, "No."

The coffin subsided further as several appalled people released it. Something tumbled out—wadded clothes—then in a thumping rush as it went over against the gatepost, *everything*, books, some closed and like paving blocks, some open and like shot birds. Then the bones fell out. A jumbled, disarticulated skeleton. I saw clean long thighbones and little finger bones like dice, or polystyrene packaging material. And I saw the holed skull.

The moon had fallen from the sky. They wrapped his bones and carried them into a cave whose mouth dripped when it rained. When it rained I lay listening. I'd unfold his letter. It's in pieces now, all its creases turned to dust.

Dear Carme,

I don't know what is in your mind but I'm afraid that whatever it is, it hurts you. Your father is a better person than any of us imagine right now because he's doing what he thinks is right although his heart isn't in it. His heart is with you and me and all his friends. I'm not sure I can say that everything will be all right, but I will be around when you need me and whatever else happens, I'm as mad as

I ever will be. Now—isn't that comforting? I love you, and not just
because you're his daughter. Write to me if you can, or would like to.
                                            Your loving friend
                                            Dev Hughes

We all lived. The cars managed to back and turn and take us away.
Maria Godshalk, fat and fiftyish, who was waiting in the palace to
receive her dead friend, rushed out at the head of a mass of soldiery
and fired into the air and bawled into a megaphone until she had the
attention of the crowd. Why were they rioting? Were they so furious
because Fernando's remains had been spirited away? "Yes!" They
roared at her. And she yelled back, "If it *had* been Fernando in the
coffin he'd be trampled underfoot by now, wouldn't he? Like whoever the hell that poor specimen is," pointing at the scattered bones.
Silence. "*Uh?*" Maria, mad as hell and telling them all off. She played
indignant mother, she scolded and soothed and sent them all home.

The assassins were never identified or apprehended. The body
was never found.

California, near Bodega Bay, October 2010

My elderly incurable patient wondered why I sat with her so often—my practice couldn't be falling off. When I told her that I *liked*
her she said, sadly, "But I'm not *myself* anymore."

I enjoyed her repose. She hadn't any strength for real trouble, no
internal inclement weather left to shake her. Her stillness had the
appearance of solidity, her last days looked like something lasting.
She asked me about my marriage, and considered each answer before going on to another question. She wasn't judicious or polite or
calculating. She wasn't even curious, really. Watching her work her
way toward the next question was like seeing a thing expertly finished, a practiced knitter casting off.

Bella was in touch with Madlena's father, Emilio Rivera. Her informant. One afternoon in October she invited me to her house, where he was too. I had to hear, and from his lips, the story he'd told her. "But you have to remember, Carme, that this man is a third of my book, at least. I need him to cooperate, and sign a consent form. So don't overreact. Actually, don't react at all."

Emilio Rivera told us that he hadn't realized that Ambre, despite her grievances against him, had always chosen to report his membership in the Pola Pastrez as something in his more distant personal past—only when he was young, and his daughter an infant. That's what Ambre always let everyone believe, perhaps ashamed of her inability to influence him. They had been separated for years. He scarcely ever saw Madlena. There had been no incentive for him to give up the luxury, the power, the *pleasure* that came with his job. Like Ambre's, his was a quest for understanding, and the mastery of nature. They were alike—for all her later piety—and they parted ways not because she rejected what she'd now call "his wickedness." There was no *falling out* over philosophy, and he wasn't a bad father—Ambre simply couldn't accept the fact that his milieu would not forget that she had once been the famous fat whore of the brothel in Leonarda. "It was her pique that parted us in the end, not her scruples," said Emilio Rivera. "But of course, Ambre would never represent it that way."

Don Ricardo Pastrez was the head of a coven of sorcerers— all men and all members of the Security Forces. Emilio Rivera was invited to join them. He completed their number. Six. Rivera was a Caribbean Lequaman—he had Spanish, Mneone, and slave ancestors—and had come to sorcery through religion, through Santeria. His mother was a priestess, a *bruja*. The first polish he put on his beliefs came from Ambre Guevara, who had dabbled in Yaqui sorcery in Mexico. Emilio was an officer in the army but transferred to the Security Forces because he met Ricardo Pastrez. As a sorcerer Ricardo was a polyglot. Magic will usually only work through the metaphors an adept acquires in childhood and youth. Magic didn't travel well, because it was so often tied to local languages, sites, or even a certain look of the land. That is why anthropologists' notions of "phenomenology" were plausible, seductive, and *reassuring*. Phenomenology says that wonders are only observed because local observers have an *eye* for wonders.

Ricardo wasn't reliant on what he had learned as a child. There was apparently no form of magic he could not enter. He had a kind of imaginative eloquence in his ability to switch from voodoo to Wiccan to Yaqui or Taoscal practices as though *nothing was foreign to him*. He was a sort of magical savant. "I wanted to be like him," Rivera said. "And so I joined him."

Emilio Rivera struggled with his description. His membership in the coven wasn't a "good alliance," it was more like obsessive love, or a shared mania. "The things we all saw!" He sounded more ecstatic than nostalgic. "The horrible, bottomless grails of power." He whispered, "The things we *did*."

He said he would tell me the worst first, the *worst*, but not the one that made him finally leave the Pola Pastrez and flee Lequama. His voice was harsh, face flushed. Then he just *came out with it*. "There were six women we buried up to their necks in the cane fields and throttled while we drank their saliva."

"This was a rite?" Bella's voice synthesizer made her sound icy but reasonable. He hadn't previously told her this story. I could see she was as shocked as I was—but the synthesizer disguised her shock.

Rivera said, "It was a very profitable rite."

I put out my hands, palms up. I had to put something between this man and me. He said, brisk, quelling, "Don't interrupt me. This rite enabled us to identify and capture the chief of the Taoscal."

In 1981 the Pola Pastrez arrested an old Taoscal sorcerer, Raphael Masolan. The group of six identified Masolan as the chief and bribed his hophead, susceptible nephew Pablito to lure him out of the jungle. Masolan was not taken to Los Muertos, since word would have got around from that prison—who was arrested, why, and what they did to him. Emilio Rivera remarked that it was astonishing how many rumors left that prison considering how few prisoners did.

I listened to his arch tone and I looked at his shoes, their worn lopsided heels and cracked stitching. I wondered, if he had murdered to gain power, what had become of that power? Why the sad shoes? I kept thinking of the wealthy, attractive monster I'd married. I kept thinking crooked.

Masolan was taken to the palace, to their blind room. "We didn't call it the Black Room. It was featureless, do you see? The windows were covered, and the wall seemed always to recede." Ricardo planned to steal the chief's power, the centuries of power Masolan believed he'd acquired when he ingested the heart of his predecessor. "It was *true*," Rivera said. "Masolan was heavy with power, he had mass like a Mass." Rivera paused, his eyes opaque. "My mouth watered," he said. "We had to dismantle him. We had to remove all those other men and women; make their power unavailable to him." Rivera went all matter-of-fact. "The ordinary thing to do, the thing that works—since torture doesn't—is to let the people you want to reduce to a more malleable state see *another* tortured, someone they care for. We had Pablito—who was a coward and corruptible—but Ricardo hit on the notion of having Pablito torture his uncle."

The old man begged and wept—"As they do," said Rivera—while Pablito too wept, implored the six to let him stop, and his uncle to forgive him. "We were working to a formula. A magic formula. Seven false reprieves. We didn't count his periods of unconsciousness, and it took days. Twice we pretended to lose interest. Twice we let him 'escape' and *dapple* the floors for a few corridors with his bloody toes. There were moments of drama—little Pablito turned a scalpel on himself, he managed to excise one of his own nipples and feed it to Masolan, who'd been complaining of hunger for some time." Rivera paused, made a steeple of his fingers and put them against his pursed lips, and looked at me over them.

Masolan was never left alone for long, although they *did* have to sleep. A little. "At the end we were exhausted, and actuality had thinned. I saw little candle flames shining through the walls, and there were footprints like stepping-stones going away at one place into the wall.

"We had built up *one hour*, concentrated worlds into one hour, all kinds of creatures seemed to be watching us from out of those sloppily creosoted panels. And Masolan—he was dismantled. All he could do was weep in a weak, slobbery voice. You see, we'd removed the last of his teeth." Again Rivera looked right into my eyes, his look intense but his voice bland. "So that he couldn't *bite us*," he said, and smirked. Then he drew a long shuddering breath. "And then it was time for the final ceremony—I don't think I need to go into its specific words and gestures, I'm not here to *teach* you. The *gist* of it was that we cut out Raphael Masolan's heart and Don Ricardo ate it. I believe we all had a taste of the rest of him. Little Pablito had rather more than his share." He sighed. "Then we slept."

They slept and Raphael Masolan's ghost slipped its bonds and walked down stepping-stone footprints from the reverse side of a painting, and into another prison cell—below the level of a river—to show my father an empty chest cavity.

"Then we slept," Rivera said again, his eyes closed and long-lashed lids fluttering gently. For a moment he looked like Aureliano, who was his grandson. He opened his eyes. "After that, from what I gather, Pablito Masolan became the most daring madman in Lequama. I left the Pola Pastrez—"

"Why?"

"Because I learned that my daughter wasn't in Costa Rica with Carlos D'Escoto—she was in Lequama and had been detained and tortured."

Bella said, "After what you just described—I mean, I realize that it's different when it's your daughter—"

"It wasn't to any *purpose*," Rivera said. "And yes, she was my daughter. I left. Don Ricardo let me leave. Nestor Galen's government was falling apart, the FDR was making weekly advances. Don Ricardo didn't have a plan, he only had an appetite. Later the Pola Pastrez arrested Aureliano Zabe, the counterfeit chief, Masolan's heir. Pablito Masolan went about trying to get himself killed before and after the revolution. He was like a holy fool—no one touched him. Until, eventually, someone had the sense to ask questions—Fernando Sola's deputy minister. She worked it out. I heard that she had one of Fernando Sola's bodyguards stalk and kill Pablito Masolan. Possibly Tomás Juiliano, though I doubt *that* simple soul ever asked why, *why* kill little Pablito, past some unknown need to protect his friend. The deputy minister kept it very quiet.

"When he was released from Los Muertos Aureliano Zabe said he was the chief. And since Raphael Masolan had vanished, and the revolution had been so disruptive, the elders decided to believe that the ceremony had been correctly performed. It suited them—because Zabe was a hero, and mortally ill, and because Zabe's heir was Sola, whom they *wanted*. As for Sola, he was defrauded, and a fraud. But I'm sure he never knew that when he became chief, he'd had to sit down to dine unnecessarily on Zabe's utterly secular, singular, lightweight heart."

San Francisco, November 2010

Ricardo was on the Alzheimer's research register. I'd signed him on when he went into long-term care. In the beginning, as a courtesy, I went along to the support and information sessions they ran for relatives. Those arrangements always needed support themselves—needed the numbers of people saying, "*I need this.*" I met a few friendly pathologists at a get-together and, being tidy-minded, I'd kept their cards. When Ricardo began finally to fail I made an appointment with one. We went over his history so that she'd know everything she'd be looking for—not just causes of death, main and subsidiary, but everything, the whole bodily record.

"The greater the age of the patient the more things kill them. There is usually a convergence of final causes," the pathologist said. "Dementia is complex and covert, but not a mystery, as such. What *seems* mysterious is how a person can change so. Anything badly altered or diminished hurts and puzzles us," she said. "You're a doctor in detentive medicine, I'm a pathologist, but even we don't always know what to make of our feelings about either your routine defeats or my being called routinely to catalogue physical calamity."

The pathologist puttered about her office as she talked. She was stocky and slump-shouldered and odd, but when she sat down opposite me I had to hold onto my seat in order not to lean forward and embrace her. She was alarmingly eloquent. It wasn't *necessary*. I only wanted her respectable credentials, her room, her Jewett-fixed stainless steel table and L-shaped autopsy station, and her practice in making Y-sections. I said, "I've had a few surprises with this man. I want to know everything. And I want to sew him up—and wash him, head to toe, as the women in my country still do."

"I see." She rummaged around and found her reading glasses. I bit the inside of my cheek. She looked at Ricardo's records. "Arteriosclerotic vascular disease, transient ischemic attack, depression, mild onset confusion. Progressive global cognitive impairment, stroke. Admission, left cerebellar infarct, changing mental status, left facial paralysis, right cerebellar infarct. Drugs drugs drugs—" She sighed. "Readmission, stroke—oh, I see—positive syphilis serology." She looked up at me through the top half of her bifocals. I asked her for her first name. She blinked, then said, "Wislava. It's Polish. I presume you've been tested, Dr. Risk? Treated?"

"I'm fine."

She looked down again. "Psychotic agitated behavior. Paranoid agitation. Placement in a nursing home. Bladder incontinence, progressive lethargy, combative behavior, generalized arteriosclerosis, myocardial fibrosis, coronary artery arteriosclerosis, anorexia." She put the notes down and took off her glasses. "Not long now."

"No. I only want to finish doing everything for him—after you've carried his brain off to your lab."

She cleared her throat. I'd offended her. "This is your *husband*. And I'm sure you haven't performed an autopsy since medical school."

"I won't be. I'll be stitching up and washing my own dead."

She put the glasses back on. "Yes. Yes you can, Dr. Risk. It'll be all right, I'm sure."

Anorexia, somnolence, acute confluent bronchopneumonia—the old man's friend.

I sat by the old man's bed and held his damp, bony hand.

I rang Ambre from his hospital bed and said there was something I wanted her to do for me. I wanted her to take her phone and hold it out the window for a minute. She did. I listened for a time, heard someone sweeping a path and the fruity gurgle of a La Host ambulance. I heard a scooter laboring loudly along the road, and a child's voice opening out, as they do, everywhere the same, uninhibited and immediate.

I stopped listening myself and held the phone to my husband's ear.

The pathologist kindly glued Ricardo's empty skull shut and stitched his scalp down. "Closed casket?" she asked, making sure.

I'd already watched her weigh and measure several of my husband's thoracic internal organs, reminded of paintings of Anubis from the Egyptian Book of the Dead. She packed the organs into plastic bags, with the rest of the glistening, ropy, lumpy jumble. She put the bags back in his abdominal cavity—each in its approximate place—and I took note as she settled the one with heart, lungs, liver, and pancreas. Filled, the maroon cavity closed with a wet sigh.

"Thank you," I said.

She stepped back, went to the sink, removed her gloves, visor, apron, cap, and gown. She disposed of all of it, and ran the taps. I waited at the table, my gloves clean. Bella sat on the stool by the door, masked with safety glass but not gowned or gloved. She was in the room ostensibly only to support me, not to lend a hand.

"I'll leave you to it," the pathologist said. "I'll be back at three." She was a few feet away from me, but I could smell the fresh antiseptic cleanser above all the other smells. I stared at her pink fingers. She said, in a shy, consoling way, "There is much still unknown about the physiology of diseased brains." Then, "Okay." She went out. The door slapped to and fro.

I told Bella I was going mad. "I can't look at that woman without wanting to kiss her. The sight of her fingers makes me weak."

"You're not going mad, Carme. You're trying to *live*." Bella sidled across the room to peer through the glass doors to the refrigerator, where Ricardo's brain sat in a Perspex-topped container, steam showing on the inside of its lid. "Cunt," Bella said, placid and cold.

I was clumsily wrestling with my husband's sternum. I was afraid that the gap wasn't sufficiently wide for me to retrieve the packed organs without rupturing the plastic. I'd rather not do that. I tried to get purchase but his ribs were elastic, and resisted. "Come here," I said to Bella. "Put some gloves on first." I pointed at the box from which protruded a strip of powdered latex.

She put on gloves and came. I pointed to where I wanted her to hold. She drew back.

"He hasn't got hepatitis B or C or HIV. Just concentrate on your hands, don't look deeper."

She took hold and I inserted my hands. The feeling on my covered skin, as my hands went in, was like that you get standing in a still-warm bathtub after the water has drained. Bella shook. Her mask didn't move, but the two layers of papery gauze wrapping her collar fluttered as she breathed fast.

I placed the bag between my husband's legs, and Bella went to the sink to wash her hands—for some time. When she turned around I had just sealed the microwave-safe plastic container I brought with me.

"Is that it?"

"I have to close up and wash him, as I said I would." The pathologist had threaded a needle for me, and I began with my best surgical stitches—the wrong ones really for this task—to seal him again from throat to groin. "She thinks she's going to find Lewys bodies and a degenerated hippocampus as well as plaques and infarcts and general arteriosclerotic degeneration," I said. "But I think he simply slipped next door. He was always next door to mad."

"I don't think he was," Bella said. "Especially if you are saying he had to be mad to do the things he did."

After a time, listening to the tiny tug and creak of my stitching, I said, "The heartless, tortured Taoscal chief chose my father. He showed him his chest cavity, his gap, took my father into his confidence. The Pola Pastrez made their chief *the* chief. They opened the door in the Black Room that my father first wandered through. The Airans transplanted my father to Lequama. He brought me with him. I married the Pola Pastrez chief, he signed himself over to me, in sickness and in health, and in helpless senility. I think it's a *conspiracy*."

Bella asked whose conspiracy it was—the Airans'? Or Ricardo's?

Or the murdered Raphael Masolan's? I said I thought there was a conspiracy behind *all* the conspiracies, shaping them. A good conspiracy.

Bella was anxious. She posted herself by the doors and peered through the glass. If she'd had breath in her nose and mouth she would have been making mist. She wanted to know how much longer I'd be. The stitching takes the longest, I said. Always. I was thinking of scars without rucks. I told her she could help by wrapping that container in a towel and stowing it in her bag.

"Are you *quite sure?*"

I said that it was in my nature to want to put the whole world into my mouth—quoting Fernando on my father.

"You've shown remarkable restraint so far," Bella said.

"Restraint is also in my nature."

Bella said she couldn't approve of all this essentialism, especially from someone acting on an idea, because it was in no one's nature, only in Taoscal culture, to suppose there was anything magical about a bit of dead muscle tissue.

I filled a bowl with water and disinfectant, found wads of cotton wool, and began to wash Ricardo's body.

"You can only exploit their belief by telling them what you've done," Bella said.

"He didn't tell," I said, carefully wiping his mouth, which was at last not set and stubborn.

"He went mad," Bella said.

Reader, I ate him.

I met the pathologist for a drink and gave her a plant. I watched her hands cup its painted terra-cotta pot and didn't feel a thing. I don't miss Aureliano yet, though I do turn right around if I hear a car coming up behind me—eight cylinders, one skipping. He hasn't called me—scared, perhaps, because he sided with the Minister of IA and his father, against his mother and me. But I know, without having asked, that he's keeping an eye on Ambre now.

Bella continued to argue with me—after the fact. I'd open her e-mails and read about the Airans' essentialism, their experimentation, their *nature*. She opposed the Airans, and their world view, to the Taoscal. To Taoscal social engineering, like the chief's "statutory" homosexuality, and the seven questions. "Whereas the Airans believe in nature, the Taoscal believe in *nurture*," Bella wrote. "Both world views imply that we are doomed. Our bodies are our destiny; or we are poured into the mold of our culture, so that none of our ideas are innocent, and none of them are our own. But—Carme—are both views not versions of the Calvinist doctrine of predestination? We are predestined by nature or we are predestined by culture. But the doctrine of predestination was always flawed, and false to its own authority—God. Because, although God gave us our selves and the world—nature *and* nurture—he also gave us free will."

Every night I dream that I'm standing by a sandstone pool, in the upper La Mula. I'm welded to various surgical instruments—welded by dried blood. Fernando comes and helps me into the water and uses his thumbs and fingers to coax the red resin to dissolve. He never speaks; he stands behind me with his marvelous mouth pressed to my shoulder. I wake up feeling that I've cheated on everyone.

California, near Bodega Bay, December 2010

I came home from my elderly patient's funeral to find my sister's Mercedes parked outside. It was a cool day, cold enough so that before the sun came out I'd been able to see my breath—at the graveside, all our breath, and water vapor in a white halo around the minister reading from the Book of Common Prayer. My patient's joke was her funeral music—Jimmie Rodgers singing his "TB Blues."

Fidela wasn't waiting in the car. I cupped my hands against its back window and saw bags and two carelessly bundled coats, one green cashmere, one fawn leather.

The front door was open and the alarm deactivated, though I didn't remember ever having given Fidela my keys or code.

I went in. My house was quiet. The linen cupboard was open; a stack of pillowcases had fallen and skated, fanned out, across the polished tiles. My cat would get in the cupboard, seeking quiet, whenever the opportunity presented itself. I put my head in, looked for it, but it wasn't there.

Out the kitchen window, which opened onto my vegetable garden and the inlet, I saw Fidela. She was narrow of shoulder and thin of leg but big in the middle like a digesting snake. She was throwing a pinecone for Miss Mansfield, who was in mud right up to her clipped belly. I must have watched them for several minutes. I scarcely ever saw my sister this way, mucky and unselfconscious but still a star, wrapped in her air of moment.

I went out through my garden and climbed the flagstones across the low breakwater I'd built from rocks and moss and driftwood. I waved—then had to walk out to Fidela as she showed no sign of coming in. She looked at me strangely. I explained, "I've been to a funeral," and touched my black coat. I asked her, "Are you cold?"

She stroked her own stomach. "I have central heating." She threw the pinecone again and Miss Mansfield plunged after it, her backside pelted by gobs of kicked-up mud. "Carme, I have to tell you something I know will shock you."

"I could probably reciprocate." I folded my arms and looked down at her. She usually wore high heels or went barefoot and lounged. It was a novelty for me to see the parting in her hair.

She wasn't interested in my defensive offer of a confession. She just went on. "Though it *hasn't* shocked others more nearly concerned. Bob agreed. We have a bargain. We plan to have two children. First mine—because it means so much to me, and he understands—then his."

I asked how she could have her own child. Apart from the pregnancy, which was evident, and birth process, which she was headed for.

"My child means my genetic material," she said. "So, a donor egg—and Edwin Money—"

"*Edwin Money?*"

"It's his clinic, Carme. And he kept Dad's sample."

"Of course." I stared at her. My inventive, determined, flourishing, dewy, unbelievable little sister. "You're having our father's child."

She nodded. Then the fresh apricot blush slowly left her cheeks. It seemed to evaporate. This couldn't be a response to my expression, which was probably stupefied or tired, but not angry. Fidela said, "And *he* isn't shocked, either."

Fidela's face was too wide—I had to read either eye; it was like those children's puzzles that ask you to spot the difference. My eyes flicked back and forth, reading, and finding no differences. I asked if Miss Mansfield had put my cat to flight. It had hidden in the linen cupboard but wasn't there now.

"*Carme*," Fidela said.

I told her I was going to find my cat—to reassure it.

"Carme, your cat is just fine."

I ran back to the house to find my cat. I ran past my lupine-lined vegetable garden, the newly turned earth, its dark geometrical clods; I ran past the still pump and the pierced hardboard tool rack with its painted shadow shapes of hammer, chisels, pliers; I ran up the stairs. I made my search.

My cat was asleep, surprised by sleep, not curled but sitting on its folded front paws and tucked haunches, its head drooped and nose resting lightly on the rise and fall, the peacefully sleeping chest of my father.

He was the same. He was the past in its power. For a moment I was the only one awake, and I sat against the door frame, six feet of rag rug between us. My life rewound and resettled around its center.

He woke fast, as usual, and sat up, quick. The cat tumbled, still asleep, and he caught it, cradled, one of its back legs up as though to call attention to a question it had. My cat wouldn't leave his arms—of course—even when he lifted it, sagging between both level palms, and kissed it. It lay on his palms, threatening to overflow, irritable, reluctant, muzzy. He poured it out on the floor. It was that kind of cat. It walked away, its fur separated in gills to let out the heat of sleep.

"Wait," I said. My father was threatening me too with those warm, comfortable hands. I was buffeted piecemeal by things I'd seen all my life and hadn't noticed because they were too familiar and I had looked with inexperienced eyes.

His attention could alter barometer readings; it was like falling air pressure. I could see that he was trying to guess what I was thinking; could see his curiosity, calculation, love—like the old Bible's translation of "charity" for "love." I realized that he had only ever been brilliant at guessing, not because some special sympathy allowed him to read people, but because he could imagine so many possibilities, consider and eliminate them so rapidly. I saw that he was waiting for a clue, while processing the clues he had. "Carme?" he said—*the sound of his voice!*—and then he observed me with his beautiful, intent expression.

I've met autistic children and Asperger adults, the hand flappers, the people who give you a cockeyed indignant look if they meet you unexpectedly, who can't act unless prepared, who seem shy or sulky or quizzical, who simply lack the grammar of feeling the rest of us are born with. Those illiterate as to human expressions, to whom the self-expression of others is never wholly real; who are attracted more to ideas than people, ideas turned merciless and inevitable, fixed ideas, but not fast or firm, only information scrolling like a computer checking its systems. *These* are human. This patient, capable, loving attention *wasn't*.

"Carme is thinking," my father said. I could see he'd crept closer to me.

"Thinking has been a great comfort to me." I motioned to him to stay back. I was afraid of my joy and my rage—all my lawless and irregular passions.

But he only gave a small gasp, as if hurt, and crossed the gap between us. I found my shoulders against the floor in his hand cupping the back of my neck. He kissed me—then looked at me—then kissed me again. "I can't stay. I can't *woo* you, Carme. I haven't got time." He stroked my face—it was the same, his sensitive, searching touch. He always touched as if he were blind, refusing to spread the work or pleasure of getting sensations into all his senses. I'd always known this about him, but how striking it was, and how wonderfully personal and sensation-seeking it made his touch.

"I was always *used* to you," I said, as if apologizing. "But you haven't changed. How is that possible?"

He blushed. "But I have!" He seemed disappointed I hadn't noticed. Then he explained that about five years ago his teeth began falling out and he grew some new ones. "It was very distressing," he said. "I felt like one of those poor girls to whom mother and peers have failed to explain menstruation. It seemed fateful and unnatural." He grinned to show me the new teeth—his incisors with their glassy tips. When he shut his mouth I could see that his jaw was a little heavier—not flesh but bone. He'd grown. But he hadn't aged.

I was being examined. He was like an animal, uninhibited. He picked up a lock of my long hair and ran it through his lips, inhaled. "I hate my patience," he said—or was it "patients"? I laughed and said, "I bury mine."

Again I was being stared at and stroked. He wouldn't be fatherly in any acceptable way— and I could feel myself falling through my fear, anger, reserve, ordinary decency, all my values and valves of safety, until I was just a lonely woman lying in the arms of a very beautiful man. I took a deep breath and his own unique scent came into my head like smelling salts. I regained consciousness. He had my father's scent and was my father.

He made a suggestion. "There's going to be a storm. The cloud ceiling is low and the satellites can't see us. We should go walk on your beach and talk." I was lifted and set on my feet. He followed me as I went to find more suitable footwear. Once he put out a hand and caught me under the elbow to steady me.

"Edwin keeps an eye on me hoping to catch whoever else is watching. Or—he keeps an eye on me because he's too scared to let me out of his sight."

"Edwin?"

"He was doomed anyway—so *I* don't mind that his knowing me puts him in danger. *He* doesn't mind—but I expect he'll revise his opinion before he gets much younger."

I shivered, not at the idea of what my father could do, but at this travesty of language. I found my walking shoes, but he had to fasten their clips for me. As he did my ankles were caressed and endearments poured in my ears. "Oh God! All right—I love you," I said, like someone breaking down under interrogation. That stopped his rapture. He helped me up and meekly took my hand as we went outside.

We trespassed through the grounds of a closed holiday home on the front road, and climbed down to where sandy soil and sage gave way to sand.

Someone had built a tepee of sticks above a pile of firewood. A bonfire planned for the weekend. The tide was coming in. There were terns on the spit—a crowd of them, bad weather coming. They shuffled nearer together in retreat from the tide. A low cloud dragged its belly across the hills behind the inlet. We crossed the stream where the water was curdy, freshwater above salt in invisible plates. We reached the long sweep of fine, packed sand and walked.

My father told me he was here because he blew his cover. Because he'd blown his cover he was able to give in to Fidela's siren song. "But only for a short while. Sorry."

He said, "When you were around five you had nightmares, and would climb into bed with me and Dev—always too polite to worm in between us. It was Dev you'd confide in by daylight, but after your bad dreams you'd fall asleep with your head on my arm. Dev would peer over my shoulder at you, curious and infatuated. I remember once being moved to say to him, 'Isn't she nice?' I was playing with one of your musky, not-quite-clean hands. Dev said he was glad I could appreciate you but why didn't I try *talking* to you when you were awake? Telling me off. I didn't defend myself. It seemed better—my love seemed better as a secret—something I could keep even from him. I thought I could communicate it to you while you lay asleep and I played with your hand. *Your hands*, Carme! They had everything in them: your health, your personality, the force of your future—life and latent life. I hoped no one would ever guess how I felt, how much I loved you." He sighed. "But of course my enemies didn't *need* to guess—they only needed to make the usual assumptions about how parents feel."

I asked him how he felt—as a parent—about Fidela's pregnancy.

"She's very resourceful, isn't she? And there's no question of consanguinity—which is the only *scientific* basis for the incest taboo. It's a donor egg."

"Space cadet," I said.

"I left when she was only seven."

"Is this the 'something must have happened to her to make her this way' argument? You abandoned her, so she grew up inhumanly autonomous? Bella told me off for using the 'something must have happened' line to excuse Ricardo. Bella would say, 'What about temperament, propensities, and choice?' "

"Ricardo's dead, isn't he?" Dad said, changing the subject.

I stamped—and the sand, filling with the sea again, gave like jelly and grew shiny around my foot. I thought of Albany in *King Lear*, on hearing Edmund reported dead: "That's but a trifle here." I said it.

My father then told me why he'd come. He'd already gone where he'd been warned not to. "I saw Fernando," he said. "Thirty-eight hours after he died. *Thirty-eight hours.*" The figure seemed to drive him wild. "If he'd died of stroke, or meningitis, or cardiac arrest, I'd have been sad, but it wouldn't have made me mad. It was *Dev*, Carme, Dev shot in the head. I'd been caught, trussed, and I had to watch Dev's last boot prints fade, the grass spring up again, the dew marred for good for *that* day, but the grass stand up again. When I heard about Fernando I went a little crazy. I thought: 'May I be annihilated, *may the world end*, before I have to see this happen again.' Thirty-eight hours later I was in the morgue at La Casa de la Mujer. And—and I suppose that whoever stole his body did so because they're waiting for it to start to exude the smell of roses. Because I mended the slashes. Death's 'ten thousand several doors.' I did what even the most artful mortician cannot do to restore the appearance of life in the corpse. But I couldn't make something out of nothing. Something was missing—and not just his heart."

We stood at the waterline, and the waves made hushing sounds at me, but my father let me cry. "I'm sorry," he said. "So that's why I'm here. Now I should tell you why I left."

Jules chose to take Ido with him to New York and Washington ostensibly because a number of Ido's translations had made it to his *Collected Poems*. But when they were boarding the first plane, La Host to Miami, the poet told Ido that he'd taken him along because Ido was the "most worldly" person he knew. "Age is insidious," Jules said. "And I find I've become rather timid."

The East Coast was a treat. Ido was tired of taking Fidela to L.A., flying into LAX over loosely knotted highway interchanges, green storm drains, and tile-roofed bungalows—everything browned by the air, as if the whole city was in a convection oven.

Jules and his minder had a fine time in New York. They went to dinner with Jules's publisher, a deep-voiced old man with cold hands; and the poetry editor; and the principal translator; and their spouses, who either taught at Columbia or were in "think tanks." Ido had never met people like that; even Jules and Anton Xavier didn't have that kind of polished, broad, humane intelligence. Jules introduced Ido as his "tenuous *outlaw*" and "a talented doctor in the underequipped La Host hospital." The host and other guests were obliged to admire Ido's dedication and ingenuity; he had to tell them, no, he was just *there*, going from ailment to ailment like a honeybee working a flower bed.

Jules did readings, and signed books for worshipful expatriate Lequamans. He'd been depressed after Lena's death. And he'd spent much of his life silenced. He hadn't had the usual opportunities to travel or to be a celebrity, so he'd jumped at the chance to attend the conference in Washington, a conference on global culture in the twenty-first century. Not what the twenty-first century *might* be like—a conference for futurists—but what it *should* be like. It was sponsored by a nonprofit foundation overseen by a respectable right-wing newspaper—a newspaper that failed to make a profit but was kept afloat by a prophet, the Reverend Moon of the Unification Church.

Jules's minder knew all this before they went. He had done some research, read cautionary tales by ex-members of the Unification

Church. He'd found a list of the businesses they owned—and got some sense of scale. He had tried to get Jules to consider his decision, to weigh up the opportunity to go and mingle with writers from other countries against the probability that he was being co-opted. Jules said he was curious. He said he'd go along, gracious and in good faith, and give the conference the best quality of his attention. "You have to remember, young man, that like a number of other writers listed here—this fellow from Ghana whose work I've admired for decades, and this fine professor from Madagascar—I come from a country with a 'soft currency' and can't normally afford to meet other writers of poor, distant nations, or to have access to our rich host nation."

Later it became clear that most of the conference's invited writers were quite innocent of their host's intentions—their host's program—and were only there as *components*, representative of their cultures, making up the international numbers. But Jules was invited because, in the early '90s, he had published a number of remarks disparaging socialism—and Lequama's sluggish efforts to "move beyond its revolution." "Socialism," Jules had said. "There's an idea that has lost its luster—its ability to reflect what we want." He was quoted in an article in *The New York Times*, one of those articles that are either faintly self-satisfied or mournful about the death of militant socialism and "the disappearance of dogma and the fashion for military fatigues." It relished Jules's quotes and used them well: "the revolutionary rhetoric that glamorizes our deprivations . . ." The article wasn't silly or unintelligent, but it was smug and tired and seemed to think it fit and witty to remark on which of the revolutionary heroes of '83 had put on weight and which hadn't. Francis Taylor was beginning to become famous about then, and this piece chose to quote him saying that he had gone to Lequama not out of a sense of vocation but because he was in trouble at home after driving his ex-girlfriend's Audi into her swimming pool. This was the reporter's idea of putting things in perspective.

The conference began well for Jules. He and Ido were picked up at Dulles by a limo whose driver turned out to be a former member of the Egyptian national soccer team. Jules talked soccer with him.

Then they discussed the split in Islam proceeding from an incident at the deathbed of the prophet. And they talked about the "bad" Arabs in Hollywood movies, and living in Washington—related subjects. Ido sat back and thought about the shuttle at Dulles that took passengers from terminal to terminal across the runway. He thought about the big trees he'd seen flying in, the flash of water lying between them. It got dark. The driver pointed out the pavilion on the lawn of the White House; the President was having a party. The limo turned into Pennsylvania Avenue and its passengers were called on to admire the Capitol—which was lit up, solid and ethereal and rather like a backlit picture of a sundae on the menu of an ice cream parlor.

Ido asked Jules, by the way, what he had meant by "worldly."

"Pragmatic," Jules said. "Morally unencumbered."

The conference was at the Grand Hyatt, which had an atrium, ten stories high, and escalators like bridges flowing down over fountains and pools, chlorine blue. The splash of fountains masked the faint trundling of escalators and echoing talk from a cafe and bar, but not the sound of the white grand piano on an island in the middle of the pool on the lower ground floor.

Jules and Ido registered. They were late, so were given a meal voucher for the restaurant—to which they repaired with the conference program. Jules read it, expressed anxiety and appetite, and let his soup get cold. Ido promised the poet he'd spend the morning with him—the opening session and first workshop. Then, Ido said, he wanted to go look at the Lincoln Memorial.

They were in a twin room—two double beds. That night Jules kept Ido talking, as if they were teenagers on a sleepover. Ido was reminded of Edwin Money. Jules and Money were both talented old men, and egoists. Jules was full of plans, he was spinning and glimmering, like a big diamond on show. He said, "My book, my magazine, my career, my reputation," as Money would say, "My studios, my satellites," or, to his fleet of physicians, "My samples, my lipids," and, like a great composer, "My *movements*." Jules was nervous—he'd given interviews in New York and seemed in some trepidation about what would come of it. "I have this bad habit," he said, "of using figures of speech, I think to clarify complicated ideas."

Ido asked the poet if he'd ever heard Fernando saying that *he* had only three rules: one, don't mix vodka and mountain wine; two, don't leave your enemies alive; and three, don't use rhetorical figures to a journalist.

Jules didn't find this reassuring. Ido had to calm the poet by reading him his new translation of a 1979 poem, "A Garden in Exile," which hadn't made it into the *Collected*.

> I went out walking to ask God
> what I could do for my people
> and about the factory in La Host making mats
> for General Motors vehicles, and bad water.
> The factory whose taxable wealth never touches
> the public coffers of its owner nation
> and whose workers earn seventy cents a day.
> What could I do about the lovely woman
> in the white gown, met at the Dean's party, who said
> "Surely, in your country, seventy cents goes a long way"?
> "All money does, Madam, ceaselessly circling
> the upper atmosphere, making clouds
> in the condensers of Head Offices only and only
> raining in the gardens of the rich.
> Besides, Madam, the tax on seventy cents a day
> cannot purchase medicines from France and Switzerland
> for our hypertensives and heart patients."
>
> In the Japanese gardens at Brooklyn Botanical
> a man is at prayer
> blowing prayer through a bamboo flute.
> A thrush alights to split a snail
> on the wet rock face, the waterfall
> isn't running today. There's no sound
> from the pump house.

Irises above the water, and again
transparent on olive darkness, a tree in bud
black cracks on a reflected sky.
Carp sulk in the iris roots, won't rise
to the scatter of stamen from a flower
unknown to me, which makes mock
craneflies stopped on the surface of the water.
Says God—
It is our eyes the Just want Justice for
good water
the diminishing force of a falling tear.

The following morning Ido woke, dry from the air-conditioning and
startled by the flap-skid of the newspaper delivered under the door.
Breakfast was held in a big banquet room. Ido thought that everyone
at their table seemed alarmingly unattractive. Jules was eager and
polite at first, then troubled—then he adopted a grand manner.

After breakfast things got nasty—and Ido watched Jules take it
all personally.

They found their seats in a below-ground, shabbily magnificent
conference room, at a table with tumblers and conference packs.
There was some bad odor over headsets. People were told they *had*
to have them, to tune into the translators, but in order to receive
one everyone had to provide security in the form of either a driver's
license or a passport. Jules had only his passport to hand over. He
parted with it reluctantly. The headsets attached to a cable that ran
to the back of the room, where sat ranks of translators, sound technicians, camera operators—four deep, like the artillery behind the
infantry. Ido felt that he and Jules and the other conferees were that
infantry, and that they were all about to go over the top.

The audience was warmed up by a master of ceremonies, who
created a big scented lather for the first speaker—the former editor
of a leftist liberal humanist magazine and a born-again Catholic. The
speaker told the room how he thought the twenty-first century was
going to unfold. It was a puzzle. The man had been an influential lib-

eral, but he seemed to have recanted his past politics and to be looking for redemption.

Jules had gone pale. He passed Ido a note: "Am I missing something?"

The next speaker was the Reverend Moon, who had an interesting vocal style, Ido thought—rather like the patriarch in a Chinese
opera, who whispers, then suddenly declaims in a huge haranging
voice. Moon spoke about himself in the third person, which tended
to make his identity merge with that of the other main third-person
subject of his speech—Jesus Christ. He read from his text, occasionally doubling back to reread some paragraphs while the translators maintained radio silence like commandos on a raid in enemy
territory. They sat, heads lowered, earphones on, listening and marking time.

Men with cameras prowled the aisles, getting proof of the distin-
guished audience the sponsors had purchased. Ido tried to look
skeptical for the cameras. The room was so full of electrical equipment it stank of hot circuitry.

Moon finished and the audience was released.

Some people came up to talk to Jules—targeted him actually,
but Ido missed this, since he was in a hurry. He went out to piss, and
to process his astonishment. When he came out of the bathroom
several minutes later, he heard, around the corner in the submarine-
like corridor, the sound of stealthy weeping. He found a woman in
tears by the pay phones in a blind end to the passage. He recognized
her. She'd been onstage with the first speaker, had spoken briefly
herself. She blew her nose and asked if he was an organizer or a
guest.

"A guest," he said. "I'm minding Jules Frei."

"Frei? I'm looking forward to hearing him read." She told Ido
that she was a professor at a university the Unification Church had
"financially rescued." "They've never interfered with my teaching,"
she said. "But now I feel I've been tricked into supporting those
speakers, lending my black face as a backdrop to their well-dressed,
hostile ideology."

She raised her spectacles to wipe her eyes. Then she thanked Ido
for his concern and said he should go back in.

In the lobby by the conference rooms women were beating triangles and urging guests into their next session. There was a choice of three workshops. Ido picked up a cup of coffee and a scone and followed Jules—who he knew hadn't eaten.

Jules seemed stunned. Ido sat him down and put the scone and coffee before him. The poet remarked how accommodating American culture was of extremes. Then he was quiet, and he and Ido listened to the man running the workshop on "teaching moral stories to children." Ido realized that Jules had been so disoriented by shock that he'd let himself be herded into the wrong room. Still, Jules listened with great attention and a strained, benign smile on his face. And Ido was embarrassed for him.

My father and I were at the end of the beach. I had settled on my throne, a natural seat in the dark "intrusive rock," as geologists call it, a smooth brown stone, still faintly warm from the quenched sun. I nestled in my big black coat, Dad sprawled beside me at an angle, facing the water but with his head and one arm braced against my leg. It wasn't a position anyone over twenty-five would be comfortable in for long, but he'd maintained it throughout his story, easy, as if he reclined on cushions, not the knobbly spine of a canted slab of rock.

"Are you suggesting that embarrassment is a failure of feeling?" I said. Then, "When I said earlier that you hadn't changed, you were embarrassed."

"Embarrassment is what's available when shame is busy with heroes," said my father. He finally changed position; sat up and swung around so his feet pointed at the water. He continued his story.

"We went up to our room after lunch. I got ready to go out, as I'd planned, with my backpack and city map to look at the Mall—"

"And your camera," I said.

"I didn't have a camera." My father stared at me, a kind of blind look, impatient and cold. It was my third interruption. He'd reacted well to my question about his embarrassment, but the other interruptions had met with this look. On both occasions I'd tried to remind him of something. "And your camera," I'd said. And earlier, "When you were in the shuttle at Dulles, Jules said you had him completely baffled, because you began to explain something he said was 'utterly bizarre.' Apparently you talked about the Shuttling Wood on the River Nith." When I finished speaking Dad had given me *that look* and said he didn't remember. I began to suspect that his recollection had exact and immovable parameters and that he couldn't be reminded of anything beyond them. This wasn't *memory*, as I had always understood it, where there are surprising recollections like a second crop of hay in one season. The story my father was telling was like one in a book—what was on the page was all that existed, there was no independent, definable world beyond.

What have they done to you? I thought.

While Ido got ready to go out, Jules sat on the edge of his bed, looking out of place, and talked. The poet had been approached to lend his name to a literary federation that the conference organizers hoped to form. "They've given me this document explaining what they'd like this federation to do. It's very high-minded."

Ido took the document from Jules. While he read, Jules went on talking. He said he'd been addressed, amid the general flattery, as a writer of "moral fictions" and "a vigilant force for the future of the world." He was told he must produce work that provided guidance, "security for the present and seed corn for the future," and that he should as an artist demand that the arts "reflect the best of us" and provide "a mighty influence in restraining the grosser appetites of the people."

Ido asked if this was why the poet wasn't eating—did he hope to provide an example of restrained gross appetite? Then he suggested the poet take a nap, and he folded down the covers and took off Jules's shoes and swung his skinny old feet into the bed.

Jules took Ido's hand and told him that he felt appalled and impotent. "The proper response to my hosts is courtesy," Jules said. "I've listened in good faith. Does courtesy extend to putting my name down for this Writer's Federation for World Peace?"

Ido picked up the prospectus and read: " 'A nonprofit organization founded under section 501 (c) 3 of the Internal Revenue Code of 1954.' Look Jules—it's a high-minded tax shelter for the church's businesses. End result—more money translated into political influence. And with your name, your famous name." Then he gave the poet's leg a brisk pat and went out into the sultry, sunny June afternoon like the careless, cheerful creature he was—leaving Jules wondering what he could do to save his soul.

Ido walked to the Mall, weaving through crowds of schoolchildren being ushered across the narrow street between Ford's Theatre and the house Lincoln was carried into to die. It began to rain, big fat drops that made no change in the heat.

In the Mall Ido walked by the Reflecting Pool, under the trees where it was cool. He was going to Lincoln, ultimately, and kept looking that way, watching the figure in the memorial get nearer and bigger. It looked to Ido as if Lincoln might just finish his thought, get up and *do* something.

Ido never did reach Lincoln—maybe that was why he kept feeling that the Emancipator was going to come to *him*. It was as if his intention knew there was something in its way, and was putting out enough energy to make a stone man come to life.

It was a strange feeling, but then everything had begun to seem strange to him. He looked at his guidebook. Its pages were printed with a ragged right margin and he kept seeing the words washed away.

Ido stopped at the Vietnam War Memorial. The black trench. He walked down a path so friendly he didn't need to watch his step. The wall grew beside him, got taller and the path deeper, toward the year of highest casualties. Ido could see himself between the lines of names, reflected in the polished stone. He noticed that when he looked straight into the stone, it wasn't black, it was all the colors of the world behind him: green oak leaves, green grass, a sky in patches blue, with high cirrus clouds.

It had been Father's Day two days before, and there were flowers, flags, photos of infants, soft toys, and shiny whirligigs heaped up against the base of the wall. When he reached its highest point Ido had to stand back so as not to crush all the offerings. He stood and enjoyed the gleaming, sober blackness, and the shade.

No one was there when Ido arrived—or no one he minded. He'd come between tour buses. But then he saw shadows moving behind him. Someone had arrived. He saw a tall shape, quite still, then a flash—a camera flash, of course—but it made the shape look, for a moment, like a lighthouse. Ido glanced behind him—at a young man accompanied by a boy of about fifteen. The man looked like an actor fresh from wardrobe and just getting into the part. He gave Ido a quick, tight smile; it occurred to Ido that the man was awkward because he was under the impression that he'd intruded on mourning. The boy behind the man—equally well turned out, but ugly—stood staring into space, picking his spots, and muttering. Ido thought he heard the boy softly chant, "Turnaround, turnaround, turn back around."

Ido turned back around to the long lists and caught sight of a name, "Cadaver"—but with initials unknown to him. He put a finger under the name and the man behind him said: "That's one that seems oddly inappropriate on a memorial, though I suppose it would look even worse on a toe tag." His voice was right by Ido's ear. Ido turned back sharply and heard the man's camera click again as his shoulder collided with the man's raised arm. The camera dropped onto the path. Its back gate shattered and the film herniated out of it in a brown loop about twelve inches long.

They squatted together, but the man let Ido pick the camera up.

"That was easy," said the teenager, behind them. Then he began to hop from leg to leg as if suddenly overcome by the urge to urinate. His face screwed up, and tears came into his eyes. "He's sealed shut. He's as tough as rubber," the boy said.

The man didn't seem to hear him. "What a pity," he said to Ido. "The camera *and* the film. My vacation shots." He was so close Ido could smell aftershave, mild and sparingly used. The man was shiny-eyed, seemed shy and cautious. He said, "Whenever I fumble, and something falls, it is so *unmeant* it almost seems possible to *replay* the moment."

Ido wondered what he was supposed to do? He knew an Airan

when he saw one. But he found he couldn't think. His head hurt—and the boy was carrying on. Ido felt himself *do* something; it was as if he gave his head a quick flick—but he didn't move. He shook himself like a wet dog, and felt the heaviness leave him.

The boy was silent for a second, then the front of his pants went dark. He fell on his hands and knees and began to vomit.

"Your friend is sick," Ido said to the man who still stared into his eyes.

"To replay the moment, to retrieve time," the man went on. "To take it all back, to restore, reinstate, mend, reanimate. Yes, my friend is sick." He got up and left Ido holding his camera. The man coaxed the boy upright, took a handkerchief from his breast pocket, shook it out of its geometry and mopped the boy's bile-lacquered chin. Then he led the boy away.

Ido took the camera back to the Hyatt. There was a one-hour photo shop in a mall off the lobby. It was around six in the evening, and a line was forming in front of one of the down escalators, before a sign, flanked by ushers in black tie, for a "Concerned Young Black Men's Awards Dinner." There were concerned young black men and proud parents, and dates in backless dresses and tall shoes and hair like confectionery. They formed a wall of fabric and flesh and scent and chemicals. Ido was going patiently through them when someone stopped him. A blocky, uniformed, graying colonel.

"Pardon me," Ido said, and stepped aside.

The colonel put out another hand and firmly fielded Ido back before him. "You don't remember me, do you?" he said.

Ido was obliged to look at the man. After a moment he said: "Oh yes—Munro. You're alive, and fatter, and promoted."

"And you have an entry visa?—I trust."

Ido told Munro that he'd been going back and forth for years between Lequama and the States. That his daughter worked in television—was Fidela Guevara of *Starting Over*.

"That's *your* daughter?" Munro laughed. "Your small contribution to the friendship between our nations." He was kidding, and all the time he kept a hand on Ido in a bullying and possessive way. He asked for a name, so Ido gave him Walter Risk's.

Munro apologized for letting down his end of the bargain. He'd never sent that microfilm of the Wall. Though it was okayed; it wasn't judged as "sensitive." He glanced at the broken camera and spilling film. "I always wondered if you saved our lives."

By this time they had an audience, a cluster of concerned young men and their cultivated young women. "I hope so," Ido said. "But I think Fernando's good behavior just coincided with my arrival."

"*I* think you did." For a moment Munro cupped his hand over one of Ido's, the one holding the camera. "I should thank you," he said. Then he let go, and let Ido through.

Ido went on to the beige marble and brass mall. There was a seat in an alcove by a pay phone. He prized the film out of the camera, discarded the camera, and used his pinky finger to wind the herniated filmstrip back into its canister. Ido closed the canister in both his hands, hung them between his knees, and began to think, or try to imagine, what it would mean to cure the film—to turn back its time.

He never could describe the process. Only Fernando had ever asked him to, and Ido's attempts to explain just seemed to excite Fernando—another narcotized soul who wanted to shiver at a marvel more than he wanted knowledge of its causes.

The day he'd first met Francis Taylor and dispatched the sick dog Ido had felt the animal's vitality around it, like dissolving steam. But that was a *conventional* description. He could feel time he couldn't pass, couldn't get by, or *put one by*. It was the same with Madlena's horse, whose death he felt as a barrier between him and its vitality. If someone died on an operating table they could be revived, started up again—but that wasn't the same as *undoing* everything. Ido had to get away from death to do his undoing. Death baffled and blocked his gift. So, for instance, if someone had a stomach wound, so fresh that it smelled of cordite as well as bowel—well—it was ridiculous. He saw wounds that way—as ridiculous, unbelievable. The wounded body had only recently been *whole*, and its wholeness was innate. Ido would look into the stomach wound—and suddenly begin to feel how *everything* was, in every moment, flowing, what people called "backward and forward" in time. Ido could feel that his body was involved in this flow, and that the universe could be coaxed to do what it did anyway—whenever an excited electron disappeared while jumping orbits, and went missing from its atom for a tiny fraction of a second, and for a tiny fraction of a second couldn't be found *anywhere*. Subatomic particles did, after all, seem to move through time. It was what the universe seemed ordinarily to do. So, for *him*, it was only a matter of coaxing it to do it more specifically. And his body was like the breath of life—he'd feel himself pouring something into the wounded body. Perhaps he took apart his own cells and taught them to be someone else's. He couldn't explain the process. He needed new words. However, soon after he'd first learned to fix things, and his rapture at fixing things had settled a little, Ido realized that the flow could be persuaded the *other* way too. He'd practice by drawing the life out of flies even as they buzzed about Ambre's kitchen, or by fading flowers. It was easy, because there wasn't any rebuilding involved, and it used nothing of his own, only what was in the flies, the roses, only where each thing was already headed anyway. Ido could kill things by hurrying them toward their own deaths, but to cure them he couldn't *pass* death. (Still couldn't. Not thirty-eight hours of cooling, and pooled blood, and a heart gone.)

But Ido could cure the film. As he did, he felt another trapdoor spring open in his body, another slight change of brain function. He felt that he was *on his way*.

The photo place said yes, they could develop it in an hour. With time to kill, Ido went to the mezzanine floor and bought a drink. It was comfortable in the bar. He sat down, relaxed, and began to make plans. Not resolutions, positive plans. He planned what to do for Jules. He would be *sunshine* for Jules.

On a couch across the table from his, one conference attendee said to another, "What I'm feeling is spiritual queasiness." They were dissenters, obviously. The man added, "I spent years at the coal face of teaching and I have to say that I can see this federation offers someone like me the chance of grants and advancement. But the question is: Can I? Can I bring myself to join?"

Ido went to get his photos. They were ready, still very flexible and warm and a little sticky. Ido stood in the brass and marble mall and looked through them—they clung together and he had to take care.

In the envelope were pictures of everyone he ever loved—everyone who was still alive—in *two worlds*. There was one of his daughter Carme at the door of her dormitory on the campus; and one of his daughter Fidela by a baggage carousel at LAX; there was Ambre, with flowers and fruit, in the Plaza market; Fernando and Madlena on a balcony, a midtown bar, New York, forty stories up at least, in their spring jackets, leaning together and excited about something; there was a photo of Astrella being handed up into a carriage by some man; and Carlin and Cassandra dockside, between stacked bales of wool sewn into sackcloth. After eight years Ido still recognized the smaller ships in the berths on either side of the *Ambre Guevara*.

He went up to the room and ordered a sandwich for Jules. Then he called Fernando in New York and asked Fernando to come to Washington. Ido said Jules needed "the family." Fernando didn't ask any questions—Ido guessed Fernando was pleased that Ambre's deputy had deputized him, and he was "the family." Fernando called back later to tell Ido to expect him, and Fidela, on the Amtrak Metroliner arriving at noon the following day. Ido arranged to meet Fernando at the station, where he'd brief him on the "Jules situation."

The poet ate his sandwich. He was scarcely awake, drowsy, demoralized.

Ido got into bed and turned out his light and before long he heard Jules snoring softly. Ido thought about all the strange beds ahead of him; and then he suspended his thinking.

Jules went grimly off to breakfast and a morning workshop. Ido took the headsets and tried to return them, to get Jules's passport and his own driver's license. The very polite, frightened, implacable Asian woman in charge of headsets kept telling Ido that he and Jules would need them to listen to the Reverend's closing address. Ido lied. He said Jules was ill. The woman was evasive. One of the more substantial male administrators arrived, a man with a *look*—shrewd, wholly without warmth. The administrator suggested that Ido need not make a fuss or be uncooperative. Ido insisted, cranked up his volume—which didn't impress them—until, genuinely angry, Ido began to show his gradual, corrosive fury, and they gave way.

He caught a cab to the station and met Fernando and Fidela in a coffee kiosk.

Fernando lifted Fidela onto a stool and bought her a chocolate milk. They talked around her. Ido told Fernando that Jules was distressed, and exactly what the conference was like. He didn't need to invent a thing. He watched Fernando frown and nod and incline closer, waiting for advice and instructions. Ido gave Fernando Jules's passport and said, "We must all go to the hotel. We must pack Jules up, and you must take him back to New York. I'll stay here to—to lodge a complaint."

Fernando nodded slowly. He thought the plan was reasonable. Fidela swung back and forth, her head cocked and her mouth applied to her straw, and looked up at her father, skeptical and assessing. And her father realized that it was never confidence she'd had, it was autonomy. His child was a great kingdom with a population of one.

Back at the hotel the poet went all helpless and tearful on them. Fernando was nice to him, which Ido found a novelty, since Fernando was usually only nice to children. "This is a bad place," Fernando said. "Home's a good place; let's go home."

Down in the lobby Ido had the bell captain call a cab, and they all waited beside the revolving door. He wanted to touch Fernando—just once—as if by touching him he could infect him forever. Because he loved Fernando. But he needed no excuse to pick up Fidela and kiss her. The cab came and Fernando ushered Jules out the door. Ido held Fidela and, on impulse, said: "Can you keep a secret?"

She didn't answer him, so he put her down and she pushed the door around, and its glass flashed, and with each flash the three—Jules, Fernando, Fidela—were farther away from him, in the courtyard, at the cab doors, inside the cab, moving away into the traffic.

———

My father shook his head. "The first thing Fidela said yesterday, when I turned up on her doorstep, was, pouting: 'You asked me if I could keep a secret, and then you didn't tell me one!' "

By the time my father finished his story it had started to rain. He stripped off his good leather coat and draped it over my head and shoulders—his gallantry a reflex. Before long rain had begun to stream off the top layer of his hair, and it formed wet tassels. But the water didn't penetrate the thicker layers, so that I could see dry hair under dripping spirals. My father said, "I'm going to go soon. I'll have Fidela drive me to the airport." He took my hand. "I don't know that love entitles us to trouble each other." Then, still holding my hand, so that I was drawn forward, he leaned out over the water, which the tide had quietly carried, deep and clear, right to the foot of my throne. He asked me to look at what the rain was doing. I saw that each fat drop that fell into the sea formed a globe, a bead of fresh water that rolled in the dimple its impact made on the sea's surface. The beads stayed discrete, orbiting smoothly on a skin of salinity, and slowly spun themselves away.

"That's something new," my father said. "I've never seen that before."

Countertransference

(A therapist's rooms, Northern California, 2022)

For six weeks I slept on my hoard of objections, like a dragon whose skin is impressed by stolen money. Hostile people call psychology a pseudoscience, and therapists have to defend their practices as *practical*, have to say: "There are things that work." At the end of the seventh week, Carme Risk said, all right, what was bothering me? In particular? And until that moment I could have defended myself as a good practitioner, I could have gone on going along with her story. Instead I answered her—with the breath I had left in me. What bothered me was what always had—her magic, her curses, and her great glistening webs of destiny. All of it with gravity, and a system—a place for everything and *a shadow of everything in its place*.

Carme Risk jumped up and grabbed an A4 envelope from my stationery box. She made alterations, passed it to me with its end gathered, and said, "There—breathe into that." She sat beside me and put her fingers into the hair at my temples.

I dropped the envelope and retreated around the far side of my desk. I said something to fend her off, said it like somebody pulling a gun. Then I told her about the research I'd been doing.

I'd been *teased* for the questions I asked, I told her. Apparently those Lequaman Miscere films were aimed straight at "my demographic," and I hadn't seen them. The people I'd talked to were generous. It must be very dull for enthusiasts to have to educate the wholly uninitiated—dull uphill work. I told Carme that I realized I'd heard about "Taoscal magic" *before* I'd read her journals. On my car radio—for instance—a hit single from a soundtrack to a cult movie. The latest of a series of movies about the Taoscal child sorcerer who became the disputed Lequaman saint, Miscere, which is Latin for "mix." I had discovered that there was a whole Lequaman film industry based around these fantastic action fantasies, which boasted no computer graphics, but acrobatics, pyrotechnics, camera trickery, flying on wires, astonishing makeup, lighting, stunts, and *very* attractive actors.

Carme was standing too—she made damping motions with her hands, as if trying to coax me to sit or to stop yelling at her. She said, "Fidela called me up a month before her first baby came and said she was going to change what she did. I was really worried. She was so successful, I wanted her to go on being successful. So I said, 'Not your career?' and she said—sounding like Dad, formidably simple—'No, Carme, what I *do*.' And she swung herself and Bob right around. They invested in Lequama. Money and expertise. And when they needed *more* money they got me to manage Carlos, and Carlos to manage the Council of Projects, so that now the tribe owns fifty percent of the studio. Nine years and eleven films later there are articles in the film trades about how Lequama is the next Hong Kong or Bombay. And the actor who played the child Miscere is a star, and has just been contracted by Disney. We are looking for a replacement—an adult Miscere. We're casting now." She smiled. "We're not casting our nets wide, rather putting a line in a deep pool where we once glimpsed a big fish."

It was a Sunday again. We were having a marathon session, not agreed on in advance—which was one of Aramantha Visistation's recommendations for avoiding bad "abreactions," deepening trauma instead of achieving therapeutic release. I heard a car come into the parking lot below my terrace. I raised my wrist to check my watch, and Carme Risk laughed at me.

I told her what I thought. That at first I'd thought she was a Miscere fan and a fantasist, and that she had been very, very lucky to happen on a therapist who was trying so hard to add gravity to his person that he didn't do what his "demographic" generally did— didn't do the music, movies, clubs, gym. She knew what I did do, which was partly why I felt mocked. Once, I'd driven her back to her house near Bodega, and we'd taken a detour to look at my horses, and she'd denuded a four-foot strip on the paddock side of the ditch in order to feed all three horses long dry grass from the flat of her palm. She knew about my horses, and my restored stone pump house.

I explained my disappointment. I had wanted her to be an *inventive* liar.

At this point Carme began to sidle around the desk. Her movements were awkward, self-conscious, but her face—her face wore the saddest expression I've ever seen a face wear. It was the patience in Carme's sadness that made it so stunning. She seemed to be looking on the work of years all gone wrong and needing doing over.

I heard another car. I decided the first couldn't have been Bella and I felt relieved, till I thought that maybe the *second* was. The sound was like an itch on the inside of my skull. I itched and my brain shrank in its quilted cover, tried to crawl back into bed. I said to Carme, "I eventually looked up the film company's management structure and found your names: Carme Risk, Fidela Guevara, Bob Renzi, the Juiliano-Guevara twins. And instead of nursing suspicions about pathological movie fans, I began to wonder. I thought, why are these people trying to teach the world about Taoscal magic? Then I noticed that a *Carme Juiliano-Guevara* has a writing credit on one of the films. Which one is it?"

"Which film?"

"Which *twin* did you marry?"

"I love to watch you wrench yourself about," said Carme. "Engines full back! Rudder hard to port!"

"If I was a plane that would tear me to pieces."

Carme had cleared the corner of the desk, and there was nothing between us. She peered over my shoulder and out the window. She seemed excited. Her excitement was as intense as her sadness—and again refined by patience, a sense of all sorts of things still waiting to be done. She looked me in the eye. She was so close that I could feel the exhaled moisture in her breath as she spoke. "Don't you believe my story?"

I pointed out that her arithmetic didn't work. If her father was sixteen when she was conceived, and she was ten in 1987, then her father couldn't cite *The Twyborn Affair* to Ulaw because that novel was published in 1979, not 1976.

Carme said that was goddamned autistic of me, and asked whether I'd been humoring her all this time.

"No. I did what you wanted. I read and I listened."

I found her fingers on my forearm, warm and maybe meaning to steady me. She said that she had needed Patrick White's Edie, Eddie, and Eudoxia—those different identities—as I needed my meaningful patio plant with its purple, pink, and white, all on the same bush. "I wrote that story," she said. "Abra's story. I composed it. But the journals are authentic. So—will you believe me?"

I asked her why she never used my name, and she said because it was a play on John Doe and she had had quite enough of serious people saddled with joke names.

This was cruel. *I'd* saddled myself. All names mocked my homelessness. John or Jon, Sean, Jean, or Jack. Or Doe, Deere, Stagge, Fawn, Hynde, or Hart. A name isn't innate, essential, like genetic material—but it is a credential, proof of provenance. What's in a name? Usually taste, fashion, family tradition, hope, affection, an attempt at the domestic magic of blessing. Everything I'd gone without. "No," I said. "I *don't* believe you. And I want you to answer me—why are you trying to share with the world your romance with Taoscal magic?"

"Because it works," she said, simply.

"Even if it works—why?"

"To change the world, of course. Into two worlds with their heads together." She smiled sweetly and squeezed my arm hard enough to stall what I was going to say next. She said, "I've been trying to change your mind. Or at least increase your tolerances. And I did hope you'd help me see my story just a little differently—no matter how infatuated I am with it just the way it is."

I retrieved the little that was left of my professionalism. I told her that I believed there were things her father had got wrong. Did she think it was possible that her father misinterpreted the message of the photographs? The Shuttling Wood had been off on its comet cycle, and if that was why Carlin didn't come, then perhaps the Airans' photographs of "everyone he ever loved in two worlds" might have been telling him that if the Airans could go to Eden, he could too. Why was that young Airan in the suit glowing like a bride, a gift giver? Because he had the pleasurable task of letting her father know he could regain his own time. Perhaps that was the message her father wasn't *intact* enough to hear or understand.

While I was saying all this I heard another two vehicles drive into the parking lot. Their engines shut off. I heard doors opening, voices, but I went on acquitting myself, doing my duty, my best. I understood that I had lost my *calling*. My job had given me peace, or gravity at least. To listen to other people was to let them top up my spilled life. I knew that now, when this woman finally left my room, I wouldn't feel alive anymore.

"Your father kept forgetting," I told her, "because he was ashamed. Ashamed of his gifts. He needed to sit down with the people he loved and ask their advice—*How should I live my life?* But Fernando was envious, Ambre was afraid, Madlena was a blockhead, and Carlin was always indignant. Those revolutionaries at least knew how terribly difficult it is to take responsibility for other people. Your father could have learned from them—not how to take responsibility, because he already had—but how to *live* with it. He never understood that he was feeling his responsibility just the same way any other responsible person does, as terrible but ordinary, fatal and fated—as if life is a disaster but, if you try to dodge it, you dodge your*self* as well."

Carme was smiling at me, very slightly. "Engines full back, rudder hard to port. You're not a plane," she said.

"Or a boat. Or a Snort." I was quoting *Are You My Mother?* Then I asked her, did she know where her father was?

"Yes."

"And can you produce him?"

"I was about to." She asked me to come out onto my terrace with her. As she went by my tricolor shrub, she plucked a sprig. The day was overcast and the jacaranda was at its best, optically illusory, like tweed cloth, purple hatched with black, or with darkness. It was gorgeous—my cheap street tree.

There were four cars in the lot. And people. When Carme led me to the concrete balustrade they all looked up at once. There was a slight red-haired woman with two children; the elder was the boy with "congenital anesthesia" from the special needs class of a client of mine. I recognized him from birthday party photos. Beside this family, shading their eyes with their hands, were two identical, dark-skinned men. There was a famous face—Madlena Guevara, her thick grizzled hair in a brush cut. She took off her shades and squinted up at us. There were two women on either side of a tall, husky, big-hipped old man. One was short and dumpy and elderly. The other was rangy, with long variegated plaits, black and gray, and bright blue eyes. She had a finger missing on her right hand, and her right arm—her sword arm—was plowed by pink scar tissue. The two women were having some trouble with the old man, who had lifted a hand to us, a hand that trembled, not with frailty but with feeling. He then dropped the hand onto the dumpy woman's shoulder and lifted a leg instead. He began hopping about on one foot while the women supported him.

I turned to Carme Risk. I asked her my last rational question: "Are you my mother?"

The old man was grappling with his free hand at his raised foot. As he jigged, I figured—I did the calculations. I looked at Carme, a fading beauty in her mid-forties, and I thought of Swift: "The black ox has set his foot upon her already." I looked at the figures right side up, and they finally worked. Worked without error or anomaly. Abra Cadaver, Ido Idea, Sean Hart; body, mind, and soul; yesterday, today, tomorrow—all in flower, and all on the same bush.

Below me in the parking lot the hopping had resolved itself into an action as, irascible and ecstatic, Carlin threw his shoe at me.